QUEENDOM:
FEAST OF THE SAINTS

Also by Kim Antieau

Novels

The Blue Tail • *Broken Moon* • *Butch*
Church of the Old Mermaids • *Coyote Cowgirl*
Deathmark • *The Desert Siren*
The Fish Wife: an Old Mermaids Novel
The Gaia Websters • *Her Frozen Wild* • *Jewelweed Station*
The Jigsaw Woman • *Maternal Instincts* • *Mercy, Unbound*
The Monster's Daughter • *Ruby's Imagine* • *Swans in Winter*
The Rift • *Whackadoodle Times* • *Whackadoodle Times Two*

Nonfiction

Answering the Creative Call
Certified
Counting on Wildflowers
The Old Mermaids Book of Days and Nights
*The Old Mermaids Book of Days
and Nights: A Year and a Day Journal*
An Old Mermaid Journal
The Salmon Mysteries
Under the Tucson Moon

Short Story Collections

Entangled Realities (with Mario Milosevic)
The First Book of Old Mermaids Tales
Tales Fabulous and Fairy
Trudging to Eden

Chapbook

Blossoms

Cartoons

Fun With Vic and Jane

Blog

www.kimantieau.com

QUEENDOM:
FEAST OF THE SAINTS

KIM ANTIEAU

Green Snake
PUBLISHING

Queendom: Feast of the Saints
by Kim Antieau

ISBN-13 (trade edition): 978-0692580271
ISBN-13 (library edition): 978-1518855849

Cover design by Ivan Zanchetta
Cover image by Nejron | Dreamstime

Thanks to:
Nancy Milosevic
Tracie Jones
Carmen Staton
Rachel Slick

http://www.kimantieau.com

Electronic editions of this book are
available at your favorite ebook store.

Published by Green Snake Publishing
www.greensnakepublishing.com

For Mario

and with special thanks to

Nancy Jo Rebhan

and

Prairie Kittin Stock

and all of The Queendom's Court

PART ONE
ARRIVALS

CHAPTER ONE
LORELEI

No official record survived of the small earthquake that shook the Queendom the day the new chef and her daughter arrived at the Hearth, home of the First Family and headquarters for the busidom. Eighteen year old Lorelei Villanueva noted the quake in the chronicle she kept on the walls of her private closet in her chambers on the third floor of the palace. She wrote, "I smelled cardamon brought in on the tresses of the East wind just before I felt the shudder."

Perhaps no one else noticed, not even the Old Oak that grew up beside the stone palace, a natural buttress against any storm or quake in the Queendom.

Lorelei felt the shift and understood what she was experiencing went beyond the trembling of the earth. She knew strangers had arrived—and something more—and her world would never be the same again. She did not hesitate. She immediately left her rooms and headed downstairs, taking the wooden steps that had been specially made for her short legs. No one was certain when the Hearth had been built, but no elevator graced this part of the labyrinthian palace.

Lorelei's stairs stopped on the second floor—a way to discourage her when she was younger from frequenting the downstairs, but she was not deterred this time, or any other time. She ran down the hall, her footsteps echoing up to the vaulted ceiling that adorned this part of the house. She heard voices coming from the Crocus Garden, and she slowed her pace.

"How could this have happened so quickly?" the Queen was saying. "You're telling me the Queendom could be bankrupt in six months?"

"I'm not sure how it happened," said Nehemiah, the Queen's right hand.

"That's not a good answer," the Queen said. "If we don't fix this, the Queendom could fall, and we will be exiled to the Hinterlands."

Lorelei gasped. "Mother?"

Lorelei heard a chair scrape across the garden floor. A moment later, the Queen came to the open door. "Did you hear all that?" Reina asked.

Lorelei looked up at her mother—tall, beautiful, and imposing as always—and didn't say anything.

"Don't worry," the Queen said. "I'm sure it is a mistake. In any case, Nehemiah and I will take care of it. We always do." She smiled. "Where are you headed? To meet the new cook and her daughter? Good. Tell me all about it later." She turned and went back into the garden. As the Queen closed the door behind her, Lorelei heard her say, "It is a good thing we have no spies amongst us."

Lorelei kept walking down the corridor. She saw her sister, Minerva, outside, with Mr. Peetall, the Foreign Minister of Berland who was visiting for the night. She was smiling and nodding while her right hand absently touched one of the ruby red blossoms on a rhododendron bush. She was the spitting image of their mother—except the Queen's hair was now prematurely white. One day, Minerva would be queen, too.

"Hello, little one." Raphael came up beside her and put his hand on top of her head. "Our sister has the bearing of a queen already, doesn't she?"

Lorelei looked up at her older brother.

"Maybe she'll give up the queenship, once she has it, like Aunt

Hildy did," he said. "Then I would be sovereign." He shrugged. "Then maybe I would give it up and you would be queen." He laughed as if that idea was the most ridiculous one he had ever heard. "Wouldn't that be something? We shouldn't wait, though. Maybe you and I should overthrow the government now and run the Queendom the way we want. Cookies, ice cream, and whiskey twenty-four hours a day. What do you say, little one?"

He knew she did not care for that particular pet name.

"I like the Queendom just the way it is, *Sonny*," Lorelei said. She pushed his hand off her head. He laughed again.

He leaned down and said quietly, "You may fool the others but not me. We should stick together, you and I, troublemakers that we are." He stood up straight and said more loudly, "Chess tonight? I'll be black to give you a head start."

She wanted to remind him that she did not need a head start. She won more often than he did. But she said nothing more. Instead she rushed down the wide hall until she reached the stairs down to the kitchen.

"You can run, sister, but you cannot hide," Raphael called after her.

But she could hide. She could hide better than any creature on Earth. It was one of her many gifts.

She half-slid on the railing and half-walked down the too tall steps until her feet hit the stone floor just outside of the kitchen where Umberto Cavallo was speaking with two strangers: a woman and a girl.

The woman held a battered leather valise in one hand and her daughter's hand in the other. She wore an old brown wool coat over a bright yellow cotton dress which peeked out a few inches below the hem of the coat. A small black hat with a tiny black feather and a dried yellow marigold blossom sticking out of it covered her hair and dipped down over her forehead. Her black shoes were cloth.

The child had black eyes and straight black hair. Lorelei wasn't sure she had ever seen another human being as white as this child, although it was not a sickly white. It was almost like fine porcelain.

Lorelei resisted the urge to touch her to see if she was real. The child looked straight into Lorelei's eyes and smiled. She didn't look away. She didn't look puzzled. She smiled and nodded, as though they had once been friends and now they had found one another again.

Umberto cleared his throat, and Lorelei looked up at him. A slight twitch on the right side of his face told Lorelei he was startled by her presence. He quickly recovered. He was the steward for the Hearth, after all. It was his job to be calm and cool under all circumstances: even when someone from the First Family kept turning up where they were not expected.

"Miss Lorelei Villanueva," Umberto said, moving a bit so that Lorelei had a better view of the woman and child, "this is our new cook, Chef, and her daughter." Umberto pulled absentmindedly on his gold waistcoat. Apparently he did not know the child's name.

"I actually prefer to be called by my given name," the woman said. "Which is Marguerite Teng. People may call me Marguerite or Teng or Maggie, and this is my daughter, Genevieve, but she goes by Viva. My cooking guild has not designated me as a chef, yet, so I don't presume that title."

Umberto pursed his lips and frowned.

"*Your* cooking guild?" he said. "*Your* cooking guild means nothing here! The Queendom's Cooking Guild has seen your papers and *they* have authorized us to employ you as chef. So chef you shall be." He paused, breathed deeply, and then continued. "But, I will allow that how you wish to be addressed is up to you."

Viva leaned closer to Lorelei and said quietly, "How old are you? I am ten."

"Miss Lorelei does not ordinarily speak," Umberto said. "Now, um, Marguerite Teng, perhaps I should show you the kitchen and give you the instruction manual for the rules of the house. Your assistants, Turnkey and Wanda, are in the kitchen garden. You'll meet them later."

Viva's mother nodded, dropped her bag, let go of Viva's hand, and followed Umberto out of the semi-darkness of the corridor and into the large kitchen that was brightened by north-facing windows on the other side of the room.

Viva continued to stare at Lorelei. She mouthed the words, "How old are you?"

Lorelei pressed her lips together. Somehow this child knew what most adults had not been able to grasp: She was not feeble or stupid. Lorelei looked around. When she saw no one else was about, she mouthed the words, "I am eighteen."

Viva moved closer. She was a little taller than Lorelei, so she looked down at her. She whispered. "You are old."

Lorelei nodded. "But hardly anyone remembers that."

Viva smiled. "So you get to see and hear everything," she said softly, "because they don't notice you. I won't tell. I like your golden curls."

"Wait until you see my mother's hair," Lorelei said. "It is white as snow. White as a lotus blossom, should that blossom be white."

"White as a swan?"

"Whiter," Lorelei said. "White as a white raven."

"Ravens are black," Viva said.

"Some are white," Lorelei said, "at least here in the Queendom. I've never seen one, but Poppie tells a story about the Raven Sisters. One is so old or so young that her feathers and hair are completely white. Her magic comes from the Sun and the Stars. One sister is so old or so young that her feathers and hair are the darkest blue-black anyone has ever seen. Her magic comes from the Moon and the Earth. They wander the desert keeping the world in balance. It is supposed to be good luck if you see a white raven. Or bad luck, depending upon the state of the world."

"What about if you see a black raven?" Viva asked.

"That's always good luck," Lorelei said. "One of our legends says that each of our queens is either a white raven or a black raven, each looking for her sister so she can balance out the world again."

"Do you think your mother was once a white raven?"

Lorelei smiled and shrugged. "Maybe she still is. She is very wise. Usually it is our oldest people, our wisest people, who have white hair. But my mother's hair began turning white when she was eleven. By the time she married my father, her hair was completely white. Whatever else it may mean, it is a sign that she is a very great queen. The first Reina—the first queen—of Queendom had white hair, too, and she was a great queen. So did the first Chief, who was my mother's great, great, great uncle."

"May I touch your hair?"

"Gold is not so nice as white," Lorelei said, "but you may see what your fingers think of my gold."

Viva reached out and gently touched Lorelei's hair. As usual, it seemed to fly about her head like something separate from her.

"It feels like feathers," Viva said. "Are you a bird, too?"

Lorelei smiled and started to answer, but then Umberto was there, his shadow like a tall oak about to keel over on her. When she was very young, she had been tempted to climb the steward, like a tree. He probably would have allowed it. She had spent more time with Umberto than she had with her own father, Talib, the Queen's consort.

Lorelei called her father Tally, and he called her "little one," not realizing, she supposed, that she hated the nickname. She saw distress in his eyes every time he saw her, although he rarely looked at her. He did what most people did: They let their gazes slide over her, trying to acknowledge her existence and not look at her all at the same time. No one wanted to stare. It wasn't polite. But no one could understand how no medicine, mage, or mystic had been able to heal what ailed her. She was the daughter of the CEO of the Queendom, after all.

Elata, the Queen's soothsayer maid who had known Lorelei her whole life, once told Lorelei she couldn't be "fixed" because there was nothing wrong with her.

"You are a foundling fairy, no doubt," Elata said, "and your mother's real daughter has been taken to fairyland. Your parents should be grateful that they have been given such a magic child as yourself."

Lorelei liked Elata's story, but that kind of fairy tale was from the long ago. Even though stories were part of the warp and weft of the Queendom, Lorelei believed that if fairies ever really existed, they no longer did. Still, for a time when she was younger, she had wandered the forests looking for Reina's and Talib's "real daughter." Although she never found a daughter of any kind or even one fairy, she had made many friends in the woods, including the Old Ones who gave her and everyone else oxygen to breath. Crows and ravens seemed to like Lorelei's company. They didn't fly away when she approached. Now and again, they visited her on the third floor of the Hearth, perching on the Old Oak whose branches stretched across much of the north and west sides of the building.

Deer did not run from her either. At first Lorelei thought it was because they didn't see her—like so many humans didn't see her, even when they did. After a while, she realized, the deer *saw* her, and they were not afraid of her.

She liked that. Too many people were afraid of her. When she was very young, this distressed her. She wanted people to like her. How could they like her when they feared her? Then people began to ignore her. Being ignored was worse than being feared.

But mostly the trees—the Old Ones—were her allies, especially the Old Oak, around which so much of their lives revolved. She believed the trees were filled with giant stories waiting to be told. Trees knew all the secrets of the Universe, just as Umberto knew all the secrets of the Hearth.

Well, he knew *most* of them.

Many Queendomers believed the Hearth was actually a living being. If human beings could create the soothsayers—biological beings who were not birthed and who could not give birth—couldn't they create a living building? The Hearth had been empty when Lorelei's ancestors and their community arrived 200 years earlier, except for a lone woman—human or soothsayer, the stories never indicated. She showed them around the place and told them how it worked, and then she walked away and was never seen again by any of the Queendomers. They called her Steward, and she was considered to be the first steward of the Hearth. Umberto was the current. He didn't know all the secrets to the place, but he knew more than most.

Lorelei shook herself. She did not like when she got lost in reverie like that. Viva was smiling at her. Umberto was talking. Lorelei stepped back a bit and made herself listen to him.

"This home is different from any other," Umberto was saying to Marguerite Teng, his deep voice booming in an almost sing-song way, as though he were telling a story to a huge gathering in the Saffron Room. "We strictly adhere to First Family Protocols which were set forth by our ancestors. These protocols—these rules of etiquette, as it were—bring order to a world that can sometimes be chaotic. We do all we can to keep chaos from our doors!" His voice rose a bit here.

Then he continued, "When the people see the First Family maintain decorum, dignity, and good cheer no matter what, the people are relieved, and life goes on as it should. All is well. That is our motto. Our purpose here, our very important purpose, is to make life as easy and comfortable for the First Family as possible so that they may do their duties for the Queendom and keep our economy flourishing and the Safran Bleu growing."

Umberto took a breath. Viva was listening to the tall steward with rapt attention while her mother fiddled with her gloves, putting them on and taking them off. And putting them on again. She seemed to be looking at Umberto's chest—maybe at the golden fob chain that came out of his waistcoat pocket. Lorelei knew today was Monday because Umberto's waistcoat was gold with blue saffron-colored threads weaving through it like blue clouds through a gold sky. At the other end of the fob chain was a windup watch his grandfather had given him when he left the employ of the Hearth and retired to a hillside in some part of the Queendom far from the Hearth.

"In any case, to help you understand our house, here is a copy of the First Family Protocols, and also a handbook for downstairs, which you may borrow." He emphasized the word "borrow" as he handed Marguerite Teng the books. They had been repaired and reinforced several times. Printing was an expensive venture, and

Umberto never wasted anything. Umberto could squeeze more dye out of spice than anyone alive. At least that was what Queen Reina said every time she went over the monthly expenses. Umberto always said, "We should care for the First Family in style, but we should not be improvident."

"Can't I read these on Nexus?" Marguerite Teng asked as she took the books from the steward.

"Certainly not!" Umberto said. "This information is not for public consumption." He frowned and nodded. "Although it is out there, perhaps even in our village library. Otherwise, how would the public know when we break protocol? Believe it when I say, they know. On the very rare occasion that happens, they let us know." He looked at Lorelei. She raised her eyebrows almost imperceptibly.

"And you, young lady Genevieve," Umberto said, "you should know you are not allowed upstairs unless you are invited by the First Family or one of the Queen's Advisors. You have the run of the downstairs as long as you stay out of the way."

Marguerite Teng twitched as Umberto talked to her daughter. She bit her lip and shrugged her shoulders. Lorelei smiled to herself. Teng did not like Umberto talking to her daughter in this way. But Umberto ran the downstairs. Teng would get used to that. The steward always had the final say in all things downstairs.

"We do not have school in the Hearth," Umberto said, "since Miss Lorelei, Miss Minerva, and Mr. Raphael are no longer children. There is a perfectly respectable school in the nearby Queen's Village, but all of that is up to your mother. Teng, I can show you around more later. Right now, one of the housebods will show you to your rooms. Abbygail!"

Abbygail came running out of the servants' dining room. She looked to be about thirty—although no one knew her real age. Her shoulder-length brown hair fell in one braid partway down her back, and she wore the one piece maroon-colored uniform that covered her from neck to foot. She was one of the first-line bods— the first generation of soothsayers who weren't quite smart enough to be mages. She'd been at the Hearth for as long as Lorelei could remember.

Abbygail smiled at Lorelei and curtsied, as she always did, and said, "Good day to you, Miss Lorelei. It's another lovely day."

Lorelei couldn't help but smile at Abbygail. When she was younger, Abbygail would pinch her cheeks and tell her how smart and pretty she was.

"I wish I were as smart as ye," Abbygail had said more than once. Lorelei did not know why Abbygail thought she was particularly smart—or pretty.

Abbygail appeared to be comfortable at the Hearth, grounded, like one of the old trees in the forest, only she had her roots in the house and the grounds. Away from here, even sometimes in the Queen's Village, Abbygail seemed a little frightened, like the pygmy rabbits Lorelei occasionally saw in the forest. They trembled whenever she went near, unlike the other animals in the forest. Only Abbygail wasn't small like the pygmy rabbits, or like Lorelei herself.

"What do you be needing from me, Sir Umberto?" Abbygail asked.

No matter how many times Umberto instructed Abbygail not to call him "sir" anything, she persisted. Like many first-line soothsayers, it seemed she could not reprogram herself.

Umberto's cheek twitched slightly, and he rolled his eyes. "Marguerite Teng and Genevieve, this is Abbygail. Abbygail, Marguerite Teng is the new cook." Umberto hesitated. "It really is most awkward to call you Marguerite Teng. It is a lot to ask of the Queen, too, should she ever need to address you. I can order you to let us call you Chef, but I'd rather it was your own decision. We are not a dictatorship in this downstairs, but neither are we anarchists."

Marguerite Teng briefly closed her eyes. She was tired. Her mouth was set hard, as though she had said her last word, ever. Then she opened her eyes, nodded, and said, "You may address me as Teng, Maggie or, if you must, Cook or Cook Teng."

"Fine," Umberto said. "Cook Teng and child, please follow Abbygail."

Abbygail picked up Marguerite Teng's bag. "Come with me," she said.

"We have more bags outside," Teng told Umberto.

Someone knocked on the back door. Umberto called, "Billy!"

Viva waved to Lorelei and then followed Abbygail and her mother down the long hallway to the servants' quarters. Lorelei momentarily wished she could go with them.

"Billy!" Umberto called again.

Billy came out of the servants' dining room, wiping his chin with a napkin. He seemed to enjoy human sensual pleasures more than Abbygail or any other soothsayer Lorelei had ever met. More than anyone, actually. He had curly red hair, wore a one-piece green uniform, and was as lean as Abbygail. He smiled when he saw Lorelei. She returned his smile. He had only been at the Hearth for a few months, but he had made an impression on everyone—or at least, he had on Lorelei.

"Yes, Umberto," Billy said. "What may I do you fer?"

"*Mr.* Umberto to you," Umberto said. "And why are you talking that way?"

"I like playing with the old vernaculars," he said. "Mix it up some."

"Well, stop it," Umberto said. "I need you to fetch Cook Teng's luggage and see who is at the back door."

"Sure thing," Billy said. He started to walk down the corridor to the door to the outside. Then he turned around and said, "You know, I have a last name, too, Mr. Umberto. My full proper name is Billy Santos. The woman at my first house let me choose a last name. She said I was like a saint, like those old-time saints. Holy people who did good for others. Santos, she called me. So I took that as my surname."

Umberto arched an eyebrow. "I seem to remember that was also what they used to call wooden statues of saints in the old world. She was calling you Pinocchio. Remember the old story of Pinocchio, the wooden boy whose nose grew every time he lied?"

Lorelei looked at Umberto. Of course, Billy remembered. He was a soothsayer. He had all of known history at his recall.

"She was insulting you, Billy," Umberto said. "She knew you wouldn't understand."

Billy's shoulders dropped a bit. "Oh," he said. Then he turned around and kept walking to the door.

When Lorelei believed Billy was out of earshot, she said to Umberto, "That was cruel."

"Maybe," he said. "But there are no saints in this house, and he is no exception."

"I am Billy Santos!" Billy shouted as he reached the door to the outside. "Saint *and* wooden boy, at your service."

Lorelei laughed. Billy opened the door, and sunshine spilled onto the stone floor.

"That boy is going to be trouble," Umberto said. "You best stay away from him, Miss Lorelei. You have too much in common."

Lorelei watched Billy step outside and look around. Then he took something from the outside of the door. He came back inside and hurried toward them.

"Mr. Umberto!" he said. "Look at this." When he was close enough, he handed Umberto what looked like an old parchment piece of paper.

"Good grief!" Mr. Umberto said. "What nonsense."

Umberto showed the paper to Lorelei. Written in red ink on the parchment were the words: "Live free or die." Someone had sketched a segmented snake below the words.

"What does it mean?" Billy asked, taking the words right out of Lorelei's mind.

"I haven't any idea," Umberto said. "But it doesn't concern us. Go get the bags, and let's get back to work."

CHAPTER TWO
REINA

Reina sat in the Crocus Garden looking at the financial figures Nehemiah projected above the round wooden table and listening to his dire predictions for the next quarter. Nearly all of the glass doors were open, but so many flowers and vines snaked up the trellises just inside and outside the garden that the area was cool and shady, comfortable and cozy. Reina gazed up through the gray vines that twisted through and over the lattice roof. The patches of blue sky felt like a balm on this day of bad financial news.

"If none of the warehouses are missing inventory," Reina said, "what has happened? Why are sales of Safran Bleu going down?"

Safran Bleu—blue saffron—was the premier crop of the Queendom and their main export. Legally, no other nation state in the Consolidated Five could grow and sell it.

"I don't believe demand has gone down," Nehemiah said, "but our exports have definitely dropped. Not enough to account for the losses."

Mathematically that did not even make sense.

"Someone must be illegally growing it and selling it," Nehemiah said. "Or stealing it and our cooperatives aren't aware of it."

"If any other nation is allowing this," Reina said, "they are in violation of our treaty." She stood, and the projection disappeared.

"Next time we meet with the Five, I will demand they put a stop to this underground—" She looked around, trying to think of the right word. "This underground *thievery*. The others have turned a blind eye to it for too long."

A few years ago, thieves from Armistead had come into the Queendom and stolen tons of red saffron before they were apprehended. The Prime Minister and CEO of Armistead, Damon Lerner, had voted with his advisors to reimburse the Queendom, and their legal system had supposedly reconciled the thieves with their communities. Prime Minister Lerner had not been specific about their reconciliation, so Reina was never certain Armistead had done anything to stop the thieves from stealing again; the criminals had not returned to the Queendom to apologize or attempt to make restitution for their crimes.

Reina would have sent them to the Hinterlands if she had had a choice.

Perhaps not. The Queendom's judicial system rarely exiled anyone, so Reina could not expect another nation to do that which she would not do to her own people.

"I wonder if we should try to investigate this on our own first," Nehemiah said. "Before we mention it to the Five."

A breeze wound through the garden, ruffling Nehemiah's red saffron-colored robes. Soothsayer mages almost all wore the saffron robes. No one had ever told Reina why, and she had never asked. It seemed too personal a question. Nehemiah was her most trusted advisor, it was true. But she knew nothing of his personal life—or even if he had one. Like most soothsayers, he worked much longer hours than any human.

"If we insist on a crackdown of the underground economy," Reina said, "the Five might guess that we're having some financial irregularities? Yes. I agree. Send out people you trust to the other four nations to see if someone is stealing. Quickly, though. We can't sustain these kinds of losses for long. If any of the Five find out we are this close to ruin, they may try a hostile takeover. We can't allow that to happen." She rubbed her face.

"Are you tired, Ma'am?" Nehemiah asked.

Reina looked at him, surprised. "I am, Nehemiah."

"Do you need to see a physician? Or a healing bod?"

She smiled and put her hand on his arm for a moment. "No, Nehemiah. I am only human, and I need to work less and play more. A healing bod might be nice. Have not had a massage in a while." She dropped her hand. "What we really need are more inventive ways to use Safran Bleu. No, what we really need is for someone to find the Moonstruck Saffron. Can you imagine what a boon that plant would be to the Queendom with its ability to cure illness and create exquisite dyes?"

"I have no record that black saffron ever existed," Nehemiah said, "moonstruck or otherwise, as I have mentioned to you on many occasions."

"Yes, I know," she said. "And as I have said on many occasions, you don't know everything. You were programmed, and whoever programmed you, didn't have access to what happened privately in every person's life. You don't know what Mary Letty Holmes had for lunch the day she created Safran Bleu."

"She had a garden salad with fresh blueberries," Nehemiah said.

Reina leaned her head back and laughed.

"Liar!" she said.

Nehemiah's lips moved into a barely smile which made Reina laugh harder.

"Truly, it was in her journal," he said. "I have no journal record of her creating a plant that was the color of night, with the 'ability to cure illness and create exquisite dyes.'"

"I hate when you quote me," Reina said. "Why do you think your creators gave you such a phlegmatic personality?"

"All the better to serve you," Nehemiah said.

"A few hundred years after the fact," Reina said.

"By the way, you have been programmed, too," Nehemiah said, "only your programming comes from the culture and from your family and friends."

"Granted," Reina said. "We are all influenced by our surroundings, including me and including you."

The door from the house to the garden opened, and Umberto stepped through and came into the Crocus Garden.

"Your Majesty," he said. "The chef and her daughter have arrived, and I've brought them up to meet you."

"All right," Reina said as she looked toward the door. She motioned with her right hand for the woman and child to come in.

They followed Umberto into the garden and stopped several feet from Reina. The woman wore a bright yellow dress that matched the poppies Reina had seen growing in one of the fields she walked past every time she went into the village. The color looked good against the woman's olive-colored skin and dark hair.

The girl was dressed in blue saffron-colored slacks and a pink top. She had big black eyes that stared directly at the Queen. The woman touched the girl's elbow, and the girl looked away from the Queen and down at her feet. Reina grimaced. She wanted to tell the woman not to suppress her child's natural curiosity. They were equals, Reina and the child. They were all equals; they just had different jobs, roles, and titles.

"Your Majesty," Umberto said, "may I present Marguerite Teng and her daughter, Genevieve."

The woman bowed her head slightly and said, "Your Majesty."

"How do you do?" the Queen said.

The girl curtsied.

Reina laughed. "My, what a fine curtsy! I had to learn that when I was a child, too. My mother wanted me to curtsy to every adult I met. She said it was a way to remind myself that I was not better than anyone else. She was right. I was not better then and am not now. We are all equal in the Queendom. Isn't that right, Genevieve?"

"Yes, Your Majesty," Genevieve said.

"Do you have other family, Teng?" Reina asked. Umberto had shared Teng's biography with her, but Reina wanted to hear what the woman had to say for herself.

"Yes, Ma'am," Teng said. "My parents and brother live in Erdom. I have a son, too, Cristopher."

"He didn't come with you then?" Reina said.

"No, Ma'am," she said. "After his time in the Service, he left home seeking adventure."

Reina said, "I heard something about him exploring the Hinterlands. Is this so?"

"It is," she said. "I didn't want him to go, but he believes he's invincible, and he's interested in the wildlife, geology, things like that, beyond the Consolidated Five. I encouraged him to go study in one of our countries, but he wasn't interested."

"I certainly understand headstrong children," Reina said. Her son Raphael had never done a solitary thing she had wanted him to do his entire life. She had believed—hoped—his time in the Service would have matured him, settled him down. That was the purpose of it: to steer young women and men in the right direction so they would not become a menace to their communities. Raphael was not a menace. He was unfocused.

"Their father was an explorer, too," Teng said. "Left us to explore the Hinterlands when Cristopher was only twelve. Never came home. I'm hoping Cristopher will return, but I have no control over that part of it. There's not much for me to do."

"I admire your acceptance," Reina said. "Are you from Erdom originally, Marguerite Teng?"

"Yes, Ma'am," Teng said.

"And why did you want to immigrate to our fair nation?"

"Because of the Safran Bleu," Teng said, "and all the spices and herbs you grow here. My mother was from Queendom. I grew up on stories of the long-lost Moonstruck Saffron."

Reina smiled. She wanted to look over at Nehemiah, but she restrained herself.

"Ah yes," Reina said. "We were just talking about the stories of the black saffron. Do you believe the Moonstruck Saffron is real?"

The child looked up at her mother. Marguerite Teng said,

"You might ask me if I believe in giants, fairies, or monsters in the dark."

"I might," Reina said. "Do you?"

"I do not," Marguerite Teng said. She hesitated and then said, "But I do believe in the Moonstruck Saffron, and I have come here to find it. I also believe in the Unified Field Theory of Spices."

"Perhaps we have bothered her majesty enough today," Umberto said, stepping toward Teng.

"No, let her speak," Reina said. "What is this Unified Field Theory of Spices?"

"My mother and father are cooks, too," Teng said. "We follow the ancient ways of plant people and cooks. Plants were the first people on this planet, and they know everything. Every dish we create has a particular set of ingredients that can make the dish perfect. It's like we are fairy tale witches weaving a spell, only we used spices instead of words. Once you have the correct ingredients in the correct proportions, magic happens and anything is possible. Only it's not magic like in fairy tales. It's science *and* ancient tales. Chemistry and magic together! In other words, if someone has enough of the proper ingredients in the right order in the right dishes, she can make a perfect meal that will bring about peace, harmony, prosperity, and good health for all who partake."

"Extraordinary!" Reina said. "Have you heard of this, Nehemiah?"

"It is in the founding stories of some of the Cooking Guilds," Nehemiah said.

"I hope you do find the Moonstruck Saffron," Reina said. "As you may or may not know, we have offered a bounty to anyone who finds or can grow the Moonstruck Saffron. In addition, if you achieved this great feat, you will be awarded the Queen's Honorary Star which would make you a citizen of the Queendom for life."

"Thank you, Ma'am!" Teng said.

"I like this idea of a Unified Field Theory of Spices," Reina said. "Please, implement it at any meal. I assume there are no downsides to this theory? The wrong mixture won't put a bad spell on us, will it?"

"No, maybe a bit of mild indigestion," Teng said. She smiled slightly.

Reina laughed. "Truly?"

"No," Teng said. "I would never put Your Majesty and your family in harm's way. I know what I am doing."

"I know you do," Reina said, "otherwise Umberto would have never hired you. And you, Genevieve. How do you find our country?"

"I have only been here a few hours, Your Majesty," Genevieve said, "but I feel as though I am home. I met Lorelei—"

"Miss Lorelei," Umberto corrected.

"I met Miss Lorelei," Genevieve said, "and we are friends already."

"I am glad to hear that," Reina said. "Now, we are entertaining the Foreign Minister of Berland tonight. I believe we will have ten for dinner. It's not a state dinner. No one will be watching us on Nexus, so it's private, casual. I'm certain Wanda and Turnkey will help you put a meal together for tonight."

"I look forward to creating something for you," Teng said. "Is there anything in particular you would like?"

"Peace, harmony, and complete honesty," Reina said. "Well, complete honesty on the part of the Minister." She smiled. "No. Umberto has a list of my family's likes and dislikes. Beyond that, feel free to express your artistic vision."

Umberto led the cook and her daughter away. Reina went back to the table and Nehemiah.

"That is an interesting woman," Reina said.

"You mean she is eccentric," Nehemiah said. "You have a soft spot for eccentrics."

"Yes," Reina said. "Mary Letty Holmes was an eccentric, and that eccentric botanist created our entire economy. Without her, there would be no Queendom. So if an eccentric chef wants to find the Moonstruck Saffron, I say let her try. Now, let me see the sales for the red saffron."

After Reina's meeting with Nehemiah, she went up to her third floor chambers. In the hot afternoon, she suddenly longed for the dark coolness of her bedroom. She got inside her front room—the room that seemed too white and bright today—when someone knocked at her door.

A moment later, Elata opened the door and stepped inside. Elata had been taking care of Queen Reina for many years, but Reina was not familiar with the peculiar expression on Elata's cherub-like face. Was it a smile or smirk or something in-between?

"Your healing bod has arrived," Elata said.

Had Nehemiah called in a masseuse for her without telling her? That would be unusual. No matter. She welcomed a massage.

"Good!" Reina said. "Send her in."

"It's not a she," Elata said.

Elata opened the door, and a tall medium-built man with short brown hair and bright blue eyes stepped into the room. He smiled at Reina and slightly bowed his head.

"Good day, Your Majesty," he said.

He was the spitting image of Outram, her first love, when Outram had been about thirty years old. Reina almost laughed as she looked at him. Sometimes the Universe had a ridiculously wonderful sense of timing.

"Elata said you weren't expecting me," he said.

"No, but I'm so glad she brought you up," Reina said. "Elata, you may go."

Elata made a face. Reina could tell she wanted to stay, but Reina nodded toward the door. When it had closed behind Elata, Reina said, "Why are you here?"

"I have an appointment with you, Ma'am," he said. He was wearing a blue saffron-colored shirt that was too tight, but it was too tight in an attractive way. His dark blue slacks were loose and comfortable looking. In fact, he looked loose and comfortable himself. As if he did not have a care in the world. What was that like?

"I had an appointment with you for a massage?" Reina asked.

"For whatever you like," he said. "I am a full service healing bod. I have agreed to all of the privacy regulations, as everyone has in our company, and I will keep anything that happens here private from everyone, as you know."

"Who sent you?" Reina asked as she walked around him, looking at him from top to bottom. The resemblance was uncanny.

"The Queen Madre Boudica sent me," he said.

Reina laughed. "Mother!" she called, activating the Hearth's privocom system. "Can you please come to my chambers?"

Reina and the man stood silently in her room for a few moments. Then Reina said, "What is your name?"

"Fan," he said.

"Are you saying deer?"

"Yes, but it is spelled like fan, like something you would fan yourself with. I choose it myself. It means 'mortal.'"

"But you're not," Reina said.

"We all are," Fan said. "Even soothsayers."

"Ahhh, you sound more like a mage soothsayer than a healing bod. Introspective."

"We are all individuals," he said, "just as you humans are."

"Yes, I know," Reina said. She suddenly felt irritated that this stranger was standing in the Queen's chamber in the Hearth—the headquarters of all of Queendom—lecturing her. Perhaps lecture was the wrong word. Perhaps he was trying to have a philosophical conversation with her. She did not care much for philosophy. She cared for her Queendom, she cared for economics (because she had to), she cared for her family and the people of the Queendom.

The door opened without a knock and her mother, the Queen Madre, stood on the threshold. She was wearing a maroon red robe with white trim. It was buttoned all the way up to her chin. Reina grimaced. Her mother had eschewed all pretenses of royalty when she was CEO; they weren't blood royalty and the Queendom was not a monarchy. The Villanueva family had been in charge for two hundred years, elected by the people of the Queendom again and again. Now that the Queen Madre was retired, she sometimes dressed as if she were a member of one of those long ago monarchies from far before the Fall. The Queen Madre had left office far earlier than most leaders of the Queendom had when she was a mere sixty years old.

"I see you have met Fan," the Queen Madre said. "Isn't he beautiful? I thought you seemed a bit tense of late."

"Your Majesty," Fan said, nodding to the Queen Madre.

"Mother," Reina said. She pulled her mother aside and whispered. "You should not speak about him as if he were a thing."

"He can hear you, sweetheart," the Queen Madre said. "He is a soothsayer, you understand."

Reina looked over at Fan, and he shrugged. Reina felt herself blushing. She was thirteen all over again. She breathed deeply and stepped away from her mother.

"I am afraid the Queen Madre is mistaken in this matter," Reina said. "That is unusual. She is rarely mistaken."

"I am never mistaken," the Queen Madre said. "When I was CEO, I often cavorted with health bods. It was the only way I stayed sane. Sexual urges are as natural and healthy as sneezing."

"Thank you for that image, Mother," Reina said. "Now every time I have sex I will think of sneezing, or the other way around."

The Queen Madre laughed.

"I have to prepare for a dinner with the Foreign Minister," Reina said. "Nehemiah is waiting for me."

He was not waiting for her that moment, but essentially, he was always waiting for her.

"Yes, speaking of someone who could use some cavorting," the Queen Madre said.

"Shall we not speak of Queendom business in front of—"

"The help?" the Queen Madre said. "Don't be a snob, daughter."

Reina felt a flash of anger. Her mother should not be speaking to her this way, not when someone else was in the room.

"I was going to say in front of a stranger," Reina said.

"He is not a stranger," the Queen Madre said. "He is now part of the staff. I may use him myself."

Reina looked at her mother.

"As a masseuse, dear," she said. "He is too young for me. Besides, Poppie would not be pleased. Fan has his own place, so he won't be living here, but he will come daily to service our needs. When I saw his image on Nexus he reminded me of someone, and I felt he would be perfect for you."

"He is the twin of Outram!" Reina said. "When he was younger."

The Queen Madre said, "Perhaps Outram is a soothsayer, too."

"How do you explain his children then?" Reina said.

"That tells us his wife is not a soothsayer," the Queen Madre said. "Not the other way around."

Reina groaned. No matter how she tried, she could not seem to extricate herself from this awkward conversation. She was not going to win this, and trying to maintain her dignity while she wanted to yell at her own mother was wearing her out.

"Fan," Reina said, turning to him. "This is not how new staff usually come to the Hearth. Mr. Umberto takes care of the hiring and firing. However, since my mother has asked for you in particular, we can bypass the bureaucracy, somewhat. Welcome to the Hearth, the People's House." She smiled. It had not been a true People's House for many generations.

"Thank you, Ma'am," Fan said.

"Queen Madre," Reina said, formally, "I can manage this from here. I will see you at dinner tonight."

The Queen Madre tilted her head forward slightly. Then she left the room.

Reina looked at Fan again. "Your services are confidential, as you said. No other human or soothsayer need know anything about what goes on between us?"

"Discretion is the better part of valor, Ma'am," Fan said.

Reina was not certain she cared for the way he watched her.

"A valorous and mortal man," Reina said. "How can I resist?" She smiled, then shook her head. No, she could not do this. She was queen. She was CEO of the Queendom.

But Talib had left her bed long ago and lived full-time in his art studio. She had no intention of being celibate the rest of her life.

"You perform your services willingly?" she asked. "You are not under any duress?"

"Very willingly," he said, "and I am not under any duress at all."

Reina gazed out her window that looked over the blue saffron fields. To the west of the fields, the Black River wound south, toward the distant ocean. It reminded her of a snake at this time of year, before the saffron blossomed. To the east of the fields was a meadow of tall grass. She remembered many hours spent lying in that grass field when she was a girl. The grass undulated in the wind like a vast always moving sea. Right now, she wished she could dive into that sea.

"If now isn't convenient for you, Ma'am," Fan said, "I can come back another time."

Reina looked back at Fan. "No," she said. "This is exactly the right time. I could use a massage. And whatever else you have to offer today. Tell me, how long can you stay hard?"

"Forever," he said.

Reina laughed. "More and more, this sounds like fun."

CHAPTER THREE
TENG

Marguerite Teng stepped out of the kitchen carrying shears and a woven cedar basket. She let out a grateful sigh. She had never seen such a large lush kitchen garden. The Hearth was shaped like a rectangle with one of the long sides missing—or like a "c" with hard angles. It had been built so that the north front entrance led into the second floor where the First Family's dining rooms, library, and drawing rooms were located, along with sleeping quarters for guests, and offices for the Queen, Nehemiah, and others who worked on the business part of the busidom. The First Family had their apartments on the third floor.

Teng had not seen any of this yet, but she remembered it all from the floor plans she had viewed on Nexus. The south back entrances led to the first floor, which was where the kitchen was, along with the sleeping quarters of the servants. The first floor got an up-close and personal view of the gardens that spilled out onto the grounds and nearly all around the Hearth.

Teng had dreamed of coming to the Queendom and the Hearth her entire life, and now she was here. She wanted to jump with joy, but her joy was muted because of Cristopher. Her poor foolish son who had gotten himself kidnapped by some kind of rebel group in the Hinterlands. At first, the Hinterlanders demanded ransom from her for his release. She had to give so much of her credit to their contact in Erdom so he could purchase supplies and bring them into the Hinterlands. If she did this for three months, they promised, Cristopher could come home. If she did not comply with their requests, they promised Cristopher would be imprisoned by them for at least three years. If she informed anyone about Cristopher's capture and imprisonment, they promised, they would change his sentence to life.

Three years. She had no idea what conditions were like in a prison in the Hinterlands. They did not have prisons in Erdom, or in the Queendom.

For several months, Teng had given them exactly what they wanted. Then the Hinterlanders changed the terms of their bargain. They had found out about her job at the Hearth, and now they demanded she spy on the First Family and the Queendom busidom until further notice.

She was not a stupid woman, but she knew her view of the world was quite parochial. She did not know how to deal with extortion or mysterious unknown persons from the Hinterlands. She should have gone to the authorities from the very beginning. Now three months had passed, three months where she had been illegally sending credits to someone to help smuggle supplies into the Hinterlands. If she confessed, the Queendom judiciary might not be satisfied with reconciliation. They might sentence her to exile in the Hinterlands. And if one member of the family was sentenced to exile, the entire family had to go.

Teng didn't have a choice, as far as she was concerned. She had to do what the Hinterlanders demanded, to save her son from his imprisonment and her entire family from exile. Cristopher may have acted stupidly by traveling to the Hinterlands, she may have acted stupidly by not contacting the authorities right away, but Teng could not let their mistakes impact Viva.

Besides, she was convinced she could salvage this, make it better. She had survived when her husband—her sweetheart since they were teenagers—left her and the children ten years earlier, left her with no credit and all of his debt. She had wanted to find the highest bridge and jump to her death. Instead, she made a cloth effigy of her ex-beloved. With her children by her side, she had burned the effigy, declaring her freedom from her husband and the misery he had caused. As soon as the stand-in husband went up in smoke, she realized her true calling was to follow in the footsteps of her parents and become a chef and learn as much as she could about the Unified Field Theory of Spices.

She breathed deeply again as she looked at the Hearth's kitchen garden. She might be a criminal, she might be exiled eventually, but for now, she was here in the Queendom, working as the head cook. She was going to enjoy the experience. She would spy as little as she could for the Hinterlanders. And maybe, just maybe, she would find the Moonstruck Saffron and use the bonus credits to free her son.

She began walking the dirt path that wound through the garden. Her steps kicked gray sand into the air. It was drier here than she had imagined it would be. She walked past rows of greens, some she recognized: arugula, leaf lettuce, rocket, dandelions. Some were strangers to her. Most of the rows grew in straight lines but a few grew into a spiral. The carrot greens were already a foot high, their crowns pushing up through the dark earth: orange, yellow, and purple. Onions and garlic grew here and there, along with cilantro, parsley, kale, rutabagas, and other root vegetables. Teng was impressed that the gardener was able to get so many different kinds of plants growing together.

She walked by the herb beds: wild ginger, cardamon, rosemary, basil, thyme, and more she did not at first recognize. Beyond the herbs were berry shrubs—not yet producing—and fruit and nut trees. Something was growing nearly everywhere, some in shade, some in the sun. She breathed it all in and felt slightly dizzy. She was in heaven, she was certain.

Suddenly, a few feet from her, a man stood up. She had not seen him until he moved. He blended into the garden as if he were a part of it. He slapped his pale hands on his dusty blue overalls and tipped the pale yellow wide-brimmed hat back on his head.

"Hello," he said. "You must be Marguerite Teng. It is a pleasure to meet you. I am Quintana." He held out his hand to her.

Teng shook his hand and squinted. She could not tell if he was very old or not old at all.

"Are you a soothsayer?" she asked.

"I am," he said. "I have been with the Hearth since the beginning of the Queendom. I can tell you the story of each plant. That rosemary bush, for instance." He pointed. "Some form of that rosemary tree has been here since the beginning, even before."

"Wasn't that two hundred years ago?" Teng asked.

"And more," he said.

Teng looked at him. He was doing that thing so many soothsayers did: They did not exactly correct humans when humans were wrong, unless they were asked. They added to what the humans had said to make it right. Quintana knew exactly when he had arrived at the Hearth. Teng supposed soothsayers understood better than anyone that human egos could be easily bruised.

"I took cuttings from the original rosemary bush," he said, "and then cuttings from those new bushes, and on and on. This garden has fed the First Family and their guests for generations. Now it is yours to use."

"I will do so with great reverence," Teng said, "and regard, I promise."

"I appreciate that," he said.

"Tonight I am feeding the Foreign Minister of Berland," Teng said. "I wanted to demonstrate the Unified Field Theory of Spices, but the time for the meal is so near. I am uncertain on what to do."

"As I understand the Unified Field Theory of Spices," Quintana said, "you rely on your instincts, intuition, and your knowledge of and connection with the plants to determine the right combination of ingredients."

"Yes!" Teng said. "It is rare to meet someone who knows the theory, besides a few chefs here and there. Most people become uncomfortable when I speak of it. They act like I have said I believe the

Earth is flat or the Moon is made of cheese." She smiled. "I wonder, did people ever really believe the Moon was made from cheese?"

Quintana shook his head. "I would wager that people never believed the Moon was made of cheese or that the Earth was flat, generally speaking."

"My mother used to tell me the Moon was made of sunlight," Teng said, "a particular kind of sunlight that knew everything, therefore the Moon knew everything. I spent a great deal of my childhood trying to get the Moon to tell me first everything and then when that didn't happen, I tried to get it to tell me *anything*."

Quintana laughed.

"Yes, even after I knew the chemical composition of the Moon," Teng said. She smiled. "That is how I knew I belonged in the Queendom. This is where stories matter. Where people understand art and storytelling. They understand that blue saffron is more than a beautiful plant. It is the culmination of the hopes and dreams of a people, blossoming every year, offering up medicine and good taste. In Erdom, the people are good people. They share the values of the Consolidated Five, but here . . . here, I always imagined everything was more poetic. More magical, in a way. In the Queendom, the citizens never forget the Reconnection, the first reconciliation, never forget that we are bound to this place and one another for all time."

"Sometimes we do forget that," Quintana said. "It is natural. People get busy with life, and we forget to nurture those connections. It is good to hear it again, especially—" He hesitated.

"Especially from a human being?" Teng said. "Yes, we have short memories, don't we? The soothsayers must constantly fear we will repeat the mistakes of our ancestors."

Quintana shook his head. "No, I wouldn't say we are in fear."

Teng put up a hand. "I apologize again. I didn't mean to get into a political tangle. I only need to decide what to make for dinner."

"Well," Quintana said, "I do know the Berlanders typically like hearty meals, with little spice."

"There is some venison marinating in the refrigerator. Working with meat is not my strength."

"I know the deer was killed with honor," Quintana said. "Hunter would never take a life unless she believed it was being offered."

"Thank you, Mr. Quintana," Teng said. "I look forward to working with you, and I hope you will allow me to ask you an ignorant question now and again."

He laughed. "Let me know if there is something you want to use in your cooking, but you don't see here, and I will attempt to grow it for you. That is, if you intend to stay for a time. Our last chef only lasted three years."

"Three years," Teng said. "That seems like a long time, although I suppose it doesn't to you."

She did not answer Quintana's question on how long she intended to say. She could not tell him that her son was being held by bandits. Instead, she said, "I can't imagine I would need anything beyond this garden for my cooking needs, except for rice and legumes, which I assume are grown elsewhere. Unless you want to grow some Moonstruck Saffron here."

"If I knew how, I certainly would. By the way, over on the other side of that juniper bush, we do have some red and some blue saffron, for use by the Hearth's chef."

"I have quite the task," Teng said. "Which you have made easier with this exquisite garden. Thank you."

Quintana nodded, then slowly walked away from her.

Teng bit her bottom lip and looked around. The Old Oak on the other side of the Hearth moved slightly in the breeze. Its branches reached so far up and so far out that it seemed as though the ancient tree were stretching. Teng smiled. One of the reasons she had wanted to come to the Hearth in the beginning, before Cristopher got caught up in whatever he had gotten caught up in, was because of this tree. She had seen a picture of it and heard the story of how the Hearth had been built around it, so that the foundation of the Queendom was rooted, quite literally, in Nature, in something older and wiser than human beings. Every large stone that became a part of the outside of the three and a half story home came from the countryside—at least, that was what the first steward claimed.

In the beginning, most of the citizens of Queendom had lived at the Hearth, until gradually, families wanted to move out and be on their own—Teng could hardly imagine why—but the Hearth and the Old Oak—and the other Old Oaks and newer trees—were always at the center of the Queendom.

In Erdom, Teng had felt separate from everything and everyone. Ungrounded in place, time, or story. She was certain it would be different here. It had to be.

But now she had a meal to prepare. Which herbs and spices and other plants called to her? Which wanted to be a part of this meal? She reached into the dark blue cloth bag around her waist and took out a small handful of dried tobacco and cedar.

"I come in peace," she said as she held the dried plants chest high and opened her hand to let the breeze take the offering. "I intend no harm and wish to ask the plants to work with me to bring good food, good health, and harmony to the meal I create today and all days."

Soon her hand was empty. Then she held the palms of her hands down, horizontal with the ground, and began walking. It wasn't that she talked to the plants, exactly, or that they talked to her, but something happened. Normally, she let herself wander around a garden and then maybe a name would drift into her mind or she would have the urge to go this way or that way. She liked to walk in the garden barefoot, but she did not want to seem too strange on her first day.

She heard Viva's laughter somewhere in the distance. She vaguely wondered what Viva was up to. Viva had an amazing capacity for making friends and allies wherever she went. Viva would certainly not hesitate to kick off her shoes.

But then she was ten years old.

Teng rolled her eyes—and kicked off her shoes. The soil was darker here and felt cool on her feet. She walked over to a silver sage bush.

"Great Sage," she whispered. "You who are wise, grant us your wisdom and allow me to take some of your leaves." She felt a breeze on her face and suddenly remembered an old chant her mother had taught her when she was a child. "They who would live for many a day must eat sage in May." Even though it wasn't May, she felt the moment was right, so she plucked several silver green leaves from the sage tree as she hummed, dropping each into her basket.

Next she got a whiff of lemon and wood: thyme. She walked until she found a patch of it growing low to the ground in the dappled sunlight not far from an apple tree. Teng knelt next to the patch of green that spread along the ground toward the nearby basil and rosemary, its leaves so tiny they hardly looked indistinct from each other. She ran the palm of her hand above the thyme and breathed deeply.

"Oh, Great Thyme," she whispered. "You who gives us good health and fills us with courage, allow me to use you in my cooking."

She breathed deeply, closed her eyes, heard the whir of something next to her ear, opened her eyes just as a blue dragonfly darted past her, hovered over the thyme, and then zipped away.

Teng pulled out the shears and gently took a handful of the thyme in her hand. She waited a moment, and then she cut the thyme while singing, "Oh the summer time has come and the trees are sweetly blooming, and wild mountain thyme grows around the purple heather. Will you go, lassie, go?" And then she heard Quintana's voice from across the garden sing, "Will you go, lassie, go?" Teng laughed and dropped the thyme into her basket.

"Thank you, Thyme," she said.

Next she found parsley and then rosemary.

"Oh, Rosemary," she whispered. "You who are everything. Healer, lover, purifier. Please become part of this dish and spread your magic far and wide. You who the Sea Mother brought into being share yourself with the First Family and company."

When she felt the time was right, she snipped off several stems of new growth and dropped them into her basket.

She looked around and breathed deeply. She felt pure joy bubbling up from the ground, it seemed, or maybe from her heart, her soul. She didn't know from where, nor did she care. She couldn't remember ever being so happy in her work, so delighted. This place was perfect, perfect, perfect. They would be happy here, she and Viva, and she would figure out some way to get her son back.

She realized then she needed one more item for her dish. She heard the song on the wind, or maybe it was the scent that called her, but she followed the garden path until it wound around to a juniper bush. It twisted up and away from her, like a woman stopped in mid-dance, its bark gray and craggy, its green boughs seeming to frame it in a kind of green halo. Only that wasn't quite right. It was as though the entire tree glowed.

"And you who protects us," Teng whispered, "you who stand at the opening of this world and that one, please allow me to take of your berries to create the perfect dish."

She stepped closer to the tree and carefully felt the dusty blue berries for those that were ripe.

She dropped them into her basket. When she turned around, Quintana stood a few feet from her.

"I apologize," Quintana said. "I didn't mean to startle you. I didn't realize you were here, at this place."

"This is an amazing juniper tree," Teng said as she turned back to the tree. "The trees here at the Hearth are all wonderful."

"This tree might be a thousand years old," Quintana said, "maybe two thousand. It was here before me, before the Hearth, before the Old Oak or the Fall. I heard your songs. I am glad someone who knows the Old Ways is now our chef. I have a feeling something is coming, and we will need all of our skills to get through it."

"I didn't know soothsayers had intuition," Teng said. "Excuse me if that's ignorant. I haven't had a great deal of experience personally with soothsayers. Please feel free to ask any ignorant questions about me, my family, my profession, or Erdom."

Quintana smiled. Teng liked the way his eyes seemed to light up when he smiled. He seemed more like a real person than most people. He *was* a person. He just wasn't a human being.

"We don't have intuition the way humans do," he said, "but there are things we know. And something feels askew. I am not certain what, yet."

"I hope it's not me," Teng said. "I have been accused of being askew now and again."

Quintana laughed. Teng thought she heard bells, but it was only Quintana's laughter. She couldn't help it. She laughed, too.

"I don't believe it is you," he said. "But I'll be on the lookout for you now." He smiled. "I probably should not have said anything. Just the ramblings of an old man. I will see you later."

Teng watched as Quintana walked away. He was the youngest looking old man she had ever seen.

And definitely the best looking.

She shook her head and laughed at herself. It was time to see if the potatoes, carrots, onions, and garlic would allow themselves to become a part of her healing brew.

Maybe if she did her job well enough, her son would be freed without her having to betray the First Family. When they first told her she had to spy on the First Family in order to get her son released, she told them she could never do such a thing. She could not, would not, do anything to harm the Villanueva's or Queendom.

That was when her son's captors told her she must send them regular communication about the First Family or she would never see her son again.

What kind of people would threaten such things?

She had to find a way out of this mess. She couldn't see it yet, but she would do it.

In the meantime, she had to cook.

She hoped none of her troubles would seep into the food she was preparing. If she used the right ingredients, the best ingredients, and applied the rules of the Unified Field Theory of Spices to the dish, everything would be fine. In fact, everything would be perfect.

CHAPTER FOUR
UMBERTO

"Don't spill a drop of that, young man!" Umberto said as Billy stepped out of the kitchen carrying a large tureen of venison stew that he lightly rested on his left shoulder.

Billy said, "Yes, Mr. Umberto."

Umberto nodded. Good. Billy was learning. If Umberto had admonished him a few days ago, he no doubt would have said something like, "Not bloody likely." Soothsayers were not perfect, and Billy needed to realize this. They could not do everything, and they occasionally made mistakes. True, Billy had been on this Earth much longer than Umberto, so he was not a young man, per se, despite his looks, but still. He needed to learn respect. He needed to understand his place in the scheme of things.

"Mr. Umberto, Billy knows more than you and me put together," Abbygail said, as she passed him carrying a freshly baked loaf of bread. "Have you forgotten that?"

Both Abbygail and Billy were dressed in the gold and white livery they wore when serving.

Umberto's eyes widened. "A soothsayer is perfectly capable of tripping, Abbygail," Umberto said. "Now, go!"

Abbygail followed Billy up the stairs. Inside the kitchen, Teng worked steadily and efficiently. Wanda and Turnkey worked beside her, the older woman humming softly as she stirred nuts into a chocolate sauce. Turnkey was cutting up fruit. Thin and fey-looking with thinning blond hair, Turnkey rarely had anything much to say. He came in, did his job, left for home. Sometimes Umberto longed for the kind of quiet Turnkey maintained.

Umberto heard someone clear their throat. He glanced over to the servants' dining room where the Foreign Minister's attendant sat drinking a cup of tea. He was a grim-looking person whose brown hair seemed too short for his long face. His dark brown clothes were too tight, and Umberto wondered how he could possibly breathe while wearing them. Perhaps that was the style in Berland. The man looked impatient and bored all at the same time. Umberto was not fond of entertaining foreign servants. What was he supposed to do with them?

Hunter came up beside Umberto. They nodded to one another.

"Miss Teng," Umberto said, "Hunter is here. It is custom for the chef to go up with the hunter before the guests eat the main course."

"Yes," Teng said. She wiped her hands on her apron and then untied it and put it on the hook near the sink. She smiled blandly at Umberto. He was not certain what to make of her yet. She was oddly . . . odd. She was a foreigner, but he was accustomed to foreigners. It was as if she was not all there—all here.

Viva was. Right away. She had been at the Hearth for less than a day, and it was as if she had been here forever. One of the first things she did was run outside and hug the Old Oak. She flung herself at the old tree, arms outstretched, face pressed against the bark, her baggy blue saffron slacks undulating in the wind. She looked like a butterfly sunning herself on the oak.

When Umberto had come over and told her it was time to let go of the tree, she had complied. She kissed the tree, then pushed away from it, and reached up and put her small hand in Umberto's very large hand. Together they walked around to the back of the Hearth and went inside.

Umberto wasn't certain where Viva was now. She either had the good sense to stay out of the way during this busy time, or her mother had instructed her to remain in their rooms.

"I'm ready," Teng said.

Umberto nodded and led the way up the stairs. He did not look at the Safran Bleu ink drawings of fish and birds on the walls on either side of the stairs, but he could see them in his peripheral vision. As always, he felt comforted by them, painted long before he had been born, even before his mother or father had been at the Hearth. He felt comforted and proud of the history of the house and the people who had lived here.

When they got to the second floor, the three of them walked down the corridor, their footsteps echoing, until Umberto stopped before the closed door to the dining room. He heard the murmur of voices inside. He looked back at Hunter and Teng.

"I will announce you," he said.

He opened the door and stepped inside the room. The First Family, along with Savi—Minerva's significant other—Nehemiah, and Mr. Peetall, the Berland Foreign Minister, sat around a long oblong table. The room was lit by sunlight streaming in from the west window. The pale blue walls were slightly stained with the golden light of near sunset. A line of fish drawings swam on the cornices of the room, along with a few depictions of sea shells and sea fronds. Above the sideboard, a huge bouquet of painted wild yellow daffodils spilled across the wall. Billy was serving the venison stew, expertly ladling the dinner into white porcelain bowls—white with a narrow red and gold border—while Abbygail used tongs to place a piece of hot bread on the gleaming bread plates.

The diners paid no attention to Abbygail, Billy, or Umberto. All was as it should be.

"Excuse me, Ma'am," Umberto said. "Hunter and Marguerite Teng are here."

The Queen, who sat at one end of the oblong table while Talib sat at the opposite end, nodded and set the wine glass she was holding down on the white tablecloth. Billy and Abbygail, their tasks

45

KIM ANTIEAU

completed, stepped back. The room became quiet. Umberto moved out of the way, and Teng and Hunter came to stand beside him.

"Tell us, Teng," Reina said, "how was it, preparing your first meal at the Hearth?"

Umberto raised an eyebrow and gazed at Teng. He hoped Teng understood the Queen was merely being polite. Teng's story of the meal was not the story the Queen or anyone else wanted to hear.

"It was a joy," Teng said. "The salad was made by Turnkey, who assures me he also follows the Old Ways when harvesting. We all prepared the stew together, after I sang the appropriate songs and asked the appropriate permissions while harvesting. The herbs we used today are parsley, sage, rosemary, thyme, juniper berries, and Safran Bleu. The bread was started yesterday and finished today by Wanda. We added rosemary, that pillar of strength and protection, to the bread as well."

Reina turned to the Foreign Minister of Berland and said, "Wanda is the best baker in all of Queendom. I hear stories that she not only feeds her wild yeast, she has named it." The people around the table chuckled. "Isn't that right, Umberto?"

"I have heard it is so," he said, "although I would not swear on it."

"Hunter," Reina said, "what have you to say about tonight's dinner?"

"Your Majesty, two days ago I asked for a vision," Hunter said. "I asked if an animal would be willing to give up its life for our lives. I dreamed of an old stag. He said he would wait for me at the trivia in the forest. In the morning I went out into the woods. It was so filled with the noises of the creatures that I felt I would lose my way. I came near the first trivia, the first crossing of paths, and a young buck ran in front of me. I thought he was the one from my dream. But he was too young. So I kept traveling toward the next trivia. Soon I came face to face with a huge old buck. His antlers reached up to the sky. He reared as I approached, as if he were a horse, and exposed his great old heart to me. I said a prayer of thanks to the

46

Old Buck. Then I shot the arrow, and the Old Buck gave his life and all of his wisdom to us."

The First Family clapped. Mr. Peetall hesitated, and then he clapped once or twice.

"We are honored to accept this meal from you," the Queen said. "Thank you."

Umberto nodded, indicating Teng could leave. Billy and Abbygail followed Hunter and Teng out the door. Umberto quietly shut the door behind them and stepped back into the shadows.

"What a nice story," Mr. Peetall said, drawing out the word "story." The Queen's mouth hardened slightly.

"Your people have such glorious imaginations," he continued.

"Do Berlanders not follow the Old Ways and honor that which has died to feed you?" Minerva asked. Her words sounded upbeat, as they often did. She could ask almost anything, say anything, and no one was ever offended. Tonight her blond hair was tied up in gold and blue ribbons, and she wore a shiny gold top with bright blue trousers. One day she would be queen, no doubt, and Umberto was certain she would do well for the people of Queendom.

"We follow the Old Ways," Peetall said. "Only we don't *talk* about it. It is assumed." He waved his right hand as he said the word "assumed."

"Our national heritage is cultivation," Minerva said. "We cultivate the arts as we cultivate herbs and spices, especially our Safran Bleu."

Peetall took a bite of his venison stew. Talib talked quietly to Savi who sat on his left, opposite to Minerva. Raphael was next to Minerva and Lorelei, with Poppie and the Queen Madre opposite them. Nehemiah and Mr. Peetall sat opposite each other next to the Queen. Umberto wondered if he should have suggested Minerva sit next to Mr. Peetall rather than the Queen Madre. Poppie often dominated the Queen Madre's attention.

"The stew is wonderful," Peetall said.

The Queen nodded. "We wanted to honor you with a simple dish that might be served in your own land."

"Yes, quite," Peetall said. He took a sip of red wine. "Although we would probably drink a white wine with our venison stew. I do like the touch of Safran Bleu in the stew, but I wonder if you don't get tired of it everywhere." He gestured to the drawings on the cornices. "And in everything." He nodded to the stew.

The Queen Madre laughed. "That is like asking you if you ever get tired of beer and beans," she said, "or long epic stories where everyone dies in the end."

Lorelei looked at her grandmother, then her mother and Mr. Peetall. Reina barely hid a smile.

Peetall nodded. "I suppose so. Although our economic base is much more diversified," he said, "so we don't have as many financial worries as the Queendom does."

Reina shot Nehemiah a look. He continued to eat his stew.

"More diversified?" the Queen Madre said. "Isn't your main export *mushrooms*. And *beer*."

"As you well know, Ma'am," Peetall said, "we export what we make from mushrooms. And we allow other countries to grow mushrooms and produce mushroom plastics. Only we are better at it than the rest of the Consolidated Five."

"We have no economic worries here," Talib said. "The saffron grows well. Our tourists are happy with our offerings. It is the most beautiful place in the world to live." Talib shrugged. "Although I am certain you would say the same about your country, and that is how it should be. Now, come, let us not talk business or politics. Mr. Peetall, we would love a story! Especially a long one where everyone dies in the end."

They all laughed, including Peetall, and the tension in the room dissolved. Talib smiled and winked at the Queen. Umberto was certain no one saw except the Queen and himself. It was good to see the Queen and her consort getting on with one another. She had chosen well when she married Talib, even if he had not proved to be a particularly faithful husband. He was a good father, good host, and good ambassador for the Queendom arts.

"I am no storyteller," Peetall said. "I would love to hear one from a famed Queendom storyteller."

"Poppie is the best of us all," the Queen Madre said. "It is his guild."

Poppie held up a hand. "Nowadays I must be drunker or sleepier to tell any tales."

"And Poppie's stories often involve sailors and naked men and women," Talib said. "I am not prepared to listen to those stories with my children gathered round tonight."

"Better love stories than war stories," Savi said.

"Yes, indeed," Reina said. She raised her glass to Savi.

"Perhaps you should tell the story of the Queen and Premier Outram," Raphael spoke up suddenly, as though the words had been building up in him. As usual, he sounded vaguely angry.

"Sonny," Talib's voice was a warning.

"The Foreign Minister might like to know that the man who is now premier was once engaged to my mother."

"Rafe," Minerva said. "I don't think the Minister would be interested in that story. It's not really a story at all, Mr. Peetall. It's old history."

"They were in love," Raphael said. "But my mother, who is now head of the Queendom, decided it was not a good idea to join the two families in matrimony."

"The end," Talib said. "Now, let's hear a much more interesting story."

Reina was glaring at her son but not in a way any stranger could tell. She had a smile on her lips. That was all Mr. Peetall could see. The Queen was the most diplomatic person Umberto had ever encountered, except perhaps, for Minerva.

"I did not know this," Peetall said. "And—"

"And Premier Outram and I have been close friends ever since," Reina said. "The bond between our countries has never been better. I must finish this amazing stew before I hear any more stories."

They ate in near silence for a few minutes.

"This has all been delicious," Peetall said, "and the company is wonderful, but I am afraid I'm feeling a bit peaked. For some reason the trip has taken a bit out of me. I hope you will excuse me."

"Yes," Reina said. "Nehemiah, can you please check out Mr. Peetall and make certain all is well."

"No," Peetall said, shaking his head as he pushed his chair away from the table. "I—I would like to see a physician, however, if one is available."

Everyone at the table stood as the Foreign Minister rose to his feet.

"But Nehemiah is a soothsayer," Reina said. "He can diagnose you much quicker—"

Umberto went to the wall, pressed a button, and said quietly, "Send Mr. Peetall's servant up to the dining room and call for a village doctor, please."

The Foreign Minister leaned on Reina as they walked to the door. Umberto opened it. Nehemiah took over for Reina as they stepped into the hall.

"I will be fine," Peetall said. "Finish your delightful meal."

Umberto heard footsteps coming toward them. A moment later, the servant was there, walking with Nehemiah to get Mr. Peetall down the corridor to one of the guest apartments. Reina returned to the dining room, and Umberto went to the front door to await the doctor. When Healer Bearsdaughter arrived, Umberto took her to the minister's rooms and left her there.

He returned to the dining room in time to hear Raphael say, "I loathe the Berlanders. They think they are better and smarter than everyone. He insulted our stories. He insulted Safran Bleu. I wanted him to understand that *we* rejected *them*!"

"Brother, our mother rejected the leader of their country," Minerva said. "That had nothing to do with us. You must learn to hold your tongue."

"Truly, Raphael," Reina said, "you want more responsibility, but then you do something like this?"

Lorelei got up from the table, crossed the room, and slipped out the door. No one—except Umberto—seemed to notice.

"I hope he doesn't think we poisoned him," Minerva said. "Berlanders can be rather suspicious."

"Not a good first meal for our new cook," the Queen Madre said.

"You can hardly blame her," Savi said. "At least, I don't suppose so."

"Maybe she's one of the rebels sent to poison the First Family," Raphael said. "The ones in the Low Mountains are getting more vocal. Maybe they're also getting more devious."

"It is not our way to poison other people," the Queen said. "Please, don't put that out into the Universe. If the rebels are true Queendomers, they would not poison anything. Our ancestors brought down a system that was destroying the planet. They did the job. What more could anyone want?"

"They want less of us," Talib said, "and more of them. They don't understand what our ancestors intended when they formed the Queendom and the Consolidated Five. They want to return to the days of rampant greed and destruction of life. They are a little crazy."

"Perhaps they want more autonomy," Raphael said. "The Guilds have gotten rather dictatorial. To move out of the guild and go somewhere else is difficult."

"And why shouldn't it be difficult?" Reina asked. "It's a lineage they have to protect. A familial lineage. They can't let everyone in. But it's not impossible. Even our small guild could change if the populace decided to vote us out. They must be happy with how we do things. We keep getting reelected."

"Happy or lazy," Poppie said. "If not the Villanueva family, then who?"

"Then there's the Service," Raphael said. "Not everyone is fond of being forced to go into a particular Service."

"Oh, you can't be fussing about that," Minerva said. "History taught our ancestors that it was the young males who needed more direction. Being in Service channels any violent tendencies. You know that's true."

"What's true is that the women get to choose what they do while in the Service," Raphael said, "including continuing their studies, so when we come home, we're already behind. It's difficult to succeed in business."

"And the males return physically stronger and much more disciplined," the Queen Madre said. "It has worked so well for so long. There are gender exceptions, but I believe it's a brilliant invention. Are you telling us you are against the Service?"

"I was having a conversation," Raphael said. "I have no complaints about the Service, beyond that it was boring."

"We all have options when we go into Service," Reina said. "Even you poor put upon men. History and biology instructs us in this manner. Young men need a tighter rein, need to express themselves in a much more physically directed way, need a bit more instruction on how to be good citizens. It's science, and I don't want to have this argument yet again. Let's change the subject."

"Friends of Poppie's saw strangers around the Lows," the Queen Madre said. "Not your ordinary strangers. Not the kind we welcome every day. They were certain something nefarious was happening. That is where so many of our fields of Safran Bleu are grown. Perhaps you should send someone to check it out?"

"If someone looks suspicious for whatever reason we're now going to send them off to the Hinterlands?" Raphael asked.

"No," the Queen Madre said, "but we need to know what's happening within our borders."

"I'll talk to Nehemiah tomorrow," Reina said. "I should find out how Peetall is doing. Mr. Umberto, do I need to go to the Minister or will the doctor come here?"

"She said she would come here, Ma'am," Umberto said.

"We haven't had dessert yet," the Queen Madre said.

"Mother," Reina said.

"Don't you think the Foreign Minister was being melodramatic?" the Queen Madre asked. "Or maybe he wanted to get away from us so he could wander through the Hearth on his own and collect information for Outram."

"I hardly think that is what is going on," Reina said. "For one thing, Premier Outram could ask me anything he wanted to know, and I would tell him. He doesn't need to send spies."

"You wouldn't tell him everything," Talib said. "For instance, I've heard we had a bad quarter. Some of the Safran Bleu seems to be missing, no? Or is this idle gossip?"

Everyone looked at the Queen.

"Where did you hear that, Talib? Suppose that was a state secret?"

"We don't have state secrets," Talib said. "It's family business. Everyone here is family, so it does no harm to bring it up here."

"We may be in for some difficult times," Reina said. "It's true, but we will be all right. Yes, our figures were down last quarter, but they will bounce up again. You don't need to worry about it, Talib. Drum up business for the arts. Raphael, you can keep up your profile in the village. It's good for the people to be interested in our lives and to see we are happy, healthy, and confident. We'll host the Summit soon. That will be good for business." She shrugged. "I am not worried."

"Mother," Minerva said, "Savi and I have something we wanted to tell you. We were going to wait until later, but maybe this will help. Savi and I are getting married."

"Wonderful!" the Queen Madre said. Everyone clapped, and the family stood to shake first Savi's hand and then Minerva's.

"This is good news, sister," Raphael said.

"That is *great* news!" the Queen said. "You'll get married here?"

"Yes!" Minerva said. "We can make it a huge celebration. The whole Queendom is invited, and we'll get tourists from the rest of the Consolidated Five. Could really help the economy."

The Queen laughed. "I hope that's not why you're getting married. Have fun with it. When your father and I got married, we threw the biggest best party you've ever seen!" She looked at Talib. He nodded.

"As long as we can have some private time with the family on the day," Minerva said, "we're OK with everything else, with it being a big public celebration. We already talked about it."

"Good," Reina said. "Do you have a date in mind?"

"September," Savi said. "It's so beautiful that time of the year."

"That doesn't give us much time," the Queen Madre said. "Your mother is useless at that kind of thing, but I've got some ideas, and I bet your father does, too."

Umberto went to stand next to the Queen's chair. He leaned over and asked quietly, "Ma'am, should we skip dessert?"

"Not on your life, Umberto," Reina said, "unless the Minister dies—and he better not—I want to celebrate this engagement. The more chocolate, the better. But could you go check on the Minister? If he is actually dying, I should probably know." She looked up at Umberto and smiled.

"Yes, Ma'am," Umberto said.

Umberto stepped into the corridor as the doctor was walking down the main corridor toward him.

"Healer Bearsdaughter," Umberto said. "What say you?"

"He will be fine," she said. "I don't believe he travels well, and something he ate has disagreed with him."

"Something he ate *here*?"

"No," she said. "The upset was too far down to be from something he ate here. Have your cook prepare him a ginger celery broth, and he should be fine in the morning. I suggested Safran Bleu tea. But he would have none of it. And he wouldn't allow Nehemiah to diagnose him. He wanted a beer, of all things. The Berlanders think anything and everything can be healed by beer. Maybe bring him a very small glass of it, to ease his mind."

"Very well," Umberto said. "Thank you."

"I will see myself out," she said. "Have a good night, Umberto."

"It has certainly been an interesting one," Umberto said.

Umberto returned to the dining room to quietly tell the Queen what the doctor had said. Then he headed downstairs.

Teng was in the kitchen with Wanda. Billy and Abbygail stood nearby. Turnkey had finished his shift and gone home, no doubt. He often left before dessert.

"So you know," Umberto said, "the Foreign Minister has become ill. The doctor prescribed ginger celery broth. Is that something you can make, Teng?"

"I can," she said.

"Second," he continued, "we've had some news. Miss Minerva and Miss Savi are to be married."

"Yeah!" Abbygail said. She and Billy clapped.

"The Queen would like to celebrate," Umberto said. "Is dessert ready? A bottle of champagne is in order, too." He glanced at Billy who nodded and then headed for the wine cellar.

"We have fruit with chocolate sauce," Teng said. "Will that do? It's ready to go up."

"Indeed," Umberto said. "Since the Foreign Minister has taken ill, he will not be needing any dessert."

Billy returned with two bottles of champagne.

"Abbygail, you take the champagne," Umberto said. "Billy, you may take the tray of desserts."

"Oh, Mr. Umberto," Abbygail said. "Billy should serve the champagne. I get nervous pouring champagne. It has to be just so and everyone watches me."

Umberto arched an eyebrow. "Are you quite sure you're a soothsayer, Abbygail?"

"Well, I—"

"It was rhetorical," Umberto said. "Fine, trade tasks. Why must everything be so difficult? Go, go."

Abbygail picked up the tray from the serving shelf, and then she and Billy headed for the stairs.

Teng was already cutting up ginger while Wanda chopped celery.

"Mr. Umberto, what is it that ails the Foreign Minister?" Teng asked, as she looked down at the knife in her hand and the ginger she was chopping.

"Something he ate," Umberto said.

Teng looked up, startled.

"I apologize," Umberto said. "I should have said it was something he ate some time ago. Nothing you served. The First Family was delighted with the dinner. Good job, Marguerite Teng."

"Thank you, Mr. Umberto," she said.

Umberto went into the servants' dining room. On the long wooden table was the message Billy had found tacked to the door earlier: "Live free or die." Umberto had forgotten about it. He should show it to someone upstairs.

"What on Earth does this mean?" he said out loud. He was free. Everyone he was acquainted with was free. As far as he knew, everyone in the world was free—and he knew for certain everyone in the Consolidated Five was free.

Perhaps he was taking it too literally. This kind of paper was expensive and hardly used any more. He tried to smudge the ink with his thumb. The ink stayed true.

Was this from one of the rebels they had been talking about at dinner?

He folded the paper and put it in his back pocket. He was about to return upstairs when he heard a knock on the back door. He hoped it was someone else coming to pin a strange note on the door so he could give them a lecture on propriety, history, and etiquette.

He ran down the hall until he reached the door. He grabbed the handle and jerked the door open.

It was night now, or nearly so, and it was raining. Standing on the threshold was a hooded figure, her head down. She looked up and pushed her hood back.

Umberto nearly gasped. For a moment, he was speechless. He finally said, "Good evening, Your Majesty—I mean, Miss Hildegarde."

"Hello, Berto. Long time. The prodigal queen has come home."

CHAPTER FIVE
REINA

Reina was ready for the day to be over. The First Family had finished dessert, and now they were gathered in the drawing room. Nehemiah had retired for the evening after reporting that the Foreign Minister was sleeping. Lorelei was not present. But she would eventually show up.

Reina sat away from her family, sipping tea. She was happy for Minerva, and the news had brought the First Family together, it seemed, at least for this night. The Foreign Minister's illness had put a damper on the evening for her. She had hoped to get him alone to talk about trade—without giving him any hint that the Queendom was in a bit of financial trouble. She was still not certain how it had all happened.

She had always been expert at juggling many things at once. She was the queen of multitasking, so to speak. Lately, however, she was bored by it. Or irritated by it all.

She wanted to be upstairs in her chambers right then, with Fan. She had forgotten how pleasurable it was to be skin to skin with another person. And Fan was an expert. He knew exactly where to touch her.

"What are you smiling about, Mother?" Raphael asked. He had

wandered away from the rest of the family and now stood next to Reina.

"Um, nothing, love," she said. She felt her face turning red. She hoped in the dim light, Raphael would not notice. "I'm thrilled about Minerva and Savi."

"Good save, Mother," he said. "But not good enough. You were far away."

Not that far. Only one floor up. Where Fan said he would be when Reina was finished for the day, in case she wanted another massage. An extra special massage.

She rolled her eyes. She did not like vulgarity—and yet here she was thinking vulgar thoughts and hoping for more vulgarity later on in the evening. Not that she considered sex vulgar.

"What is it you want, Sonny?" Reina asked.

"Do I have to *want* something?" he asked. "Couldn't I just want to talk with my mom?" He sat in the chair next to her. The rest of the dinner party remained on the other side of the room, laughing and murmuring to one another.

Reina looked at Raphael. "I like the way you're wearing your hair these days. It's very flattering. You look good on NexusView."

"Mother, I would like to do more than look good on Nexus-View," he said. "If the Queendom is having problems, I would like to help."

"We will be fine," she said.

"I want to be part of the busidom," he said. "I could be a great asset."

"You are a great asset," Reina said. "No matter what happens the people need to see us doing well. We are a reflection of the land and the people. And you are often our public face. Your service is invaluable."

"I don't feel very useful," Raphael said.

Talib called to them from across the room, "We're going for a nightcap in my studio. Care to join us?"

"You all go," Reina said. She appreciated her husband's invitation. It had been a while since he had asked her to come to his house. Most days she could barely stand the sight of him. Tonight, she had not been bothered by him. "Enjoy your party!" she said. "I have an early day."

"I'll be along," Raphael called.

The group left the room, their voices low as they headed out. Reina felt a strange relief as soon as they were gone, but then she realized she was alone with her son. She did not want to argue with him. That was all they seemed to do.

"Sonny—"

"I wish you would not call me that," he said. "I wish you would all stop calling me that."

"Raphael," Reina said. "What is it you truly desire? Every time we discuss this, it seems like you only want to be at the top, to be in charge, without doing any work."

"*Discuss* this? I don't remember us ever *discussing* this. I want more of a role. More than being the public face of the family. I want a mission in life."

"After you finished your Service," she said, "you could have gotten membership into any number of guilds. They would have taken you on as apprentice. I know you don't like the guild system, so you could always do something where membership in a guild isn't required. Finding your mission in life is something you need to do on your own. I can't choose your mission."

"I am interested in politics," he said. "I would like to run for town council or even national council, but I am barred from doing so because I am a member of the First Family. Can't we get that rule changed? Besides that, you won't let me have a hand in the nation's business. What is it I should do then?"

"Find a spouse," she said. "Raise a family. Grow a garden. Do volunteer work."

"That is Minerva's work," he said, "as she waits to become queen. I'm not interested in that. Mother, listen, what if Minerva decided she didn't want to be queen. Then it would be up to me, right? Shouldn't I be trained for that eventuality?"

Reina looked at her son. She sighed. "I never wanted you to spend your life waiting for your sister to give up her destiny. Or worse yet, waiting for her to die. Look at your uncle Jeremy. He has made such a good life for himself away from the Hearth. He never wanted to run the business. He never wanted any of this." She looked around. "He was fortunate. I want you to have that good fortune, too."

"But I am interested," he said.

"All right," she said. "I am listening to you. I have heard you. The only way to learn the family business is to learn the family business. You would have to apprentice to someone. You'd have to learn it from the ground up, which is the only way to learn anything."

"Can't I apprentice to Minerva or Nehemiah?" he asked.

Reina chuckled. "Nehemiah would crush you like a puffball. Not on purpose. And Minerva has her hands full. Besides, if you want to know the business of the Queendom, you should know all aspects of it. We all started that way. That's the only way to do it. It's the only good way."

"Mother, you can't mean that. I'm twenty-one years old."

"Yes, you are a child," she said. "But not too childish to sweep floors!"

Raphael stared at his mother. She could see his face flush with anger—or embarrassment.

"Raphael, the way to learn the business of the Queendom is to learn how the cooperatives work," she said. "We could send you to one of the farms or warehouses. We need to find out what is happening to the Safran Bleu. It's being stolen or—misplaced. We are losing a great deal of credit. You could be our eyes and ears. But consider it carefully before you say yea or nay. You cannot go and then quit after a day or two. It would not look good for us."

"You think of me as a quitter, Mother?"

"It's just that your attention wanders, doesn't it?" Reina said. "You are interested in so many things, for short periods of time."

"When I was twelve that was true," Raphael said. "But I have been quite focused on the idea of being part of the busidom for some time."

"Having eclectic interests is an endearing quality," Reina said.

Raphael groaned. "Will you ever take me seriously? You treat me like a child."

Reina wanted to say, "Stop acting like a child, and I will stop treating you like one." He was always whining about not being respected or not having a job he liked. That seemed childish to Reina. One did what one had to do, for country and family.

Reina heard footsteps in the corridor. Perhaps something was happening in the busidom that she needed to deal with immediately. That would be much easier than having this conversation with her son. She loved Raphael, but she felt at sea with him so much of the time. He did not seem like a man of substance. She couldn't say that to him. She didn't even want to think it. But he was his father's son: He wanted success without effort.

She wished life was like that. It hadn't been for her, but it was for some people. Her sister, for instance. Even their mother seemed relaxed when she was queen; she got the job done without putting in long hours. She got the job done without having a spouse, since her husband—Reina's father—had hightailed back to Armistead a few years after her brother Jeremy was born. Poppie hadn't shown up in her mother's life until after she had resigned as queen and CEO.

Umberto stepped through the open door.

"Ma'am," he said. "We had an unexpected arrival at the back door this evening."

"The bad sheep of the family has returned," someone behind Umberto said.

Umberto stepped aside, and Reina's older sister Hildegarde walked into the room. She was dressed all in black. Her short wavy brown hair framed her face like a fuzzy dark aura.

Reina immediately got to her feet.

"Look what the cat dragged in," Raphael said. He got up and walked to his aunt, his arms outstretched.

"Now this is the greeting I expected," Hildegarde said. "How are you, Raphael?"

The two embraced.

Reina looked at Umberto. He shrugged almost imperceptibly. She said, "Thank you, Umberto. That will be all."

Once Umberto had gone and closed the door firmly behind him, Reina put her hands on her hips and said, "What on Earth are you doing here?"

Hildegarde let go of Raphael and smiled at her sister.

"No embrace from my sister?" she asked. "One queen to another?"

Reina went to Hildegarde and cautiously put her arms around her. Hildegarde gave her a hard squeeze. Then the women let each other go and stared at one another.

"Yes, I'd love to sit down and chat a while," Hildegarde said. "Umberto already fed me, so no, I don't need anything to eat. Thank you for asking."

"You've been here thirty seconds," Reina said. "I haven't had a chance to ask anything."

Hildegarde pulled off her jacket, tossed it on the arm of the sofa, and then sat in one of the chairs.

"I don't know how you stand these things," Hildegarde said. "You have to sit so straight."

"It's healthier," Reina said. "Those chairs you had were terrible for your posture."

Hildegarde had been in the room for two minutes and already Reina felt defensive. She took a breath.

"Mother will want to see you," Reina said. "Shall I have Umberto fetch her?"

"I'll go," Raphael said. "It will give you two time to catch up."

Raphael squeezed his aunt's shoulder as he went by. When the door closed again, Hildegarde said, "He has grown to be such a handsome man. And diplomatic. I remember him as being a bit selfish and self-centered, always wanting to be the center of attention."

"That sounds like a description of you, Hildy," Reina said. "Would you like something to drink?"

Hildegarde shook her head. "No. I never touch the stuff any more. Or were you offering me water? That I do touch. But I don't need anything. I met your new cook. She seems nice. Her food is delicious. And the new housebod, Billy Santos. He is funny. It was nice to see Abbygail again, and Umberto. He didn't know what to do when he saw me."

"As much as I hate to interrupt this trip down memory lane," Reina said, "I need to ask: Why the hell are you here? I thought you were in a monastery or something."

"You know I left there years ago," Hildegarde said. "I have been wandering. On a saunter, if you will. A pilgrimage of sorts. I've been painting some. Maybe I take after Dad a bit. No one recognizes me any more. That is wonderful. Even when I mistakenly say I am Hildegarde Villanueva, no one notices. Or cares. I cannot tell you how liberating that is."

"But you are here," Reina said. "People will notice. They'll remember. You'll be back on NexusView."

The door opened, and the Queen Madre strode into the room. Raphael followed her.

"She was already on her way back," Raphael said.

"Oh my word!" the Queen Madre said. "I can't believe what I'm seeing. What are you doing here?"

Hildegarde got up. "I have come to reclaim the queenship," she said. "As is my right as the oldest child."

The Queen Madre's eyes widened. The room grew unnaturally quiet.

"I am joking," Hildegarde said. "Come give your old daughter a hug."

"You are a bad child!" the Queen Madre said as she approached her daughter with open arms. "At least one out of two of my children is good!"

"Mother, you have three children," Reina reminded her.

"Oh, my, I forgot about Jeremy," the Queen Madre said as she embraced Hildegarde. "Don't tell him! I would never hear the end of it."

"I wouldn't dream of it," Hildegarde said as she let her mother go. "But seriously, I would like to stay the night and maybe more. And I need to speak with the Queen. Privately."

"All right!" the Queen Madre said. "Come up to our apartment before you go to bed. We must catch up. Oh, we're having a wedding soon. Minerva and her beloved are getting married. You will come to that, won't you? And then if I can get Jeremy here, we will be one big happy family again." She took Raphael's arm. "Come, grandson. We know when we're not wanted."

Raphael nodded to his mother, and then the two left the drawing room and closed the door. Hildegarde and Reina sat down again, in chairs that nearly faced one another.

"I've been traveling," Hildegarde said, "and I've heard rumors about the Queendom and some kind of financial trouble."

Reina bit the inside of her cheek. How could there be rumors? She only found out herself not long ago, and she was CEO.

Hildegarde continued, "And the rebels in the Lows may be planning demonstrations in some of the villages."

"We have had demonstrations before," Reina said. "It is their right as citizens."

"That's the thing," Hildegarde said. "I'm not sure they are citizens. Some of them may be infiltrators or spies from the Hinterlands."

"I'm not worried," Reina said. "Besides, if a plurality of citizens want change, we will have change. Our system has worked for two hundred years. We have peace, we have prosperity, we have happiness."

"You're singing to the choir here, sister," Hildegarde said. "They're either from the Hinterlands or it's possible they're from Loveland."

"Loveland? Why?"

"The Lovelanders want to become part of the Consolidated Five," Hildegarde said. "Make it the Consolidated Six."

"They've tried before," Reina said. "We have no interest in

them. They are geographically too far from us. They don't share our values—and they are clearly demonstrating that they don't share our values if they've sent spies. Friends don't spy on friends."

"I'm only telling you what's in the wind," Hildegarde said. "I don't know how much of it is true. I have also heard rumors of a hostile takeover attempt. Has it happened?"

"No," Reina said. "As far as I knew, our financial difficulty was a state secret."

"Apparently not," Hildegarde said. "It's possible you already have a spy here."

"No one knew about the financial problems except Nehemiah and myself," Reina said. "None of my advisors knew. No one who works for me knew." She didn't mention that Talib had brought up the subject at dinner: Obviously it wasn't a state secret. But Reina carried on with the ruse. "I didn't realize the extent of the problem until today."

How could everyone in the Queendom seem to know more than she did? She was head of the whole country!

"I suppose now you think I've bungled it and you want to take back the queenship?" Reina said.

"I don't think you've bungled it," Hildegarde said. "I've come to help, if I can. I thought you would want to know what's being said. Something could be happening on the borders. Maybe one or more of the Consolidated Five is loosening restrictions at the border. People from the Hinterlands get into their country and then once in, they can more easily come here."

"Why us?" Reina asked. "Why would we be targeted for theft or revolution or whatever it is they want? Why not one of the other countries?"

"Because we are the most beautiful," Hildegarde said. "Or because we are regarded as the best. Or maybe they want the saffron. I don't know."

Reina nodded. "Tomorrow, let us meet and talk with Nehemiah."

Hildegarde nodded. "I'm tired. Is my old room unoccupied?"

"It is," Reina said.

The two women rose.

"Thank you for coming," Reina said. "I'm guessing it wasn't easy returning to the Hearth."

"Easier than I thought," she said. "See you in the morning."

Once her sister had left, Reina headed for her office, down the corridor and around the corner. She wasn't certain what to make of her sister's visit. Hildegarde had been queen for less than a year when she suddenly resigned, fifteen years ago. Reina was next in line. When it was put to a vote, Reina won easily, keeping the Villanueva family in power.

Reina had not been prepared for Hildegarde's abdication—she had not been prepared to be queen. But she had done it, with Nehemiah's help, with her mother's guidance.

Once Reina was inside the office, she closed the door, sat in a chair, then turned on her private Nexus channel and called Premier Outram. A moment later, the image of Outram hung in the air before her. She smiled—she couldn't help it—and he grinned, too.

"Premier Outram, how nice to see you," she said.

"Your Majesty," he said. "How wonderful to see you. To what do I owe this pleasure?"

"Your Foreign Minister became ill at dinner," she said.

"I heard," he said.

"The doctor assures us it had nothing to do with what we served him."

Outram laughed. "That never crossed my mind when contemplating the cause of Mr. Peetall's illness. He is what you would call a sensitive man. Every wind, every change in temperature, ever bump in the road upsets him."

"Really? Berland has sensitive men?" She smiled.

"I am afraid so," he said.

"And he was chosen to be foreign minister why?"

"Are you questioning my hiring practices?" Outram asked.

"Not at all," Reina said. "I assume you have reasons for appointing a man like him to such an important position. I was curious what that reason was."

Outram shrugged.

"Not much diplomacy was happening at our dinner table tonight," Reina said. "Mr. Peetall didn't seem much enamored with our culture, so my son proceeded to tell Peetall that you and I had once been engaged. Apparently Peetall did not know that story."

"Why did you contact me tonight?" Outram sounded annoyed.

"Frankly, I needed a friend." She flinched. She had just told another head of state that she needed a friend.

She must be losing her mind.

Outram nodded. The irritated furrows disappeared.

"I apologize," he said. "I don't like being reminded of that time, when we parted ways. That was over twenty-five ago. Can you believe it?" He looked away for a moment. Then he looked at her and smiled. "In any case," he said, "I am always here to serve you. What can I help you with?"

She felt like she could lean on Outram, albeit temporarily. She had chosen Talib because she thought he was a good man, a temperate man. She had not been certain Outram was a good man; she was never certain he actually shared her values. When they were engaged, she had feared he would try to dominate her. Their relationship had been volatile. Too many arguments. Too much fire.

So she had broken off their engagement.

"Are you alone?" she asked.

"Yes," he said. "I'm in a secure room. Why? Are you going to ask me what I'm wearing next, Rey?"

She laughed. "I can see what you're wearing, Bay."

"Ahh, I have not heard that name in years," he said. "I miss it."

They were quiet for a moment as they looked at each other across time and space.

"I was hoping we could talk about more trade restrictions at the next meeting of the Five," Reina said. "We've had some losses this quarter that we could have been prevented."

She didn't know if that was true. She had no idea where the losses had come from.

"Are they heavy losses?" he asked. "Do you need a loan?"

When the Armistead pirates had wreaked havoc on Queendom crops a few years ago, Berland had lent them credit enough to get out of the hole. The Queendom had paid back two-thirds of it, and Berland made a good return on their investment. So far. Their final payment was due in the fall.

"Thank you," Reina said. "We're not there yet. But I appreciate the offer."

"Could be problems with Armistead again?"

"I hope not," she said. "If it is, we may consider a trade embargo. They need to get tougher on their thieves."

"Let's cross that bridge when we need to," he said.

No one liked trade embargoes. It felt too much like declaring war, and none of them ever wanted anything like that.

"I wanted to make certain I have your support," she said.

"You might get a hold of Ixchel," he said. "She'd do anything for you, *too*."

Reina nodded. She was fairly sure Erdom—and Ixchel—would back her up.

"How is your family?" Reina asked. "Everyone well?"

"Everyone is well," he said. "Boann is still studying law, as you know, and Axel is studying history with a soothsayer in Bremen Province, at a monastery there. Can you imagine that?" He shook his head. "I suppose you have heard that Terra has gone to live in Paquay State. That's where her people are from."

"I had not heard," Reina said. "Is this permanent?"

He nodded. "I have not been a good husband," he said. "I have not been a bad one. I was faithful—with one exception." He cleared his throat. "But I was not attentive. I suppose you suspected I would be a bad husband."

"We were children," Reina said. "I didn't know one way or

another. But you and Terra made two wonderful children and had many successful years together. I feel the same about Talib and me. We had our children. He has been a great ambassador to the arts." She shrugged. "The rest doesn't matter."

"So it's true what I have heard," he said. "You live apart."

"I wouldn't imagine you listen to gossip," Reina said.

"When it is about you, my ears perk up," he said. "I can't help it."

"He has lived in his art studio for many years," Reina said. "He has his young women and men. And I have a nation to run. It works out."

"Do I detect bitterness?"

"No. I don't know. Life never turns out the way you think it will, does it? The people one believes will be steadfast aren't. I have never thought monogamy was necessary for a good relationship, and I still don't—as you know—but I did assume that the man I married would love and respect me above all others, including himself."

Reina briefly closed her eyes.

"I am so sorry, Outram," she said. "I—I don't know what has come over me. I do apologize. Please forget this conversation."

"No apologies necessary, Ray," he said. "I am glad you can confide in me. Again. It's been a long while."

Reina's face flushed. She shook her head.

"It's been a long day," she said. "I will see you at the Summit?"

"I am looking forward to it," he said.

"We have a new cook," she said. "She should be up to speed by then. You will be amazed."

Outram laughed. "You Queendomers put too much stock in food."

"And you Berlanders put too much stock in drink."

"In any case, I always look forward to seeing you in person, even if it is only once a year," he said, "and I'm glad it's your turn to host. I haven't been to the Queendom in a very long time."

"I'll see you then," she said. "Good night, Bay."

She cut the connection and then sat in the room, alone, for a minute, listening to the pulsing silence.

Fan was waiting for her upstairs. She should tell Elata to send him home. She did not want to face him now. Sex was the last thing on her mind.

She closed her eyes and saw Fan in her mind's eye. She smiled. He did look so much like Outram.

Perhaps a massage would do her good before she went to bed.

CHAPTER SIX

LORELEI

Lorelei moved away from the Foreign Minister's room and walked down the corridor. Her footsteps made no sounds, and her movements did not activate the autolights, so she walked in semi-darkness. She did not mind. She knew every corridor and nearly every room in the Hearth by heart. Yet even she had not discovered all the nooks and crannies of this building that held many secrets. The builders—whoever they had been—must have been wise, mysterious, and playful when they created the Hearth. Lorelei believed they had hidden many treasures within the mansion, treasures that would be discovered when the time was right.

Lorelei was always discovering something new. Last week she had gone into a guest room on the second floor and found a hidden compartment in the floor moulding. Inside the compartment was a tiny cloth mouse dressed in a tiny white vest. She had no idea who had put the mouse there or why.

Now she walked by the barely lit drawing room and saw her brother sitting alone by the open windows. The sounds of frogs and crickets and whatever other creatures wandered around in the night floated in through the window. Lorelei walked over to the windows to stand next to her brother.

"Mom wants me to go live on a saffron farm," Raphael said,

staring out at the darkness. "She should have taken me to one when I was younger. She took Minerva. She even took you. Although I can't understand why. What could you get out of it?"

Lorelei didn't say anything. Even though she had learned a great deal from her time with her mother in the saffron fields, Raphael did not need to know that. No one needed to know anything about her. Not yet.

He sighed. "We're in big trouble, Lorelei. If the Queendom goes bankrupt, we'll be ousted for certain."

Lorelei curled her fingers into fists, a reflex she had when she wanted to scream at someone. She realized she was doing it so she told herself to relax. She did not want anyone to know what she was feeling merely by looking at her. She knew it was possible because she could tell what people were feeling most of the time. Not soothsayers, but human beings. Their true emotions were written all over their bodies.

Raphael appeared to be more worried about his own fate than the fate of the nation. She supposed he couldn't help it. He had always been self-centered. She didn't want to leave the Hearth. It was her home, and it had been the home of her family for centuries. But they all knew it was temporary. Any election could potentially put them out. It had never happened, but it could.

"Mother will take care of it," Lorelei said. "She always has."

Raphael regarded her. "I can't tell if you know nothing or you know everything."

"No one knows nothing or everything," Lorelei said.

Without another word, she left her brother's side and headed down the corridor toward her mother's office. Her mother was just opening the door when Lorelei got there.

"Lorelei," the Queen said. "I've been wondering where you've been. I was going up. But I can wait. Come in."

The two of them went into the office. Reina shut the door, and then they sat on the burgundy couch together.

"So tell me everything," Reina said.

"I met Marguerite Teng and her daughter," Lorelei said. "I really liked the daughter, Viva. Something seems a bit different with the mother. She was guarded. Or nervous. But I don't know many people from Erdom. Perhaps that is their culture."

It was wonderful to speak freely to her mother. She was always so circumspect with everyone else. Now, sitting here with Reina, Lorelei felt like she could breathe again. More and more it was getting harder and harder to pretend.

"While I was downstairs, Billy found something attached to the back door. It said, 'live free or die.' With a drawing of a segmented snake. Has Umberto showed it to you yet?"

"No," Reina said. "What on earth could that be about?" She touched her privocom bracelet. "Umberto," she said. "Please come to my office when you get a chance."

She turned to Lorelei. "What about the Foreign Minister?"

Lorelei smiled. "What a complainer. He was certain our food poisoned him. He is not the right man for that job. He told his assistant that his mission was a failure, but he didn't say what the mission was, specifically, beyond lifting some trade barriers. Oh, and I saw Raphael."

Reina put up her hand. "I don't want you to report on your family," she said. "I was just saying we shouldn't be spying on our friends."

Lorelei had no intention of spying on her brother. She had merely wanted to tell the Queen that Raphael was concerned. But she didn't say anything else. Reina smiled and took her daughter's hand.

"What a relief it is to speak with you," Reina said. "I appreciate all that you do. I hope this charade is not too stressful for you."

"I do feel somewhat duplicitous in all aspects of my life."

"Please, don't do anything that makes you uncomfortable," Reina said. "I know it started out fun, but it must be difficult when people treat you as though you're stupid. I can stop that. I will speak up, if you want me to, tell people you've been helping me." She let go of her daughter's hands. "I am the worst mother in the world."

"Not the worst," Lorelei said.

Reina laughed.

"It was my idea, Mother," Lorelei reminded her.

"You were too young to make such a choice," Reina said.

Lorelei shrugged. "Back then I couldn't talk to anyone except you. You believed I would come out of my cocoon. Umberto believed, too. Because you believed, I believed. And it happened. My mind came out of the cocoon. My body did not."

"You are beautiful. You are a beautiful little person."

Lorelei smiled, but she felt butterflies in her stomach.

"In any case, my daughter," Reina said, "you need not pretend. Be yourself. You are the brightest most intuitive person I have ever met."

"You are my mother," Lorelei said. "Of course you would say that."

"You know, Healer Bearsdaughter says sometimes even someone your age can have a growth spurt."

Lorelei looked at her mother. Her words stung. The Queen was talking to her as though she were a child.

"I'm sorry," Reina said. "I don't know where that came from."

"You are being rather odd tonight, Mother," Lorelei said.

"Minerva and Savi announced their engagement at dinner," Reina said.

"Without me being present?"

"They probably hadn't noticed you left the room," Reina said.

"Or that I was ever in the room," Lorelei murmured.

"What, darling?" Reina asked.

"Nothing."

"Did you hear that your aunt Hildy is here?" Reina said.

"Why?"

"I'm not sure why she's here. I don't know why she does anything she does. I was never sure why she abdicated in the first place, beyond her feelings for her lover. Fortunately, Mother had raised all three of us so we understood the busidom. I have tried to do that with you three also."

"With Raphael, too?" Lorelei said. "He believes you're keeping him away from the business."

"I have tried everything with your brother," Reina said. "Whatever task I put to him, he stays interested for about a month, but then he's on to something else. It would be one thing if he learned all he needed to know in a month, but he doesn't. He does the least amount of work he can do to get by." She shook her head. "I believe I should stop speaking tonight. I will soon get the award for worst mother and worst queen. I need a friend to confide in besides my youngest daughter."

"I am glad we can talk, Mother," Lorelei said, "but I will leave you now."

Lorelei got up, kissed her mother on the cheek, and then walked to the door. "Sometimes I feel as though I am a hundred years old," Lorelei said. "Sometimes I feel as though I am five."

Reina nodded and smiled. "Join the club, sweetheart."

Lorelei left her mother and walked down the corridor again. When she turned the corner, she saw Minerva and Savi standing in the hall, kissing. She did not want to disturb the couple—or talk with them. She was glad they were happy, but seeing them now—so joyful—reminded her that she would never have that kind of happiness. No man would ever love her. No boy ever had. So why would any man?

Not that she thought of such things very often.

She needed to be outside with the trees. She had spent too much of the day inside the Hearth. She loved the Hearth, but she needed to feel the ground beneath her feet, needed to see the sky above.

Something about tonight or the day or the phase of the moon was making her feel out of sorts. Like she did not belong in her own house.

She retraced her steps and went down the stairs. Perhaps Umberto and the rest of them would put her at ease, as they always had when she was a child.

Downstairs was dark, too. Seemed like it had been an early night for everyone. As she walked down the hall, she noticed a low light on in the servants' dining room. Then she heard soft voices.

"And that is why horses don't have cloven hooves," Billy was saying.

Lorelei heard gentle clapping. She walked around so that she was standing in the opening to the room, although still in the dark. Teng, Viva, Abbygail, Wanda, Turnkey, Billy, and Umberto sat around a long wooden table, a single light in the middle of the table. Each of them had a bowl of something in front of them—the venison stew, no doubt. They looked so cozy together, as though they were outside under the stars.

"Miss Lorelei!" Viva said.

The others, startled, looked toward the entrance to the room. Lorelei stepped closer so they could see her. It seemed Viva was not so easily taken in by her "invisibility."

Turnkey stood. He was the only one. Whenever anyone else from the First Family came downstairs and the servants were seated, they got up. But not when Lorelei came down. She assumed it was because they were accustomed to her: She had roamed these hallways since she was a child. Maybe they didn't stand because they saw her as a child. Or maybe it was because they did not respect her.

Viva jumped up and came over to Lorelei and grabbed her hand.

"We're having stories and stew," Viva said. She pulled Lorelei into the room. Lorelei sat next to Viva and Turnkey, across from Billy and Abbygail.

Turnkey said, "Good evening, Miss Lorelei."

Lorelei nodded to him and looked at Billy. He grinned at her. She smiled. She was sorry she had missed his story. She enjoyed listening to him talk. Once she was settled, Umberto nodded, as if to say to everyone that it was all right to continue.

"Tell us again the story of the herbs in this stew, Teng," Wanda said. "Will we all be healed of what ails us?"

"That is the intention when working with the Unified Field

Theory of Spices," Teng said. "It matters where the herbs and spices were grown, who planted them—human, soothsayer, bird, or the wind—it matters how they were harvested. Unfortunately, it can't all be codified. In this stew, I used many herbs and spices."

"That isn't a story, Teng," Umberto said.

"Ah yes," Teng said. "All right. There is an ancient song about parsley, sage, rosemary, and thyme. There are different versions of this song, but in all the versions one person lists several impossible tasks for the other person to perform before he or she will accept the other as lover. In response, the other person also requires the first singer to perform seemingly impossible tasks."

Several people at the table giggled.

"What?" Teng asked.

"Still not a story, newcomer Teng," Billy said.

"A story begins with once upon a time," Umberto said, "or there are seven continents and this story comes from the eighth continent."

"A story, a story! Let it come, let it come," Wanda said.

"In the long ago," Abbygail said.

"I heard from a crow who heard it from an old oak tree who heard it from a grapevine," Billy said. "Or you could sing the song. Abbygail, my girl, shall we show her?"

Abbygail grinned and nodded. Billy got up, held out his hand, and Abbygail took it. Then they stood off to the side, a little ways from the table and whispered to each other for a bit.

Viva and Lorelei looked at one another. Viva smiled. "Isn't this fun?" she whispered.

Then the two soothsayers turned to the group. Billy said, "They ask each other to do three impossible tasks. We shall only ask one each, but we'll keep the old lyrics. Ready?" Abbygail nodded. Then Billy began to sing, "Are you going to Scarborough Fair? Parsley, sage, rosemary, and thyme. Remember me to the one who lives there."

Lorelei felt a lump in her throat. Please keep singing, she thought. Please don't stop.

Billy looked at Abbygail and continued, "For once she was a true love of mine. Tell her to make me a cambric shirt. Parsley, sage, rosemary, and thyme. Without any seam or needlework. Then she shall be a true lover of mine."

He nodded to Abbygail. She pulled on her fingers nervously, looked at Billy, and began to sing to him, "Now he has asked me questions three. Parsley, sage, rosemary, and thyme. I hope he'll answer as many for me. Before he shall be a true lover of mine. Tell him to buy me an acre of land. Parsley, sage, rosemary, and thyme. Between the salt water and the sea sand. Then he shall be a true lover of mine."

Billy took Abbygail's hand in his, they looked at each other for a moment, and then they bowed. Everyone clapped.

"What is a cambric shirt?" Wanda asked.

"I have no idea," Umberto said. "But the difficult task was making it without seam or needlework."

"How would one do that?" Wanda asked.

"Magic," Lorelei whispered.

"Yes, Miss Lorelei, magic," Billy said. "Isn't that what love is all about? Magic?"

"Why are the herbs in the song?" Wanda asked. "They don't figure."

"I believe it's a chant," Teng said. "Maybe our ancestors are trying to tell us that we can do impossible tasks by using parsley, sage, rosemary, and thyme."

"Will you sing the rest?" Lorelei asked.

Everyone looked at her, apparently surprised by her question. Maybe it was because she rarely said more than two words when she was with a group of people. Stringing five together must seem like quite an event to them.

"Please," she said. "If you know the words." They were soothsayers: They knew the words.

"We can sing it all," Billy said. "And who knows? Maybe it's an enchantment, the entire song. We'll enchant us all into finding our true loves."

"Or we'll enchant ourselves into doing the impossible tasks to find our true loves," Teng said.

Billy nodded. "Either way," he said, "it's magic."

CHAPTER SEVEN
HILDEGARDE

The autolights faded on and then out again as Hildegarde walked down the second floor corridor. Everyone had gone to bed long ago so she was free to wander her old homestead without being observed.

She stopped at the closed door to Reina's office. This had been her office once. It was the Queen's office, and she had been queen. She put her hand on the door to push it open, but it didn't budge. She pushed again. It still didn't move, and this time a holographic message bloomed in front of her: "Attempted unauthorized access. Please see administrator."

Hildegarde made a noise. "No respect," she murmured before continuing down the corridor.

She wandered into the library. The auto lights came on, and Hildegarde stood at the entrance looking around her childhood refuge. The two large rooms that made up the library were filled wall to wall and ceiling to ceiling with old books. Around the corner, in the other room, she knew, were two reading nooks that looked out at the south gardens. In the center of the rooms were tables and straight-backed chairs. Dark blue comfy chairs with foot rests were situated nearby. Hildegarde smiled: So Reina had not thrown out all of her things after all. She assumed Reina would have gotten rid of all traces of her. Maybe she hadn't remembered Hildegarde had bought these chairs. Reina had never been one to pass a day inside reading, even a rainy day. Reina liked being outside, running wild with the wild things. The library had been Hildegarde's place.

Directly across from where Hildegarde stood, inside a glass case, was a framed copy of the Queendom Constitution. It wasn't the original. Unsigned but dated, this copy had been made around the same time as the original, about 200 years ago.

Next to the Constitution, in the same case, was one of the Hands of Peace which had also been created around the time of the Reconciliation, when the Treaty of the Consolidated Five was signed. Made of clay, this Hand of Peace sculpture—an arm from the elbow up to the hand—was covered in a deep blue glaze that spiraled up the inside of it, with a light green glaze winding up the outside of it. Safran Bleu plants seemed to grow up from the elbow, the flowers blooming on the forearm and hand. Multicolored stars blossomed from each finger.

Artists had made several Hands of Peace during the Reconciliation and spread them around the Queendom as "Milagros," symbols of the miracle of Reconciliation. As children, Hildegarde, Reina, and Jeremy had been warned by their mother never to touch the Hand of Peace. As far as Hildegarde knew, none of them ever had. Even as adults.

Hildegarde had spent countless hours in this place when she was a child. She had preferred this quiet place over almost any other place while Jeremy and Reina were outside with other children or adults.

Even though Hildegarde had been trained to be queen, she had not felt prepared for it. She had begged her mother to wait to abdicate. A late bloomer, Hildegarde had been in the midst of a passionate love affair when Queen Boudica retired. The love affair had been her priority then. She knew once she became queen she would be pressured to get married, to have children, and that would not have been possible, not with the man she loved. She hadn't been ready to give him up then.

She hadn't been ready to be queen either. She'd been afraid she would take down the entire Queendom with her incompetence, so she had resigned six months after her election. She wanted to stay at the Hearth, but she had to leave, had to make a clean break of it. She couldn't be a shadow on Reina's reign.

Now she was back. She wasn't afraid any more. She could breathe. She no longer believed she was incompetent. Something had gone wrong in the Queendom, that was true, and maybe it had all started when she abdicated her responsibilities all those years ago.

Hildegarde left the library and went downstairs. She walked down the corridor, past the now-deserted kitchen and staff dining room to the back door. Once there, she opened the door and stepped out into the moonlit garden. It smelled like home here, on this spot, like humus and lavender. She looked over her shoulder at the huge Old Oak and whispered, "Hello, old friend."

She walked down the garden path until she saw the long nursery building and the gardener's small round living quarters next to it.

A light was on inside the gardener's place.

Hildegarde walked toward the light. Her stomach fluttered, and she could feel her heart beating inside her chest.

Quickly she was at the door. She put her palm on the wood, waited a moment, and then lightly rapped her knuckles on the door.

A moment later the door opened and Quintana stood on the threshold.

"Ahh," he said. "Now I know who caused the earthquake."

Hildegarde smiled, and Quintana moved aside. She stepped into the warmly lit house.

"It looks the same," she said. "It smells the same."

"I didn't change anything," he said, "on the off chance you would return."

"Liar," she said.

He laughed. Then he held his arms open, and she went into them and embraced Quintana.

Hildegarde turned her face to him, and they kissed. It was a long kiss, and she could barely breathe for it.

She knew, in those moments as she held Quintana in her arms, that she had made the right decision to come home.

PART TWO
SUMMIT

CHAPTER EIGHT
LORELEI

Lorelei sat in the back of the chambers of the Reconciliation Council in a spot where she knew the shadows fell on her in such a way that she was invisible to most people—and she was certainly hidden from any of the NexusView cameras.

Lorelei often came to these proceedings. The Reconciliation Council was a kind of living history—a reminder of how their ancestors had stepped up, how they had saved themselves, their descendants, and the world from certain destruction.

Savi was one of the three rotating judges in the Queen's Village: two from the community and one from the Village Council. Savi was from the Village Council. She sat at the front of the room with the other judges while everyone else in the courtroom sat in a semi-circle around them. Behind the judges on the wall were the words: "Everything Is Connected To Everything Else."

Today Bob Jihnston was seeking help with his neighbor Lemeula Fragard who had recently dug up his lilac bush.

"Your neighbors have told us what they observed the day you pulled out the lilac bush," Savi said. "What say you, Lemeula?"

"I agree with their version," she said. "It is my version as well, but I only did it because of the smell. I asked them before if they could move it, and they refused. I hadn't slept for several nights. I deeply regret my actions. I am willing to replace the lilac bush with something else, please."

Savi said, "What about the lilac? Does it live?"

"It does, your honor," Jihnson said. "We put it right back and dosed it with some flower spirits. We sang to it until we figured it was rooted again. We'll see what happens. We only came to court because this is the third time she has damaged something in our yard. We tried to heal it in our neighborhood, but it didn't work."

"Lemeula," one of the other judges said, "have you been to a healer? Perhaps there is something wrong with your sense of smell."

"No! I am not to blame for their stinky flowers!"

"You cut another neighbor's roses," Savi said, "without any regard to the plant or the neighbors. There is an undercurrent of violence to what you keep doing."

"No undercurrent," Jihnson said. "Very over current!"

Savi said, "Our foremothers and fathers recognized that violence is most often a mental illness or the result of stress. Which is it with you, Lemuela?"

"I am not crazy."

"And yet you keep destroying your neighbors' peace," Savi said.

"I suppose I have felt stressed about not sleeping," Lemuela said. "No sleep, no dreams, no relief."

"What is your work?" Savi asked.

"Textiles," she said. "Everyone knows I make the prettiest Safran Bleu scarves in the Queendom. Maybe you don't know because you spend so much time up there with them. Congratulations, by the way on your upcoming marriage. Lately we haven't had as much demand for the scarves. I suppose that has been worrying me. Yes, it has."

"Excuse us," Savi said. The judges conferred, quietly.

Lorelei looked around the room. She recognized some people but not most. She should know them. They all knew one another, as it should be in a community. She guessed they would know who she was, too, if she came out of the shadows for a moment. She should have made more friends over the years. If things go sidewise in the future, having friends could help.

She entertained the notion that everyone in Queendom was a friend, of sorts. Everyone was rooting for them because when the First Family succeeded the nation succeeded. That was how it had been since the Queendom began. So if Lorelei did not have many intimates, what did that matter in the grand scheme of their lives?

The judges moved away from one another. It was time for the ruling.

"Lemuela," Savi said, "we wish this had been handled in your neighborhood with your neighbors. However, since it has come to us, we advise you to consult a healer to see if you have a medical problem. You need to make restitution to your neighbors. You must work it out together. Talk with them. Jihnson, you and the other neighbors should be aware of and sensitive to Lemuela's feelings. Why not talk with her before you plant? We're sorry you aren't getting enough work, Lemuela. You can find work or get a hobby. Maybe horticulture."

The people in the room laughed. Lemuela half-smiled.

"But you must have known the cohesion of the neighborhood was in danger. We're curious why you didn't get help."

Lemuela shrugged. "If they'd plant the right things everything would get back to normal, including my work."

"Jihnson," Savi said, "are you satisfied with this judgment? We'll have a check back in a month."

"I am," he said.

"Community members," Savi said, "is this outcome satisfactory to you?"

The people in the room clapped.

That had been an easy case, although Lorelei wondered if Lemuela would actually comply with the orders. Lorelei sensed something was amiss with her. Once Lemuela mentioned the problem with her work—with the economy—Savi seemed to rush through the proceedings. Perhaps the judges were afraid that any mention of the Queendom's economic woes would exacerbate the situation.

A stable economy meant a stable nation. It wasn't common knowledge yet that the Queendom was having financial difficulties. The Queen did not normally hide the truth from the public—that would be wrong—but she didn't want to say too much before they worked out what had happened and how to fix it. For one thing, they couldn't let any of the other nations in the Consolidated Five find out. If one of the Consolidated Five was financially unstable, it could bring down the others, so the leaders in the Consolidated Five would not tolerate economic instability for long.

Ten years earlier when Erdom had been on the brink of economic collapse, Armistead geared up for a takeover. The Queendom had come to the rescue, loaning them the credit they needed to start the road back to stability.

Lorelei slid off the bench, left the court, and went out into spring sunshine. The village was busy this morning, lots of people out and about because of the Annual Consolidated Five Summit which would kick off tonight with a dinner and celebration of the first Reconciliation and the Treaty that formed the Consolidated Five.

Lorelei looked north toward the Hearth up on the hill. She could not see much of the building except the pointed roof on the cupola on the abbreviated fourth floor. But the Old Oak and other old trees were clearly visible, along with the garden that spilled out from the backside of the Hearth, making the whole place look wild and mysterious. Splashes of color here and there showed her where wild flowers and other spring plants were blooming. No place in the world was more beautiful than the Hearth in spring.

A group of people passed by her, laughing and talking. They nodded to her and said, "Good morning, Miss Lorelei." She answered them with a nod. That was enough. She guessed most of the population of the Queendom did not know she could talk. If she was going to come out of her shell, as it were, she supposed she should do it slowly, so she didn't shock the world.

Although maybe a shock would be a good thing.

Lorelei smiled and ducked down one of the side streets to get away from the crowds. She loved the Queen's Village. Every building fit into the landscape as well as any natural ridge, any rock, any flower. Each building was a part of the land, yet every one was also a unique architectural wonder. Each was a piece of artwork.

Today, Lorelei was headed to Wanda's Patisserie, which was just ahead. The sous chef from the Hearth had her own shop, too, which her wife and daughter ran when she wasn't there. The exterior of the one-story shop was blue and rust-colored with a purposely crooked yellow roof so that the whole thing looked like some kind of magical cottage out of a fairy tale. The windows were framed in material that imitated light blue candy sticks beautifully. The door looked exactly like gingerbread with a chocolate cupcake as the handle.

Lorelei wanted a few pieces of Wanda's Queendom Lemon Drops to give her mother as a surprise at the end of the evening. At the center of each heart-shaped drop was a tiny piece of chocolate wrapped in one blue saffron thread. Nothing tasted better, especially after a long day.

When Lorelei was a child and having a bad day, her mother would come into her room, get under the covers with her, and they would suck on lemon drops together, noisily, waiting for the wonderful bitter taste of the chocolate at the center. And then they would talk, and her mother would reassure her that one day, she would find her mission in life, one day she would have friends and she would feel as though she was a part of something wonderful.

Lorelei still did not know her mission in life, and she had no true friends, beyond Viva and maybe the downstairs crew. But she knew she was part of something wonderful. She was a part of the First Family, dedicated to the protection and nurturance of the Queendom.

As Lorelei reached out to open the door of Wanda's shop, she spotted Marguerite Teng—or someone who looked like her—out of the corner of her vision, walking into the alley. Lorelei turned to look and saw no one at first. She took a few steps and peered down the alleyway. It was Teng, and she was talking to a man Lorelei didn't know.

Teng had twenty-six different dishes to prepare for the Annual Consolidated Five Summit. At the very least, she had to supervise the preparation of twenty-six dishes. How could she have time to be here in the Queen's Village? The last time the Queendom had hosted the C5 Summit, when Lorelei was thirteen years old, the Hearth had been a mad house. Not only did the staff have to prepare five dishes to represent each country, the chef had to come up with one original dish. And then all the dishes would be on display on NexusView for the entire country to see—and duplicate if they wished.

Lorelei did not recognize the man. She couldn't hear what they were saying, but both speakers were quite animated. That was not unusual for Teng.

"Lorelei!" Viva was suddenly beside her.

Teng must have heard her daughter's voice because she looked over and caught sight of Lorelei watching her. Teng waved; Lorelei did the same. Then she turned to Viva.

"Hello," Lorelei said. "What are you doing here?"

Viva held her hand out to show Lorelei two pieces of Wanda's lemon drop candies. Viva popped one in her mouth and then said, "The other one is for you."

Lorelei hesitated. Viva moved her hand closer. "Take it," she said. So Lorelei did. She put the candy on her tongue and the sour flavor filled her mouth.

Viva laughed. Lorelei couldn't help it: She laughed, too.

Most of the time, Lorelei was wary of being friends with children because she was afraid people would continue to think of her as a child. Yet this particular child, Viva, was difficult to resist. She was so vibrant, exuberant, and persistent.

"Dee-lish!" Viva said.

"I can only agree," Lorelei said.

She glanced in Teng's direction. The cook was now walking

toward them. The man she had been conversing with was nowhere in sight.

"I needed some air," Teng said when she reached them. "It's going to be quite a night! That gentleman is visiting and wondered where he could get a good meal. I told him anywhere in the village!"

She talked fast and loud. As though she was nervous or lying.

"Some of the restaurants are duplicating the dishes from my menu," Teng said. "Can you believe it? It's very exciting. Viva and I should get back. You got your lemon drops? Good. Do you want to walk back with us, Lorelei?"

Lorelei shook her head.

"Can't I stay with Lorelei?" Viva asked. "That would be more fun."

"Miss Lorelei has things to do," Teng said, "including getting into her costume. We'll see her later."

Lorelei did not correct Teng. It wasn't exactly a costume she needed to don. It was traditional dress.

Viva rolled her eyes at her mother.

"You can come up and help me get dressed later," Lorelei said.

"Oh, yes," Viva said. "That'll be fun. It'll be like dressing a giant doll!"

Teng's eyes widened in horror. "Viva! Oh, Miss Lorelei, I am so sorry."

"For what?" Lorelei asked. "No one has ever referred to me as a giant anything before. Maybe I'm getting that growth spurt at long last."

Teng appeared shocked. Viva looked confused. Her mother grabbed her hand, and they hurried away.

Lorelei waited until the two of them were out of earshot, she hoped, and then she laughed.

She went into Wanda's Patisserie, purchased several lemon drops, and then headed back toward the Hearth via a side trail that went nearly straight up and then around through the forest. She liked this trail because she rarely met anyone else on it—at least not anyone human.

Today she was grateful when she stepped out of the sunlight and into the cool dark woods.

"Hello, Old Ones," she whispered as she followed the path through the forest.

A hawk called out above the canopy. Lorelei waved. Soon the ground leveled off. She hummed as she skipped down the path, suddenly feeling like she was ten years old again. Ten years old: the age when she stopped growing.

For a time, she had measured herself every morning to see if she had grown overnight. After a while, she realized she was as tall as she was going to get. One morning her grandmother—the Queen Madre—saw her measuring her height. She said to Lorelei, "Some of the strongest and most beautiful trees in the world are small. Look at the juniper trees, the ones twisted as if by some unseen wind—or dancing with some unseen partner. They are tougher than the tallest trees in the forest. They can take drought, harsh winds, and climate fluctuations. Yet they remain. Or the bristlecone pines. Short and sturdy and thousands of years old. Can you imagine what they could tell us? Size has nothing to do with what kind of person you'll be. You get to decide that. I already know you are kind and wise. Time will tell the rest, no matter how tall you are or aren't."

Lorelei wasn't sure then how her grandmother knew she was kind or wise, since she hardly ever talked. Maybe it was because her grandmother believed as her mother did: "Most often the smartest person in the room is the one who is talking the least."

Lorelei didn't know if this adage was true or not, but she liked to believe it, especially those days when she could not bear to utter even one word.

She looked up at the tall tree next to her, following the line of the trunk up, up, up, until she saw patches of sky. She flexed the muscles in her arms, and cried, "Strongest woman in the world!"

Then she laughed. Suddenly a figure dressed all in black, wearing a black mask and a black jacket with a hood, stepped out from behind a wild rhododendron bush just up the trail. The forest quivered, as if signaling this was all a dream. Only it wasn't.

"Don't be afraid," he said—a man's voice, she thought—as he held up his left hand.

Adrenaline shot through Lorelei's body. She hadn't been afraid until he told her not to be.

"I am not afraid," she said. "Who are you? Show yourself to me." She could easily outrun him in this forest she knew so well.

The man moved forward slightly and then stopped.

"It is the Consolidated Five Summit," she said, "not May Day. We don't wear masks this day."

"I am masked to protect myself," he said.

"From what? We are a people of peace."

"Yes," he said, "but what I have to say might be considered heresy."

"Nonsense," she said. She had never spoken to anyone so boldly before, especially no stranger.

"We have no such thing as heresy in the Queendom or anywhere in the Consolidated Five," she said. Perhaps the man was unbalanced. "I must be on my way. If you are lost, I can point you in the right direction."

He shook his head. "I have been waiting for you, Lorelei Villanueva. We have been watching you, and we believe you can save the Queendom."

"The Queendom is not in need of saving!" she said. "How do you know me?"

"I can't say," he said. "But I only have the best interests of the Queendom and the Queen in my heart. Difficult times are ahead."

"How do you know?" she said. "Are you a soothsayer? Even soothsayers cannot predict the future."

"No, I am no soothsayer," he said. "We follow ways even older than the soothsayers. We follow the Old Ways."

"We all follow the Old Ways," she said. "What is your point?"

"I can see I am trying your patience," he said. "It is only because we believe we have seen what is to come that we are breaking our silence. You could see the future, too. People like you can intuit things, including the future, by using information from your surroundings."

"Anyone can do that."

"Not like you," he said. "You are special. Your gifts are special."

Lorelei stepped back until she was leaning against one of the ancient oaks. She couldn't remember anyone ever praising her like this before.

It made her suspicious.

"There are some, with training, who can see beyond this present to the future," he said.

"I don't believe anything you say," she said. "What kind of difficulties are coming?"

"It stems from the very core of the Queendom," he said. "A rotten core. We want to bring to the Queendom a true monarchy. A rule of one, based on bloodline, where the Queen commands for a lifetime, and we are her loyal subjects. Not what we have now, a semi-monarchy which could be toppled at any time after any election."

"But it hasn't toppled!" she said. "For 200 years the Villanueva family has been in charge."

"Haven't you ever wondered about that?" he asked. "How have the Villanuevas stayed in power so long?"

"No, I have never wondered," she said. "The election results are checked and double-checked. My family has stayed as the First Family because we have done a good job and the people reelected us."

"And now the rebel group in the Low Mountains is threatening the Queendom," he said, "and the missing Safran Bleu has caused economic instability. Your family could be out soon."

"How do you know any of this?" Lorelei asked. "My mother knows what she's doing. The Queendom will be fine. The Queendom *is* fine! And if my mother isn't reelected, so what? The next elected ruler will do a fine job. That is our system of government."

"That's the point," he said. "We don't know that the next person will do a good job. Your mother was born, bred, and trained for the job. You or your siblings have been trained to take over when the time is right."

"Obviously you are not from here. Neither my brother or myself will ever be CEO! I am the idiot dwarf daughter and my brother often acts like a two year old. Only my sister Minerva is fit to be leader."

Lorelei put her hand over her mouth. She could not believe she had said all of those words out loud, to a stranger.

"You must be some kind of mad man," she said, "or magician, to make me say such things. I am not listening to you or saying another word."

Lorelei stepped off the path and went around the man. He smelled like cinnamon.

"You would make a great queen," he said gently. "And we'd like to help you become queen."

Lorelei gasped and backed away from him. "You dare believe I would ever do anything to hurt my mother, sister, or the Queendom so that I could be queen? You are crazy! I have no desire to be the monarch. My mother is a great queen, and my sister will be a great queen once my mother retires."

"We are not suggesting anything nefarious," he said. "Your mother might retire early, as your grandmother did. And my sources tell me Minerva will not become queen."

"Why? Why wouldn't she be queen? Are you saying something will happen to her?" Lorelei felt panic. Maybe this was why she did not normally talk to strangers. It was all too confusing.

"No," he said. "Please try to trust me. I mean you and your family no harm."

"Trust you? Are you kidding? I don't know who you are or what you want with me! If my sister does not become queen, then my brother will become Chief of State."

"The Queendom will need a leader," he said.

The implication being that Raphael was not one.

"You have all the qualities and gifts that would make you a good queen," he said.

"Stop trying to flatter me," she said. "I am going home." She rushed down the path, away from the man.

"We believe there is more than one page to the Constitution," the man called after her.

"I've heard that rumor," she said, still walking away. "So what? No one has ever found anything more, and the soothsayers who were there say there isn't anything more."

"The soothsayers say a great deal."

She stopped and turned around.

"All we know about history before the time of the Reconciliation was told to us by the soothsayers," he said. "They told us what went wrong. They told us a true monarchy never worked well in times past. But we don't know. Not really."

"I won't listen to this," she said. "The prejudices against the soothsayers have always been unfounded and bigoted. The soothsayers were created to help us, not harm us."

"They were created for the corporate busidoms," he said. "They were created for those people who took down our civilization."

"No," Lorelei said. "That isn't true. They saved us. You are a bigot."

"It's not bigotry," he said. "It's only a question. We can't know what we don't know. Shouldn't we question everything? We believe— my people and I—we believe the lost pages of the Constitution must be in the Hearth somewhere. You know the house better than most. You could look for the lost pages, and if you found them, you could read them first. Perhaps the rest of the Constitution was a blueprint for a true monarchy. Perhaps not. We will accept whatever it says. We only want to know what our ancestors intended for our country."

Lorelei backed away. "Ah, now I see the truth of this. All your flattery was to get me to do your bidding and ransack my home."

"No," he said. "My name is Patra. We call ourselves the Queen's Court. We stay hidden because we fear exile."

"You can't be exiled for your beliefs no matter how stupid they are!" Lorelei turned and ran down the path, away from the man.

"I am at your service," she heard him call.

Later, she would have to tell her mother all about the crazy man in the forest, so they could laugh about it while sucking on lemon candies.

He *had* to be crazy. That was the only explanation.

Only a crazy man could possibly imagine that she could ever be queen.

CHAPTER NINE
BILLY

Billy began the morning of the Annual Consolidated Five Summit celebration the same way he began every morning: He stood outside in the Hearth garden in his bare feet singing up the sun. Sometimes other members of the downstairs staff sang with him, sometimes he was the only humanoid. This morning, he was surrounded by the regular staff.

Since Teng had arrived, more members of the staff had started practicing the Old Ways. She was so excited about being in the Queendom: "You people *live* the Old Ways. You are dedicated to meaning, to story, to ritual. I so admire that." It was difficult to disappoint her, to not live up to her expectations.

Billy liked singing up the sun. He always had. This morning, the singing seemed more ebullient. Abbygail did a little dance as she sang. She always sang a little off-key, and Billy wondered about that. How could a soothsayer be out of tune? Sometimes he had to remind himself that soothsayers were not perfect. They each had their own quirks and foibles. And he liked that Abbygail sang off-key. She was different from any other soothsayer he had met. She was different from *anyone* he had ever met. She was always so happy once the sun came up, as if their songs were actually responsible for the sun rising.

Mr. Umberto never joined them when they sang up the sun. He said the sun had been rising and setting no thanks to him forever and would continue to come up and go down without his help.

"It's not that the sun won't come up without our songs, Billy told Mr. Umberto once. "But every Being in the Universe deserves recognition, especially this particular Being who provides a living for all of them."

Billy had only been at the Hearth for a few months, but already it felt like home, his place on this Earth for the foreseeable future. He loved the feel of the house, the land, and the people. He liked how the gold of sunrise and sundown changed the entire feel of the place each dawn and dusk. The house and gardens looked betwixt and between then, and he sometimes wondered if it could all just slip into another world and disappear. It wasn't that it looked preternatural during those times: It was that it looked completely natural, as if the house itself was growing up from the land just as the trees, bushes, and flowers had.

He loved the smell of the place, too. Even when he was indoors, he could smell the gardens. Sometimes it was a distinct scent—like the daffodils when they first bloomed. Sometimes it was lavender or lilac. But most of the time it was something more, a collective scent—a mingling of the smells of humus, flowers, cooking herbs and spices, and human sweat.

And sometimes, when he was in a particular room, one of the many murals seemed to come alive, moving slightly just outside of his vision so that when he turned and looked, all was still again. The vines that snaked across the walls in the large dining room always appeared to be on the move. The mural of the daffodils in the small dining room seemed to get bigger or smaller, depending upon the phase of the moon. He couldn't explain the painted moon on the wall above Miss Lorelei's dresser: It changed with the phase of the real moon. When he asked Mr. Umberto about it once, Umberto said, "Our ancestors knew far more than we ever will. They were artists, visionaries. Ours is not to reason why. Ours is to be in constant awe."

Every day Billy found whimsical details in the Hearth he had not observed before. Yesterday, he spotted a mysterious red shadow in the corner of the First Family's drawing room. He thought for sure they had missed something when they were cleaning. As he got closer, to sweep it out, he realized it was a tiny painting of red porcini mushrooms.

In his room, gigantic colorful fluorescent dragonflies arced across the ceiling and out the windows. It was weeks before he noticed the dragonflies glowed in the dark; in daylight, they were barely noticeable. He always turned off his light while lying on his side. One night he woke in the middle of the night, on his back. When he opened his eyes, he wasn't certain where he was as he looked at the dragonflies. The longer he stared, the more the dragonfly wings seemed to flutter.

The only thing he didn't like about living and working at the Hearth was his work schedule. He and Abbygail, the only downstairs soothsayers, usually worked twelve hours a day. The other servants worked eight hours, sometimes ten if they were short-staffed or something special was happening at the Hearth.

When Billy complained to Mr. Umberto about this, the steward said, "How fortunate you are that you don't need as much rest as we human beings do. Don't brag too much about it. The others might resent it."

Abbygail said she had always worked that much, and she enjoyed it.

"But don't you want time off to do whatever you want to do?" he asked her.

She had looked around the room for a moment, and then she said, "I hadn't thought about it much before. I like my work. I like knowing everything that is going on in the house. When I'm gone, I feel as though I might have missed something. And you know, they seem to need us. I feel like we are helping all of the Queendom. What we do is important. And I do get one day off a week. But, yes, perhaps now I would like to do more."

"Why now?" he asked. "What has changed?"

"You are here, Billy Santos," she said. "And you are as interesting as this house."

He laughed.

He had pledged to her to bring their work schedule up to Mr. Umberto again. Now was not the time. Today they would all be working extra shifts. Mr. Umberto had brought in help from the village for the Summit, but he had warned Billy and Teng—the newcomers—that it would be a very busy twenty-four hours.

So Billy began the day barefoot, singing up the sun. Afterward, he got dressed in his livery and then ate breakfast with the rest of the regular staff. Mr. Umberto had a rule that they could not talk about work while eating.

"Life is not all about work, even here at the Hearth," he often said. "Let us expand our horizons by steering our discussions to something besides our duties here."

Sometimes that meant no one said anything for long stretches of time. This morning, they talked about the full moon that had kept most of them restless in the night. Wanda regaled them with her dream about walking and talking cupcakes. "The vanilla cupcake had such a bad attitude," she said. "So the other cupcakes ate her. They had white frosting all over their mouths."

Abbygail started laughing and couldn't stop. Soon everyone around the table was laughing, even Mr. Umberto.

When they stopped laughing and were finished with their meal, Mr. Umberto said, "It will be a long day. We are witnesses to history each and every time we host this event. And good hosts we will be. Our helpers from the Queen's Village will arrive any minute. You all have your instructions. Have a good day, and I will see you along the way."

Billy was paired with Abbygail for most of the day. The other four leaders in the Consolidated Five would be lodging at the Hearth during the Summit, so Billy and Abbygail needed to make certain their rooms were spick-and-span splinter new. They dashed up the steps together.

"I thought of you as I got up and stared at the Old Moon last night," Abbygail told him. "I bet myself that you'd have a tale to tell about it."

"Indeed," he said, "I might have. But right this minute I am dumbstruck. What about you? Did the Silver Disk have anything wise or wonderful to tell you?"

She shook her head and let her fingers trail along the wall and across the stenciled fish that swam up alongside them. "I'm not much of a storyteller. I do like your tales. They're funny."

"You like funny stories?"

"Doesn't everyone?" she said, "they almost always have a happy ending. Who wants to hear stories where everything ends badly? Mr. Umberto says we're all fish food in the end. And then we start all over again." She shrugged. "That may be true for him—if any fish would eat him." She laughed. "But what about us? What's our happy ending?"

Billy smiled. "I never thought of death as a happy ending," he said. "I will have to consider that."

They walked down the main second floor corridor.

"But for now," Billy said, "once more into the breach, dear friend, once more."

Abbygail giggled. "The game's afoot. Follow your spirit!"

They opened windows, fluffed pillows, and put out pitchers of water in each room. When Billy went to open the window in the corner spare room on the third floor, he looked down and saw Lorelei running out of the woods, toward the house. Her face was flushed, and she looked frightened. Billy wondered if he should call down to her, see if she was well. She looked up at him and stopped running. She waved.

"Is everything all right, Miss Lorelei?" Billy tried to call down softly.

"It is," she said. "Thank you. We have a big day today." She glanced behind her, into the woods, and then up at Billy again. "Have a good one!"

Then she disappeared under the apple trees near the entrance.

Abbygail came and stood next to Billy at the window. "She's a dear one, Miss Lorelei is. She barely talked most of her life, except when she was down with us, but even then, it was odd. It was always as if she were listening to someone or something else. She has her ear to the Great Unknown, that is for certain. Never seen her do an unkind thing, even though she got teased when no one was about. Her brother, especially. Don't tell anyone I said so, but I'm not so sure about him. And she has something bubbling up inside of her. She has taken a shine to you, I'm sure you've noticed."

They turned back to finish up the room.

"It is difficult to resist my charms," Billy said. He grinned.

Abbygail laughed. "It certainly is."

When they finished opening up the rooms, they helped set up a buffet in the Heron Room just off the Coneflower Garden, at the opposite end of the house from the Crocus Garden. On one of the light blue walls of this long rectangular meeting room, a great blue heron looked away from them, over her shoulder at something more interesting in the distance. The artist had painted her as tall as the ceiling. Someone had put a tablecloth the same color as the great blue over the oval wooden dining table at the center of the room.

Abbygail and Billy shuttled pies from the kitchen to the Heron Room and set them on linen-covered tables near the wall across from the heron. One table was covered with meat and vegetable pies; another table was filled with dessert pies. Teng helped Billy and Abbygail arrange them prettily on the tables and the pie stands.

"I choose pies because the idea of the Consolidated Five and the Reconciliation was a pie in the sky idea," Teng told Billy, Abbygail, and Umberto as she looked over her dishes. "No one thought it was possible to have a just and peaceful society. Yet we have attained it." She smiled as she turned one of the pies. "Mr. Umberto, tell me five minutes before they are to eat because I want to start dinner with a particular dish. There will be a string on the dish, and the Queen will need to gently pull the string up."

"The Queen must pull a *string*?" Mr. Umberto asked. "You aren't playing some kind of prank on her, are you?"

"I would not do that," Teng said. "It is elegant, simple, and it will be wonderful. Now, I have to get back downstairs. Remember, five minutes, Mr. Umberto."

Teng left the room.

Not long after, the Queen arrived, along with Nehemiah. She stood tall and confident. Her hair was piled atop her head with a gold and blue ribbon woven through it. She wore aquamarine pants and top, close-fitting, with a sheer bluish half-cape tied loosely around her neck. Her shoes were light blue. Nehemiah wore his usual saffron robes. He walked alongside the Queen as nonchalantly as always, seemingly unimpressed—or unmoved—by all he saw.

The Queen greeted the staff and then said, "It looks wonderful. You and your staff always do such a marvelous job, Mr. Umberto. I am quite certain no one will go hungry. Marguerite Teng is doing well under this pressure, I gather."

Mr. Umberto held his hands behind his back, as he often did, while the Queen talked. When she was finished, he said, "All is well, Your Majesty. If you could let me know five minutes before you want to eat, I would appreciate it. Cook Teng has a *plan*." He sounded dubious.

"How are you, Billy?" the Queen asked. "This is your first Summit, isn't it?"

"Yes, Your Majesty," he said. "Very exciting."

She smiled. "Yes, it is. It's part of the weft and warp of our particular tapestry, eh? Abbygail, I hope this day finds you well."

"Yes, Your Majesty." Abbygail made a small curtsy. The Queen smiled.

"Not your first Summit," the Queen said.

"About my twentieth," Abbygail said. "I look forward to them every five years!"

"And what's your favorite part?" the Queen asked. "The glittering conversation? The presence of these great leaders? The traditional dresses at dinner? The music? The stories?"

"Why, the food, Ma'am," Abbygail said.

Reina laughed and clapped her hands once. "How could I have left that out!"

The Queen continued walking alongside the tables, gazing at the feast.

"It is called 'Pie in the Sky,'" Mr. Umberto said, "in honor of the history of the Consolidated Five."

"Marvelous," the Queen said.

"Laudable," Nehemiah said.

The Queen and Nehemiah moved away as the guests began trickling into the dining room from the Coneflower Garden.

Billy and Abbygail stayed at the buffet tables, ready to help cut and serve the pies as needed. They'd been told to expect about twenty-five leaders, diplomats, and advisors, and come they did, men and women talking quietly and intently with one another. Abbygail knew most of them, and she whispered their names to Billy as they came into the room.

"President Ixchel of Erdom," Abbygail said when a small dark woman entered the room, "and her aide."

Ixchel had green eyes that looked directly at Billy when she went by the tables.

"Hello, Abbygail," Ixchel said. "Nice to see you again. I cannot believe this food! The Queendom has outdone itself again."

"President Ixchel," Abbygail said, "this is Billy Santos."

The president held out her hand to Billy. He took it.

"Ah, Santos," she said. "A good name for a good man?"

It was a question, but she did not wait for an answer. She kept walking.

"Reina!" she said when she reached the Queen.

"Shelly," Reina cried. The two women embraced. "Always good to see an old friend."

Soon after, Chief Flora Diaz from the Paquay State made her way into the room, followed by her aide, Teasdale—a soothsayer. They nodded to one another—Teasdale and Billy—as Billy felt that bit of frisson in his brain each time he encountered another soothsayer. It was some kind of bio-mechanical signal that they were connected with one another on the great soothsayer communications web: the

Nexus. This soothsayer did not wear the saffron robes, so he was not a mage like Nehemiah, yet Billy sensed he was looking down at Abbygail and him—because they were mere housebods.

"Pay no attention to him," Abbygail whispered. "He's that way with everyone."

Most soothsayers came from the Paquay State; that was where they went if they needed medical care—or an upgrade. Billy wasn't fond of the country. He didn't find the soothsayers there particularly friendly.

"Prime Minister Damon Lerner of Armistead," Abbygail whispered when a tall pale man dressed in a green suit coat sauntered into the room followed by a heavy set woman with the reddest hair Billy had ever seen. "And Mauve. She's called his assistant, but they say—whoever they are—that Mauve knows more about the Consolidated Five than anyone alive, even more than the soothsayers. I heard someone once say she knows where all the bodies are buried. That confused me somewhat since anyone can find out where the bodies are buried. It's public record. But then I realized that was an idiom. Metaphor, analogies, idioms. Sometimes they go right over my head." She ran her hand over her head.

Billy laughed.

From across the room, Mr. Umberto shot them a look.

Abbygail looked down at the buffet table. "Oops. I'm sorry I got you in trouble."

Billy smiled. "Don't you worry, Abbygail. I'll explain later that you were telling me who everyone is, and that knowledge allows me to do my job better. Is there anyone else? Are all the leaders here?"

Abbygail looked around the room. "No. One more. Premier Outram of Berland."

The noise level in the room went up as it filled with people. Then suddenly a hush fell over the group. Billy looked toward the entrance where a lone man stood. He wasn't tall or short—maybe Billy's height—with thick and wavy salt and pepper hair and eyes bluer than the sky. He appeared completely at ease as he stood there, gazing around the room with this hands in the front pockets of his black pants, yet the room practically vibrated with his intensity.

Nearly everyone in the room turned to watch the man. When he stopped looking around, when he had finally found what he was seeking, his face softened slightly. The other guests followed his gaze. He was looking at Queen Reina. She must have felt his eyes on her because she looked up from her conversation and saw Outram. She smiled.

In that moment, conversations began again. The guests looked away. Billy watched as Reina walked across the room, as Outram strode across the room, as the two walked toward each other.

When they were face to face, Reina held out her hand to Outram. He took her hand in both of his. Billy couldn't hear what they were saying, but they leaned toward one another. Reina kissed Outram on first one and then the other cheek. Then they let go of each other's hands.

Billy looked away and saw Nehemiah watching Reina and Outram. Mr. Umberto was watching, too, as he walked over to the buffet table, his left eyebrow arched.

Billy couldn't help himself. He whispered, "Mr. Umberto, what was that?"

"*That* was Berland's Premier Outram," Umberto said.

"The Queen's first love," Abbygail whispered.

"No gossiping," Mr. Umberto said.

Abbygail frowned. "Is telling the facts gossiping?"

The Queen looked at Mr. Umberto then and nodded. He went to the privocom in the room. Billy didn't hear him but assumed he was contacting Teng. A few minutes later, Teng appeared, carrying a pie. She put the pie on the top of one of the pie stands, and then she moved to the back of the room. Mr. Umberto went to the Queen and whispered something to her. Then the two of them walked to the buffet table.

"Excuse me, everyone," the Queen said. "I would like to welcome you to the Annual Consolidated Five Summit. We are honored to have you in the Queendom. We hope that you will stay long enough to enjoy our art, food, stories, and hospitality. This year we kick off the Summit with the Pie in the Sky lunch buffet dedicated to our shared values and the great work and play we've done together over the last two centuries." The Queen stepped closer to the pie. She was so close to Billy—who stood across from the table from her—that he could smell her scent. She smelled like the gardens: of sage and lavender.

The Queen picked up the delicate-looking maroon-colored string on the pie and gently pulled up. The string lifted half of the pastry on top of the pie—it was like opening a door on the floor. As it lifted, Billy saw a flurry of color and then wings as five butterflies—one yellow, one blue, one red, one black, and one brown—burst out of the pie through the open pastry door. A collective "ahhh!" went up around the room. The butterflies fluttered around the pie for an instant, and then they flew out the door toward the garden.

"No butterflies were harmed in the process," Reina said.

The crowd roared with delight.

"Now," the Queen said, "let us eat."

The Queen got a small plate and put a slice of quiche on it. After that, the leaders of the free world—and their advisors—lined up to eat. Once they had their plates, some of them wandered out of the room again and into the garden.

"You two go on your break," Mr. Umberto said to Billy and Abbygail. "They'll be down to business soon, and they'll kick out all except for the leaders and their immediate advisors anyway. I'll stay then. Go on now."

Umberto shooed them away. Billy laughed, and then he and Abbygail left the Heron Room. Marguerite Teng followed them.

"Well done, Teng," Billy said. "That was very impressive."

"I've never seen anything like it at any of our other summits," Abbygail said. "How did you do it?"

"Not long ago I was out in the garden asking the spirits I see and the spirits that be what I could do for the Summit and these butterflies flew right up to me." She clasped her hands together.

"It was so beautiful. I took it as a sign. So this morning I made a friendly butterfly trap. I promised them I wouldn't keep them long, and when I came back, the trap was full. I had already prepared a cold pie for them—with food inside I thought they'd like—and there you are!"

"You are a trusting soul," Abbygail said. "What if it hadn't worked out? What if the butterflies hadn't shown up?"

"Then I wouldn't have done it," Teng said. "No one would be disappointed because no one knew what I was planning. That's what I do: keep those surprises to myself. If I fail, no one is the wiser. But I continue trying!" She grinned.

Billy laughed. "I should keep that in mind."

"I must be off," Teng said as they reached the busy kitchen. "We have more magic to create. I left some food for you two in the dining room."

Wanda called out to Teng, "How'd it go, lovey? All well with the world?"

"It's all well, Wanda," she said. "Worked like a charm."

"That's 'cause we were up all night fixin' the charms," she said.

Teng and Wanda laughed, giggling like girls, and Billy smiled. They were all getting a bit giddy. Wanda looked over at them.

"Best be eatin'," she said, "or we're gonna find you something to do."

"Don't have to tell me twice," Billy said.

Abbygail and Billy went into the dining room and picked up the covered plates Teng had left for them.

"Outside?" Billy asked.

Abbygail nodded, and they headed down the hall and out the door into the bright sunshine. Billy pointed to a grassy spot under one of the old oaks. They walked to the shade and then sat next to each other, facing the village—although from their viewpoint, they couldn't see it. They could see the rest of the garden and the smoky blue hills in the distance.

They ate their respective spinach quiches in silence. A crow called out above them, and Abbygail waved.

"How are you liking our little part of the world?" Abbygail asked. Several crows landed on the grass a few yards from them and began picking at the ground. "Look at them. Must be a buried treasure they're looking for."

"I do enjoy it here," Billy said. "Very much. Everyone is kind and interesting."

"Interesting?" Abbygail said. "Really? Everyone?" She gazed at him, but then turned away when he looked at her.

He chuckled. "Yes, everyone. I could stay here a while."

"You've had an interesting life I'll wager," she said. "You've done so much traveling."

He shrugged. "Couldn't find home. You know, the soothsayer restlessness syndrome. It's what happens when we don't have family, I guess. I lived for quite a few years with a band of traveling musicians and storytellers. It wasn't a very comfortable life, but we had a lot of joy."

"You didn't stay?" she said.

"After a while, people get old," he said. "They start to die—while I don't get old or change or die. It got uncomfortable. And sad. It was sad. Don't you feel that, being here for so long? Watching the march of time?"

"It could be," she said, "if I thought along those lines. For some reason, I haven't. It's like watching the garden come into its own every year and then watching it die out again. It is sad when it dies out or when it's fallow. But when it is in bloom, oh my! And that's the same with the people here. I watch them bloom. If I can be here for that, it only seems right I stay around for the rest of it."

Billy nodded. "I hadn't thought of it that way. You are very wise, Abbygail. Abbygail what? Do you have a last name?"

She shook her head. "Never have. Maybe I should."

"What name would you pick?"

"I don't know," she said. "I like yours. I like Santos."

"You are welcome to it," he said. "You are certainly more saintly than I am."

"If we had the same last name," she said, "wouldn't that make us related?"

"Ah yes," he said. "We could be brother and sister. Except you were activated before I was, so we could be mother and son."

Abbygail shook her head. "No, I don't think of you as a son. Although I wouldn't know what having a son actually felt like. I wonder why our creator didn't design us so we could reproduce? Have you ever wondered?"

"I suppose it's because we live so long she didn't figure we'd need to reproduce. Don't humans and others reproduce because they're going to eventually die? Reproduction helps them carry on."

Abbygail looked over at Billy. "Now I never thought of it that way." She laughed. "You are funny, Billy Santos."

"In this case, I was not trying to be," he said. "So can you tell me about Premier Outram. Do you know him?"

She took another bite of quiche and then looked around. "When he was younger—when they were younger—he was here a great deal. I'd see them in the garden together. They'd go out hiking, exploring. He always filled whatever space he was in. She did, too, but not in the same way. She wasn't going to be queen, you know. He was always going to be premier, at least it seemed that way. They were in love, but they fought. He got angry a lot."

"Why?" Billy asked.

"Who knows," she said. "But Reina had planned on marrying him and moving to Berland. And then suddenly it was over, and she married Mr. Talib. He was so relaxed and friendly. The Queen is not an angry person, so it was better for her to leave him. But Outram loved her, almost desperately. I bet he would have given up everything for her. He would have given up his country, I believe, if she had asked."

"I wonder what it is like to love or be loved that way," he said.

"It was uncomfortable, at least for her," Abbygail said.

"Have you ever been in love like that?" Billy asked.

Abbygail ran her fingers through her hair. "No," she said. "I have loved." She shrugged. "I did have feelings for someone in the First Family a long time ago. And that was strange. But I got over it. They age so rapidly, you know. Plus, it would have never worked."

Billy nodded. It was not illegal for soothsayers and humans to be together, but it was not entirely socially acceptable.

"What about you?" Abbygail asked.

"Oh, I loved a woman in our traveling show," he said. "But she wanted to marry and have children. Which is what she did. She married and had children with a man. The kids are grown now, and the woman and man are still together."

"What about another soothsayer?" she asked.

"Now and again," he said. "But nothing long term."

"Maybe you haven't met the right person," she said.

"Maybe. Isn't it nice to be talking about ourselves instead of them? The First Family, I mean. We have lives, too. I don't want every minute of my life to be focused on them."

Billy heard the squeak of a door opening. He and Abbygail looked to their right, through the tall decorative grass to where the door to the gardener's home had just opened. Quintana was standing on the threshold, and Hildegarde stood on the step. Quintana smiled. She laughed, and he took her hand and pulled her into the house and closed the door.

"Speaking of them," Billy said. "I had no idea that was going on. I thought she was leaving."

"We all thought she was leaving," Abbygail said. "And everyone was hoping *that* wasn't going on again."

"Why?"

"Because that's why she abdicated," Abbygail said. "She wanted to be with Quintana, and no one believed that was the right thing to do, even Quintana."

Billy turned to face Abbygail. "And everyone knew it was going on back then?"

Abbygail shook her head. "No! It was all deadly secret. It would have been a huge scandal. Interest in it would have died down, but they couldn't risk shaking the confidence of the electorate. When her mother, Nehemiah, her brother, and sister all were against their relationship, Hildegarde resigned. She thought Quintana would leave the Hearth with her. He didn't."

"That must have been devastating for her," he said.

"I don't know," Abbygail said. "It was very difficult on the rest of the family. On everyone here. Many people felt betrayed. Everyone here has made sacrifices for the greater good. It was a relief when she finally left."

"You were relieved?" Billy asked.

"I don't know," she said. "I felt sorry for her. She fell in love. She didn't want to hide it. It seems in this day and age you shouldn't have to hide anything about your private life—it should be private. But yes, I was glad when she left. I'm a little uneasy about why she's here. But the Queen will take care of it. I have faith in her. She is steady as it gets."

"Did the First Family lie to the public about why Hildegarde resigned? I remember they publicly told everyone that she resigned because she decided she wasn't cut out for the life, that she didn't like the attention or the work."

"That wasn't a lie," Abbygail said. "She obviously was not cut out for the life, and she didn't like the attention or the work."

He shrugged. "I guess I haven't been here long enough. It feels like a lie."

"Even if it is," Abbygail said, "does it matter? Why should the rest of the world know she was in love with a soothsayer? All they needed to know is that she quit and Queen Reina stepped in."

"Queen Reina. You know that essentially means queen queen."

Abbygail laughed. "When Reina was born, the Queen—who is now the Queen Madre—said she called her that so that she would always feel like a queen, since her sister Hildegarde would *actually* be queen. Little did she know."

"Maybe the name was a way of tempting fate," Billy said.

"Do you believe in such a thing as fate?" Abbygail asked.

"No," he said. "Things just happen. What about you?"

She made a face. "I don't know. I wasn't built brilliant like Nehemiah. Or even like you. So I don't know. Whether it was an accident of fate or a plan of fate or neither, I'm glad you have come to the Hearth. We will be great friends."

"We already are," Billy said. "Now, I suppose, it's back to work."

CHAPTER TEN
HILDEGARDE

Hildegarde could not resist Quintana's house. Even on a warm sunny day like this one, the first day of the Annual C5 Summit. It was like being in a very comfortable cave. Or like being part of an art piece. The Hearth was like that in a way, too, with all the murals and artwork everywhere. But it was so big. Cavernous.

Quintana's place was small. Hildegarde walked in and observed the small kitchen to the left, a worktable to the right, and the bed in the middle, against the back wall. The golden rumpled blankets on the feather mattress looked so inviting, as did Quintana's silk golden robe on the end of the bed.

Hildegarde wanted to pick up the robe and smell it, hold it close. But Quintana was standing right next to her, holding his arms out to her. She fell right into them, as she had the last time she had been here, and the time before. Soon they were naked and on the bed together. She kept her moans to herself. She couldn't let the attendees of the Summit hear her. Couldn't let her mother or sister or anyone else know what she was doing.

Not that any of that mattered. She just wanted to feel Quintana against her. His weight on her as she sank into the feather bed, as she sank into her own ecstasy. He knew where to touch her, what to do when. She had never had a lover like Quintana. Never would. Soothsayers had been engineered to be good lovers.

The Queen Madre had told Hildegarde about Fan, Reina's sexbod lover. Only as a tension relief, the Queen Madre said.

"She hasn't fallen in love with him," the Queen Madre said. "She knows the difference between a human being and a soothsayer. Falling in love with a soothsayer would be like falling in love with a Nexus communication outlet."

"Not in the least bit similar," Hildegarde told her mother. "Thank you for your support and understanding, as always."

But now, now, as she pulled Quintana closer and deeper, she didn't want to think of any of that. She only wanted to look into his green eyes and see his love. She wanted to know that he loved her. *Loved her.* For now and always.

"I'm ready," he whispered. "Are you? I can wait. I can." He closed his eyes briefly. "I can try to wait. God. You feel so good."

"Stop," she said. "Just stop."

He gently moved away from her. "What is it?"

She grabbed his silk robe and slipped it on as she got out of bed.

"I don't believe you," she said. "I don't believe anything you've ever said to me. You're a machine. You can control your erection and ejaculation! Why did you say that to me?"

He sat up and pushed himself to the edge of the bed. He looked confused. She paced back and forth in front of him.

"I gave up everything for you!" she said.

Quintana grimaced slightly and then said, "I never asked you to do that."

"I thought you loved me," Hildegarde said. "I thought you wanted me as much as I wanted you."

"I did," he said. "I do. But I had no idea you planned on resigning."

"Neither did I," she said. "But when they said it wouldn't look good if we stayed together, I had to do something."

"What did it matter what they said? It would have been all right. We could have continued as we were."

"With you out here as the gardener and me in there as the Queen? With me sneaking out to see you?"

"Why not?" he said. "Besides, it wouldn't have lasted forever."

She snorted. "Why do you say that? Because you've done it before with other queens? Or because I'll age and die and you won't?"

"Because you were young," he said, "and you didn't know what you wanted."

"How patronizing is that?"

She stopped pacing and looked at Quintana. His skin was brown and leathery from spending decades—centuries?—in the sun. He was so beautiful it nearly took her breath away.

"Did you have an affair with me because I was going to be queen and then was queen?" she asked. "Once I was no longer queen— once I resigned—you weren't interested, isn't that right? Isn't that why you wouldn't go away with me?"

"That is absurd," Quintana said. "And you know it."

"I know nothing of the sort!" Hildegarde said. "You're a machine. I don't understand how you think. How you feel. Maybe you don't feel."

"Stop saying I am a machine. I am not a machine. I had no idea you held these kinds of prejudices."

"How can a fact be a prejudice?" she asked. "You *are* a machine, essentially."

"I'm as much of a machine as you are," he said. "We were made in your image, after all."

Hildegarde made a noise. "I wouldn't have resigned if I had known you wouldn't come with me."

There. She had said it out loud. The truth. How ghastly was that?

"I never told you I would leave," he said. "I had and still have a responsibility to this place, to these gardens, to these plants and their seeds, to the people who live here."

She grabbed her pants and pulled them on. She took off the

robe and flung it at Quintana with one hand while picking up her shirt with the other hand.

"And I didn't have responsibility? The entire Queendom was my responsibility."

"Yes," he said. "It *was*."

Quintana got up and put on his clothes.

"I gather from your tone that I disappointed you by leaving? You didn't think it was great, wonderful, even mythic how much I loved you and how much I was willing to sacrifice for you?"

"No," Quintana said. "It did not feel good. You didn't do it for me. You did it for yourself. And now you're here again. Why?"

"I wanted to come back and show you what you've been missing," she said. "I came into my own, sexually speaking, at the monastery."

Quintana laughed. Hildegarde shrugged. "Well, maybe not there. Maybe in your bed. But that's beside the point. I actually was hoping it wasn't as great as I remembered, being with you. I wanted to see if you had become boring."

"That can't be the only reason you came back."

She walked over to him and kissed him on the mouth. He returned the kiss. When she pulled away, she said, "Things aren't going well in the Queendom. I've come back to help. I abdicated my responsibility once. I want to make amends."

"They don't want you here."

"I know," she said. "But I am here. They can't do anything about it."

"The Queen doesn't need you," he said. "She is good at her job, and she will weather this storm. She is well-respected here and abroad."

"Good for her," Hildegarde said.

Quintana moved away from her. "Bitterness is not very attractive," he said. "Reina did nothing wrong. She took over when you left even though being queen was not something she planned or wanted. She has done a yeoman's job."

"We don't need a yeoman," she said. "We need a queen. We need a leader."

Quintana was silent for a moment. Then he said, "We have a queen and a leader. They will fix this."

Hildegarde nodded. "Of course, of course. And I am only here to offer any assistance should she need it. I want to be a good sister. Reina always played things very close to the vest, so I'm guessing she has few people with whom she can confide. Perhaps I can become a confidante now."

"That is admirable," Quintana said, "but building a relationship takes time. You have been gone fifteen years."

She sighed. "I know how long I've been gone. And now I've been back for a while. I'm getting into the swing of things again. Reina has stopped leaving the room when I enter, so that's a start." She smiled. "Once we have this latest problem solved, I'll be on my way. It doesn't really feel like home any more."

"It doesn't?" he asked.

"No," she said. She looked around. "This does. I could live here forever, with you, I'm certain. I'd take up art again. I was pretty good when I was a girl."

"It's difficult to imagine you sitting still long enough to paint," he said.

"Don't you remember I used to bring my easel out to the garden and paint when I was a kid?" she asked. "I did it to get closer to you."

Quintana made a face. "Don't remind me that I knew you as a child. This is one of the many reasons soothsayers and humans should not have intimate relationships."

"I can't be your first," she said.

Quintana didn't say anything.

"At least tell me you didn't have a relationship with my sister," she said. "Or my mother. Or my grandmother."

"How is your grandmother?" he asked. "I was sorry when she decided to move away. I miss her presence."

"You didn't answer my question," she said.

"It wasn't a question," he said. "It was a plea. I have had relationships with all of those people. I watched them grow up. But no, I haven't had a sexual relationship with any of them. Despite all the progress we have made over the years, you humans still have strange notions of what sex is and isn't. You think if you have sex with someone they belong to you."

"I understand you don't belong to anyone," she said, "but apparently you belong to this place. And I can't compete with a place. This conversation is exhausting me. I need to go prepare for dinner tonight. Are you coming?"

Quintana laughed. "When have I ever come to any kind of political dinner?"

"The Villanueva women are all dressing up as queens."

"You are not." He sounded horrified.

Hildegarde laughed. "Ha! Wouldn't that be something? Now that would cause shockwaves through the Queendom. No, Reina will be dressed as a queen, a la Elizabeth I. I think that's who. I was never good at history before the Reconciliation. I shall be dressed as one of her Ladies in Waiting, no doubt. I didn't pay much attention when she was talking about it."

"Marguerite Teng has invited me to sup with them, after the Summit attendees have been served," he said. "I might stop by. She's promised a taste of everything she's serving."

"You would prefer her company to my own?" Hildegarde asked.

"I prefer *their* company to the company of the summiteers," he said. "All politics all the time. I prefer talk of seeds. Or food made from seeds. All the deal-making and plotting is not for me."

"No one plots," Hildegarde said.

Quintana laughed. "Everyone plots," he said. "You remember I have been here from the start."

"I never attended one of these as queen," she said. "So I am vaguely interested. Would you like to meet later and finish what we started here?"

"I don't know," he said. "Are you going to scream at me again?"

"Maybe," Hildegarde said. "I'm still very angry and hurt." She put her arms up on his shoulders. "Or we could try again, now. How long does it take to put on a dress?"

Chapter Eleven
Raphael

On the morning of the Annual Consolidated Five Summit in Queendom, Raphael had a headache, his back hurt, and he was certain he would never get the stink of the fields out of his nostrils. The omnibus he'd taken from the saffron fields to the Queen's Village had been too slow and his fellow field workers had been too jovial. Raphael had wanted to join in and have a good time, but he could not make himself, not this time. They were all so excited about the Summit celebration: a few days off to dance, drink too much, and have sex with as many of their co-workers as they could. Ordinarily that would have sounded like nirvana to Raphael, but lately he could not seem to shake this sense of shadow or ennui that had sunk into his bones.

Or maybe it was tamped down anger. He felt useless. He felt ignored. Granted, he had not been the most dedicated student when he was a child, he had loathed his time in the Service, and he had shown little interest in the running of the Queendom until recently. To him, his father's lifestyle seemed more enjoyable than his mother's. She worked too hard and too much. His father enjoyed the pleasures of the world. Raphael would have bet anyone that his father had never had an unhappy day in his life.

Yet his father also didn't have much of a purpose beyond the day's pleasure—at least as far as Raphael could tell. This was fine, this was even, perhaps, laudable; Raphael wanted something else. He wanted to be recognized for more than what clothes he wore when he went out dancing.

Raphael had thought he could help out by going to the saffron fields as his mother had suggested. He thought he would learn about how the business of the country was conducted. He believed he would get to know ordinary people and become one of them. He fantasized that he would even discover how the Queendom was losing millions of credits, and he would become the hero of the nation.

None of that had happened. He learned how to work in the fields. It was back-breaking work that went on from sunup to sundown. Actually, before sunup! And he could not understand how anyone got a decent night's sleep on those thin mattresses with sheets that felt like burlap.

He was glad field workers got paid well above the GMI, but even that was not worth it to him. Every part of his body hurt. One night he wept into his pillow from the pain. Someone must have heard because the next day, the healer brought him cream and told him to rub it on his arms and legs. It had helped.

Hardly anyone spoke to him on the farms. Figuring they might have been intimidated by him because he was a member of the First Family, he tried to engage each of them in conversation, but they wanted to talk about yields and soil and what they were going to eat for dinner. He could not imagine more tedious subjects to discuss.

None of them were good storytellers either. To be fair, he usually fell asleep when they started telling tales. They had urged him to share a yarn once or twice, but he had begged off. He didn't want them to know he was absolutely useless as a bard: He couldn't even tell a joke.

His mother had warned him not to quit, and he had stuck it out for an entire month. A month of being tired and uncomfortable. A month of feeling completely out of his element. If this was how the common ordinary person lived, he was grateful he was not one.

So this morning, as the fieldworkers all spilled out of the omnibus and went their separate ways in the Queen's Village, Raphael was ecstatic to be away from them. He hurried home, up the main trail to the Hearth, and he tried to devise a convincing excuse of why he could not, would not, return to the fields.

That was when he came upon Marguerite Teng and her daughter, Genevieve, walking to the Hearth. Swallows followed them, diving down as Genevieve walked through the taller grass and kicked up insects. When the swallows swept down closer to the ground, Viva held up her hands to be closer to them.

Raphael thought about turning around and finding another path. After spending more than an hour on an omnibus with very enthusiastic people, he wasn't certain he could bear speaking with anyone human right now. Marguerite Teng looked over her shoulder and saw him.

"Good morning, Mr. Raphael," Teng said. She slowed so that he could catch up. Genevieve waved and ran ahead of them on the path, this time following two yellow butterflies.

"Good morning, Madam Teng," Raphael said. "I'm surprised you are out and about on such a day as this."

"You mean because I am supposed to be preparing twenty-six dishes for tonight's dinner celebration?"

"'Supposed to be?'"

Teng laughed. "Have no worries. Everything is on schedule."

They continued walking up the hill. The fields on either side of them were awash in color as the wildflowers—blue bells, daisies, and black-eyed susies—swayed in the morning breeze. Raphael breathed deeply. It was good to be home.

"You must have very good nerves," he said.

"I am steady in most storms," Teng said. "I've had a few to weather. I was hoping the biblioteca was open. I wanted to find out as much as I could about Mary Letty Holmes. I should have guessed it would be closed today."

"Queendomers love having any opportunity to close up shop," he said. "But why are you interested in Mary Letty Holmes?"

"I want to find the Moonstruck Saffron," she said. "If it exists, I intend to find it. It would be a great boon for the Queendom."

"Why do you say that? What have you heard?"

"Heard?" she said. "I haven't heard anything except that there is a reward for the person who finds it. I would like that reward."

"Oh," he said. He laughed. "And what would you do with this newfound wealth?"

"I have plans," she said.

"Ah, a woman with secrets," he said.

She squinted as she gazed at him, briefly, and then she looked up the hill again. "Well also, wouldn't it be something to discover a plant that has such extraordinary abilities? All plants have abilities. For one thing, they eat sun. How grand is that? And the Safran Bleu is a healing plant, but if the stories are correct, the Moonstruck Saffron has the medical properties of Safran Bleu multiplied by a thousand."

"Yes, indeed," Raphael said. He looked over at Teng as they walked side by side. Could someone like her actually find the Moonstruck Saffron?

"Are you good at finding things?" Raphael asked. "Have you done so before?"

"I have," she said. "I'm good at discovering plants that don't want to be found. Or maybe I should say I'm good at finding plants that are hidden away. I once found a type of violet no one had seen in decades, a wood violet with dots on it like a face, but I uncovered it in an old growth forest one spring, clear as day. Sometimes you have to be very still to find plants. Once you see one, usually the other ones will appear around it. Once you've respected them— you've honored them—by being still and quiet, they're willing to show themselves to you."

"Then I doubt I will ever find a lost plant," he said, "as I am rarely quiet or still."

"I had to learn it," Teng said. "It does not come naturally to me. Now your sister, Miss Lorelei, I imagine she would be great at finding lost plants. Maybe lost anything. She can be very still and blend in. Viva is the same way."

"Yes, Lorelei blends in," he said. "She actually disappears. I do not have that talent of fitting in or blending in. I often stick out like a sore thumb."

"Are you feeling sorry for yourself, Mr. Raphael?"

He laughed. "Indeed I am! If you want to find out more about Mary Letty Holmes, the library at the Hearth is the best place to begin and end. We have most of her works, most of her letters. They've been gone over before—others have looked for the Moonstruck Saffron. But maybe you will discover something new. I'd be happy to help you, or at least to be your sponsor, as it were. If we found it, you would get the reward, of course, but I would love to be of service to the Queendom. Perhaps this is one way."

If Raphael told his mother he was searching for the Moonstruck Saffron, maybe he would not have to go back to the fields. Instead he would find the next great healing plant that would solve all of the Queendom's economic woes.

"I would like that," Teng said. "First, can you tell me how I can use the Hearth's library?"

"Just go upstairs and use it," he said. "You don't need permission. Anyone in the Queendom has access to it. If they don't live in the house, they need to make an appointment, but you live in the house. You're free to go there anytime."

"Wonderful!" Teng said. "Thank you, sir."

"Call me Raphael," he said. "Or Rafe."

"I couldn't, Mr. Raphael," she said. "Mr. Umberto is very strict about protocol."

"I am not in elected office," he said. "I am only an unworthy son. I have few friends. Maybe you and I can become friends as we embark on this new adventure." He stopped and held out his right hand. She hesitated, and then she shook it.

"It is done," she said. "When we are alone, I shall call you Raphael. And you can call me Marguerite or Teng. Or even Maggie."

"Too many choices!" he said. "What is your preference?"

"You can call me Maggie. I have a son almost your age. He always called me Mother Maggie. It would be good to be called Maggie again."

"Where is your son?" Raphael asked.

"He is in the Hinterlands," she said. "He is an explorer, of sorts. Maybe one day soon, you will meet him."

Raphael began to relax as he walked up the hill with the cook and her child. Genevieve—Viva, Teng called her—ran back to them now and again to point out some wonder she had discovered yards ahead off the path: frogs in a marshy place; dragonflies skimming a small pond, a patch of greens in the shade of a copse of trees further up.

Raphael enjoyed the way Teng talked to him. She did not treat him with feigned respect because he was part of the First Family nor did she speak to him disrespectfully because he was so much younger and less experienced than she was. When any member of his own family talked to him—with the possible exception of Lorelei—he always heard disapproval in whatever they said to him. So far, no matter what Teng said, he could detect no judgement in her words.

"You've been away," Teng said.

"Yes. The Queen wants me to learn the business of the Queendom. I want to learn, too. So I went to work in the fields for a time."

"You didn't enjoy it," she said.

He laughed. "How could you tell?"

"Look at your hands," she said.

He held them up, turning them so he was looking at his palms.

"They're soft," she said. "Someone with soft hands would not enjoy field work, at least not in the beginning."

"I don't see how anyone could enjoy it, ever."

Teng held up her hands, palms toward her. She had calluses on the middle parts of her fingers.

"And you enjoy it?" he asked.

"I did," she said. "When I am working in the earth, with the plants, I think of nothing else. I don't worry about the past, future, or present. There is only the work."

"You don't strike me as a worrier."

"I have two children," she said. "That predisposes one to worry."

"My mother doesn't worry about us," Raphael said.

"Why would you think that?"

"Maybe about Lorelei because—well, because she is a strange little one. Minerva and I are adults, of a sort."

"I worry about my son more than I worry about Viva," she said. "And Viva is definitely a strange little one. Aren't you, love?" She called out the last little bit. Viva turned around and waved and then hastened ahead into the forest.

"Why your son? Does he get into trouble?"

"He has," she said. "He . . . well, he has. He's like his father, who disappeared into the Hinterlands ten years ago, never to be heard from again—at least not by us. Now Cristopher—that's my son—he's gone there, too."

"He'll be back, though, won't he?" Raphael asked. "You hear from him."

Teng hesitated, and then she said, "Sons never contact their mothers as much as they should." She smiled. "So will you go back to the fields?"

Raphael knew she was trying to change the subject, so he followed suit. "I believe my mother wants me to go back. I would rather not, but I don't want to disappoint her."

"Perhaps your father could help pave the way for you," she said. "He must have some influence on your mother."

Raphael shook his head. "I am not certain anyone has any influence with my mother, aside from Nehemiah. Perhaps you're right, though. I could talk to my father about this. He thinks I should be an artist, or a philosopher. I can't imagine anything more tedious than being a philosopher—besides working in the fields." He shuddered. Teng laughed.

"I suppose I could be an artist," he said, "if I had talent, but I don't believe I do. My father thinks me working for the Queendom is a waste of time because I won't ever be the head of the nation."

"That's a strange notion," she said. "We all work for the good of the Queendom, and only one of us is ever queen. Most of us work at something where we aren't necessarily the head, the one in charge, or the best. But we still do that work."

"You are the head," Raphael said. "You are chef. That literally means 'head.'"

"Yes, in my case," she said, "but we were speaking about you. Or people in general."

"I believe what my father means is that I would have to work under my sister when she becomes queen," he said. "He has his doubts that we would work well together, and he's right. Family dynamics and all that. My father rarely talks to me, so I tend to listen when he does. Maybe I shouldn't."

"Tell me," Teng said. "Did you learn anything new about Safran Bleu while working the fields?"

Raphael shook his head. "No. I was supposed to uncover any theft or wrong-doing. As far as I could tell all was well."

"Why theft?"

"Queendom profits were off last quarter," he said. "We're trying to find out why. Wait. All of that was supposed to be secret." He made a face. "I probably shouldn't have said anything."

"It will go no further," Teng said.

When the three reached the Hearth, Raphael said, "Later you and I will make plans on how to look for the Moonstruck Saffron."

Teng nodded. "Yes. First off I will comb the papers of Mary Letty Holmes for any indication of where it might be. I know many others have done this, but I may see something they didn't. Who knows? I will let you know if I find anything."

"Thank you," Raphael said. "I look forward to your feast tonight."

Viva and Teng headed around the Hearth to the kitchen entrance. Raphael watched them until they were out of sight. Then he peered at the huge wooden doors at the entrance to the Hearth. Above these doors was a concrete arch. In that arch were the carved words: BEHOLD THY MOTHER. Next to this arch was a stone relief of the Sheela-Na-Gig, the short naked goddess with a wide face who grins as she opens both sides of her vulva with her long fingers, like someone opening the curtains right before the show begins. Raphael smiled. Seeing the sheela always made him chuckle and feel as though he had come home.

He decided to talk to his father. He walked down the forested path toward Talib's studio, pausing to touch a tree here and there. He had played in these woods since he was old enough to crawl.

He came out into a small clearing where his father's studio stood. The small square building had no character and little charm on the outside. Inside it was filled with artwork. As Raphael neared the house, he heard voices. Sounded like they were out back. He started to take the path around through his father's herb garden, but he changed his mind and instead stepped onto the porch and knocked on the door. No one answered. He opened the door and called, "Dad!"

No response.

He stepped into the house and walked across the main room. He could see his father and Minerva sitting on the porch, facing the bottom of the clearing and the woods.

He stopped.

And listened.

"You need to think long and hard about this, Minerva," Talib said.

"That is all I've been doing. I won't make a hasty decision. I am going to ask for a twelve month leave after we get married. Savi and I want to travel for a while. And Savi wants to get pregnant very soon."

"You can still be queen and have children," Talib said. "Most of them do."

"I know," Minerva said. "It's not that. I'm not suited for the political part of the job."

Raphael frowned.

Talib laughed. "You think your brother is?"

Raphael moved closer, quietly, hoping to hear better.

"No," Minerva said. "I'm not sure what Raphael is best suited for. But I can't think about any of that."

"But you must," Talib said. "Do you want to be like your aunt, throwing the Queendom into a tailspin because she was in rut for a machine?"

"Father!" Minerva said.

"I'm sorry," he said. "But why is she here?"

"I have no idea."

"Now is not the time to be having doubts about becoming queen."

What?

Raphael stepped back.

Minerva had doubts about becoming queen? That was not like her. She was the perfect child, the perfect worker, the dutiful daughter, always.

"Your mother is young," Talib said. "She could be queen for another thirty or forty years. So don't worry about it yet. Live your life. Have fun. And don't frighten anyone with the idea that Sonny might one day be chief. I doubt he could win an election, and if he did, may the Old Oaks help us all."

Raphael's face flushed.

He turned around and quickly left his father's residence. He felt like he'd been slapped across the face or punched in the stomach.

He rushed down the path toward the Hearth.

No one he cared about believed he was capable of doing anything.

How could that be?

He had to find some way to redeem himself in the eyes of his parents—and the entire queendom.

And he would.

Unless he failed, as he always did.

Suddenly someone crossed in front of him, a human blur, and

he had to reach out to keep from falling over. But the blur stopped and grabbed a hold of his elbows, so they could keep each other from falling. Once they both had their balance, they looked at each other.

"I should have known it was you," Raphael said. "The perennial troublemaker."

The young woman was about his age and size, with dark black hair. A small zigzag of red and white lightning decorated her cheek.

"It's been ten years," she said. "How could you still know me?"

"I could say the same thing to you," he said, "but you obviously know who I am since you know it's been ten years since last we saw one another."

They let go of one another but didn't move far away.

"You had a huge crush on me," Raphael said.

"Ha! Then tell me my name."

"Never to be forgotten, she who creates rivers," he said, "she who is the watcher at the well, the keeper of wisdom." He bowed. "Boann."

"I never had a crush on you," she said. "You had a crush on me. You asked me to marry you."

"How do you know that wasn't political expedience? Uniting our two tribes."

"You were thirteen!" she said.

"Then tell me my name," he said.

"Ah, you who in the time before were a grand angel," she said, "called upon for healing. Nowadays I don't know what your story is. Perhaps that of a great painter? I hear they call you Sonny: He who is a son."

Raphael shook his head. "I hate that name," he said. "And why do we use the words like angel or saint any more when the religions that used those words are extinct?"

"Angels are messengers," she said. "They don't have to be messengers from God. Are you a messenger, Raphael? And saints are just people who have dedicated themselves to something beyond themselves. The word can also refer to an important relic."

"So a saint is a person or a thing?" he asked. She nodded. "You're learning all of this studying law?"

"Yes," she said. "Words are important."

Raphael took one of her hands in his. "It is good to see you, my old friend. You look the same, only bigger, more beautiful, and just as smart. When did you get here? You wanna get something to eat at the Hearth or—" He shrugged.

"No, I want to go to your room so you can show me your boy parts," Boann said.

Raphael's eyes widened. "Really?"

Boann laughed and slugged his left shoulder. "No, not really. I've seen boy parts. They're no big thrill."

"Are you trying to tell me you prefer girl parts?"

"Oh how I wish I preferred girl parts," she said. "Men are so difficult. But really, I was trying to say: let's go eat." She shrugged. "The rest we can work out as we go. I'll race you back." She leapt passed him and ran down the path.

"We aren't thirteen any more!" he shouted. But she was almost out of sight. "OK then." Off he raced, like he hadn't since he was a boy. He spread his arms out as he ran and laughed.

CHAPTER TWELVE

TENG

Marguerite Teng's first Annual C5 Summit was going off without a hitch—at least if she didn't think about the man who was black-mailing her or her son who was being held hostage. She managed to do that for most of the day.

Before dinner was served in the Grand Dining Room, Teng left Wanda, Turnkey, and their helpers to finish up downstairs while she went up to the dining room to see how it all looked. As she stepped into the room, she gasped.

"I assume that means it meets with your approval," Mr. Umberto said. He was dressed in a long black tailcoat with a white tie and a dark gold vest.

"It is exquisite," she said.

The long table, covered in white linen, was already set. A deep red band around the edges of the gleaming plates framed cobalt blue crocuses that circled the white centers of the china. Each white napkin had been folded into a flat flower with the colorful blossom of a real flower at the center of each: some red, some blue, some yellow. Four silver candelabras with three tall white candles each took up the middle of the grand table, to be lit just before the guests came in.

Valances cascaded across the tops of the open French windows that took up most of the north wall. Right outside the dining room, wildflowers of all heights and colors filled the garden spaces and moved playfully in the spring breeze.

Quintana had told Teng that he created this garden for the diners in this room. Beyond the wildflowers several flowering fruit trees grew, their dark green leaves creating a kind of calm after the tumult of color. No mural or painting adorned the burnt orange walls of this room: The view and the table itself were decoration enough.

Despite the formality of this room, tonight's dinner was a buffet, as always, with five different buffet tables set up next to one another. The only dish that would be served at the table was the Elementals dessert: the twenty-sixth dish. That dish would come at the end of the night.

"Are you ready to begin bringing up the food?" Umberto asked Teng. "The Queen said they would start coming in at half-past, after the storyteller and the blessing. President Ixchel is actually giving the blessing this year. She is a powerful medicine woman. I have heard her speak before."

"Wouldn't it be better to say grace here, where the food is?" Teng asked.

"The acoustics are better in the Grand Ballroom," he said, "and the NexusView cameras can get a better sense of what's happening than the ones in here. It looks rather small in here from the perspective of the Nexus viewers. Shall we begin?"

Umberto and his staff brought up the food and arranged it on the buffet tables. When the tables were filled with food, Teng started to leave. Mr. Umberto stopped her.

He said, "You need to stay for a bit."

Teng patted down her hair and took off her apron. She looked around for a place to put the apron and couldn't find anywhere appropriate. Abbygail reached out and took it from her, and Teng was grateful.

The Queen and Talib were the first to come into the dining room. Talib was dressed in tails, just as Umberto was, only his were green. No one was paying any attention to Talib, however. The Queen was the star. She had painted her face and arms ocher. Blue stars bloomed here and there on her skin, like comets in the night sky. Her gown was white and gold, tight at her bodice, with her skirt flaring out at the waist. Ruby-colored ribbons snaked through the dress almost haphazardly, making it seem alive. A pleated ruby-colored ruff with gold lace adorned her neck. Wrapped around her golden hair—which was piled on her head—was a coiled dark blue snake, made out of cloth, whose head jutted out at the Queen's forehead. The snake's red tongue was out, and her eyes were black. On either side of the snake was a golden crescent moon: one facing to the Queen's right, the other to her left. The Queen wore no shoes, just a string of tiny bells around her ankles.

She came to stand by the food as the family and the rest of the guests filed into the room, found their place names, and stood by their chairs.

Except for Talib, the entire First Family was dressed in variations of the gold, white, blue, and ruby, including Savi and Poppie. Lorelei and Minerva were dressed in slacks, waistcoats, and vests. They had also painted their arms and faces. Everyone except the Queen wore shoes. Teng guessed the Queen was barefoot to show her connection with the Earth.

"Good evening," the Queen said, when all twenty-six were inside the dining room. "Welcome distinguished guests. All of Queendom welcomes you to this celebratory dinner. We are grateful for these blessings given to us by the gardens, the fields, and the forests. They have all been harvested or taken with love, devotion, care, and blessings. This year, our new chef Marguerite Teng has been at the helm of our kitchen. We have her and the staff to thank for this magnificent feast." She indicated the tables of food with a slow wave of her hand. Everyone clapped. Teng bowed her head for a moment.

"Teng is also a proponent of the Unified Field Theory of Spices," the Queen continued as the clapping died out, "so all of these dishes were prepared with your good health and happiness in mind. May it be so. Let us begin."

Mr. Umberto brought the Queen's plate to her and Talib's plate to him, and they began the buffet line. Soon, everyone else was lined up behind them.

Teng looked at Umberto. He nodded. He and the two helpers from the village would stay to serve while the downstairs staff ate their dinner. Teng left the dining room and headed for the kitchen.

"Wonderful looking food, Teng!" Billy said as he and Abbygail ran to catch up to her. "It's only my first Summit celebration, but I have never seen a spread like that before in my life. Colorful vegetable dishes, scrumptious looking meat dishes, side dishes galore! I could look at it all day."

"I agree," Abbygail said. "You did a great job."

Teng smiled. "Thank you, both. Let's hope it tastes as good as it looks."

The rest of the kitchen staff were waiting for them in the servants' dining room. Someone had set the table so that it was almost as fancy as the one upstairs. Teng grinned when she walked into the room. Viva ran up to her and grabbed her hand.

"Isn't this beautiful?" Viva asked.

"It is indeed," Teng said.

On the half-wall countertop between the hall and the dining room and on the sideboard below the countertop were several servings of most of the twenty-six dishes. The staff looked at Teng.

"Do you usually wait for Mr. Umberto before you eat?" Teng asked.

"We do," Abbygail said, "but he told us to go ahead."

Quintana walked into the room, followed by Hunter.

"I could smell the magic of this meal all the way in the garden," Quintana said.

"And I knew it was time to eat!" Hunter said.

"Shall we begin then?" Teng asked.

She picked up a plate from the table and began ladling a bit of each dish onto her plate. The mixture of aromas was odd but appetizing. Viva moved in front of her mother and began scooping food onto her plate, too.

"There's a lot to eat," Teng said to her daughter. "You might want to pace yourself."

"I know, I know," Viva said. "But I'm ready for magic, too."

When the staff had all filled up their plates and they were gathered around the table, Teng said, "Abbygail or Quintana, you have been here the longest. Have you any wisdom to impart to us before we begin?"

Quintana nodded to Abbygail. "Abbygail will no doubt have more to say than I do. All the wisdom I know comes from the plants which we are about to consume. May their wisdom become our wisdom." He looked across the table at Abbygail.

She smiled shyly. "I am grateful we are here together," she said, "on this glorious day. I am proud to work with all of you, and I thank Marguerite Teng for this meal."

"Very nice, Abbygail," Teng said. "I want you to know that I did use this spice and that herb and the other plants to create healing dishes for us all. My intent was that each dish contribute to the peace, to the enchantment, that will bring us all good days ahead, good days behind, and good days in-between. I thank all the beings that are a part of this meal. I thank all the beings who contributed to the creation of this meal. May it be grand. And may it be so."

"Now let's eat!" Billy said.

Hardly any words passed between the people around the table for some time, besides an occasional, "This is delicious."

Teng ate slowly and watched her fellow workers. As they ate, they started to relax, smile, nudge each other. It had been a long day. At one point, Quintana challenged the crew to guess which ingredients Teng had used for each dish. Quintana usually guessed correctly; most of the others did not.

"You have done this boar proud," Hunter said. "I have never tasted it so tender. You have made the boar's strength available to all of us. Thank you. And these carrots are cooked to perfection—and so sweet. Is that orange or lemon?"

"Neither," Teng said. "It's *when* I picked the carrots. At dawn, before any light, when all the power and glory is still in the root. That's when they should be pulled up out of the ground."

"Brilliant," Hunter said.

"I was skeptical of this rhubarb chutney," Wanda said, "but it is just the right thing for both meat dishes. It's got quite the bite."

Teng nodded.

"Everything my mom makes tastes good," Viva said.

The others laughed.

"I'm sure it does, darlin'," Wanda said.

"Except boar's tail," Viva said. "I didn't much like that."

"I doubt I would either," Wanda said.

"I don't like eating animals," Viva said.

"I understand that completely," Hunter said. "I don't always like eating vegetables. I'm never quite sure they've been harvested correctly. I wouldn't want to eat something some person just ripped out of the ground without thinking. But I've watched Teng. She knows what's she's doing. Speaking of such, I've been noticing some people in the woods I don't recognize. Strangers, if you will. Anyone else?"

"There are strangers everywhere," Quintana said. "It's that time of the year. The Summit, you know."

Hunter nodded. "I hope that is all it is. They acted strange. Didn't want to be seen by me, which is odd. Why wouldn't they want to be seen unless they were doing something wrong?"

"Maybe they were Hinterlanders," Billy said.

Teng almost choked on her food. She hoped they weren't talking about the Man Who Was Blackmailing Her.

"I've heard rumors there are some hereabouts," Billy said.

"Isn't it all right if they're here?" Abbygail asked. "We welcome anyone."

"Not Hinterlanders," Wanda said. "They could be criminals. They could be the ones who are stealing our saffron."

Quintana looked at Wanda. "Someone is stealing our saffron?"

"Something is going on," Wanda said. "Our business is down in town, and I've heard others talking about it, too."

"I dreamed last night that the Hearth burned down," Turnkey said, "and all of Queendom collapsed."

Everyone looked at him.

"That's cheery," Wanda said. "You don't say a word all night, and that's what you come up with?"

Turnkey shrugged and looked down at his plate. "It seemed part of the gist of the conversation."

"Part of the *gist*?" Wanda mumbled.

"Do you have prophetic dreams?" Teng asked Turnkey.

Turnkey glanced at her and then down at his plate again. "I can't say."

Teng frowned. She looked at Wanda. Wanda shrugged.

"Turnkey often knows more than any of us," Abbygail said.

"Because of dreams?" Teng asked.

No one said anything for a few moments. Then Turnkey said, "Sometimes I dream what others fear," he said. "Sometimes I dream what others hope."

"I hope no one is hoping that the Hearth burns to the ground!" Teng said.

Mr. Umberto appeared on the threshold and clapped his hands together. "Time enough for a quick bite, eh?" He smiled. He seemed inordinately happy.

Teng got up. "I'll serve you," she said as she went to the side board and began piling food on a plate.

"Thank you, Marguerite Teng," Umberto said as he took his usual place at the table. "I will only say this before I eat: Our guests are enraptured with the food! You are a success, Marguerite Teng!"

"*We* are a success," she said, setting the plate in front of him.

"Hear, hear," he said.

Teng stayed in the servants' dining room for a bit longer. Then she excused herself. She and Viva walked to their room, hand in hand. As soon as Teng opened the door, Viva ran into the room and plopped down on her bed.

"What a day!" the little girl said.

Teng smiled. It was a homey room—large, with two beds, a dresser, table and four chairs, with a bathroom door (and a bathroom) next to a small closet. Teng had not hung any pictures on the walls yet, but the resident before her had left a large painting of a datura flower on the wall opposite their beds. Every night Teng fell asleep staring at the white blossom that seemed to give off light in the dark. Next to the datura flower were French doors that looked out at the Hearth's kitchen garden. Right now, nearby lavender and rosemary bushes were blooming, and their scents wafted through the screen doors and into the room.

"Are you ready for bed?" Teng asked. She sat on the edge of Viva's bed.

"No!" Viva said. "It's still light, and I haven't had dessert."

Teng laughed. She had hoped Viva would go to bed so she could wander the Hearth on her own for a bit before she had to serve the twenty-sixth dish. She needed to uncover some tidbit of information about the Queendom that would sound important to the Man Who Was Blackmailing Her—would sound important but was not. She had no idea how to do that.

She sighed. She could not betray this family. Could not betray the Queendom. She had to find the Moonstruck Saffron, collect the reward, be a hera, and then she could turn in the blackmailers and get her son back.

That would work.

She hoped.

"Momma!" Viva said sharply. "Where are you?" She reached her small hands up and pressed them on either side of her mother's face. "Is anyone home?"

Teng put her hands over her daughter's for a moment, and then she moved them off of her face.

"I'm sorry," Teng said. "I have been worried about your brother."

"Why?" Viva asked. "Because he never contacts us any more? Is he dead?"

"No!" Teng said. "He's in a place where it's difficult to keep in touch."

"Like Daddy?" Viva asked.

"I suppose," Teng said.

"I miss Cristopher," Viva said. "I miss Daddy. But I miss you most of all. I've been lonely since you've been away."

Teng hung her head. Out of the mouths of children.

She was not cut out to be a spy. She had to find another way.

"How about this, sweetheart," Teng said. "You can watch us serve dessert. Then let's go to the library. I can look for ideas on how to find the Moonstruck Saffron."

Viva clapped her hands. "Yes! Yes!"

"Comb your hair," Teng said. "Splash your face. You'll be with the Queen, so we want to look our best."

Viva jumped off the bed and headed for the bathroom. "This is the best day ever!" She giggled as she ran across the room. When she reached the bathroom door, she looked back at her mother.

"Come on, Momma," she said, her hand on the doorknob. "You want to look your best, too."

Teng got up. "I'm coming," she said. "Now, where did I put my crown?"

CHAPTER THIRTEEN
REINA

The day of the Annual C5 Summit had not gone according to plan, although it had started out well. Elata brought Reina breakfast, as usual. After she finished eating, Fan gave her a massage—with all the fringe benefits. She hadn't even been in the mood, but something about seeing him, something about feeling him in close proximity to her, changed all that. When it was time for lunch, he helped her dress.

"I wish you could come to this," she told him as he stood behind her, slipping the sheer cape up her arms and over her shoulders.

"I would be bored," he said.

She turned to look at him. "I didn't know soothsayers ever got bored."

He smiled, but the smile didn't go to his eyes. "We're just like humans," he said.

"Only different," she said.

"Do you always think of me as a soothsayer?" he asked.

"Do you always think of me as a woman?"

He grinned, and this time it was genuine. "I guess that's why you're queen and I'm not."

She reached between his legs and cupped his testicles through his loose fitting pants.

"That and these," she said, squeezing ever so slightly.

Fan put his arms around her and pulled her close. "You don't have to include me in any thing beyond what happens in this room between the two of us," he said. "I am pleased with the way things are. I have a job to do, and I happen to enjoy doing it."

Reina smiled and pushed him away. "You are the best of everything. Now where are my shoes?"

She was well-fed and well-rested when it was time to meet her guests. She discreetly took off her shoes and stood barefoot on the earth in the Coneflower Garden that was open to the sloping grounds of the Hearth. Later she would purposely be barefoot, as part of her role as queen, as a way of embracing her heritage and their connection to this Earth. Now she felt a bit childish standing in the dirt with no shoes, so she pulled herself up straighter and made her smile less bright.

Eventually, President Ixchel found her. The two leaders greeted each other with a kiss and a hug. Later, at the lunch, they would formally meet, but now, Reina slipped on her shoes again, put her arm across the shoulders of her shorter friend, and led her away from the others who were streaming into the garden.

"Shelly," Reina said when everyone else was out of earshot. "No one knows yet, but we're having financial problems. Someone is stealing our saffron and selling it, we believe. Or else one of the Five is growing it and selling it. Our sales are way down, and we are in trouble."

"I know," Ixchel said. "All of the Five know. Have you tried to find out what's happening?"

"Of course I have," Reina said. "It appears to have happened quite suddenly. Within two quarters. After Armistead's thieves bled us dry five years ago, we've been doing all right, but we do have some debt. We've almost paid off Berland. One more payment is due, but we can't seem to get ahead. I've got my economic counsel working on it, but whatever they come up with will take a while to implement."

"I've told you you needed a more stable economic base," Ixchel said. "You couldn't rely on one product forever."

"We've done well for two hundred years," Reina said. "I didn't see any reason to change." She felt butterflies in her stomach. "That is water under the bridge. For now, I want to know that you'll back me when I demand that the Consolidated Five crack down on the underground market. We need to enforce the treaty. We need more inspectors."

"The Queendom helped us out when we were in trouble," Ixchel said. "And I will always support you, within reason. It's perfectly acceptable for you to send around more inspectors, but not everyone is going to be on board with that. They might want to use your desire for inspectors as leverage to get Loveland into the Consolidated Five."

Reina looked down at her old friend. "You are joking, right? Lovelanders do not share our values. They have a huge incarceration rate. They do not do any kind of rehabilitation or reconciliation."

"They say we discard our people by throwing them into the Hinterlands," Ixchel said. "They believe that is more cruel than incarceration in their own lands."

"We send few of our citizens to the Hinterlands," Reina said. "We work on reconciliation for most people. But at least in the Hinterlands, they are free to be whoever they want to be. We do not want Lovelanders as part of the Consolidated Five."

Ixchel put up a hand. "Reina, you're preaching to the choir. But we might want to hear their spiel."

Reina nodded. "I can listen." Or she could feign listening. "Will Chief Flora agree to shutting down the underground markets, to allowing our inspectors in?"

Ixchel nodded. "Yes. The problem might be Outram. If you've got a payment due soon, or if he feels the economic stability of the Consolidated Five is threatened, he'll do anything to alleviate that threat."

"The Consolidated Five is not threatened," Reina said. "There are no hordes on our borders trying to get in or take us over. It's a rough patch. We all would do anything to protect the Consolidated Five, anything that fits with our value system. We're not going to throw away two hundred years of peace because one of us is experiencing problems."

"Are you prepared to show the Queendom numbers?" Ixchel asked.

"I'd like to wait until next quarter," Reina said, "to get a handle on this."

Reina didn't mention to Ixchel that Nehemiah had already sent out his spies to see if someone else in the Consolidated Five was growing Safran Bleu. As far as they could tell, no one was. And no Safran Bleu was missing from their fields or warehouses. Someone must be covertly growing it, stealing it, and/or selling it underground.

"There is a growing concern amongst the Five about your monopoly on growing saffron," Ixchel said. "It's a living entity. Why are you the only nation that can grow it? Isn't that like saying no one can grow an oak?"

"Who has these concerns?" Reina asked. "Others can grow saffron and do. But Safran Bleu is our invention. We should benefit from it."

"It's been two hundred years," Ixchel said. "Hasn't the Queendom benefited enough? You can't patent a living thing. Safran Bleu is a living thing."

Reina held up a hand. "Wait. You seem rather vociferous in your arguments. Are you sure this isn't what *you* believe?"

Ixchel sighed and shook her head. "I can see both sides of this argument."

"I will argue to my last breath that Safran Bleu is ours," Reina said. "It grows in our soil, tended to by our people, created by one of our own. Our soil and our people are what gives the plant its healing properties. If someone else wants to grow it, they can't call it Safran Bleu. Period. If it's grown out of our region, it is no longer Safran Bleu. It can't be marketed as such."

"Are you willing to consider letting other countries grow it but not call is Safran Bleu?" Ixchel asked.

"No," Reina said. "I might consider it if it was an issue that was dividing us. Otherwise, if another country grows it, it is theft."

"Compromise is a good thing," Ixchel said.

Reina said, "I know that. And I know we need to diversify."

"No people are better at art, storytelling, producing great food," Ixchel said. "Exploit that. No people are better at producing the best herbs and spices in the world, even beyond Safran Bleu. Exploit that. You are the visionaries. You have the best monasteries in the Consolidated Five."

Reina laughed. "Yes, that will get us out of debt: People coming to our monasteries."

"We are good at hype," Ixchel said. She shrugged. "Truly. I have some great PR people. I bet you could hire one. I'd send you recommendations. You've already taken one of our best chefs. Why not our best public relations people?"

"I haven't taken anyone," Reina said. "We hired her. Fair and square." She grinned. "I better go do the meet and greet. We'll talk later."

At the meeting after the lunch buffet, with the Consolidated Five leaders and their one closest advisor, Nehemiah told the leaders about the Queendom's drop in revenue. He said they suspected someone was selling Safran Bleu to the underground markets.

"We would like to send in inspectors to other countries," Nehemiah said. "To see if any Safran Bleu got mixed in with the regular saffron."

No one said anything at first. Outram sat across from Reina. He didn't look at her.

"So we are no longer friends?" Prime Minister Lerner of Armistead said. "You don't trust us to conduct our own inspections?"

"We do trust you," Nehemiah said. "We believe our own inspectors could come in, do their jobs, and be out quickly. It would cost nothing for you, and it wouldn't interfere with any of your work flow."

"How very considerate of you," Mauve said. Reina looked at

Lerner's assistant. When she spoke, everyone listened. "But we know you have already sent your own inspectors, and they found nothing."

Chief Flora said, "Do you have other theories about what is happening?"

"Demand has not changed," Reina said. "But our sales are down. People are getting it somewhere else."

"Perhaps now is the time to consider relinquishing your control over this plant," Chief Flora said. "It doesn't seem to be working any more. We can't go through this every few years."

"This?" Reina said. "You mean people stealing from us? I agree with you. It is against the law to sell products which have been stolen or to grow and sell Safran Bleu in any country but our own."

"It's a cherished plant," Mauve said. She shrugged. "You can't keep such a thing out of the hands of the people forever. Perhaps it is time the people of Queendom invented something new."

"I have been in touch with the other soothsayer mages and advisors," Nehemiah said. "None of them knows of any Safran Bleu smuggling operations."

"You say nothing has been stolen from your fields or warehouses?" Chief Flora asked.

"That is correct," Nehemiah said.

"What makes you believe demand has not gone down?" Chief Flora asked.

"We did a trendsetting survey," Nehemiah said. "We detected no difference from last year or the year before."

The others nodded. They had all done similar surveys.

"Perhaps your people are growing their own," Outram said, "and selling it. There is nothing illegal in that."

"They can grow whatever they want for their own use," Nehemiah said, "and they can sell a certain amount, but after that, they need to divide the profits with the government."

"But that doesn't mean they don't do it," Mr. Peetall said.

"That's true," Nehemiah said. "We will check on that, although it hardly seems like that would account for the discrepancies."

"Perhaps now is the time to talk about Loveland," Prime Minister Lerner said.

Ixchel raised an eyebrow as if to say to Reina, "I told you so."

"What does Loveland have to do with this discussion?" Reina asked.

"If you would allow the Foreign Minister of Loveland to attend our next virtual meeting," Lerner said, "we might be open to allowing your inspectors."

Outram said, "Why is it that you are so interested in Loveland joining the Consolidated Five, Damon?"

"I believe they have a great deal to offer our coalition," he said.

That was vague.

"Like weaponry?" Reina said. "They have an extremely high incarceration rate. They want access to our goods and our soothsayers. What do they have to offer us? Chief Flora, I would think this would concern Paquay State the most."

"It does concern me," Chief Flora said, "but if they were under some kind of legal framework, perhaps that would stop them from sending people in from the Hinterlands to wreak havoc on us. They might be the ones pilfering or selling your spice underground."

Reina nodded. "If you don't want to allow our inspectors in," she said, "then I won't press that. But we need to get to the bottom of this. What happens to one happens to us all. And any of your goods could be next. If this is a criminal enterprise, we need to suss it out. I would appreciate it if you could check your numbers. Find out who is buying and selling Safran Bleu in your countries. Is it different from last year?"

"Our exports are down in Armistead and Berland," Nehemiah said.

The table got very quiet.

"What is different about Armistead and Berland?" Mauve asked.

"What do you mean?" Nehemiah asked.

"What has Armistead and Berland done this last year or so that is different from the rest of the Consolidated Five?" Mauve asked.

Outram said, "In Berland we have cracked down on illegal sales to the Hinterlands."

"As have we," Mauve said, "as the Queendom requested."

Everyone looked at Reina. She glanced at Nehemiah. That had not occurred to her: They had no way of measuring how much was eventually sold to the Hinterlands or to the underground. When the countries actually did what Reina had been requesting they do for years, the Queendom lost money.

Reina felt her face flush. She should have figured this out herself. Nehemiah should have thought of it, at the very least.

"The decrease in exports to these two countries does not account for all the losses," Nehemiah said. "But we will redo the numbers and get back with you."

"And Loveland?" Lerner said. "Shall we vote on it? Everyone who is in favor of inviting the Foreign Minister to an upcoming C5 meeting, raise your hand."

Lerner raised his hand, soon followed by Chief Flora, and then President Ixchel.

They didn't need any more hands; they had a majority.

"Shall we make it unanimous?" Prime Minister Lerner asked.

"I will abstain," Reina said.

Outram nodded.

That ended the meeting. Reina stayed in the room until her guests had filed out to rest or recreate before dinner. Then she walked with Nehemiah to her office. She closed the door once they were inside and then pulled down the blinds.

She took a breath, and then she said, "I have never felt more humiliated and incompetent in my life. I am so angry, Nehemiah. How could this happen? How could we not see this? How could *you* not see this! This is supposed to be your forte."

Her hands were shaking as she spoke.

"I can only apologize, Ma'am," he said.

Reina tilted her head slightly. "Is something going on that I don't know about?" she asked. "I thought you soothsayers were on top of all of this. The numbers. The pluses. The minuses. I thought you had spies everywhere."

"I've told you everything I know," Nehemiah said.

Reina rubbed her face. "I feel like a fool. I feel like a child." She pressed her lips together. Maybe she had not studied enough economics. Hildy was always better at it than she was. Her mother was better at it than she was. She briefly closed her eyes. No, she was not going down this road. She was the leader of the Queendom. It was her job to fix this.

"All right," Reina said. "After the Summit is finished, let's get together with our economic advisors and council members from all over the Queendom, before the May Day festivities. And send someone to Loveland. Find out if they are stealing our saffron and if they're actually as bad as I believe."

"Yes, Ma'am," Nehemiah said. "We will fix this. All will be well."

"If someone or some group is doing this on purpose—to bring down the Queendom—I will personally build a prison and put them in it."

Nehemiah looked startled. Reina rolled her eyes and put her hand on his arm.

"I'm not serious," she said. "Come on, old man, acquire a sense of humor."

Nehemiah arched an eyebrow. "Does this mean you've found yours?"

"Ouch," Reina said. "I'll see you at dinner."

She swung open the door and found Outram on the other side of it, his hand raised as if to knock.

"Hello," he said. "May I speak with you for a moment?"

"Certainly," she said.

Nehemiah nodded to her and then to Outram as he passed by him on his way out.

Reina stepped away from the door. Outram came in and shut the door quietly behind him.

"I'm not sure that's wise," Reina said. "The others might get the wrong idea and believe we were plotting against them."

"Then let's plot," Outram said. "That was an interesting meeting."

"Perhaps for you," Reina said. "I don't understand this rush to bring Loveland in. We know so little about them."

Outram shrugged. "Armistead has goods to trade and sell. Loveland has buyers. Pretty simple."

"We've maintained a thriving consolidated economy for 200 years. We shouldn't throw that all away for a few more sales."

"No one is proposing that."

"No?" she said. "Let's not dissect the meeting. It's exhausting. We will get the Queendom economy under control here, and all will be well. Berland does not have to worry about getting its last payment."

"I am not concerned about that," Outram said. "I wanted to see how *you* are doing."

"Why should you be concerned about me?" Reina said. She was suddenly uncomfortable with this conversation. He was physically too close to her. She preferred their long distance communication to this. The room seemed too small. She could smell him—and she wanted to breathe in the smell of him.

Outram was nearly physically irresistible to Reina. She was the one who broke off the engagement, it was true. She was the one who decided to marry someone she thought would be a kinder man. She had been wrong. Talib's silences, his passiveness, were unkind. He was a good father and a devoted champion of the Queendom arts, but that was it.

"Outram," Reina said. "Personal space."

He laughed and stepped away from her. "I thought the Berlanders were the ones with the reputation for being cold and aloof. Queendomers are always making love and art. The closer the better, no?"

"No," Reina said. It wasn't that she didn't want him close. It was that she wanted to touch him when he was close. She was not going to tell him that.

"I have a solution to the Queendom's problems," Outram said. He walked to the window and looked out at the Queen's Garden. Reina stood beside him for a moment and then opened the door and stepped outside. She breathed deeply. Yes, this was better. Outram's scent was now diluted by the scent of flowers.

"This is charming," Outram said as he came outside. "I've never been here before."

"This garden is only for the CEO," she said. "Quintana designed it at least a century ago. It's private, it's fecund, and it leads out into the forest, should I want to get away without anyone knowing."

"Why should you want to do that?" He was standing beside her now, too close again, their arms nearly touching.

"The path leads to the forest and then to a clearing," she said. "A temenos—a holy place. The grass is softer than any sheets, the ground is better than any bed. Sometimes I take off my shoes and walk barefoot all the way there and then lie on the ground and look up at the sky. It's glorious."

They began to walk down the path through the garden until they reached a wooden gate attached to a wooden fence. Beyond the gate, a path wound into an evergreen forest.

"Remember when we used to make love in the woods?" Outram asked.

"I do remember," Reina said. "I never thought you enjoyed it much."

"Truly? Did I not perform satisfactorily?"

Reina put her hand on the latch to the gate. She was tempted to take Outram to the clearing. Where they could make love until dinner. It had been a long time since they had been together.

"No, your performance was quite satisfactory," Reina said. "If memory doesn't fail me."

"What's going on with you, Reina?" Outram said. "I don't

remember you ever being nostalgic or regretful before. Are things worse in the Queendom than you've let on?"

"No," Reina said. "All is well."

"Don't spout Queendom mottos," Outram said. "Talk to me."

"I'm sure it's an age thing. You and I are not getting any younger. We're not soothsayers. We will be leaving this mortal realm one day."

"Later than sooner I hope," Outram said. "Shall we go out to this clearing, and see what it would be like to make love all day? You and Talib aren't living together. I'm not living with my wife. Perhaps it is time we begin anew. We can be together. We can join our countries. We have the manufacturing. You have the art and stories. It would be a great combination. And you and I could be together."

Reina dropped her hand from the gate and turned to look at Outram.

"What are you talking about?" she asked.

"You know what I'm talking about," he said. "I've never stopped loving you. I don't believe you ever stopped loving me. I've proven myself to be a good man, to be a good leader for my people, to be a good father, even a good husband. Your worries that I would be cruel or vindictive or whatever it was you feared have not come to fruition."

"Bay, our people have given us no indication that they want to merge countries," Reina said. "You can't believe we are in such dire straits. I will take care of my country."

He shook his head. "Yes, yes, I know. The Queendom always comes first."

"And doesn't Berland come first with you?" Reina asked.

"No," he said. "It does not. My children come first, or did when they were younger and needed me. And my wife, when we were truly together. Even now I want only the best for her. You would have come first with me. I would have given up Berland in an instant if you had asked."

Reina shook her head. "I wouldn't have asked," she said. "I would not ask any man or woman to give up their country. The land beneath our feet and the sky above our heads and all that is in-between make us who we are."

Outram took her right hand in his left hand. "I believe it is into whose arms we fall every night that makes the biggest difference. Nothing else is as important. I love you. I miss you."

"I don't know what to say," she said, gently squeezing his hand. She stared into his blue eyes. "You know I love you. That has never gone away. And I want you. I want to run away into the woods right now and forget everything that is happening. But I understand that is only a biological urge. I don't mean to minimize it or my feelings for you. I only mean that I'm not my sister. She threw away everything to be with Quintana, and it was for nothing. He didn't go away with her. He didn't love her the way she loved him. And I have a duty to my people and my country."

Outram let go of her hand. "Being with me and loving me does not hurt your country or your people."

"Unless I am making decisions based on my desire to be with you rather than what's best for my country. Can you honestly say merging our countries would be the best for our people, or is it primarily a way to get us together?"

Outram laughed. Something about it sounded forced, or maybe embarrassed.

He threw up his hands. "It was just an idea. A way to help the Queendom financially. If you do well, the Consolidated Five does well. That was all."

"Talib hasn't done anything to deserve me divorcing him," Reina said.

"Marriage and divorce is so outdated," Outram said. "We should have never brought it back."

"Maybe, yes," Reina said, "but I made a commitment to Talib. The people love him."

Outram shook his head as he turned away from her. "He does not treat you well. I've never understood what you see in him!"

"Outram," Reina said, "I'm not rejecting you."

"No, you did that long ago," he said.

Reina put her hand on his arm. "Bay," she whispered.

"Don't pity me," he said.

"Oh, good grief," Reina said. "I can't imagine ever pitying you!"

Outram turned to face her again. He grabbed her elbows. "Then let us be lovers," he said. "Like old times. Although I'd prefer not to meet once every ten years, or whatever it was. I've heard you have a soothsayer who looks like me to satisfy your lust." He grinned.

Reina laughed and pulled away from him. "You have spies even here?"

He shrugged. "I'm the real thing," he said. "Much better than a soothsayer."

"I don't know," Reina said. "He's pretty good."

Outram took her hand again and kissed it. Butterflies tickled her stomach. He kissed her arm. Kissed her ear. She shivered. It would be so easy to let go.

He whispered, "I'm better."

Reina smiled. "Yes, I think you would be." She turned toward him.

And then she heard someone clear her throat.

Elata was standing on the path a few feet from them.

Reina and Outram moved slightly away from one another.

"I'm sorry, Ma'am," Elata said, "but the dressmaker is here. It's time."

"I'll be right there," Reina said. Elata walked a few feet and then stayed put.

"Thank you for this interesting discussion, Premier Outram," Reina said. "I will see you at dinner." She bowed slightly.

Outram said, "I need you for another moment. And then I'll let you go."

Reina hesitated, and then she said to Elata, "Wait for me in my office. I'll be right there. And close the door."

After Elata had gone and shut the door, Reina turned to Outram.

She smiled. "Yes? What else do you have to say to entice me into your bed?"

He shrugged. "I can see that is futile right this moment. I wanted to talk to you about our child."

Reina stiffened slightly and moved back from him.

"No, no, hear me out," he said. "She might benefit from coming to Berland for a while and seeing how our country works."

"She isn't *our* child," Reina said.

"I am her father," Outram said.

Reina put up her left hand. "We can't be sure," Reina said. "Besides, I am mother to all of my children. Who provided the sperm is of no matter."

"Tell that to Talib," he said. "Tell that to every father in existence."

"Don't try to hold some barbaric outmoded beliefs over my head, Outram."

"Reina, please, just listen," he said. "I'm not trying to upset or change anything. I am only suggesting she could benefit from seeing more of the world and learning how different countries handle different situations. She may be queen one day. I have only her best interests at heart. And yours."

Reina sighed. "I'm sorry," she said. "She doesn't know, and it would break her heart. She's very close to her father."

"If it's not important who the sperm donor is, as you say," Outram said, "why don't you tell her?"

"It's still important in our culture," Reina said, "and why upset things now? It only matters, as far as the Queendom goes, who her mother is."

"Is it that you don't want your children knowing you had sex with another man while married to their father? It is common knowledge he has had dozens of lovers since you've been married. See. This is why we should not have brought back marriage: It is another way to fail at relationships."

"I'm not going to argue the merits or drawbacks of marriage with you," Reina said. "It's not my favorite institution either. I'm well aware of Talib's dalliances. I'm sure you had quite a few yourself."

"No," he said. "Only you."

She turned away from him. "I don't believe you," she said. "And it's not important. I wouldn't care. I've said before that monogamy is not a natural state of being. I've had lovers through the years. It's natural."

"Why do you keep saying the word natural?" Outram said. "Are you trying to prove that I am unnatural because I have continued to love you all these years, because my desire for you has never gone away? I believe it is perfectly natural to love someone with your whole heart for a lifetime. I'm sorry if that embarrasses you."

Reina looked at him again. His features were soft. She saw no trace of the anger that she was so wary of when she was younger. He looked like a man in love.

"It doesn't embarrass me," Reina said. "I don't know what to do with it. I'll think about a trip to Berland for—" She lowered her voice. "—for our daughter. But now I need to get dressed."

Then she turned away, rushed down the path, and went into her office. She nodded to Elata and together they went into the hall. When they were on the stairs, Elata said, "I hope I wasn't too late. You told me to separate you two if I found you together. You know the dressmaker isn't actually waiting for you, although she is in with Minerva."

"No, you weren't too late," Reina said. She almost wished she had never said anything to Elata. Now she wondered why she was resisting. What would it matter if she and Outram became lovers again?

It mattered because they had made commitments to other people and to their countries. Reina did not want to lose herself or her perspective to another person. What she was feeling for Outram was a biological need. She could fill that need in other ways.

"Get Fan for me," Reina said.

"Now?" Elata asked.

Reina looked at her. "Yes, now. Why? Is that a problem?"

"Certainly not," she said.

Reina went into her rooms and closed the door behind her. She was trembling. She walked to the window and looked down at the gardens. She loved the view from here: It was like looking at a living painting. She breathed deeply and watched Teng and Wanda close to the house, harvesting some kind of plant. They both peered briefly behind them and then went back to the plant. Reina followed their gazes. Ah, there was Hildegarde going into Quintana's house. So that was still going on. The idea of it made Reina slightly queasy. Quintana was so old and wise. And Hildegarde was neither of those things.

Hildegarde had given up everything because she loved that old man. And she had done it for nothing. Now she was back. Had she come for the Queendom or for Quintana?

Reina gritted her teeth. Hildegarde could have Quintana. She could not have the Queendom.

She turned away from the window. Perhaps she shouldn't judge her sister so harshly. If Quintana was as good a lover as Fan was, she could almost understand Hildy's decision.

Reina didn't know how old Fan was. He could be one of the original soothsayers or maybe he had been in hibernation, part of the second wave of soothsayers. She had never asked. It seemed too private. She wasn't sure why. Most people eventually asked each other where they were born or where they were from. She vaguely remembered him mentioning the Reconnection, which meant he was from the first batch. Or was first-line. Probably better to think of him as being first-line rather than coming from the first batch. Made him sound like a chicken or beer.

She rubbed her face. Actually, she didn't want to think of him any way. She wanted him now so she wouldn't want Outram. That was a mistake. She had things to do. She couldn't cower in here like a child. Or spend all day having sex like a teenager. She was the Queen. She needed to put on a good face. She needed to display confidence that they would turn things around.

Mostly, she needed to see her children. *Her* children. They had a celebration to attend. Nothing was going to get in the way of that: not some thieves stealing Safran Bleu. Or Outram. Or Hildegarde.

Reina pinched her cheeks and strode out of her rooms. She passed Elata in the corridor.

"I don't need Fan," Reina said to Elata without stopping. "Tell him he can go home for the night. All is well in the Queendom."

"Ain't that grand then," Elata said. "Ain't that grand."

Chapter Fourteen
Lorelei

Lorelei tried to forget about the man in the forest. She did not want to think about him or the Queendom being in trouble. She did not want to think about lost pages of the Constitution. That was an old rumor.

Mostly, she did not want to think about herself as queen. It was ludicrous. She wanted to find her mother and tell her all about the man in the forest. She tried. The Hearth was swarming with people, and every one of them wanted an audience with the Queen.

Lorelei wandered in and out of the house, listening in on conversations surreptitiously so she could bring information to her mother later. She couldn't seem to concentrate, though, and she heard nothing useful.

After lunch, she spotted Minerva out in the front gardens with Savi and one of the delegates from somewhere. Lorelei usually knew everyone who came to the Hearth, but not today. She watched her sister and Savi from inside the house for a few minutes. They looked beautiful together, one so light, one so dark, both of them comfortable mingling with friends or strangers.

Maybe one day, Lorelei would ask them how they managed to do that.

Savi and the delegate moved away from Minerva. She stood alone for a moment looking down at the camellia plant next to her. The fingers of her left hand gently touched one of the pink blossoms—and she looked forlorn.

Lorelei watched her sister. Could it be the man in the forest was right? Maybe her sister didn't want to be queen.

Lorelei dashed outside before anyone else could approach Minerva.

"Hello, dear," Minerva said, reaching for her sister's hand as she approached. Lorelei took Minerva's hand in hers, and the two of them began walking down a path that would lead into the old oak forest.

"Have you ever heard that the Constitution might be more than one page long?" Lorelei asked.

"Yes, I have heard that rumor," Minerva said. She sounded surprised. "Why on Earth do you ask?"

Lorelei shrugged. "Curious. Do you give the rumor any credence?"

"No. Why would the quote unquote real Constitution have remained hidden all these years? Who would benefit from the Queendom having lost part of its Constitution?"

"It depends upon what the rest of the document says."

Minerva stopped next to a huge old rosemary bush. "Are you suddenly interested in politics, sister?"

Lorelei shook her head. "History."

Minerva stared at her sister for a few long moments. Lorelei knew Minerva still saw her as a child—probably thought she was as ignorant as most children.

"Are you looking forward to being queen one day?" Lorelei asked.

Minerva let go of her sister's hand. She laughed: It was more like a snort than a full-fledged laugh. "What has come over you? Our mother will be queen for a long time yet, and that's all I care about. Now, it's almost time to get dressed for dinner. Meet you back at the house?"

And just like that, Minerva turned and headed back to the house.

As Lorelei watched her walk away, she knew Patra, the man in black in the forest, was right: Minerva was not going to be queen. What if he was right about the other things he said, too? The elections. The Constitution.

Lorelei looked up at the Old Oak. "Tell me, Ancestor, what does it all mean?" she whispered.

Lorelei headed into the woods again. As soon as she stepped into the light darkness of the old woods, she felt herself relaxing. This was what counted: the earth beneath her feet, the trees all around her, the sky and birds above her.

She walked a short ways before seeing two people on the path ahead of her. She sped up, quietly, so she could see who it was. Billy and Abbygail. Must be getting a breather before dinner. Lorelei was about to call out to them when Billy reached for Abbygail's hand. Abbygail looked at Billy and smiled. He leaned down and kissed her lightly on the lips. Then they continued down the path, hand in hand. Lorelei stopped walking and let them get further ahead of her.

Lorelei swallowed. She felt a bit sick to her stomach. She cocked her head to one side. A crow called out above her. She didn't look up. She hadn't liked seeing Abbygail and Billy kissing or holding hands. Why? She liked Billy. But they were not going to ride off into the sunset together.

She was never going to ride off into the sunset with anyone. That wasn't what her life was about. Yet lately, she had been feeling melancholy. She longed for human company. She wanted someone to look at her the way Savi looked at Minerva. Or the way Outram looked at her mother.

Although that was a completely different story.

She wanted to *feel* about someone the way the Queen Madre felt about Poppie and the way he felt about the Queen Madre.

She was not going to spend much time longing for something

that would most likely never happen. Instead, she would work toward protecting the Queendom.

Yes.

She nodded and silently wished Billy and Abbygail good luck. They were a sweet couple.

She walked back toward the Hearth, taking the path she had been on earlier in the day. She had only gone a few steps when Viva stepped out of the woods and onto the path. She was holding something black in her hands.

"I think death was in the forest today," Viva said. "He left behind some of his clothes."

She held out the clothes to Lorelei: a black jacket with a hood and a black mask.

"I saw you talking to him earlier," Viva said. "Has he come to take someone?"

"He's not death, Viva," Lorelei said. "What made you think that?"

"You looked afraid when you were talking to him. I've never seen you look afraid before. And he was wearing black."

Lorelei didn't know what to say.

"Do you want his clothes or should I put them back?"

"I'll take them," Lorelei said.

"I was talking to the trees just now," Viva said. "They said change is coming. Do you know what that means?"

Lorelei shook her head. "The birds have told me the same thing. Change is probably always coming. Don't let it worry you."

Viva stared at her. "You have a secret."

Lorelei smiled. "We all have secrets."

"You used to be a child," Viva said. "Now you're all grown up."

"You've only known me a short time. Have I changed that much?"

"The house is alive," Viva said.

"Of course it is," Lorelei said. "Everything is alive in the Queendom. Everything is alive everywhere. That's why it's important to be kind and courteous. We're in constant communication with the world whether we know it or not."

Viva nodded. "I wish there were more kids here," she said. "Sometimes it's lonely. Will you play with me later?"

"If I can," Lorelei said.

"Oh, my mom is calling," Viva said, and then she ran away.

Lorelei listened to the silence and heard nothing beyond bird songs and a breeze winding through the trees. She wished she could hear what Viva had heard.

She looked down at the clothes in her hand. What was she going to do with these? If she gave them to Nehemiah, he could analyze them for genetic material and probably track down Patra. The man would face reconciliation or even exile.

Maybe not. He hadn't done anything illegal. He hadn't harmed or threatened her.

She heard twigs breaking, and she looked up. She expected to see a deer or some kind of animal, but it was Turnkey coming out of the forest.

Turnkey nodded to her and bowed slightly.

"Hello, Turnkey," Lorelei said, making herself speak up since she knew he was too shy to do so. "You don't need to bow. I'm not the Queen. Even if I were, she works for you, for us, for the Queendom. So you don't need to bow." Now she was talking too much.

"Hello, Miss Lorelei," Turnkey said. "It's a beautiful day. I was taking a break before dinner."

Lorelei nodded. Those were the most words Turnkey had ever said to her at one time.

"Can I help you with anything?" he asked.

"Viva found these clothes in the woods," she said. "They're not yours, are they?"

She held up the jacket.

Turnkey shook his head. "No, that would never fit me."

"I actually know whose they are," she said. "I saw a man wearing them earlier. He told me all kinds of things about the Queendom. Said there was more to the Constitution than one page. Told me something was wrong with the elections, and he said he wanted me to be queen. He was a crazy man."

Turnkey nodded. "That all sounds strange. Except the queen part. You'd make a great queen."

"I'm eighteen years old!" she said.

"OK," he said. "Maybe not right this minute." He smiled.

Lorelei laughed.

"You could give these to Nehemiah," he said. "He could determine who was wearing it."

Lorelei looked down at it. "I know. The man didn't seem like a bad person."

"You don't want to get him in trouble?" Turnkey said.

"No."

"I could take the clothes," he said, "and burn them. Or wash them. Whichever you like. I know you have a lot to do today."

"So do you," she said.

"I would be glad to do this for you."

"All right," she said. She handed him the hooded jacket and black mask. "Burn them. I appreciate it."

"Do you want to walk back together?" he asked.

"Sure," she said.

They walked down the trail together without saying another word.

When they arrived at the Hearth, Turnkey bowed slightly again and headed around the building to the back entrance. Lorelei cut across the yard to the path that would eventually lead to her mother's flower garden behind her office. Lorelei knew no one else would be on the path, and she could escape the inquiries of any good-natured stranger she met. She was a few yards from the gate, hidden by the overhanging bushes, when she heard voices.

She stopped instead of going forward. She couldn't see anyone, but she heard Elata say, "I'm sorry, Ma'am, but the dressmaker is here. It's time." Her mother said something Lorelei couldn't quite make out. Then Outram said, "I need another moment of your time."

Lorelei couldn't hear anything for a moment. She almost stepped forward, and then Outram said, "I want to talk to you about our child."

Our child?

"Hear me out," he said. "She might benefit from coming to Berland for a while and seeing how our country works."

"She isn't *our* child," Reina said.

"I am her father," Outram said.

"I am the mother to all of my children. Who provided the sperm is of no matter."

Lorelei suddenly felt like she was going to throw up.

The breeze blew their words away. Lorelei took a step forward so she could hear better.

"I don't want to upset or change anything. I'm suggesting she could benefit from seeing more of the world and learning how different countries handle different situations. She may be queen one day. I only have her best interests at heart. And yours."

Queen. Ah, so they were talking about Minerva.

Minerva was Outram's daughter.

"She doesn't know," Reina said. "It would break her heart. She's very close to her father."

How would Talib feel if he knew his favorite child wasn't even his?

Lorelei felt a rush of glee at the thought, and she was horrified. She backed away and then turned and ran. She stopped when she was far away from Reina, Outram, and the Hearth. She sat on the ground and tried to get her breath.

Minerva was Outram's daughter. And he wanted to take her to Berland. What would this mean to her family? To the Queendom?

Lorelei sat in the forest for a long time. When she walked back to the Hearth, she felt like she was in a fog. Everything she had thought about her life with her family and about the Queendom seemed wrong.

As she got dressed alongside her mother and Minerva, she watched and listened while they talked about clothes and politics.

At some point, her mother asked her what was wrong. She shook her head. She was dumbstruck again, just as she had been when she was a child.

When her father and Raphael joined them, Lorelei watched Talib. He was cool and polite around Reina, as always, but he was warm and affectionate with Minerva. Raphael stood away from the family and left the group as soon as they all went downstairs together.

Lorelei watched Raphael make his way through the crowd to stand near Boann, Outram's daughter. Lorelei was tempted to tell him he shared only one parent with Minerva. Maybe if he knew this, he would be nicer to his one full sister.

Doubtful.

When it was time, the entire assembly went outside to stand under the Old Oak. President Ixchel gave the blessing. Then everyone sang, drummed, and danced under the tree, giving thanks for all they had and would have. Normally, Lorelei loved these celebrations. But she felt like she was only half there, and she couldn't seem to snap out it and make herself enjoy it.

She kept thinking about her mother lying to them all these years about Minerva being Outram's daughter.

At dinner, she barely tasted any of the twenty-five courses. She perked up a bit for twenty-sixth course. Five servers—one at each table—poured brandy over every dessert and then lit the brandy on fire as Teng talked about what she was calling the Elemental Dessert. It had five layers to represent each nation belonging to the Consolidated Five. At the center was a lemon candy with a piece of Safran Bleu at the center. The candy was surrounded by ice cream. Cake enveloped the ice cream. As the desserts all flamed for a moment together, the guests oohed and aahed.

Lorelei looked around the room at the faces glowing by the fire light. Her mother was laughing. Her father clapped. Minerva smiled and leaned against Savi. Even Raphael was grinning. Umberto stood at the back of the room, his hands behind his back. He looked at

Lorelei and winked. Lorelei smiled. Umberto could always make her feel better.

Almost all at once, the servers quickly dropped lids on the desserts and then just as quickly, they pulled the lids off. The fires were now out.

"Please, eat!" Teng said. "Enjoy. As with the rest of the dishes, this recipe employs the Unified Field Theory of Spices with the particular intention for your happiness and great communication for all."

The twenty-six guests clapped. Lorelei picked up her fork and dipped it into the dessert. She took a big first bite. As she chewed, she looked around the room. Outram was talking to the woman next to him. Then she looked at Minerva. Then back at Outram. She supposed there was some resemblance, but not much. Minerva looked more like Reina. All the children looked like Reina.

Lorelei took another bite. The dessert was delicious. They had had many delicious dishes tonight, but this one was the best. It melted in her mouth. The heart-shaped lemon candy with the Safran Bleu at the center slipped out of the ice cream to rest in a small pool of melting cream. Lorelei smiled. Lorelei had never been drunk before, but she felt pleasantly altered. Her mother was right: It didn't matter who was Minerva's father. It mattered who her mother was. Everyone had secrets. Her mother had told her that long ago. Even members of a very public family.

"How is everything, Miss Lorelei?"

Lorelei looked up. Umberto was standing over her.

"This is wonderful," she said. She held the plate up to him. "Please, you must finish it."

"I'll have some later," he said. "But thank you."

Lorelei stood. "No, please, Umberto, you must."

"Very well," he said. He didn't look pleased, but he took the plate from her, picked up an unused fork from the table, and then ate a piece of dessert. He nodded and tried to hand the plate back to her. "Yes, very good, Miss."

"No, you finish it," Lorelei said. She got up and began walking around the room. The musicians came in quietly, set up in the back, and began playing. Three fiddlers. As the other guests finished their desserts, many of them left their tables to wander. Some got together and began singing.

Lorelei smiled. This was the Queendom. This was what life was all about. All was well. No men in masks asking her to spy on her family. No man trying to lure her sister away from the Queendom.

All was well, all was well, it was well.

"Hello, Lorelei."

Lorelei turned and looked up. Outram stood next to her.

"Hello, Premier," she said.

"Are you having a good time?" he asked.

She nodded. Outram pulled up a chair and sat in it, so that now he was almost at her height.

"I should be asking you if you are enjoying yourself," Lorelei said. "You are the guest."

"It is a good party," he said. "And maybe we got some business done, or will yet." He was silent for a moment. Lorelei wondered why he was talking to her. What did he want from her? Did he think he could be nice to her and then she would take his side about Minerva going to Berland?

"I wanted to say," Outram said, "I mean, I wondered if your mother ever told you that my grandparents were your height. They are your height. They're still alive."

Lorelei frowned. "They're dwarves?"

He shrugged. "I know that word is a pejorative in your culture, but in ours, it's one of the names for our ancestors."

Lorelei cocked her head. "Your ancestors?"

"Many Berlanders believe we're descended from the fairies," he said. "And dwarves were part of the fairy race. The stories of fairies are just stories, but I do know many of our ancestors were smaller than people now. And my mother's parents were—are—dwarves. It's in our blood."

"Did the soothsayers try to fix them?" she asked.

He shook his head. "There was nothing to fix," he said, "so no."

"They tried to fix me," she said. She started to say, "Especially my father. He thought I was broken so he wanted to take me back and get me fixed. Only that doesn't work with people." But she didn't. She would never say anything bad about her family out loud. No.

"In Berland," he said, "you would not be anything remarkable."

Lorelei looked at him. "I'm not anything remarkable here either."

"I put that poorly," he said. "I only meant you wouldn't feel like an outsider because of your height."

"I know what you mean," she said.

"I was talking with your mother earlier," he said. "I was wondering if you wanted to come to Berland for a time. See how we live. Learn another economic system."

"Me? Don't you mean Minerva?"

"No," he said. "Why?"

Lorelei could suddenly hear her heart beating in her ears.

His grandparents were dwarves. It was in the blood.

He had been talking to Reina about *her*? But her mother had said Outram's daughter was close to Talib: That was Minerva, not Lorelei. How could her mother not see that?

Lorelei stared at Outram. He smiled. She suddenly saw herself in his smile, in the wrinkles around his blue eyes.

Outram was *her* father, not Minerva's.

She backed up. *Outram was her father.*

That explained so much.

It explained why her father—why Talib—could hardly stand to be near her. It wasn't that she was small. It was that she wasn't his.

She felt like she was going to throw up again.

"Lorelei?" Outram said. "Are you all right?"

She looked across the room at her mother. Reina looked at her and waved.

The crowd shifted or moved, and Lorelei hid behind everyone as she ran from the room, ran out and into the hall. She felt breathless. What was happening? What had just happened? She hurried down the corridor. Ahead of her, Hildegarde was striding to the stairs, heading out to see Quintana, no doubt. He had been missing from dinner, apparently uninvited this year because of Hildegarde. Why should Reina care about Quintana and Hildegarde being lovers? Wasn't that hypocritical when she had been lovers with Outram? When she had birthed a child fathered by Outram.

And she was that child.

Her ears were ringing. Her heart was racing. She ran past the library.

"Lorelei!" It was Viva calling to her from the library. Lorelei heard Teng say, "Leave her be."

Lorelei ran toward the stairs. Turnkey was suddenly there again as she put her foot on the first step.

"It's all taken care of, Miss Lorelei," he said.

"What?" She stopped and looked at him. She could barely see him.

"The clothes and mask," he said. "They've been incinerated."

Clothes. Mask. What was he talking about? Oh, yes. The man in the woods. Patra or Pater. She shook her head. None of that mattered.

"Thank you," she said. "Thank you, Turnkey."

"Can I help you?" he asked. "Tell me. I will do whatever you need."

She shook her head. "It's all wrong." She rubbed her face. "It's all different. I don't know who I am. I don't know what's going on."

"You are Miss Lorelei Villanueva," he said. "You are part of the great Villanueva family. You are part of the grand tradition that is the Queendom. And you are the kindest person I have ever met."

"They have lied to me my entire life," she whispered.

"Who?" he asked.

She heard the swish of robes. Or something that sounded like wings. She peered down the corridor. Nehemiah was headed her way. He was looking at her. He never looked at her. He never paid her any attention. He never paid attention to anyone but the Queen. He was going to ask her something she did not want to answer.

"Thank you, Turnkey," Lorelei said.

And then she ran up her stairs. She was faster than Nehemiah. She got into her rooms and locked the door. She didn't want to speak to Nehemiah or to any of them. She didn't want to answer their questions, whatever they were.

She went into her closet and closed the door. She sat in the darkness on the floor and pulled her legs up to her chest and hugged them. The walls began to lighten. Soon the whole closet glowed. She could see her writing all over the walls. Saw the pictures she had drawn over the years. Words she had pressed into the walls. She rested her head against the wall behind her. It yielded slightly, like her mattress did when she lay on it. She wept for a time. Then she wiped her eyes and picked up the pencil on the floor of the closet, the one that was always there, and she wrote in big bold letters, "Outram is my father." The words floated above the wall for a moment, and then they sank into it, became a part of the story of her life. Then she wrote, "They are all liars, and I trust no one."

PART THREE
MAY DAY

CHAPTER FIFTEEN
UMBERTO

Umberto stood on the step of the back door, looking out across the kitchen gardens that were golden with early light. Sun glimmered in the dewdrops on the grass, making it appear as though thousands of stars had fallen to earth during the night.

Musicians were already setting up on the Hearth grounds, down in the village, and along the path to the Hearth where the Queen, in her capacity as Sovereignty, and Talib, dressed as the Green Man, would lead a procession up the hill.

The Hearth staff had the day off, essentially, but Umberto and some of the others had last minute chores to finish before they left.

This year was a bit different than other years. The Queendom had waged an intense public relations campaign to get tourists from the other Consolidated Five countries to join the festivities. Every Queendom artist, musician, actor, storyteller, magician, and chef in the entire realm was working this week. The Queen had asked all citizens to welcome visitors, to put their best feet forward, and show the world what the Queendom had to offer.

Umberto was certain the Queen and her advisors and councilors would fix whatever was wrong with the Queendom economy.

"Nothing can be wrong for long in the Queendom," Umberto

mumbled. It was one of those colloquial sayings about the Queendom that Umberto never much cared for, but, lately, he had found himself muttering it under his breath now and again.

Something was wrong. Or off. Umberto could not quite put his finger on what it was. They had weathered economic travails before. Those came and went.

For one thing, Hildegarde was still there. Umberto wished she would leave. He wouldn't tell anyone that. She was part of the First Family. This was her home, but she had chosen to relinquish her responsibilities long ago. She had put herself and her desires above the Queendom. She had no right to come back and believe she had a place at the Hearth.

As far as Umberto was concerned, Reina was queen, she would always be queen, she was destined to be queen.

Besides all of that, Hildegarde and Quintana were indiscreet. Umberto had known Quintana his entire life, and he was appalled by his behavior. When Quintana and Hildegarde were in his cottage together, others could *hear* them.

Umberto turned away from the gardens and went back into the Hearth. He did not want to think about Hildegarde and Quintana or the recent conversation he had had with the Queen about them. It was one thing that their noisy lovemaking was embarrassing to the staff—as well as disconcerting to be in the garden with Viva or Lorelei while their cries emanated from the cottage—but when delegates from Armistead were visiting and asked him what "that noise was," Umberto felt he had no choice: He had to speak to the Queen about it.

The Queen listened to his report. She did not react, except to say she knew it was difficult for him to come forward, and she would take care of it. Her decorous response was one of the reasons he held her in such high esteem. Since his talk with the Queen, he had not heard a sound come from the cottage.

"Good morning, Marguerite Teng," Umberto said when he reached the kitchen. "How goes everything on this fine morning?"

The staff usually ate breakfast together after the sun singing, but today, it was a cold breakfast for those who were about. Everyone else was gone already.

"I can scramble you an egg if you like, Mr. Umberto," Teng said. "I know you're not fond of a cold breakfast."

"How considerate of you," Umberto said, "but I made myself a little something this morning in my apartment." Umberto had a small kitchen in his room. He didn't use it much, but this morning he had made himself hot porridge with dried fruit and nuts. He had eaten with his windows wide open, listening to the birds awaken and begin to sing.

"All right then," Teng said. "Mr. Raphael and I will be up in the library for a while. Send Viva up if you see her, will you?"

"I will," Umberto said. They walked down the corridor together and then started up the stairs.

"This holiday of yours," Teng said, "sounds wonderful on paper— we have something similar—but it's essentially a day of coupling, isn't it? What about those of us who aren't part of a couple?"

"There are celebrations everywhere," Umberto said, "and I'm sure you could find a willing partner. That is to say—"

"I know what you mean. But I am not looking for a partner. I was wondering what one does on a day like today if one doesn't want to partner."

"It's not a requirement," Umberto said, "if that's what you're thinking. Many of us enjoy the ceremonies, the art, the musicians, the great food."

They stepped onto the second floor and walked to the entrance to the library.

"Why, Mr. Umberto," Teng said as they stopped by the library, "I thought for certain you would go wild on a day like today."

"Yes, that is my nature," he said. "I am a wild man."

Teng laughed. "Ah, thank you for that, Mr. Umberto. I will imagine you as a wild man all day."

"I am glad to be of service," he said.

"If you see me standing alone at one of the dances," Teng said, "you know what to do, right?"

Umberto looked at her. "I'm not sure."

"What would a wild man do?" Teng asked.

"Um, I haven't a clue."

"Actually, I haven't a clue as to what a wild man would do either. But you could ask me to dance."

"Oh, well, certainly. But I don't know why you would want to dance with an old man like me."

"Hah!" Teng said. "You can't get out of it with an excuse like that."

"I assure you," Umberto said, "that I am not trying to 'get out of' anything."

"Good," Teng said. "Then I'll see you later."

Umberto nodded—feeling somewhat confused—and headed for the stairs while Teng went into the library.

Umberto liked Teng and was glad she had joined the staff. The food had never been better. She had a good sense of humor and didn't let him take himself too seriously. She was a blunt person, but she was not rude. Just truthful. And little Viva was a joy to be around. If he had ever had children, he supposed that Viva would be about the age of his grandchild. He was too old to think of Viva as a daughter. Too old to think of Teng as anything more than a colleague.

Not that he was that old. Just older than Teng.

He shook his head as he walked up the stairs. It must be the day that was making his mind wander in such strange ways. In any case, whatever was wrong at the Hearth or in the Queendom was not the fault of Marguerite Teng. She was doing a good job. She was spending quite a lot of time in the library, often with Mr. Raphael, looking for evidence of the Moonstruck Saffron. They were an odd pair—Teng and Raphael—but they had the blessing of the Queen to look for the spice. Everyone in the Queendom had the Queen's endorsement to search for the Moonstruck Saffron.

Umberto doubted that Moonstruck Saffron existed. If it did, someone would have discovered it by now. But let people dream. What did it hurt? Umberto believed in live and let live but don't upset the rhythm of life at the Hearth. Sometimes he had to be tough to keep things running smoothly. That was his job. From time to time he had to shake things up.

Like now. He thought he knew why things seemed so strained at the Hearth these days. It wasn't only that Hildegarde was now in residence. Something was wrong with Lorelei. She rarely came down to the kitchen. When he saw her at meals, she barely looked at him. She had always had a knack for being almost invisible, but lately, it seemed she actually was invisible.

When he reached the third floor, he saw Elata coming out of the Queen's chambers.

"There you are, Mr. Umberto," Elata said. "The Queen would like a word with you."

Umberto nodded, stopped at the Queen's door, and knocked.

"Come," the Queen said.

Umberto opened the door and stepped into the room. The Queen was standing by the window, looking out, her arms crossed. In the distance, the saffron fields were a sea of purple. Umberto never tired of seeing them.

The Queen turned to her steward.

"Ah, Mr. Umberto," she said. "Is everything ready?"

"Good morning, Your Majesty," he said. "Yes. Everything is set. At the end of the procession, the Hearth will be empty except for you and Mr. Talib."

She nodded. "Sometimes I wish I could skip the entire thing," she said, "and have a quiet walk through the woods, celebrating nature on my own." She smiled at him.

"Not feeling up to it today, Ma'am?"

She laughed. "That's one way to put it. I had a disturbing dream last night. Was your sleep unencumbered, Mr. Umberto?"

"Indeed," he said. "I slept like the dead. Would you like me to call in a mage?"

She shook her head. "No. I don't wish to talk to anyone about it. I hope it's not predictive. I dreamed of fire. The Hearth with everyone in it—the whole Queendom—burned to the ground. It was hideous."

"That does sound troubling," Umberto said. "We've all been worried about the weather and the potential for fire. That's probably where it came from. We could certainly use some rain."

"Yes," she said. "Mr. Umberto, is everything all right with the staff?"

"It is, Ma'am," he said. "Everyone is well and happy, I believe. Well, Billy Santos has mentioned a few times that he believes their workload is unfair."

She frowned. "He believes the staff is overworked?"

"No," he said. "The soothsayers. He and Abbygail. Maybe he feels the same about Elata, Nehemiah, and Quintana. I don't know."

"Those three work whatever hours they want," the Queen said. "And your staff?"

"The rest of the staff works between six and eight hours," he said. "Billy and Abbygail work eight to twelve hours, depending."

"I have to side with Billy here," the Queen said. "That seems unfair."

"But they have so much more stamina than we do," he said. "They can work longer hours without getting tired. It's standard throughout the Queendom."

She nodded. "I know. But I have been thinking about it for some time. I hadn't mentioned it before, I suppose, because it hadn't come up. The soothsayers don't get paid any more than the humans, but they work longer hours. Either they should get paid more or they should work the same hours."

"If they get paid more, it will appear that they are getting special privileges."

"Yes," she said. "The better solution is to have a job with particular hours and no matter who is hired—human or soothsayer—they work x number of hours and get x amount of pay. Put them on the same schedule or hours as the rest of the staff."

Umberto nodded. "I will need to hire another person then to make up for the lost hours."

"I understand," she said. "But not yet. Perhaps we can work

out ways that the family can do more, so the staff will not be over-burdened."

"I will find ways to cut, Ma'am," he said. "The family need not worry about doing more. You have your own duties."

The Queen sighed. "I was not presuming that we would or could do your jobs. We could do away with afternoon tea, perhaps. Think on it."

Umberto's eyes widened. "We will not have to resort to such uncivilized cuts," he said.

The Queen laughed. "Ah, I can always count on you to make me laugh."

"At your service, always," Umberto said. He was not trying to be funny.

"Now let's both have some fun and put these worries behind us."

"Thank you, Ma'am," he said. He went to the door and opened it.

"You are going to dance this year, aren't you?" the Queen asked.

"I do every year, Ma'am."

"No coming back here to work or read a book," she said.

"No, never," he said.

"Don't lie to me, Umberto," she said as he stood on the threshold.

"I would not lie to you!" he said. "I will definitely try to dance this year. Marguerite Teng mentioned the dances to me just now, and I promised to ask her to dance. I believe that's what I promised."

"You believe?"

"I believe." He did not elaborate.

He left the room and closed the door behind him.

He walked to the end of long corridor until he reached Lorelei's door. He knocked. No one answered. He knocked again and then opened the door. He leaned in.

"Miss Lorelei," he called as he stepped into her apartment. The blinds were drawn, and only a bit of light seeped into the rooms.

"Lorelei," he said again. She wasn't in the sitting room. The bathroom door was open, and the bathroom was empty. The door to the bedroom was open, too. Inside, the bed was made. The dark purple quilt had nary a wrinkle in it. Abbygail was so good at her job.

The closet door was closed. The closet had been Lorelei's favorite place to hide since she was a child.

He knocked on the door and said quietly, "Lorelei, it's Umberto. Is everything all right?"

No answer.

He put his hand on the knob, hesitated, and then opened the door.

The inside of the closet was lit, not from auto lights or any other kind of light Umberto had seen before. The walls glowed fluorescent green and yellow, highlighting the streams of writing that covered every inch of the closet. The letters—and some drawings—appeared to be separate from the walls, floating above before dropping down into the walls again, sinking, and then showing up in another part of the closet, all of it moving, twisting, winding, getting bigger and then smaller again. Only he couldn't read any of it. He recognized the letters but not the language.

It all circled him, like some kind of carnival game.

"All of my secrets," Lorelei said as she stepped away from the closet wall to stand next to Umberto. He shivered, startled. Where on Earth had she come from?

"Good grief, Miss Lorelei," he said, "you scared me to the Bad Old Days and back again. How did you do that?"

"Do what?" She looked up at him.

The light faded, and they were standing in the semi-darkness together.

"Out," Umberto said.

They left the closet and walked into the sitting room. Lorelei opened the blinds and climbed into her window seat.

"This house is alive," Lorelei said. "You knew that, right?"

"As much as anything that is built is alive," Umberto said. "Yes."

She shook her head. "No. It's different than that."

Umberto looked at Lorelei. He was not certain he was ready for this particular conversation today.

"Never mind," Lorelei said. "Did you need me for something?"

"I wanted to inquire if there was anything I could do for you," he said. "It seems you haven't been yourself lately, and I've noticed a difference in the house."

Lorelei looked at him. "A difference in the house? How can that be? No one notices me. No one knows who I am."

"Miss Lorelei," he said, "you know that is not true. You are the heart of this place."

"If any person is the heart, you are. I am . . . nothing."

"It is not like you to feel sorry for yourself," he said. "Tell me what has happened."

"I can't," she said. "I will say that I have been lied to my whole life. And I don't know what's true any more."

"I have never lied to you," he said. "It is my job to make life easier for the family, but I have never lied to you. So what can I do to help now?"

She shook her head. "Nothing. It's done."

Silence throbbed between them for a few moments. Umberto moved closer to the window and looked out.

"It's a beautiful day," he said. "It will be a glorious celebration. It is a good day to live."

Lorelei didn't say anything.

"As we get older," Umberto said, "we learn more about life, and about our parents, about those in power. It is sometimes startling and often disappointing. But then you realize they're all human beings—even those who are soothsayers. They have foibles. That's life."

Lorelei looked over at him. "Are you telling me to grow up?"

Umberto smiled. "Certainly not. You have been grown up for a long while."

"I'm not getting any taller," she said. "Umberto, did you know

Premier Outram's parents are dwarves? Or not average-sized people. They believe their ancestors were fairies, and dwarves are fairies."

"I did not know that," Umberto said. He felt slightly uncomfortable. He did not like talking about Lorelei's size.

"You know my—you know Talib can hardly bear to be around me," she said. "I always thought it was because of my size."

"If there's any way you can not take that personally," Umberto said, "I would encourage you to do so. Some people need an audience and aren't good at intimate relationships, especially with their children."

"He's close to Minerva," she said.

"Exceptions to every rule," Umberto said.

Lorelei smiled. "You'll say anything to try and make me feel better, won't you?"

"Only the truth," he said. "What are your plans for today?"

"I was going to run away from home," she said. "But now that I've told you, I suppose I've spoiled that plan."

"I suppose you have," Umberto said.

"I will be part of the Queen's court," she said, "as usual."

"Then all is well in the realm once again," Umberto said. "I'm sure I'll see you later today."

"Save a dance for me," Lorelei said.

"I will," he said. His dance card was getting full.

"I dreamed you were dancing," Lorelei said. "Last night. It was a strange dream. Odd things were happening everywhere. Were your dreams troubled?"

"No, but others had strange dreams last night, too," he said. "You didn't see a fire in your dream, did you?"

She looked up, as though thinking, and then she said, "I don't believe I did. I did dream of flowers blooming at night. Some flower I didn't know with dark petals. When it bloomed, it was light inside, like tiny moons were hidden within."

"That sounds lovely," Umberto said.

"It was," she said, "but something about it felt sinister." She shrugged.

"You are all right, though," Umberto said. "You would come to me if you needed anything?"

She smiled at him, but the smile did not quite reach her eyes. "I will."

Umberto didn't know what else to say. He started to leave, and then he turned back to Lorelei and said, "The closet. Whatever's happening there, should I be concerned?"

"It's a closet, Umberto," she said.

Umberto nodded. "As I suspected."

He opened the door.

"Thank you, Umberto," Lorelei said. "I understand what you've said to me. And I know you wouldn't lie to me."

"Thank you, Miss Lorelei," he said.

He left the rooms and closed the door behind him. His strides were almost jaunty as he headed for the stairs. He hadn't fixed everything, it was true.

But he knew he was going to dance today. That was enough for now.

CHAPTER SIXTEEN
TENG

Marguerite Teng flipped through page after page of Mary Letty Holmes's journals. The faded ink was not helping her decipher Mary's terrible handwriting.

Still, Teng enjoyed sitting in the beautiful library at the Hearth, across from Raphael who was also trying to read one of Mary's journals. A fragrant breeze wafted in from the open window, and all seemed right with the world. Relatively speaking.

This morning, she had spoken with Cristopher via the Man Who Was Blackmailing Her's Nexus connection. Cristopher looked well. She wanted to yell at him for getting into this mess—for dragging her into this mess—but she didn't. She was so grateful to see him, to hear his voice. He urged her to do whatever the Man said. The Man wanted information she didn't have. But she kept telling him things, little things, private things, but nothing that would upset the balance of the Queendom.

"The Queendom is losing money," she told the Man during one visit. "They've put out a public call to find the Moonstruck Saffron." Another time she said, "The Queen and her consort are living apart. She was once engaged to Premier Outram. Minerva and Savi are getting married in the fall."

"None of this is new," the Man said. "We will not release your son until we have better information."

"I am not privy to any of the Queendom's business," she told him again and again. "I am a cook! I can give you details of what I cook and what ingredients I use. I can tell you about the Unified Field Theory of Spices. But I can't tell you anything about the business of the busidom. How about credit? I can get you credit or get you supplies, which is what you wanted in the first place."

He shook his head. "What you know or will know is much more valuable."

What the Man was asking of her was impossible. So Teng came up with another solution just in case she did not find the Moonstruck Saffron: She would employ the Unified Field Theory of Spices to concoct a dish that would cause the kidnappers' hearts to melt in compassion, and they would release her son.

Right this moment, however, she needed to concentrate on Mary Letty Holmes's journals. Mary wrote about what she ate, where she walked, what plants she encountered. She only occasionally mentioned black saffron or a black crocus as the plant that "would save us all."

Unfortunately, her journals were incomplete. Some had been lost in a fire at one of her homes.

Teng sighed. Raphael looked up from the journal he was perusing.

"You're not finding anything?" he said.

"No," Teng said. The Hearth was so quiet this morning. She heard no other voices, no footsteps. The staff had the day off, and everyone else was out celebrating. "But if Holmes was trying to keep it a secret, we wouldn't find anything in her journals. Lots of people have already looked at these journals and found nothing. If they're like the old alchemical texts, perhaps there's an inherent code."

"Or it's in some kind of invisible ink," Raphael said.

"Is there any such thing as invisible ink?"

Raphael shrugged. "Anything is possible, but I don't know

where the invisible ink writing would be. She's written or drawn on every part of her journals. And we've read the reports from other researchers. They tried reading the journals backwards. They looked for codes. Someone did an infrared scan. No one could figure out if the Moonstruck Saffron was real, and if it was, where it grows."

"I bet this passage is significant," Teng said. "'One day this will save the Queendom, and it will be found in the most obvious of places. I have dreamed it, so I know it to be true.'"

"Yes, I remember that quote," Raphael said. "But what does it mean?"

"Seems like the most obvious place would be around the Hearth," Teng said. "But we've looked. Everyone has looked. There is no black saffron growing here—no black petals and no black stigmas."

"That's an interesting word," Raphael said. "Stigma. It's a mark on someone because they've done something wrong, it's part of a plant, or it's the mark of someone religious. I wonder how it happened that that word means three different things?"

Teng looked across the table at him. "A religious person? They have stigma because they're religious?"

"No, it's marks on the body that correspond with another holy person," Raphael said. "They called it stigmata when someone would bleed from the same places as Jesus bled, when he was murdered."

"Jesus?" Teng said. "Remind me who he was."

"They don't teach you anything in Erdom, do they?" Raphael said. "He was a holy man. Or a holy god. Depending upon your belief system. He was murdered by being nailed to two pieces of wood and speared in the side. Apparently some people used to bleed in those same places on their bodies. Stigmata." He shrugged. "I don't know why. I only thought of it because I had a dream last night that I had a stigma. My hands and sides were bleeding."

"I'm so glad we don't have religion," Teng said. "I loathe the idea of millions of people blindly following some invisible being."

Raphael leaned back in his chair. "Some people would say having a monarchy is equivalent to having a religion. Aren't people blindly following one person? That person is visible, sure, but not infallible."

Teng frowned and pushed the journal away from her. "No one thinks the Queen or any of the leaders are infallible. We vote for them. I didn't vote for the Queen because I'm not a citizen of Queendom yet. One day, I hope. I don't think it's the same at all. In religion, people relied on dogma supposedly sent down by an invisible being or beings. Our constitutions and the rules of confederation were created by us—or by our ancestors. And those documents are flexible. We can change them if we think it's necessary."

"But we haven't changed them," he said. "And our ancestors were no saints, you know."

"Of course they were," Teng said.

Raphael laughed. "You really don't know history, do you?"

"They were trying to do good," Teng said. "If you strip away any religious connotations of the word saint it means a person who is doing good. Or a holy person. To make something holy is to make it whole. That's what our ancestors were doing: they were trying to make us whole again, to make our world whole again. Were they perfect? No, absolutely not. Were they saints? Yes. They were trying to do the right thing."

"I suppose given that definition I'm a saint, too," he said.

"I would agree with that."

Raphael leaned his head back and laughed. Then he looked at Teng and said, "You are the only person in the world who would agree with that. I am the screwup in the family. Everyone will tell you so."

"So stop screwing up," she said. "Then everyone will tell me something else."

"I can't argue with that logic," Raphael said. "And we, my friend, are no closer to finding the Moonstruck Saffron."

"Holmes does mention the Low Mountains quite often," Teng said. "That was her favorite place to study plants.

"I really want us to find it."

"Me, too," Teng said. "I can use the reward money."

Raphael leaned forward and said quietly, "And I want to leave behind the screwup moniker, in case my sister decides not to be queen."

Teng's eyes widened. "Is that a possibility? Would you then be Chief? Premier?"

"Chief," he said. "Chief Executive for the Queendom."

"What have you done that's so bad anyway?"

"Nothing," he said.

"I don't understand."

"I have done nothing," he said. "That's the problem. When I was young, I was the one who was always breaking something or losing something or saying the wrong thing at the wrong time. But then I didn't find anything I was good at in the Service. I hated all of it and couldn't wait to get out. For a few years before going into the Service and a little after, I enjoyed going out with friends. I drank too much sometimes. There always seemed to be so much excitement wherever I went, but I know it didn't have anything to do with me. None of those people were actually friends with me. I know, it's an old story. Poor little famous kid. I'm trying to find my place, you know."

They both stood and began gathering up the journals.

"I wish I could do more to help the Queendom. My mother doesn't tell me much, but the numbers keep getting worse. Somehow people are getting Safran Bleu somewhere else. It's almost as if there is a glut of Safran Bleu, but we don't know how."

"Maybe if there weren't so much of it, the price for what there was would go up."

"We have warehouses full of it," Raphael said. "We always have enough."

"But what can you do?" Teng asked. "You must leave it to those who know what they are doing, to those in charge of such things."

Together they put the journals in the cabinet and locked it. Teng set the key on top of the cabinet.

"Is that what you do?" Raphael asked. "Leave things to those in charge."

"Yes," Teng said, "if they are the experts. If it's something to do with my life and I can do something about it, I decide what to do and then I do it. I decide what my responsibility is: what my ability to respond is. If I try something and it doesn't work, I try something else."

"It must be great to be so certain," Raphael said.

Teng nodded. "I am not always certain," Teng said. "But you either act or you ruminate. Where does rumination get us?" She shook her head. "Absolutely nowhere."

"My mother used to tell me I should think before I act," he said. "Then maybe I wouldn't keep doing stupid things."

"That's you," Teng said. "Me, I usually know what I'm doing."

Raphael laughed. "OK. I give up!"

They parted from each other at the door to the library. Teng glanced back once. Raphael was walking down the corridor away from her, his hands in his pockets, his head down. She wished she could say something to keep him from feeling sad or mad or whatever it was he was feeling, but she knew he had to find his own way. As did everyone. Although in the Queendom, everyone was supposed to find his or her own way alongside kin and community. Secrets were anathema to the Queendom way. And Teng had many secrets.

She guessed Raphael did, too.

Teng went down to the kitchen where Viva was sitting on the counter, swinging her legs. She smiled when she saw her mother.

"Momma!" Viva cried. "When can we go? I want to see all the magic. I want to see all the dances! And everyone will be dressed up. I have our masks ready."

"It's very early," Teng said, "and we will not miss anything. We're going to make cookies that will help Cristopher come home."

"Oh, cookies!" Viva said. "I'm ready."

Teng took Viva's hand and closed her eyes.

"All my ancestors," Teng said softly, "all the ancestors of this holy place, I ask that you help me in this task to bring my son home. All the plants, all the food, all the spices, we ask you to weave your healing, your nourishment, into this dish and do as we wish: bring our son and brother home to the bosom of his family. Let it be so."

"Let it be so," Viva said.

Teng let go of her daughter's hand.

"Good," Teng said. She got butter and eggs from the larder and honey from the cupboard, along with a mixing bowl.

"Beat these three together," Teng told her daughter, "while you imagine your brother peacefully home." She picked up an egg. "This—this egg—has all of creation inside of it. Every egg you ever eat, every egg you see, it is the most profound magic: It is life. It either becomes a bird or it becomes part of you." She rubbed the egg up and down her chest, between her breasts. Then she rubbed it on Viva's head. "Bring my boy home," she whispered. "And this butter has transformed. It was once something else, a liquid, and now it is a solid. Like a butterfly that was once a caterpillar. It will help us transform this situation for the better. And the honey is a gift from the bees. You know the saying, Viva."

"Ask the wild bees what the druid knows," Viva said.

"Yes," Teng said, "and the honey gives us the wisdom and healing of the plants."

"Eat the wild honey to learn what the flowers know," Viva said.

"And flowers know everything," Teng said. She held the jar in her hands for a moment. "Help bring my boy home to us."

"Momma," Viva said, "Cristopher would not like you calling him a boy. I thought he was on a vacation. Why are you making him come home?"

"I—I think he wants to come home," Teng said, "so I'm helping him."

Viva expertly mixed the three ingredients while Teng sifted some leftover rice and wheat flour together. She whispered to the ingredients as she worked. She imagined Cristopher walking through the doors of the Hearth, happy, whole, healthy.

She grated nutmeg into the flour mixture and then pressed her finger into the spice and put some on her tongue. "We are linked now. Once my son eats these cookies, he will come home to me."

Teng added cinnamon, apple cider, and a pinch of Safran Bleu. Then Viva poured her mixture into her mother's, and they stirred everything together.

"We're like two witches over a cauldron," Teng said as they stirred. "What way ye, Witch Viva."

"I say bring my brother back to his mother," Viva said. "Sooner than later."

"May these cookies bring peace and happiness to all who partake of them," Teng said. "May the Unified Field Theory of Spices reverberate through these ingredients and bind them together to bring my son safely home."

They used big spoons to drop the batter onto a tray, tablespoon by tablespoon, slid the tray into the oven, and waited for the cookies to bake. The kitchen smelled of lavender and possibilities. Teng smiled. Yes, she smelled possibilities.

"Viva," Teng said. "Later I will give these cookies to the man you have seen before. If he doesn't want to take them, I want you to grab them and say something like, 'If you don't want them, I do.' And then I want you to take one and eat it. I will then retrieve the bag from you and give it to the man again. Do you understand?"

"Yes," Viva said. "It's like a play. Umberto said much of today is like a play. We can play act and be whoever we want to be. Who do you want to be, Momma?"

"I only want to be me," Teng said. "Only me. Me, with the ability to protect my children always."

When the cookies were out of the oven and cooling, Teng and Viva put on their May Day clothes—matching blue and gold slacks and tops. Viva slipped on a gold mask decorated with blue feathers. Teng wore a twin to Viva's mask, only hers was blue decorated with gold feathers. They put the cookies in a bag and headed outside and down the hill.

Viva ran ahead and talked to everyone she met on the way.

People dressed in costumes were dancing, singing, and selling food and artwork alongside the path. Teng smiled as she looked around, as she walked through it. She felt like she was a part of it all, even though she was striding through it while others stopped, others participated. Teng couldn't stop, not yet. She had magic in her bag. Real magic, true magic. She believed with her whole heart there was a recipe for every situation—a recipe that would make everything whole, everything well, everything healed.

She hoped the bag full of cookies was a recipe for getting her son out of the Hinterlands. She understood most people would think she was delusional. No, she would say, she was hopeful. Sometimes it amounted to the same thing.

When they were halfway down the hill, the Man suddenly came out of a crowd. Viva was talking to a woman who was giving away colorful twirling stars on a stick. The Man fell into step with Teng.

"What have you learned today?" the Man said, without a hello or how do you do.

"Very little," Teng said. "As I've told you again and again, I am the cook. What could I possibly tell you? I've looked in the library. I've befriended the son. I have learned nothing. They are decent people trying to get through their days. The Queen and her advisors will determine why the Queendom is in dire financial straits. But they won't tell *me*. I don't know what you expect of me."

"Can't you break a lock?" he asked. "Or get into the Queendom's accounts?"

"Break a lock?" Teng asked. "What lock? I don't even know what that means. And you can't get into the Queen's office unless you're her or she invites you in. The door will not open for anyone else. I've told you all of this before, and yet you keep insisting I can find out something for you."

"You aren't trying hard enough," the Man said. "You need to listen to conversations. Private conversations."

"How do you suppose I do that?" she asked. "I am the cook! I'm in the kitchen all day long."

She was raising her voice. Someone from the crowd they were passing through looked her way. She smiled, pretending all was well.

The Man said quietly but clearly, "Next time I see you, I expect financial reports or detailed plans on how they intend to fix the economy. If you don't have them, you will never see your son again. We will send him to the far side of the Hinterlands. Have you ever heard what goes on in those places? You all believe you're so safe here. You've got your little paradise of the Consolidated Five where people live happily ever after. Not everyone is so fortunate. Some of us have to do anything we can to survive."

"This is why you threaten my son?" Teng said. They were stopped now, and she was facing him. "This is why you threaten me? Because you don't like the way you live?"

"Yes," he said. "It is. Not only will we send your son to the hinterlands of the Hinterlands, but we will inform on you. We will tell Queen Reina that you have been spying on her. You will lose this job you love so much."

Teng pressed her lips together. How could he possibly know what she did and did not love?

"What good would that do you?" Teng asked. "I would be fired and sent to the Hinterlands myself. I couldn't spy for you then."

"You aren't spying for us now," he said. He shrugged. "Sending your son away would be our revenge."

"What kind of people are you?" Teng asked. "You have no integrity."

The Man smiled. "So you say."

Teng swallowed. She hesitated, and then she held out the bag of cookies to him. "I made these for you, and for Cristopher. For all of your people who are holding him. The cookies will bring you peace and happiness." She considered telling him about the Unified Field Theory of Spices, but she bit her tongue. This man did not want to hear about spices.

At first, the Man did not take the bag. Viva came running up to them. She snatched the bag from her mother, reached in, and pulled out a cookie. She began to eat it.

"Yum," she said. "These are the best."

Teng gently took the bag from Viva and held it out to the Man again.

"Please," Teng said, "for your peace and happiness."

The Man took the bag. "I don't care about peace or happiness. I care about justice."

With bag in hand, the Man strode away from Viva and Teng.

"He does not deserve your cookies, Momma," Viva said.

"He does not," Teng said. The crowd hid the Man for a moment. When the people parted, as if to make way for something, Teng saw the Man drop the bag of cookies into the trash. She watched the bag fall, and the world suddenly seemed to be moving in slow motion. He hadn't eaten a cookie. None of his compatriots had eaten a cookie. So the spell, the enchantment, the science of the Unified Field Theory of Spices would not take hold.

She wanted to cry.

It had been a ridiculous idea.

As most of her ideas were.

"Mom! Did you see that?" Viva asked. "What a waste. Can I run and fetch the cookies out of the trash?"

Teng put her hand on her daughter's shoulder. "No," she said. "Leave them."

The cookies had been her last hope. She shook her head. Believing a cookie could save her and her son was insane. No Queen ever shouted, "A cookie, a cookie, my queendom for a cookie." Although some queen somewhere should have.

Truth was, Teng did not know how to stop these people or save her son. She couldn't do it on her own. She had to tell the Queen about the blackmail. There was no way around it. She should have done so long ago.

"Can we go play now?" Viva asked.

Teng looked down at her daughter. The girl grinned. What a

happy child she was. This might be the last day she was happy for a long time. Most certainly they would be sent to the Hinterlands now.

"Sure," Teng said. "Let's go have fun."

She would tell the Queen. At the end of the day. For now, she would hold her daughter's hand and be amazed at the wonders of the Queendom.

CHAPTER SEVENTEEN
LORELEI

Lorelei put on her May Day costume: a one piece green and brown suit, with leaves and flowers sewn throughout the outfit. Her mask was green, like the forest.

She went downstairs. She hesitated before going outside. She did not want to interact with any strangers. She didn't want anyone staring at her either. Her costume did not hide her stature. She supposed she could pretend she was a child, and then no one would notice her. She shook herself. Why worry? She still knew how to make herself essentially invisible. She stepped outside and walked through the crowds, skipping now and again so that she would look like a child and not as the Queen's dwarfish daughter.

She did not see any of her immediate relations. Maybe they had already gone into town. She had hoped her uncle Jeremy would attend the festivities this year, but he had decided to stay home. His husband's father was ill, so they wanted to remain nearby. Lorelei's great grandparents—the Queen Madre's parents—hardly ever travelled these days. They were quite content in their home in the East, far from all the madding crowds. Lorelei's grandfather—Reina's father—did not come to the Queendom any more. Once he had fathered the three children and they were well on their way, he had packed up and returned to Erdom. Reina had never told Lorelei why, and she had never bothered to ask. Her father's relatives visited occasionally but weren't coming to the May Day festivities this year.

Her *father*.

Talib.

Only Talib was probably not her biological father.

She wasn't certain that mattered. He had raised her.

She bent down slightly to peer at the inside of an orange poppy. Talib had not actually raised her. He had had very little to do with her. Minerva was his favorite. Everyone knew that. Even she played second fiddle to the men and women who visited her father's house. They used to come to the Hearth, although Lorelei had not been aware of their presence at the time.

One morning when Lorelei was much younger, she ran into Talib's bedroom to wake him, and she found him in bed with a man and a woman—thankfully they were all sleeping. She ran out of the room, went to her mother's chambers, and asked who Daddy's visitors were.

Soon after, Talib left the Hearth to live in a building on the property that was converted into a studio. Reina had sat Lorelei on her lap and explained it wasn't Lorelei's fault that he left. Reina said, "Your daddy has not done anything wrong. But it's better if he has his own place where he can work and play undisturbed."

Lorelei never knew if Reina had been upset or surprised by the entire episode. Maybe she felt nothing about it. Reina hardly ever showed her true emotions. Or any of her emotions. Maybe because she was even-keeled, always in charge of herself. Lorelei wasn't sure. She knew Reina tried to do the best thing for everyone. She admired her mother for that. She was not a selfish person. If she lied about who Lorelei's father was, she must have had a good reason.

On the other hand, her father—Talib—was selfish. Her brother was selfish. Aunt Hildegarde, too. They all put themselves and their desires above others, above the Queendom.

Minerva didn't. Lorelei had always believed Minerva was the model of a leader in training. But if it was true that she wasn't going to become queen, she was being selfish, just like Talib. Raphael could not manage the Queendom. And no matter what the masked man in the forest had said to Lorelei, she was not fit to be queen either. She knew little of business, and she knew even less about people. A queen had to have the confidence of the people. Lorelei doubted she could ever garner anyone's confidence.

"Does it smell?"

Lorelei looked up. Turnkey was standing next to her. He wore a ruby-colored mask—along with burgundy-colored slacks and a white shirt—but she knew it was Turnkey. He knelt on the ground by the poppies and leaned over to sniff at the flowers.

"I don't smell anything," he said. "Do you?"

"It's faint," Lorelei said, "and perhaps I'm making it up. It's more of a sound than a color."

"A sound?" he asked. "Can you describe it?"

Lorelei closed her eyes. "It's as if the sun is saying hello," she said. She opened her eyes. Turnkey nodded.

"I can see that," he said. "I can't hear it, but I can see it."

Lorelei smiled. Turnkey was the only person, besides Viva, who sought her out. She didn't know why. He was shy around her, but he was comfortable with his shyness.

"Have you heard from the man in the black mask again?" he asked quietly.

Lorelei shook her head. "Maybe it was all a joke."

"You haven't seemed the same since," Turnkey said.

"It doesn't have anything to do with that," she said.

He nodded. He looked like he wanted to say something else, but he didn't.

Lorelei said, "I better get going."

Turnkey nodded and got up off of his knees. "Sure. Sure. Maybe I'll see you later?"

"Yes, OK," Lorelei said. She didn't know where she was going, but she suddenly felt uncomfortable. Turnkey was trying to be nice to her, just as Mr. Umberto had been earlier. She did not feel like accepting their gifts of kindness, their courtesies, their niceties. They had no idea who she was, not really.

As she walked away from Turnkey and from the vendors on the grounds of the Hearth, she felt childish. Perhaps she was becoming a brat. She had never gone through a bratty stage. According to her grandmother, Minerva and Raphael had both been difficult children at different points of their maturation; Lorelei never was.

Maybe this meant she was finally growing up, literally. Maybe she was growing taller: That was a better way of saying it. At eighteen years old, she should be all grown up. She had heard of boys suddenly shooting up in their late teens. Maybe it could happen to girls, too.

She shook her head. She didn't care about any of that, not now. Instead of hiding in her room fuming about her mother's possible lies about her paternity, she should find out the truth. Was she Outram's biological daughter? Once she knew that, she would know her next step. If there was one.

She stopped, turned around, and peered into the crowds. She lifted up her mask so she could see everyone better. Normally, she loved May Day. She loved the colorful costumes, the masks, the day of pretending to be whoever you wanted to be. And it was a gorgeous blue sky day. She wanted to love it again. She wanted to stop being angry with her mother. She wanted to celebrate this day with everyone else.

She spotted Mr. Umberto. He was dressed as usual except he wore a light blue vest that was not buttoned all the way to the top. His brown eye mask was hardly visible against his skin. Umberto had been an ally of hers for as long as she could remember. If she told him she needed a paternity test done without anyone else finding out, he would figure out a way to do that for her. But he would have to get someone else involved to actually do the test. Plus she was fairly certain what he would say first. "What does it matter who your biological father is? You don't need a maternity test. You are the Queen's daughter and a Queen's granddaughter and another Queen's niece. Pater isn't important."

He would be right. Still, she wanted to know the truth. The truth was important.

Lorelei kept scanning the crowd. Who else could help her? Who else did she trust?

She spotted Quintana, standing away from the crowds by the plant nursery. His arms were crossed over his chest as he, too, watched the people. His face sagged a bit, for an instant, and he looked old and leathery. Then he squinted and age disappeared again. He looked over at her and smiled. She nodded.

Quintana. He could do it. Any soothsayer could do it. And he wouldn't tell anyone. As long as it wasn't something that would hurt the Queen or the Queendom, Quintana would keep it to himself. He had kept his affair with Hildegarde a secret. In the end, their affair had affected the Queendom. But it hadn't harmed it. Not really. Reina was a better queen than Hildegarde would have been. Everyone knew that.

Didn't they?

Lorelei walked over to Quintana.

"Hello, Lorelei," he said. "Are you enjoying the day?"

She didn't answer him. Instead, she said, "I need a favor." She glanced around and saw no one was within hearing distance.

Unless that person was a soothsayer.

"I need to ask you something in private," she said.

Quintana held his hand out, directing her to the nursery. "Only the plants will hear us."

She walked into the nursery, followed by Quintana. He shut the door behind him. Inside, it was so quiet Lorelei could hear the plants growing. She closed her eyes for a moment and listened: Yes, there it was.

When she opened her eyes, Quintana was watching her.

"I need to know if I am biologically related to Talib," she said quietly.

"You humans are all related to one another," he said, "to one degree or another."

"I need to know if he's my father," she said.

Quintana sighed. "Lorelei—"

"Please," she said. "And I don't want anyone else to know. Not my mother and certainly no other soothsayers."

"All right," he said. "Give me your hand."

She held out her hand. He took her hand between his. A few moments later, he said, "No, Talib is not your biological father."

"Can you tell who is?" she asked.

"Yes," he said.

"Is it Premier Outram?"

"It is," Quintana said. He let go of her hand. "I wish I did not have this information so readily at hand, as it were. I know your family values privacy. As do I."

"I've never thought of you as being queasy about the truth," Lorelei said.

Quintana looked almost startled. She hadn't seen that reaction from him before either.

"I'm not—" He shook his head. "I apologize," he said. "I certainly understand your need for the truth, and I won't tell anyone that you asked."

"I'm the one who should apologize," Lorelei said. "I didn't realize this might put you in an awkward position. Do you feel like you have to tell my mother? Or Hildegarde?"

"I don't need to tell anyone anything," he said.

"Are you upset with me?" Lorelei asked. "I'm not understanding you."

He shook his head and put his hand on her shoulder. "I am not upset with you," he said. "I realized you were right. I was a bit *queasy* about having this information. I don't know why. I have so much information, I know so much, and some of it isn't pleasant, but I have no attachment to who is or isn't your biological father."

Lorelei stared at him. Something else was going on, and suddenly she knew what it was. "It's because it's Outram," she said. "You don't like him! Why? What's wrong with him? You've never lied to me. Don't start now."

Quintana dropped his hand from Lorelei's shoulder and moved

away from her, just slightly. He looked over at the plant starts on tables all around them.

"I don't like or dislike him," Quintana said.

"Then you know something about him," Lorelei said. Every soothsayer had access to every other soothsayer's memories and knowledge: except those few things they chose to keep private from one another.

Quintana looked at her. "No, I don't know anything about him specifically. When he and your mother were together, he was a little intense. I'm sure you've heard that. It's why she ended the engagement."

"But she didn't end the relationship," Lorelei said, "because apparently they kept having sex."

Quintana shrugged. "That happens. Your mother leans toward monogamy, I suppose. Your father—er—Talib does not. She probably needed a stable relationship in her life back then." Quintana shook his head. "This isn't a conversation we should be having."

"I have known you my entire life," Lorelei said. "I have never seen you upset or flummoxed by anything until now. Is there something else you are keeping from me?"

"Of course!" he said. "Aren't you keeping things from me? We all do that. Even soothsayers. Look at you. A few months ago, you barely spoke to anyone. Now, you are completely changed."

"I am not changed," Lorelei said. "I am now more verbal. It's as if a door opened somewhere a few months ago. I don't know why or what it means. I suddenly became tired of pretending."

"Pretending what?"

"That I was nothing," Lorelei said. "We are all something, even me."

"Yes," Quintana said. He looked like he was going to cry. But that was unimaginable. Quintana wouldn't cry, would he?

"What about Outram?" Lorelei asked.

"Is there something specific about Outram that I know and you should know? No! Is he a good man or a bad man or something in-between? I don't know. Most people are something in-between."

"Truly?" Lorelei asked. "And that is true of soothsayers, too? Are you something in-between? Or are you primarily good or bad?"

Quintana sighed. "I'm afraid you have caught me off my stride today, Lorelei. I wish I could answer your questions wisely, knowledgeably, but I can't. The older I get, the more complicated and the more simple things appear."

"That doesn't make any sense," Lorelei said.

Quintana shrugged.

"Thank you for telling me who my biological father is."

"Why did you even wonder?" Quintana asked.

"I heard my mother talking with Outram," Lorelei said. "He asked her if he could take his daughter to Berland for a while. I thought it must be Minerva. Later, I figured out he was probably talking about me."

He nodded. "That explains a great deal. I have had several people ask me if I knew what was troubling you."

She frowned. "Why? Why would they ask you?"

"Because I've known you all your life," he said.

"Who asked?"

"Your mother, your aunt, Mr. Umberto."

"And now, what if they asked now? What will you tell them?"

"They've already asked. Why would they ask again? But my advice to you is to talk to your mother about this, especially if it is upsetting to you."

"I'm not ready for that conversation," Lorelei said.

"We seldom are ready for those kinds of conversations," Quintana said. "Best to get them done and over with."

"You've had to have big conversations?" Lorelei asked. "Like what? You know everything. You live forever. What kind of awkward conversations could you have?"

Quintana laughed. "This particular conversation isn't exactly easy. And I don't know everything. I have loved and lost. I have wondered about my purpose in life. I have wondered if I'd done enough with my life."

The nursery suddenly felt stuffy. Lorelei stepped over to the door and opened it, and a rush of fresh air came in. She breathed deeply.

She looked back at Quintana. "Is there more than one page to our Constitution?"

"I've heard that rumor," Quintana said. "As far as I know, it is only a rumor."

Lorelei squinted. How could she know if he was lying or not? Soothsayers were capable of deception.

"Have you ever wondered how the Villanueva family has won all the elections since the Queendom came into existence?" she asked.

"Because more people voted for a Villanueva candidate than for any other candidate," Quintana said.

"Is it possible the elections have been rigged," she said, "to make certain my family wins?"

"How?" Quintana said. "And why?"

"I don't know how," Lorelei said. "You would know that better than I. Why? Maybe my family wanted to stay in power all this time."

"I've known your family for generations," he said. "Not a one of them has been particularly power-hungry."

"Has anyone ever suggested there's been election tampering?"

He shrugged. "Every once in a while, someone will challenge an election. After each investigation, no fraud is discovered. And no human, no matter how clever they are, could keep something like that hidden from the soothsayers. We'd know."

"Maybe the soothsayers wanted us to win again and again."

He shook his head. "No. And we've made a pledge, a commitment, a promise. We don't interfere. We participate, we counsel, we help. But we don't manipulate. We've had bad apples now and again, and we find them and pluck them out. No one has wanted the Villanuevas to keep winning elections. It makes no difference to us."

Lorelei felt relieved. She had not wanted to believe her family could have been involved in anything like election fraud. The man in the woods must have been some kind of crackpot. She should have kept his clothes. Maybe Nehemiah could have tracked him down.

"Thank you, Quintana," Lorelei said.

She stepped outside. For the first time in many weeks, Lorelei felt more like herself. Now she knew why Talib had never felt affection for her. He must have sensed something about her all along. Maybe she felt better because she knew her real father, her true father, didn't see her as defective. She had options. She could leave the Queendom and find a home in Berland should she ever have the desire.

She heard the songs of birds on the East wind. She closed her eyes.

"What do you hear?" Quintana asked as he came up beside her.

Lorelei opened her eyes. "Birds. They are singing about fire."

"Let's hope that's a metaphor," Quintana said.

"For what?"

"For anything but fire."

Chapter Eighteen

Billy

On the morning of May Day, after singing up the sun and then eating breakfast, Billy stood in front of the mirror in his room adjusting his trousers, shirt, vest. He was excited. It was his first May Day spent at the Hearth, even though technically he would not be spending the day at the People's House. But it was the first time in his long life that he would witness the Queen and her consort in the procession that would end at the Hearth. Then as the Queen and Talib reaffirmed the bond between Sovereignty of the land, the Queendom, and Nature by making love, the rest of the citizens would eat, drink, and dance.

Mostly, Billy was glad to be spending the day with Abbygail. He could hardly wait to tell her the news. He could let her know the way soothsayers let each other know things, via their soothsayer Nexus connection, but he wanted to see her face when he told her. A human had once accused Billy of reading minds. He had to reassure the man that he could not read minds, but he and other soothsayers could share memories and information with one another, no matter where they were on the planet. It was handy, but it was difficult to pick out an individual mind. In other words, if he wanted Abbygail to know something, he could let all the soothsayers know, and this meant she would know, too. But it would be like sending a message that was meant for one person to an entire crowd. Some people were better at it—like mage soothsayers. Billy was just the run-of-the-mill soothsayer.

He grinned at himself in the mirror. He liked that expression: run-of-the-mill.

In any case, before Mr. Umberto had left the house this morning, he had informed Billy that he and Abbygail would now work the same hours as everyone else. Umberto had presented Billy's arguments to the Queen, and she agreed with Billy. Their working hours had been unfair.

"Ah, thank you, Mr. Umberto!" Billy had said, patting Umberto on the arm, and restraining himself from hugging the big man.

"Now, now," Mr. Umberto said, "it was the Queen's decision."

"And what it says about her!" Billy said. "This is grand."

Mr. Umberto had smiled and said, "Very well. I will determine how to divide the extra work load later and give you your new schedules soon. Have a good day, Billy Santos."

Abbygail would be pleased, Billy was certain. She didn't care about working more hours, but she would be happy for Billy, he knew.

Billy had never met anyone quite like Abbygail. Perhaps this was because he had spent little time with soothsayers during his life. Most soothsayers lived and worked in the cities, in important positions or as part of important households, and Billy had been a wanderer for most of his life. He had even spent some years in the borderlands near the Hinterlands.

For some years he had worked to help the plight of those cast off into the Hinterlands, but he hadn't made much headway. The people in the Consolidated Five didn't want to hear about those sent to the Hinterlands. Too many of the exiled thought they deserved their punishment. If a person showed they had mended their ways after a number of years, they could petition to return. When they came back, they seldom talked about their experiences.

Didn't matter right now. Billy was done with crusades. He needed to get his mask—the one Abbygail had made for him—and meet her. He had made a mask for her, too, and had secreted it inside a box. Billy had woven Abbygail's mask himself, from straw and flax, and hung beads and tiny colorful stones from it on pieces of gold ribbon. He wanted her mask to be sparkly and golden, just like Abbygail was.

Billy went to his bed where the unopened box with his mask in it was. He lifted the lid off and set it next to the box, on his dark green bedspread. Inside the box was a mask almost identical to the one he had made for Abbygail, only the straw was a bit darker, and a few tiny feathers dangled from the ribbons alongside colorful stones.

Perhaps they could read each other's minds.

He lifted up the mask and put it on.

He gazed into the mirror. He looked like a wild man. A cultured, suited-up wild man. He laughed. He had never felt like this. He had loved, he had lusted, he had befriended during his lifetime. But he and Abbygail fit together like two puzzle pieces that made up a whole puzzle. He knew if he said any of this out loud he would sound sentimental and clichéd. He didn't care. It felt good. He felt good. His first thought when he woke up was of Abbygail; his last thought of the day was of Abbygail. Not in a desperate way. In a comfortable way—as if he had known her for his entire existence. Known her and loved her. Perhaps this was what human beings felt like with their families, with their blood relations.

He didn't know, but he hoped his feelings for Abbygail would last. He shook his head. No, that was wrong. He knew their love would last. He hoped he would always be with her. And he knew she felt the same, although she was more pragmatic than he was, less inclined to romantic fancies, he supposed, or flights of imagination. Once, when he asked her if she wanted to leave the Hearth and travel the world, she told him no. "Not even if we went together?" he asked.

"All right," she said, "I would do that with you, for you. But not for always. This is my home, and these are my people."

Billy had never really had people. He remembered the time before the Reconnection and Reconciliation; he remembered running for his life as the humans hunted him and others like him. It wasn't good to dwell on that event in history, and he didn't. Things were different now. Still, he did not completely trust humans. He wouldn't admit that to anyone—probably not even to Abbygail. He didn't like to think it himself. Those he knew and worked with at the Hearth were certainly good and honorable people.

The house was quiet now, except for Viva and Teng in the kitchen. He could hear them talking but wasn't able to quite make out what they were saying. And someone else. All of a sudden.

Billy left his room, walked down the corridor, and went into the kitchen. Teng and Viva were making cookies.

Billy heard someone else. Upstairs.

"Is someone else here?" Billy asked Teng and Viva.

They looked over at him.

"I don't believe so," Teng said. "Everyone has left. Why?"

"I hear something," Billy said.

Teng and Viva listened.

"Must be your soothsayer ears," Teng said. "I'm sure it's nothing."

Billy nodded, but he remembered the note pinned to the door a few months back. They still didn't know what that had been all about. From his journeys on the border with the Hinterlands, Billy knew not everyone wished the Queendom well.

Billy ran up the stairs. Mr. Umberto had told him to keep an eye out for anything strange, so he was only following orders. Still, when he reached the empty corridor to the second floor, he felt peculiar being there, as though he were an intruder. He walked softly, turning up auditory senses so he could hear every breath in the place.

Then he went into the library. Someone wearing black pants and a black hooded sweatshirt stood in front of the glass case that held the Hand of Peace and a copy of the Constitution.

Billy moved so that he stood squarely in the entranceway. No one was getting around him.

"May I help you?" Billy asked.

The figure turned around. He or she wore a black mask and black gloves.

"I wanted to visit the library." It was a man's voice. "I was told it is open to the public. This is the People's House, right?"

The man didn't seem afraid, but he was nervous, almost panting. Billy turned his hearing down. He didn't need to hear that.

"Normally, yes," Billy said. "You must not be from around here. On May Day, the Hearth is only open to the Queen and her consort."

"I didn't realize that," the man said.

Billy knew he was lying. Billy held out his hand. "Welcome to the Queendom," he said. "I am Billy Santos."

The man hesitated, but then he held out his gloved hand. Billy had wanted his bare hand, so he could get his DNA, but even with his gloved-hand he got enough to find out who he was.

"Patra Davis," the man said. "Good to meet you. Could you show me the way out?"

"Of course, sir," Billy said. He led the man to the front door. Once there, Billy opened it and the man left. Billy shut the door and locked it. He closed his eyes. The man's DNA was not showing up anywhere in Nexus.

How was that possible?

Billy opened the door again and stepped outside. He looked around for "Patra Davis," but he had already slipped away. Billy went inside and closed and locked the door again. Then he ran downstairs, waved to Teng and Viva, and went out the back door.

He looked around for Mr. Umberto in the crowd and soon spotted him talking to a tall woman who was handing out large colorful hats. She was trying to get Mr. Umberto to put one on.

"You are such a handsome man," the woman was saying. "On you, this hat could die happy and fulfilled."

Mr. Umberto was laughing, almost giggling. Billy couldn't remember ever seeing him laugh. It was almost alarming.

"Oh good," Umberto said when he saw Billy. "I am saved. Take me away."

Umberto grabbed Billy's arm, and the two of them moved quickly away. Umberto looked back once and waved. When they were some distance from the woman, Umberto let go of Billy and said, "Today I seem to be catnip to the ladies."

"They aren't your cup of Safran Bleu?" Billy asked.

"I am not opposed to the ladies," Umberto said, "if that is what you are trying to assess. But I am old-fashioned. I am married to my job."

"Your job won't keep you warm at night," Billy said.

"It most certainly will," Umberto said. "The temperature at the Hearth is always perfect. But I take your point. You needed me for something?"

"I just escorted a man out of the Hearth," Billy said. "He said his name was Patra Davis and he wanted to see the library. He was standing at the Hand of Peace case. I searched for his DNA, and I couldn't identify him. I'll pass along the DNA results to Nehemiah. Perhaps he has better access to that kind of information."

"Yes," Umberto said. "Thank you. It's probably nothing, but I'm glad you told me. Now go and enjoy your day."

"Thank you, Mr. Umberto," he said. "You, too!"

Elata stepped out of the crowd and came toward Billy. She motioned him away from everyone. She was wearing a dress with an apron over it, like she did every day, but she also sported a maroon-colored mask.

"Can I help with something?" Billy asked.

Elata wiped her hands on her apron and then pushed the mask up onto her head. She squinted as she looked at him.

"Have you heard anything about first-line soothsayers being recalled to Paquay State?"

Billy thought for a moment, seeing if he had missed any Nexus communications. He even closed his eyes and scanned his memories.

"No," he said. "I haven't heard anything. What kind of recall?"

"Upgrades or something," Elata said.

"I don't understand why you would have heard and I didn't," Billy said. If something was sent out through the network, all the soothsayers "heard," unless the messages were only for specific soothsayers.

"You aren't first-line," she said.

"Neither are you," he said.

"But I have a friend in Berland who is," she said. "And she got a message that she needed to report to Paquay State as soon as possible."

Billy frowned. "Report? That sounds like an order. Who has the authority to order us to do anything?"

"I thought it was odd, too," she said. "Has Abbygail said anything?"

He shook his head. "Have you asked the Queen?"

"She wouldn't know," Elata said. "And I hesitate to ask Nehemiah. Maybe it's a virus. You know, a false message of some kind. But my friend knew several other soothsayers who had gotten the message, too. I'm sure it's nothing. It's odd though, and so many odd things are happening lately. If something nefarious is going on in Paquay State then we are all in trouble."

"And why would soothsayers have to report to Paquay State?" Billy asked. "They can do most upgrades long distance."

Elata nodded. "That was my thought." She shrugged. "Just be aware, I suppose."

"Thank you, Elata," he said. Elata nodded and then left him alone.

Billy rushed through the throng. Once he reached the perimeter of the forest, he was glad to step out of the sun and onto the path that wound through the trees. He practically ran down the trail until it forked away from the Hearth and the Queen's Village. He was meeting Abbygail deeper in the woods, at a clearing that looked out over distant saffron fields.

He grinned and waved when he saw Abbygail standing under a tall old Douglas fir. She waved. He ran to her, and they embraced.

"The mask you made is perfect," Abbygail said. "They look nearly the same."

"Brilliant minds think alike," Billy said.

"No one has ever called me brilliant before," Abbygail said. They held hands and gazed at one another.

"But you are brilliant," Billy said. "You have a natural wisdom."

Abbygail smiled. "Come on. I want to show you something." She let go of one of his hands and tugged on the other.

They ran through the woods together, matching strides. It was invigorating, refreshing, freeing, to run with someone who could match his speed and strength. They ran until they came to a wooden fence. Billy slowed, but Abbygail leaped over it without hesitation. She laughed and motioned him on. They ran a little further until they broke out of the woods into a small clearing, a place where the tall trees leaned away from each other a bit, and sunlight pooled in one spot, falling directly on a bed just off the forest floor.

Billy and Abbygail stopped and looked at the bed. Then they looked at one another.

"What is this?" Billy whispered.

They walked slowly to the bed. The frame was made from distressed metal. A white comforter covered the mattress. Scattered over the comforter were flower petals: orange and red poppy petals, pink rhodie petals, golden marigolds, red and orange rose petals. Abbygail reached out and carefully pressed down on the mattress.

"It's a feather bed," she whispered. "Like out of a fairy tale."

"Maybe it's for us," Billy said. He reached for Abbygail's hand. "Shall we try it out."

"It's not for us!" Abbygail said, pulling her hand away playfully. "This path—" She pointed to a trail that wound south. "—leads to the Queen's garden. It is for her and her consort."

"I thought they consummated inside the Hearth," Billy said. "Isn't that why the procession ends at the Hearth?"

"Yes," Abbygail said, "but it used to happen in the woods. Long ago. We better go. I wouldn't want to spoil it for them, but I wanted to show it to you."

Billy sat on the edge of the bed.

"Billy!" Abbygail said. "We might jinx it!"

He laughed, grabbed her hand, and pulled her over to him. "Sit next to me. It's very comfy. I think I'll take a nap."

"No," she said, but she sat next to him. She bounced a little bit. "It's quite wonderful, isn't it?"

He smiled. "Abbygail, will you marry me?"

She looked at him. "Soothsayers don't get married. That's an institution the humans brought back for their own reasons. It's not what we do."

"I'm sure some soothsayers have gotten married," Billy said. "It's not against the law or anything."

"But why?" Abbygail said.

"Because I love you," he said. "I want us to live together. Married couples at the Hearth get bigger apartments."

Abbygail laughed. "That is a very good reason to get married." She leaned against Billy. "Do you ever wish you could have children?"

"You mean biologically?" he said. "No. Do you?"

She shook her head. "I don't have that urge, no. Because we don't have that in our biology, I guess. Sometimes I think it would be nice to have family though, like what Wanda and Turnkey have. And the First Family. The Queen says we are part of her family, but it's not true. Not in any real sense." She shrugged. "Not that I mind that. They've had their troubles over the years."

"You love parties and celebrations," Billy said, "and I love parties and celebrations. That's what a wedding is. We get to tell the whole world that we love each other."

"We could do that now, without getting married."

Billy put his arm across her shoulder. "If you don't want to do it," he said, "that's fine. It would be grand, though. I want to live with you. I want to be by your side always."

"I would like that, too. All right. We can get married."

"Yes!" Billy stood and clapped his hands together.

Abbygail slid off the bed. "This place is so beautiful," she said. "The Queen will like it very much."

Billy and Abbygail began walking away from the bed and the circle of sunlight.

"Abbygail, have you gotten a message from Paquay State lately," he asked, "saying you need to report for an upgrade or anything?"

She looked at him. "Yes, didn't you? We could go together and make a vacation out of it."

Billy felt his heart beating a little faster, or maybe it was just a dump of chemicals into his system as he felt a burst of anxiety.

"No, I never got any message," Billy said.

Abbygail frowned. "Oh. You don't think they're trying to put me out to pasture or anything, do you?"

"Good grief, no! Why would you think that?"

"I'm first-line," she said. "I got the message, and you didn't. That must be the difference. Maybe they think we're too old."

"I don't know who 'they' would be," Billy said. "But no one can decide we're too old and get rid of us. That would be murder. We are protected under the law."

"Billy," Abbygail said, "you sound so alarmed. I was kidding. Or maybe I wasn't. I don't know. I do feel some anxiety about this."

"Me, too," Billy said. "Must be something going on in the network. Don't worry. You don't have to do anything you don't want to. And we have a wedding to plan. That's up first."

Abbygail nodded and squeezed Billy's hand. "Yes, that is up first."

CHAPTER NINETEEN
HILDEGARDE

Hildegarde let herself get lost in the crowd of revelers who were singing and shaking rattles and tambourines as they followed the Queen and her consort up the hill. Hildegarde wore a mask that covered her entire face and most of her hair. Her long flowing green pants and shirt did not give her away as part of the First Family. Most people had not seen her in a public role for fifteen years, so they wouldn't recognize her. For a while, at least, she wanted to remain incognito. Perhaps this way she could help the Queen.

Not only was the economy in shambles, but they kept hearing rumors of rebels in the Low Mountains—and she couldn't forget the note that had been pinned to the door the night she arrived: Live Free or Die.

She knew Nehemiah suspected she was responsible for that cryptic message. She was not. Reina was suspicious of her, too. It was the same with the rest of the family. They watched her. They were waiting for her to do . . . something. After that first night, no one had confronted her again. Now they acted as though she had always been there. They were courteous, but they were not intimate.

Except for Quintana.

Now, as she walked up the hill, following the procession, she spread her arms out and tipped her head back to feel the sun on her face through the mask. They could not have asked for a more perfect day. She whispered a thank you to the Weather Spirits. A woman walked by carrying colorful wooden star wands. Colored ribbons swung from each one.

"For you, my dear?" the woman said, holding out two handfuls of wands. "All your wishes could come true. What color, what color?"

"Blue," Hildegarde said.

The woman peeled off a blue wand and handed it to Hildegarde. Then she continued up the hill, holding out her wands.

Hildegarde waved the wand as she walked. She looked around at the masked people who walked with her. Everyone seemed happy. No one was acting as though the Queendom were on the brink of collapse. And it wasn't. It couldn't be. She wished Reina trusted her. She wished she would ask for her help. She had been trained to be CEO, while Reina had not been. Reina now had more experience being queen than Hildegarde had. Hildegarde had been too young, too inexperienced, too willing to let it all go because of love.

She still did not understand why her family had been so angry with her. Maybe they still were. She had given up everything for love, they believed. She had argued back then that she was only following the precepts of the Queendom: Love superseded everything. And they had said that love of family and love of country should have superseded her love of a soothsayer. Her love of family and love of country should have superseded erotic love.

She shook her head and waved the wand more vigorously. She had not given up everything for Quintana. No. It had been the will of the Universe. She wasn't meant to be queen, at least not then. And now she was ready to be of whatever use she could be to her country.

Not long before she came back to the Hearth, she had dreamed of home. Someone called to her in the dream, so she flew home. As she came over the northern rise, she saw the countryside around the Hearth was in flames. She awakened terrified.

She made plans to return the next day.

She had stopped by her brother's place on her way to learn what she could about her sister and her family. Jeremy told her what he knew, but even he had not been warm. Maybe it was because Dale's father was ill. She didn't know. When they were all children, Jeremy and Reina had been close to one another, and she had been the outsider: the future queen.

She didn't understand why she and Reina had never been true sisters to each other—great sisters, always looking out for one another. She watched sisters in other families, and they always appeared to be so close. When she tried with Reina, she felt rebuffed.

Sometimes Hildegarde thought of Reina as a kind of cipher. Minerva, too. Perhaps that was the wrong word. Robotic was a better word. As if they were approximations of human beings. Soothsayers were more human than they were. Neither seemed emotional, ever, and both looked perfect. Without a hair out of place. Always saying the right thing. Exactly the way a sovereign should act, she supposed. Maybe that was why Hildegarde abdicated. She knew she could never be above it all. She couldn't say and do the right thing always. She cared about it all so deeply.

She was not sure her sister did care. If she did, wouldn't she be more emotional? She appeared so calm in the midst of this storm. Perhaps calm was the better part of valor. Why be upset when everyone else was upset? Better to act as if all was well.

When Hildegarde was queen, her mother had told her, "Others may fall to their knees and weep, but we stand tall, we stand confident. We weep, too. But we have to appear to be better, stronger, more capable, especially when events make the future look dire."

Perhaps Reina had taken her mother's advice to heart more than Hildegarde had. Hildegarde had never been able to divorce her emotions from her body. That wasn't healthy. She didn't believe it was what their founding mothers and fathers would have wanted.

Hildegarde slowed a bit to allow the revelers to pass her. She could barely see her sister and her consort up ahead. Reina was dressed as Sovereignty: in gold and green. And Talib, her consort, was costumed as the Green Man. Once they reached the Hearth, the Queen and Talib would go inside and make love—to symbolize the marriage of the natural world with the government and culture of the Queendom. The Queendomers would continue the celebration outside.

In the old days, the Queen and her consort made love in the forest, while the citizens celebrated around them. Hildegarde always hoped that meant the citizens were at a discreet distance. Otherwise it might be a bit awkward.

At some point in the Queendom's history, the Queen and her consort moved indoors, where they made love in private.

That was how Reina and Talib did it. Or how Reina and her consort did it. They didn't know for certain who was in the Green Man costume. Nowadays May Day was less about the mythology or symbolism: It was more about having a grand celebration once the Queen had retired to her bedchambers. Let the parties begin!

As the crowd moved more swiftly past Hildegarde, her fingers started to ache, her palms pulsed. She flexed her fingers and hoped no one noticed. Even now, after all these years, she was afraid she might be found out.

When Hildegarde was a girl—five or six—she found an injured baby rabbit near the Hearth, bleeding from the neck. Her fingers began to ache, her palms pulsed. Without thinking about it, she knelt on the grass next to the animal and put her hands on it. Within seconds, the bleeding stopped. And then the panting stopped. The rabbit twitched and looked up at her. They gazed at one another—creature to creature—for a few moments. Then it hopped away, whole and healthy.

"What have you done?" she heard her mother, the Queen, whisper as the rabbit ran away. She sounded terrified and angry all at the same time.

Hildegarde hadn't known what to say or do. She had never seen her mother upset about anything. Until now.

"S—she needed a hug," Hildegarde told her mother, trying to say something about the rabbit that would calm her mother. She had no idea what she had done wrong, but even as she scrambled to come up with the right words, her neck began to ache, and she was certain if she did not do something, a gaping wound would open on her neck. She put her hands on her neck and hoped her tingly fingers would fix it.

"You can't do that again," her mother said quietly and gently. "Only soothsayers can do that, and only a few of them. You don't want anyone to think you are a soothsayer, do you?"

Hildegarde looked at her mother. She was puzzled by her mother's reaction. "Um, why would it matter if someone thought I was a soothsayer? And they couldn't because there are no children soothsayers."

"First off," her mother said, matter-of-factly, "after the Fall, humans hunted soothsayers to punish them for what had happened. Some of the soothsayers had healing abilities. To this day, we don't know how or why. They hid these abilities to some extent and passed themselves off as folk healers. Gloria Stone was one of those soothsayers. She's the one who brought the soothsayers and the humans together for the Reconnection and the Reconciliation."

"No one hunts soothsayers now," Hildegarde said to her mother. "So why are you afraid?"

Her mother looked at her and smiled. "You're right." She bit the inside of her lip. "Still, it would be better if you forgot about this. Can you do that? And try not to do it again."

"But, Mom, the rabbit is alive now," she said.

"Maybe it was her time to die," the Queen said, "and you have interfered with her destiny."

"It couldn't be her destiny to die, could it?"

"Hildegarde, you are too young to be so old," the Queen said. "Trust your mother on this. Trust the Queen on this matter. Don't do it again."

Hildegarde did as her mother instructed. Over time, her hands stopped tingling when she was around someone sick or wounded. She soon forgot about the incident. She only knew she was afraid of rabbits.

When she was a teenager, her hands and fingers began to tingle again, and she had gone into a full-blown panic. She didn't tell her mother, but she did mention it to her Grand Mother who still lived with them. Grand Mother sent her to the town healer who hypnotized her and guided her on a journey to discover why she was terrified of her hands tingling. That led to a rabbit. Then she remembered saving the rabbit.

She did not tell the healer what she recalled. She went home and pushed away the panic when it came up again by reassuring herself and resting her tingling hands on her chest. And then the tingling went away again for many decades. Until recently. She went around to healing centers and monasteries and worked as an aide, never using her real name. She would casually put her hands on the sick until the tingling stopped. She knew that healers were supposed to ask permission before they healed, and she decided that by going to a healing center the people within had implicitly and explicitly asked for healing.

In the monasteries, she would say something like, "I've heard the human touch helps with the healing process. May I?" No one ever refused. None of the healings were as dramatic as the one had been with the rabbit. Yet nearly every person gradually got better. Whether that was because of her touch or not, she couldn't say. If anyone noticed a direct line between her touch and their healing, Hildegarde always moved on.

And then she had the dream of the fire. So she returned to heal the Queendom.

She didn't know yet what that meant.

As she walked amongst the revelers now, because her hands tingled, she assumed some of them were sick and needed healing, but she couldn't—or wouldn't—do anything about it now. She kept slowing down until most everyone had gone past her.

Then she heard a growl in her ear, "Hello, Miss Hildegarde."

She looked to her right. Nehemiah was now walking next to her, dressed in his saffron robes as usual, with a black mask fitted across his eyes.

"You sounded like a wild cat in my ear," Hildegarde said. "What are you doing here? Shouldn't you be up with the Queen? You're attached at the hip, aren't you?"

"No more than I was with you," Nehemiah said. "Today is about the Queen and her consort, about the mating of the Earth with Spirit, Nature with Intellect, the Green with Sovereignty. My place is with the celebrants."

"Thank you for a speech about May Day," Hildegarde said.

"Twenty-nine words constitute a speech?" Nehemiah said. "You must have spent your time away alone if you now classify *that* as a speech. By the by, when do you intend to continue your time away?"

Hildegarde laughed. "Ahhh, so we come to it finally? Did the Queen send you to ask me?"

"No, she did not," he said. "What is your answer to my question?"

"This is my home, and I can stay as long as I like."

Nehemiah nodded. "This was your home, and it is the family home, for now. You must want to look for meaningful work somewhere. Everyone needs that. There is no meaningful work for you here."

"Whether I stay or go isn't any of your business," she said.

"Of course it is," Nehemiah said. "Everything in the Queendom is my business."

Hildegarde looked at her former advisor. She arched an eyebrow. "I suppose it is," she said. "However, I will stay or leave as I will it. I want to be of help in these desperate times."

"I hardly think the Queen would call these desperate times," he said.

Hildegarde stopped and faced Nehemiah.

"Then she would be foolish or ignorant," Hildegarde said, "because things are not going well for most people."

Nehemiah clenched his jaw.

Hildegarde put her hands on her hips. "The truth stings, does it?" she said. "We are not doing enough to stop this economic free fall."

"There is no free fall," he said, "and we have taken measures that will help."

"Maybe you've been here too long," Hildegarde said. "Perhaps it is time for new blood. Have you thought of that? When was the last time you left the Hearth? Do you have any idea what is happening away from here?"

"If the people believe we are not working effectively," he said, "the Queen will be voted out. If the Queen believes my counsel is unwise, she will relieve me of my duties. The Queen travels often, and I am privy to what's happening everywhere because of my fellow soothsayers." He smiled.

"I want to be of use to my queen and country, too," Hildegarde said. "You must understand that. The Queen Madre does charity work. I can, too. I will find meaningful work here."

"Beyond having sex with the gardener," Nehemiah said.

Hildegarde sucked in her breath. Her eyes widened.

"How dare you," she said. "How dare you speak to me this way? I was once your queen."

"I held you on my knee when you were a babe," he said.

"I cannot imagine that," Hildegarde said. "I've never seen you ever do anything as human as that."

"I am not human," he said.

"You are human in all ways but one," Hildegarde said. "So don't try to argue semantics with me."

"Some humans can't reproduce either," Nehemiah said, "but they are still humans."

"You know what I mean! You are a cruel man. You've never understood me."

"I am not cruel," he said. "I have never committed a cruel act in my life. You know that. I was outside your mother's door when you were born. I watched you grow and become yourself. You were always different from your sister and brother. We thought that marked you as queen, as a future monarch of the Queendom. But we were wrong. You let your desires and emotions get in the way of your duty."

Hildegarde shook her head and turned away from him. She began walking up on the hill again.

"I will not be talked to in this way," she said. "I am not a child you can scold! This is all old news. We are a country built on creativity, on intuition. We are brought up to trust our feelings, our gut. So I left. I can't be punished for that forever. Besides, Quintana didn't come with me. I didn't get what I wanted."

"You won't get it now either." Nehemiah easily kept up with her. "Quintana will never leave the Hearth, and you cannot be queen again."

Hildegarde stopped and faced Nehemiah again. "I don't want to be queen," she said. "I never wanted to be queen."

"What is it you wanted to do with your life then?" he asked.

Hildegarde blinked and looked beyond Nehemiah, up to the Hearth. She had no idea what she was talented at. She had been wandering for so many years. At each place she stayed, she helped where she could, but nothing sent her heart aflutter. Even when she started doing healings on people, she was not filled with any particular sense of purpose. She did it because she felt she should: If one had a gift, one should share it.

She admired people who were artists or carpenters, builders or musicians, bakers or teachers. They knew what they wanted. They knew what they were good at. She wished she felt some kind of whisper of destiny. When she decided to abdicate, she had felt she would find her way on another path. She had thought she was doing the right thing because she was in love. What could be more holy, more sacred, more a part of her destiny than love?

She did not say any of this to Nehemiah, then or ever.

"Leave me be," Hildegarde said. "I am still part of the First Family, and I am certain I could come up with some excuse to get you exiled."

Nehemiah stared at her. She shrugged and smiled.

"Your threats are meaningless," he said. "You tarnish your name and your station in life with such threats."

"What station in life?" She started walking up the hill again. "You pointed out I have no station."

"Help the Queendom," Nehemiah called after her. "Help your sister. Leave the Hearth and the Queen's Village as soon as you can."

Hildegarde kept walking up the hill. She wanted to look back and see if Nehemiah followed, but she didn't. She felt her face flush. How could she have spoken to Nehemiah like that? He was an icon. He was a hero of the realm.

She groaned. Maybe Nehemiah was right. Maybe she should leave.

She should at least apologize. She stopped and turned around. Nehemiah was nowhere in sight.

Oh well. She hurried to catch up with the others. She would find a way to prove Nehemiah wrong. She would do something so glorious for the Queendom that he would forget this conversation, and everyone else would forget that she ever abdicated.

CHAPTER TWENTY
REINA

The Queen enjoyed May Day; she always had. Now, as she danced up the hill with her consort and the revelers, she felt a rush of happiness.

When she was younger, she had liked coming back to the Hearth where she and Talib were alone. They would make love and then wander their home, often naked, eating and giggling while the rest of the world celebrated away from them. As the years went by, they spent less time making love on May Day, less time naked or laughing. Some years they did not make love at all. Most years now, actually. They would march up the hill together, take their bows at the entrance to the Hearth, go inside, close the door, and then go their separate ways.

Talib would say, "Your Majesty," and he would bow slightly or dip his chin. She would nod, and they would part.

Reina was not certain when it happened, but she did not particularly care for her husband. She had loved him once, almost desperately. Perhaps that should have been a clue that it was not a love that would last. Love should not be desperate. Desperate love was what Hildegarde had for Quintana. That had nearly destroyed Hildegarde, and it could have taken down the Queendom with her.

Maybe Reina had wanted to love Talib desperately so she wouldn't wonder if she had been wrong to leave Outram.

She still didn't know if she had made the right decision. Now, she did not even like being in the same room with Talib. She tolerated his company for the children and for the country. She wished he would return to his own country, just as her father had. One day, perhaps, she would ask him to leave. She wasn't able to do that yet. This year, though, she had sent him a message that she would prefer to find another Green Man for the procession. For appearance's sake, he should stay away from the parade, so that the public didn't know her consort was not Talib. He responded that he was glad to be relieved of the onerous duty.

"Onerous?" Reina had practically hissed when she got his answer. "I wish he would go away."

"You only have to ask and he would leave," Elata had said. "Why don't you?"

"How should I word it?" Reina asked. "Dear Talib, now that you've had sex with most of the men and women in Queendom, it's time you moved onto the men and women in another country. Let them have the benefit of your dick."

Elata laughed. "If you do say that, I want to be there to see his reaction."

"I'll have Fan as my Green Man," Reina said. "Then we can come back here and make love according to our customs."

Elata shook her head as she folded Reina's clothes and put each piece carefully away in her dresser. "It is not custom to make love with a soothsayer," she said. "It must be a flesh and blood man. To symbolize fertility, communion of nature and nurture, logic and emotions. You know that."

"No one will know," Reina said. "And he is the best masseuse I've ever had."

Elata rolled her eyes. "Yes, I understand."

Reina looked over at Elata. "Have you been having sex with Fan?"

Elata slapped her thighs and laughed. "Good grief, no! Fan.

That would be like having sex with a child. But I do have a great . . . masseuse, too."

Reina's eyes widened. "Male or female? Someone I know? Why did you never say?"

"Because it's none of your business," Elata said. "Sometimes I need a little relief, and sometimes he needs a little relief. Does us both good."

Reina tried to think of the other soothsayers in the house. "You did say he," she said. "Hmmm. Not Billy. Quintana? Oh yuck. He's having sex with my sister. Which is disgusting in itself, so don't tell me it's with him."

Elata shook her head. "Let's spend more time on who you want your Green Man to be and less on my sex life."

Reina flopped down on the bed and stared at the ceiling. "There's only Nehemiah," she said. "And it wouldn't be him. Must be someone in the village."

Elata didn't say anything. Reina sat up and stared at the soothsayer.

"Not *Nehemiah*? Oh my goodness. Mother never told me."

"Your mother never knew," Elata said. "And it's not as if we're in love. We have sex now and again. If you let on that you know, he will be mortified." Elata sat on the bed next to Reina. "Sometimes he will pass me in the corridor and pull me into a closet and lift my dress. Sometimes I lift his robes. It's all very discreet. Very fast. And very satisfying."

Reina held up her hand. "I have heard enough. I will never be able to look at either of you the same again."

"Why?" Elata got up and went back to the clothes. "You humans are so silly about sexual matters sometimes."

"Are you saying I'm a prude?" Reina asked. "Talib hinted that I was. That's male propaganda left over from the patriarchy. If we don't want a particular male, he accuses us of being sexually prudish. I didn't want Talib. When Fan and I are together, we have quite an adventure."

"Oh, I must hear the details," Elata said blandly.

"Don't make fun of me just because you are older and more experienced," Reina said. "I am your queen." She grinned and stuck her tongue out at Elata.

"And I have seen you naked more times than Fan, Talib, or Outram have."

"Ew!" Reina said. "Why not say you have seen me naked more than anyone else because you used to change my diapers. Don't link yourself with the people with whom I have had sex."

"Yes, Your Highness." Elata smiled. "Will that be all?"

"So you'll find someone who is built enough like Talib that he can fool the populace?"

"They wouldn't care, you know," Elata said. "You could tell them it's not Talib."

Reina knew it was wrong to be deceitful, but she couldn't help it. She didn't want to announce to the world that her husband no longer loved her. Or that she no longer loved him.

"But yes, I will find someone," Elata said.

"And stop wearing dresses," Reina said.

"Pardon me?" Elata asked, stopping midway between the dresser and the door.

"Every time I see you in a dress I'll think of you and Nehemiah," Reina said.

Elata shrugged. "You'll get over it." She left the room.

"Traitor!" Reina called as Elata shut the door.

Now, Reina danced up the hill as Sovereignty to the Queendom and the land. She wore a light blue mask over the top half of her face. Her gown was gold and cream-colored, and it opened at the front to reveal brocade slacks with colorful flowers winding up her legs to merge with a blue flower pattern on the front of her dress. Her hair was loose, flowing to her shoulders, weighed down a bit by the live flowers and pearls Elata had wound through it. Her shoes were made of light blue cloth.

Beside her danced the Green Man. His costume was more elaborate than Talib's usually was, the vegetation sprouting several inches out from his green mask. The green and brown cloth clung to his body, revealing his well-formed chest, buttocks, almost flat belly, and what appeared to be an erection—must be a codpiece. Talib had worn a codpiece in the early years, too. Many of the Green Men did. It was a symbolic way to demonstrate that they were ready to serve the Queen.

Reina enjoyed dancing up the hill with this man, whoever he was. She would have to thank Elata later. She liked being under the blue sky, surrounded by her compatriots. She liked playing the role of the strong, fertile, vivacious queen who would save them from all harm, ready for her consort.

"Plow my vulva, plow my vulva," she whispered to herself.

Today, she wasn't going to worry about the economic crisis. She was not going to think about the tinder dry countryside. She was not going to worry about her son who seemed lost and obsessed all at the same time. She was not going to fuss about her daughter who did not want to be queen. She was not going to worry about her other daughter who suddenly did not want to talk to her. She was not going to think about her sister, the ex-queen, or wonder why the hell she had come home. Reina had spent too many restless nights ruminating on that. No, all was as it should be on this particular day. The customs, the ceremonies, the celebrations would renew the Queendom. She would renew the Queendom, by force of will if she had to.

She and her consort and the crowd were almost at the Hearth. They had taken the path that skirted the woods. She heard a hawk call out from somewhere. When she looked up, she saw smaller birds diving at a red-tailed hawk as it flew across the sky. She looked toward the dark forest and felt the pulse of life coming from within. She smiled.

Then they were at the Hearth. Her consort squeezed her hand and let go of it. She strode forward to the front door of the Hearth and stood on the threshold, beneath the arch and the letters BEHOLD THY MOTHER. The crowd stayed back from her. The Old Oak towered above them.

Reina held her arms out and looked at her daughters, mother, sister, consort for the day, Elata, Umberto, Teng, Quintana, Nehemiah, and hundreds—thousands?—of citizens of the Queendom. She breathed deeply as she waited for any stragglers to catch up. She breathed and tried to recall the Sumerian poem she recited every year on the threshold of the Hearth. For a moment, she didn't know where to begin. She felt her almost bare feet on the ground. Yes, yes, there it was: The power flowing up from the Earth, the words streaming into her brain.

The crowd went silent.

"What I tell you," Reina cried. "Let the singer weave into song.

"What I tell you,
"Let it flow from ear to mouth,
"Let it pass from old to young:
"My vulva, the horn,
"The Boat of Heaven,
"Is full of eagerness like the young moon.
"My untilled land lies fallow.
"As for me, Reina,
"Who will plow my vulva?
"Who will plow my high field?
"Who will plow my wet ground?
"As for me, the young woman,
"Who will plow my vulva?
"Who will station the ox there?
"Who will plow my vulva?"

The world became still. Then the Green Man stepped toward her, away from the colorful crowd. He stood his ground so well. She could feel power emanating from him, just as she had felt it from the forest.

"Great Lady," he said, his voice gruff, "the consort will plow your vulva. I, Green Man, will plow your vulva!"

"Then plow my vulva, man of my heart!" Reina cried. "Plow my vulva!"

The crowd roared. Reina laughed as the stranger who was the

Green Man stepped forward and took her hand. They stood together, their clasped hands raised in the air as they faced the crowd. Then they turned, opened the doors to the Hearth, and stepped into the quiet, semi-dark stillness.

The doors shut, the crowd noise disappeared, and Reina could only hear their breathing. She had told Elata to make certain Fan was waiting for her so she could go to him after she dismissed the Green Man. She almost wished she hadn't. She liked the feel of this man's hand. She liked his presence.

"A kiss for the road?" Reina asked.

"Of course, my queen," the man said.

They moved together and kissed, despite their half-masks. The man put his arm around her waist and pulled her closer. She leaned against him. He felt familiar. His smell was familiar. She didn't care. She wanted to keep kissing him. When the kiss ended, she reached up and pulled off his mask.

"Bay," she said.

"Ray," Outram answered.

Reina laughed.

"Premier Outram, what a pleasure," she said.

He grabbed her hand. She smiled and moved closer.

This seemed right. Perfect.

Only Fan was waiting upstairs. Unless Elata had arranged all of this.

"Elata?" Reina asked.

Outram nodded. "It was my idea, but she liked it. I had heard through the grapevine that you had asked Talib to stand down as your consort."

"The grapevine? Who is gossiping about such things? No one is supposed to know."

"Does it matter?"

Reina leaned against him. "No. Let us go to bed to consummate this coupling. Otherwise, we will be in taboo." She took his hand and started to lead him to the stairs.

"No, not there," he said. "Not where you have made love to

Talib or that soothsayer or others." There was a question in his voice that made her want to laugh. What did he care about her sexual partners?

"And you," Reina said. "You and I have made love in that room, on that bed."

"That's true," he said, "but I would rather follow another custom. Come."

They ran down the hall, went into her office, and then out the back way, through her garden and out into the woods. Once they were in the forest, they slowed. Reina took off her mask and hooked it on the branch of a vine maple she passed by.

They held hands as they walked. The sounds of the celebration faded away. Reina heard only an occasional bird song and the creak of one tree rubbing against another when the wind flew through the forest. The world felt primeval. New. She looked at Outram. He walked slightly ahead of her while holding her hand. For a moment, she saw him as the boy she had fallen in love with all those years ago. She squeezed his hand.

And then the forest opened to reveal a bed in a pool of sunlight; forest shade trembled on the edges of the light. The bed was a four poster with green vines snaking up each post. It had a big fluffy mattress, and flower petals were strewn across it.

"Just like your ancestor queens," he said as they walked slowly to it.

"It is exquisite," she said. "But why not on the forest ground, like my other ancestors?"

"We're old," he said. "I thought this would be more comfortable."

Reina slugged Outram in the arm and laughed.

"I hope no one is wandering the woods," Reina said. "I have no desire to have sex in front of an audience."

"Sex?" Outram said. "I thought we would take a nap."

"Right," Reina said, turning to him. "Because we're old." She began to unbutton his shirt. He sighed and leaned his head back. "You know this means nothing," Reina said.

"It means everything," Outram whispered. "On this day, it means we are united, just as the land is united and merged with Sovereignty. It means—"

"Are you going to get undressed?" Reina asked. "Or are you going to talk?"

Outram did not say another word as he pulled off his clothes and watched Reina take off some of hers. Then they got onto the bed together, laughing. They sank down into the mattress.

Reina put her arms around Outram's neck, "Plow my vulva, consort." She smiled.

"At your service," Outram said.

As they pressed their bodies against each other, Reina felt herself sinking—sinking into the mattress, into Outram, into her true self. She should have never left Outram. They were destined to be together. Even though she did not believe in destiny. Maybe if they had stayed together, the Queendom would not be suffering now. She had failed in every way as head of the busidom.

Outram kissed her breasts, and she closed her eyes. She did not want to think of any of that now. If destiny was real, then she was queen because it was written in the stars or in the core of the earth. She belonged right here, in Outram's arms, as queen of the Queendom. All was not lost. All was not doomed. She would save the Queendom. They all would. And she would start by participating in this ritual, this creative act of lovemaking.

She laughed. What could be better? Her laugh echoed in the trees, and several birds took flight, becoming black dots on the blue sky.

All was well, all was well.

Reina closed her eyes again. "Plow my vulva, consort, plow my vulva."

In the distance, Reina heard thunder. Good, she thought, maybe rain was finally on the way.

Chapter Twenty-one

Quintana

Something was wrong. Even as Quintana moved inside of Hildegarde, even as he listened to her sighs of pleasure, he knew something was wrong. He was enjoying this too much. He wanted her closer. He wanted to go deeper. He wanted her body against his nearly constantly.

It was strange. It was abnormal. He knew he should get himself checked out, but it felt too good. His body spasmed with orgasm just as hers did. And then they moved away from one another, breathing quickly, shallowly, as if they had both just run a race.

"Quintana," Hildegarde said, "I can't keep doing this. I'm not a robot, you know. I can't keep going day and night."

"We can stop any time you like," Quintana said. "Only say the word."

His darkened room vibrated with silence. And then they both laughed.

"I wonder if my sister and Talib are going at it right now," Hildegarde said.

She turned away from Quintana. He ran his hand down the curve of her bare hip. He didn't answer her. He knew the Queen was not with Talib. He knew the Queen despised her husband. Or, at the very least, she did not particularly care for him. Quintana doubted they had sex any more, even on a day like today. Besides, her Green Man consort hadn't been Talib. Quintana had not recognized the man's shape, but he could tell it was not Talib. Maybe it was that soothsayer, Fan. He didn't know or care.

"I dreamed of fire again last night," Hildegarde said.

"I did, too," Quintana said.

She turned to him. "You dream? I didn't know soothsayers dream."

"Yes," he said. "I dream, and I fuck. Just like a regular person."

She reached down and grabbed his penis. It was already hard again.

"You are not like any regular person," she said. "Certainly not like any regular man. I can't believe you are ready to go again."

"It's you," Quintana whispered, pulling her closer. "I can't get enough of you."

"All right," Hildegarde said. "I guess I can go again. What else do I have to do?"

"Oh, you're such a romantic," Quintana said. "It leaves me breathless." He grabbed her and pulled her on top of him.

"Plow my vulva, consort," Hildegarde said. "Plow my vulva."

Quintana said, "I will. I am the gardener, after all."

CHAPTER TWENTY-TWO

NEHEMIAH

Nehemiah felt uneasy. Something about the day was off, although he did not know what it was. He stood amid the crowd, watching the Queen call for her consort. As she cried, "Let the singer weave into song," Nehemiah let his mind wander through the Nexus, the public one and the one just for soothsayers. He did not detect any kind of anomaly. No reports of uprisings or violence, which was what he feared. He had been hearing more reports of rebels in the Low Mountains. He was not clear on their agenda. No one he knew was. But all seemed quiet in the Consolidated Five, even in the Low Mountains.

Except it wasn't.

It was almost as if someone were blocking him. Only that wasn't possible. Ever since the Reconciliation, the soothsayers communicated freely with one another and did not hide their activities from the humans or each other. For the most part. Some soothsayers kept sexual encounters with humans to themselves. It wasn't illegal, but it was not something anyone encouraged, either the soothsayers or humans. It just happened sometimes.

In any case, Nehemiah wished he could feel more easy about the day.

"What is it?" One of the other soothsayers found him tripping around Nexus. "How go things in the Queendom?"

Nehemiah recognized the pattern.

"Gloria Stone," he whispered in his head and out loud.

She didn't say anything. No doubt waiting for an answer to her question.

"Something does not feel right," he said.

"The economy?" she asked.

"I don't know," he said.

"Sounds vague," she said.

"It feels secretive," Nehemiah said. "I wonder if someone is trying to sabotage the Queendom."

"Who would do that?" Stone asked. She seemed to be asking herself rather than Nehemiah.

"I don't know," he said.

"If you have anything more specific, let me know."

Then she was gone. She left no trace behind. He had heard rumors no one could travel the Nexus as invisibly as Gloria Stone. Now he could see the rumors were true.

Nehemiah tried to retrace his steps on Nexus, too, in the hopes that no one else would wonder about his wanderings.

Reina cried out, "Who will plow my vulva?"

Nehemiah mumbled, "I, your consort, will plow your vulva."

Nehemiah's eyes widened. The crowd was silent, waiting for the consort's answer. He looked around. No one was paying him any heed, so either no one noticed or they assumed he was only reciting well-memorized lines, like singing along to a song.

Only he hadn't been. As he watched the Queen, he felt a sudden rush of something. Affection?

Naturally he had affection for her.

This was different.

This felt like longing.

Horrified, Nehemiah turned away and walked to the back of the crowd. He kept walking until he could no longer hear Reina's voice.

The longing was still there. He felt mildly anxious that he could not see her. He scanned the crowd for Elata, but he couldn't find her. He searched for her on the Nexus, but she did not respond to his calls. He got out quickly so no one would detect his stress.

He walked to the path that led into the forest, anxious to get far from any humans. On this day especially, they were everywhere—and mating everywhere. He got off the path and went deeper into the forest. He didn't notice the old trees, hear any birds, smell the dryness. He kept walking until he realized he had travelled in an arc and was heading back toward the Hearth. He stopped, breathed deeply, listened to his heart beat.

He closed his eyes and meditated for a while as he stood in the forest.

When he opened his eyes, his stomach felt nervous. What did the humans say? They had butterflies in their stomach. Yes, that was what it felt like. He did a quick and dirty diagnostic on himself. All came up normal. He still felt that strange block. He couldn't explain it, even to himself. It almost felt like it did when he put a finger in one ear. That kind of block, only it was in his brain.

He sighed and looked around. In the near distance he saw a man standing by the Queen's fence, the fence that wrapped part of the forest and her garden in a loose barrier to discourage strangers from heading into it. It was an attempt to give the Queen and her family some privacy. It wasn't meant to seriously stop anyone.

Nehemiah briefly wondered who the man was, but he decided he didn't care enough to find out. He looked like he was guarding the fence, which was odd. The Queendom did not have guards, not here, at least. At the border between the Queendom and the Hinterlands, they had guards, but they didn't look like this man. He wasn't in uniform, but he stood as though he was a military man. How could that be?

Nehemiah jumped over the fence in a way that prevented the man from seeing him. Some soothsayers were good at stealth. Some were not. Nehemiah prided himself on being a true mage, if pride was the right word.

He wanted to be able to do anything he could to be of service to the Queendom—and to the Queen. So he practiced his physical skills. He studied the ancients. He watched and kept track of anyone who came and went from the Hearth. He noticed everything. Or tried to.

And he had never noticed he had any attraction to the Queen. He was present at her birth. He had watched her grow into a woman and then into the Queen. He had great fondness for her, an affection even. But he had never been sexually attracted to her. That would be absurd. Even wrong. One had to observe a code of behavior if one worked with the First Family. Especially if one worked as closely with them as he did. His opinions, his advice, had to be clear and unbiased.

He glanced back at the man. He had not moved, had not noticed any stirring in his environment. Where could such a man come from?

Nehemiah strode through the forest, moving as swiftly as a deer. He took care not to step on any branches or dead leaves. He did not want to warn animal or person that he was about. The Douglas firs rose above him like the old giants they were. They hadn't existed longer than he had, yet he still thought of them as his elders. Maybe because he knew some species of trees were older than he was, older than any soothsayer. He liked to imagine that some creature on this planet had more experience and wisdom then he did. Most of the time he felt like he knew the answers to life's mysteries. On the days he didn't, he liked being with the trees.

Nehemiah sighed as he walked. If he had feelings for Reina, that would make him no better than Quintana. He had known Quintana for nearly as long as he could remember, and he did not approve of his assignations with Hildegarde. Their relationship was unseemly. When it first began, it had almost toppled the Queendom. It could have easily done so.

The people expected the Queen to marry and have children. That was how it had been since the first Reconciliation. Not every queen or chief had children, it was true. But they did marry. The humans had brought back the covenant of marriage to promote stability for the nation. It was no longer about property or one person having dominion over another. It was a public commitment to family and country: As a couple they commit to instilling the values of the Queendom into their children.

Nehemiah assumed some human somewhere must have married a soothsayer, and some soothsayer had married another, he knew, but it wasn't common. And it seemed beside the point. Soothsayers could not reproduce. Hildegarde had wanted to marry Quintana. She said she would still have children, they just wouldn't be Quintana's. She had been queen, but she had begged her mother, Nehemiah, and all of her advisors to allow the marriage.

In the end, they did not have to act. Hildegarde resigned to be with Quintana, to create a life with him where she wouldn't have to worry about what the public thought about her choices. And then Quintana refused to leave with her. His home was at the Hearth.

So Hildegarde had left, and Reina became queen.

Reina.

Nehemiah caught a whiff of the Queen. He stopped and sniffed. Yes. She was near. He tried to turn down his sense of smell, but that did not seem to work. He still smelled her.

Like dogs of old, he felt he had to follow the scent.

He walked a ways until he heard two voices. One of them was the Queen's. He didn't know who the other person was. Male. Vaguely familiar.

He walked slowly forward. In the near distance, he could see a spot of light coming through an opening in the trees. He stopped when he realized he was looking at a bed in the forest with two people on it.

He heard laughter. He moved forward again, slightly, and pressed himself up against a tree. The Queen and her companion were nearly naked. The man wore the Green Man's mask. The Queen's bare legs were open and up around the man who was pushing himself into her. Nehemiah could clearly hear their grunts and groans.

He knew he should turn away. He knew he should run away.

Especially because he felt aroused.

Who was the man who would dare have sex with the Queen on this sacred day? It couldn't be Talib. The Queen hadn't had relations with Talib in years, at least, not to Nehemiah's knowledge. Could it be Fan?

Nehemiah felt angry that he didn't know.

As the Queen cried out in pleasure, Nehemiah could barely contain himself. He wanted to run to her. He had never felt desire like this.

"Turn away," Nehemiah whispered. "This is wrong. Turn away."

Suddenly the man arched his back. He reached up and flung off his mask.

Nehemiah saw him, recognized him.

Outram, the Premier of Berland.

The Queen laughed.

Nehemiah turned and ran away.

He could hardly believe what he had seen.

Not Outram. Nehemiah did not trust him.

Why did humans keep going back into relationships which did not bring them happiness?

He turned off his smell completely, and then he began to run. Whatever he was feeling, it was not natural. It was foul, and he would figure out a way to stop it.

Chapter Twenty-three
Raphael

Raphael walked quietly down the hillside, creating his own course through the brush as he headed for the saffron fields. He used the dim light of the near-distant warehouse to help him find his way. He could hear the celebrations coming from outside the Hearth, above, and from the Queen's Village, off to his right. The moon was above the village, no doubt, and would soon light up this path. Raphael did not want that.

Lately, Raphael loved the darkness. He sought it out. When it was night, when he was in the dark, the humming did not feel so pronounced. The humming, the dizziness, the anxiousness: whatever it was. He didn't know. The healer didn't know. The cosmos didn't seem to know. He only knew he did not feel right, and he hadn't for a long while.

He didn't like to think about it. Didn't like to acknowledge it.

If he found the Moonstruck Saffron all would be well. He would settle down. The humming would abate. The feeling that everything was off-balance would disappear. It was as if he were constantly at sea—and he hadn't gotten his sea legs yet. Maybe he never would.

Soon, he and Teng would search in the Lows for the Moonstruck Saffron. He was hopeful.

And he was desperate.

Teng seemed desperate, too. Raphael didn't know why. She wanted the reward, she said. But she had everything she needed. Her life would not be substantially different whether they found the Moonstruck Saffron or not. Unless the Queendom went bankrupt. Then, they would all be in trouble. The Consolidated Five would take over. The Villanuevas would be run out of office. The Queendom would be under the thumb of another country.

Tonight, Raphael realized the Queendom could no longer wait for someone to discover the Moonstruck Saffron. For one thing, the plant could be a myth. For another, the Queendom was in dire financial straits.

Raphael wanted to help, but no one believed he could do anything. No one had any respect for him, and he was tired of it. Maybe his father, sister, mother were right. Maybe he wasn't good at anything. It wasn't his fault. He was born useless.

He tripped over a bush, almost fell, and steadied himself.

No. He wasn't useless. He just didn't feel passionately about anything. Wasn't any kind of job or work that interested him. He had never even fallen in love. For a time, he had liked the attention he got because he was Raphael Villanueva. He liked being the face of the carefree but hardworking family.

He paused and listened. He had to be especially careful now. He couldn't let anyone see him. He had left a message for his mother, Teng, and the others that he was on his way to the Low Mountains. He wanted everyone to believe he was far from here.

When he heard nothing nearby except crickets rubbing elbows, he kept walking. No one thought of him as Nature boy, he knew, but he could get around in the forest—in the great outdoors—as well as most anyone.

And at this moment, he was filled with a sense of purpose for the first time in his life.

At first he had been disappointed when Boann had told him she wasn't coming to the May Day festivities. They had hit it off so well when she visited during the Summit. He had thought about starting a relationship with her. He had envisioned them getting married and becoming joint rulers of Berland and the Queendom.

He had laughed at himself for entertaining this fantasy. Still he had enjoyed thinking of Boann. But once she said she couldn't come, or wouldn't come, he was glad. Her absence freed him to implement his plan to save them all.

He reached the warehouse and went inside. The auto lights flickered on as he walked through the building. He wished he could stop them from turning on, but he had no idea how.

He called, "Anyone here?"

No one answered.

When he was certain the place was deserted, he left the warehouse and walked into the saffron fields. He stopped and took a deep breath. He smiled. The plants smelled slightly of the sea and honey, sweet and salty as they breathed out sunlight.

He pressed his lips together and kept walking to the other side of the field. The air was slightly cool. He could feel storm clouds above. It wouldn't be too long before it rained, he was certain. It hadn't rained in weeks. In months, actually. Perhaps tonight the drought would end.

But first he must do this. He would prove to his mother and father that he was capable of taking decisive effective action. He did understand the economy. The price of Safran Bleu was too low because the market was glutted with it. If there was less Safran Bleu on the market, people would then be willing to pay a premium price. Then the Queendom would be economically whole again.

It seemed simple enough.

In the distance, lightning streaked across the sky.

Raphael smiled. Good. All was working in his favor—and in the favor to his country.

When he got to the end of the field, Raphael retrieved a long box of matches from his front pocket. Then he crouched in the dirt and pulled out one of the long wooden matches and scratched it along the side of the box. The flame caught with a hiss. Raphael held his breath for a moment, feeling a rush of excitement.

"I ask that the sacred saffron plant understand what I am doing," he whispered. "I ask that the mother plant of all the saffron bless this deed. I do it for the good of all. May your sacrifice bring about prosperity. Fire, you are my tool. You are my weapon of good. Make it right."

Raphael held the fire down under a saffron plant until the fire caught. Soon flames leapt out and caught several other saffron plants on fire. He moved around the field and set several plants on fire in one area. By doing this, he hoped if anyone investigated, it would look like lightning had started it.

The fire spread rapidly, leaping from plant to plant, like some kind of demented circus act. Raphael stepped back, away from the field. He knew he should get far away, but he couldn't help but watch. The fire looked strangely geometrical as it went down the rows. In some places, the growers had let the saffron run wild through the fields, but here they were planted in rows. It made for a strangely neat and tidy fire. At least at first.

In the distance, Raphael saw lightning again and heard thunder. At the same time, the fire leaped up and caught a branch of an oak tree. It almost instantly exploded into flames. Raphael felt a knot in his stomach.

That wasn't supposed to happen. He hadn't even realized that tree was there.

The fire raced across the field in a matter of seconds and headed for the warehouse.

The fire was not stopping at the edge of the field as he thought it would. It was moving so fast. Raphael didn't understand. He had seen wild fires before, when he was in the Service. Those fires had moved slowly across the land. They had easily put them out.

Except no one was here to put this one out.

He was going to have to do it. He would tell his mother he happened by and saw it. So he did what he could and saved the day.

Raphael ran toward the warehouse. He realized he didn't know where the faucet was. Didn't even know if they had any kind of hose or contraption to pump or move water.

The fire was spreading to the next field of saffron. A breeze stirred the cottonwoods around the warehouse, and Raphael saw the fire shift, move, come alive as though it had been asleep before and now it was truly awake.

Raphael froze. He couldn't think. He had been so certain the fire would fix everything. He had been so certain he had been led to this solution to the Queendom's problems.

Led by whom? A crazy god he didn't even believe in?

He suddenly heard shouts. "Fire!" someone cried.

Raphael couldn't see anyone, but he heard them coming.

He turned around and ran. His life was over if he was caught. He couldn't do anything now to help. If anyone in the Queendom found out he had started the fire, the scandal could bring down his mother's government.

He stumbled and fell into someone coming in the opposite direction. They both moaned and scrambled out of the other person's way. Raphael thought he saw the whites of someone's eyes, but then they were gone—whoever they were. He hesitated, wondering what to do. What if that person had seen him better than he saw that person? What if the person recognized him? Recognized the Queen's son running away from a fire.

He shook his head. Nothing he could do about that now. He had to get away, far away, before anyone at the Hearth found out about the fire.

Behind him, he heard the fire roaring and crackling—and people shouting. He couldn't think about what he'd done. He couldn't think about how it had all gone wrong. Later, he would make amends. Later, he would confess and ask for forgiveness, if he had to.

He heard more people coming to fight the fire. He was never going to get away—at least not far enough away. Perhaps he could turn around now and run with the others to fight the fire. He could tell his mother he had been in the village when he heard shouts.

He pressed on up the hill.

No, it wasn't smart to lie about something like this. Someone might check—and he didn't know if the shouts could be heard from town. He looked up the hill. If he did it just right and timed it just right, he could go up one of Lorelei's hidden pathways, get into the Hearth from the back way, and go to his room. Later, he'd tell his mother he had changed his mind about going away. She would believe that. It confirmed her view of him as the constant screwup and layabout.

The moon was up now, and Raphael could clearly see the way. It also meant someone could see him. He was glad now he had disguised himself in black. And he wore a black cap over his blond hair.

Maybe he wasn't as stupid as everyone believed him to be.

He glanced back at the fire that was racing across the land.

It looked out of control.

Maybe he was stupider than they believed him to be.

The climb was steep, and he lost the path once or twice, but he finally came to the Hearth. He sprinted through the gardens and opened the back door and went inside. He pressed his back against the door and tried to catch his breath. He heard no other sounds besides his own breathing. Maybe no one else was there yet. He ran down the hall and up the stairs. He went up Lorelei's steps to the third floor. So far, he had not encountered another being.

When he got to the third floor, he glanced at his torn and dirty clothes. His arms were scratched. He could only imagine what his face looked like. But he had made it. No one had seen him. He would take a shower and then go to bed. No one would be the wiser.

And then Lorelei was standing in his path. Where had she come from? She stared at him but didn't say a word. His stomach lurched.

He put his finger on his lips. "Please don't say anything," he whispered.

Lorelei watched him. He could not tell what she was thinking or what she would do.

He opened the door to his apartment—glanced back at Lorelei—then stepped inside and closed the door firmly behind him.

CHAPTER TWENTY-FOUR
REINA

Reina was a little giddy as she sat in her office. She closed her eyes and imagined Outram's fingers on her again. She could almost feel the bed beneath her, the sky above her, could almost taste the forest and Outram.

But Outram had left when it began to turn twilight, after he walked Reina to her garden gate and kissed her one last time. Then he donned his mask and ran into the forest. She could see the muscles in his legs rippling as he ran. She had almost called him back.

But she hadn't.

She went into her garden and through the back door to her office. And then she had walked down the corridor and flung the front door to the Hearth open, letting her family and her staff—and anyone else who was paying attention—know that the deed was done, the ceremony and ritual complete. They could come home.

She had returned to her office with the intention of looking up figures and summaries of the last quarter. She couldn't make herself do it. She wanted to be back in the forest. It felt wrong to be in her office. Everything felt wrong.

Especially the way they were running the Queendom.

When the Fall happened, when the busidoms crumbled and they were wrenched finally and fatally from power, those who were left vowed to create a new and better world. Gloria Stone, the greatest webster and soothsayer of all time, had helped them shape a world that was saner, fairer, and more livable: She orchestrated the Reconnection and Reconciliation.

Yet over the years they had crept back to an economic model that wasn't working. They even still called themselves busidoms, ostensibly to prevent them from ever forgetting their history.

Instead, Reina feared, they were repeating it. They had been running their country like a business. They had to sell so many goods to so many people or the business, and therefore the Queendom, would fall. It was a model designed to fail, designed to create the haves and have nots. She hadn't been able to see it before, but now it seemed so clear. They should have been producing enough goods to provide for themselves so that they would never have to depend upon another country.

She rubbed her face. In theory, she supposed, that was a fine idea. It seldom worked in reality.

The Queendom did not produce much of the stuff of modern life. They grew food enough for their people. They had art and culture. They had the Safran Bleu to export. But they didn't create building materials like the Berlanders did. They didn't take care of the soothsayers like Paquay State did.

It had worked for so long that none of the Queens had ever questioned it. Or if they had, it was lost in time.

Reina still was not certain what had caused the economy to list. She only knew they had to get it back on track. After the May Day festivities, she was certain all would be well. She had had contact with most of the Queen's Advisors in each of the regions, and all reported an increase in sales.

Still, she should probably talk to someone she trusted on the subject. Her mother advised her as best as she could, but she had relied heavily on Nehemiah when she was queen, just as Reina did. Economics was not their strong suit. Reina didn't know if it was anyone's strong suit.

Perhaps they should go back to the trade and barter system that had been in place before the Reconciliation. They had not prospered, but they had lived good lives, decent lives.

Reina looked out her open door into the garden that was invisible in the night. It was time to go to bed. She had hoped to see her family before she went to sleep. She got up and stretched.

The door opened, and Nehemiah stepped into the room without knocking.

"Your Majesty, the saffron fields near the village are on fire," Nehemiah said.

"What?"

A live image of the fire appeared and hung in the air between the Queen and Nehemiah. "That's south of us. Three other fields in other parts of the country are on fire, too," he said.

"Is our country being attacked?"

"We don't know," Nehemiah said. "We've had reports of thunderstorms all over the country today. Maybe because it's so dry, lightning strikes started several fires."

"In the middle of our saffron fields?" the Queen asked. "I doubt it. Have the fire brigades been called out?"

"Yes, Ma'am," he said. "There's more. The wind shifted, and the fire is coming up the hill. We may need to evacuate the Hearth."

"Way to bury the lead, Nehemiah," the Queen said. "Sound the alarm. Alert the rest of the Consolidated Five."

Reina came into the hall as the alarms began ringing. Three rings, silence, three rings again. Everyone knew that meant fire.

Elata came running down the hall toward her.

"Make certain my children are accounted for," Reina said. "I'm going to see if the fire brigade needs me."

Minutes later, Reina was up on the ridge. Many of the villagers were there, too, waiting for instructions. Reina could see the fire in the saffron fields and smell the smoke, but the land was so steep from here she couldn't tell the fire was spreading uphill.

Savi was in charge of the Hearth fire brigade. "We need to widen the fire break," she shouted. "Grab shovels and picks and follow Minerva."

Reina did as Savi instructed. She felt relief in following someone else's orders. Soon most of her family and all of the staff were helping. Hildegarde arrived, along with Quintana. Lorelei and Raphael dug right into the work. They all knew how to widen a fire break.

"We worked on this last month," Savi told Reina as they dug in the dirt in the wind and darkness, "because of the drought. We should set a backfire, now that the wind has shifted again a bit."

"Do whatever you think is right," Reina said.

Umberto came over to Reina and asked, "Do you want us to move anything out of the house for safekeeping?"

Reina turned to Savi. "Should we get anything of value out of the house?"

"We won't know for a couple of hours," Savi said. "We could stop it, or the entire countryside could go up in smoke."

Savi moved away. She and Minerva huddled together with several other firefighters.

Reina stood with Nehemiah—who had taken off his robes and now stood beside her in a T-shirt and slacks. Umberto stayed with them.

"Put the valuables in one of the buses," Reina said to Umberto. "But don't leave unless it looks like the fire will overtake the house."

Umberto motioned to Billy, Abbygail, and Teng to follow him.

Raphael was suddenly next to her.

"They're taking valuables out of the house?" he asked. "The fire is coming to the Hearth?"

Reina put her hand on her son's shoulder. "We don't know yet. I'm glad you decided to stay home. You've been a great help."

"I'll do anything," Raphael said.

"I know, son," Reina said. "Be careful."

Raphael nodded and walked over to his sister and Savi.

Nehemiah said, "We should get you out of harm's way. You are more important alive and well, no matter what happens."

"It is important for the people to see me out with them," the

Queen said, "so they understand I am one of them, no better, no worse. When this is done, I'm not even certain the Queendom will be left standing. I don't know what we'll do. So I will stay here and do what I can. You can run the rest as you see fit, Nehemiah. I trust you." She squeezed his arm.

"Ma'am, I—I think I might be ill."

"What are you saying?" Reina wasn't sure she had understood him, given the chaos of the evening: people shouting, the world burning, water spraying.

"I need to go away," he said.

"Now?" Reina said. "Our country is burning down."

"Not this instant," he said.

"If you're sick, go to a healer," she said. "Or heal yourself. Do a self-diagnosis. Do something, because you can't leave me now. I need you."

Savi was motioning to her.

"Let's talk about this later," Reina said. "Right now, we need to save the world."

"Yes, Ma'am," Nehemiah said.

Reina instantly forgot about Nehemiah and anything except the fire as she went over to Savi. They had to stop it somehow, before it reached the Hearth. If the Hearth went, she was certain, the Queendom would never survive.

"We're gonna set the backfire," Minerva said. "Do you want to start it? For the symbolism of it?" Minerva's face was black with darkness and dirt.

Reina couldn't help but laugh. "No," she said. "Give that honor to whomever is the most qualified. And say a blessing to the fire spirits. It couldn't hurt."

Minerva nodded. Then she and Savi and the others stepped into the darkness. Reina watched them go. She stood alone for a moment listening to the sound of the fire coming nearer.

"Oh my ancestors," Reina whispered. "If you're listening, now is the time to do us a favor. Call off the dogs of fire and failure. The Queendom could use some good news."

CHAPTER TWENTY-FIVE
LORELEI

Lorelei curled up on the couch in the sitting room, near her mother and sister. Raphael sat across from them, next to the open window. The night was giving way to dawn. Outside the trees were gray, with a touch of pink.

The house smelled of smoke.

"Close the house up," Reina said. She was talking to Umberto, Lorelei assumed, but Lorelei couldn't see him. "Turn on the air cleaners. We need to get this smoke cleared out."

"Yes, Ma'am," Umberto said. Lorelei looked behind her. There he was.

Savi and Minerva sat in chairs next to one another. Quintana and Nehemiah were in the room, too. Hildegarde stood in the corner, behind the Queen Madre's chair, in near darkness.

Poppie said, "Where is that father of yours?"

Everyone knew he meant Talib, and no one answered him.

Lorelei glanced at Quintana, but he didn't look at her. She was sorry she had embarrassed him earlier in the day by asking him to determine who her biological father was. She hoped she hadn't damaged their relationship. At the same time, she was glad she knew the truth.

A kind of truth, she supposed. She didn't understand how it had happened or why or even if her father—if Talib—knew the truth.

Didn't matter. None of it mattered. Tonight the Hearth had almost caught fire, and part of the Queendom had burned. Four fires in one night pointed to arson, and that was terrifying. And strange. Who would want to hurt the Queendom? Lorelei looked down at her hands. She hoped it wasn't the man in black and the others in the Queen's Court. She would be crushed if someone had done something like this because they thought it would benefit her in some way.

Billy and Abbygail—looking a little more ragged than usual—came into the room carrying trays. Teng followed them. Billy and Abbygail handed around steaming cups to everyone. Billy winked at Lorelei when he held out a cup for her.

Reina said, "Thank you so much. Thank you, all of you, but you have worked harder than any of us. We didn't expect you to cook or to wait on us!"

"It's a soothing broth," Teng said, "created with ingredients that, according to the Unified Field Theory of Spices, should bring you restoration and sweet dreams. Tomorrow is another day, and we could all use the rest."

"Indeed," Reina said. "Thank you so much. Umberto, please see that the staff takes off part of the day tomorrow. We can eat leftovers. And now, all of you, go get some rest. We saved the country tonight. You should all feel proud."

"We couldn't have done it without you, Ma'am," Teng said. "We looked to you and your family for the strength to do it. Thank you."

"Come now," Umberto said.

Quintana said, "I'll go down to the fields tomorrow and see if I can lend a hand."

"Thank you, Quintana," Reina said.

He stood, nodded to them, and then left with the other servants. Lorelei looked toward her aunt, but she couldn't see her face clearly in the near darkness.

The family sat quietly for several minutes, sipping their broth. Outside, as the sun rose, birds began singing. For a moment, everything felt normal.

Reina said, "We should all get some rest." She stood. Everyone else rose from their seats. One by one, they went to the Queen.

Minerva kissed her mother. Savi shook the Queen's hand and kissed her check.

"You both did a fine job," Reina said.

Poppie and the Queen Madre kissed Reina and Lorelei.

"And you," the Queen Madre said, pointing to Raphael. "You did the Villanuevas proud tonight. You helped save home and hearth." Then they were gone.

Hildegarde passed by her sister and stood on the threshold leading into the hall.

"I'm so sorry this happened," Hildegarde said. "Let me know if I can help."

"What will help now is to know who did it," Reina said. "So we can know it won't happen again."

"I didn't do it," Hildegarde said.

"It never occurred to me that you did," Reina said.

Hildegarde raised an eyebrow. "At least you can check off one person from the maybe guilty list."

"There is one thing you could do, Hildy," Reina said. "Some of the fields burned are near Jeremy's place. Why don't you travel out there and see how it's going? Determine whether they need the government's help in any way. Help people get on their feet. The fires are out. Thank heavens. None of them traveled to the woods, except this one, and this one should be out by tomorrow. That's what Savi says. She's the expert. Yes, that would help the busidom. If you go to Jeremy's. Can you do that for us?"

"Of course, my queen," Hildegarde said. "I'll leave when I get up."

"Thank you."

Then she was gone.

"Nehemiah," Reina said, "you should get some rest, too. I am going to bed."

"May I walk you up to your room?" he asked. "I have some things to discuss."

"Can it wait?" Reina asked. "I've never been so tired."

"Yes, it can wait."

"If it's about that other thing," Reina said. "You go take care of yourself if you're sick. Do whatever you need. We will be fine."

Nehemiah didn't say anything at first. Lorelei had never seen Nehemiah hesitate about anything. She had never seen him out of his robes before tonight. He looked bigger, stronger. She could see the muscles in his arms as he moved his hands as if to say something.

He appeared to be speechless.

Finally, he followed Reina to the entrance of the room. "It can wait," was all he said.

Nehemiah went by the Queen and disappeared from Lorelei's view.

Reina looked at Lorelei and Raphael.

"You both did yourselves proud tonight," she said.

"I'm glad the alarm woke me," Raphael said. "I could have slept through the whole thing."

Lorelei looked at him. What was he talking about? She had seen him wide awake only minutes before the alarm sounded.

"Raphael," the Queen said, "if you and Teng are still looking for the Moonstruck Saffron, now would be the time to find it. Nearly our entire crop of saffron was destroyed. We are unofficially broke. Goodnight."

Reina went into the corridor. Lorelei listened to the sound of her footsteps fade away.

Lorelei and Raphael sat alone, on opposite sides of the room. Outside, the light was golden. Inside, the room pulsed with tension.

"Whatever you think you know," Raphael said, "you know nothing."

"So you have believed my entire life," Lorelei said.

"Not true," Raphael said.

His voice sounded squeaky. That usually meant he was lying.

"I was the one in the family who always believed you would come into your own one day," he said. "And I was right."

Lorelei rolled her eyes. "Brother, you don't believe in anyone or anything."

Raphael got up, walked over to the couch, and sat next to Lorelei. She scooted away from him.

"You may be right," Raphael said. "But I'm different now. I've changed. I had an epiphany tonight. I realized I don't know what I'm doing. I know I have to make it up to the family, to the Queendom."

"What do you mean you have to make it up to the family?" Lorelei said. Her eyes narrowed as she looked at her brother.

"For not living up to the family name," he said. "For being who I am."

"You can be yourself," Lorelei said, "but don't be so nasty or cynical. You're always conniving."

"What you call conniving, I call problem-solving." He grinned. His voice was back to normal. Lorelei knew that meant he thought he had fooled her about something.

Raphael got up. He looked almost happy.

"You know the Queendom is ruined now," Lorelei said. "You understand that, right?"

"Yes I understand that," he snapped, his grin gone. "*I'm* not the idiot in the family."

Lorelei sucked in her breath. He heard it, he knew he had hurt her. Regret flashed across his face. For only a second.

He finally said, "We'll be OK, baby sister. No need to worry. Teng and I will find the Moonstruck Saffron, and then all will be well."

Raphael stepped nearer to her. She thought he was going to lean down and kiss the top of her head like he had done a thousand times before.

Lorelei moved back, away from him, and looked up. "What is it that you've done, brother?"

"Done?" He laughed. "Nothing. Don't you see? That's the point. I want to do something. And I will. Good night, little one. Or should I say, good morning?" He smiled and then sauntered out of the room.

Lorelei sat by herself for a few minutes. The silence throbbed in her ears.

Something was not right.

Why had Raphael not wanted her to see him earlier in the evening? Why had he lied about being asleep before the fire alarm?

Her chest felt tight, and her stomach hurt.

She left the room, headed down the hall, then went down the stairs to the kitchen. She could hear the staff in their dining room laughing and talking. She went by them, not wanting to talk to anyone, but then she heard Billy say something, and she stopped and listened.

"We wanted to let you all know, since you're our friends," he was saying, "that Abbygail and I have decided to get married."

At first no one said anything. Lorelei pressed herself up against the wall, in case anyone came around the corner.

"Someone say something!" Abbygail said.

"Congratulations!" Wanda said.

"Yes," Teng said. "Congratulations. It's wonderful. When and where, *and* can I cook for this great occasion?"

"We don't know those details yet," Abbygail said. "We decided today."

"I hope the Queen will let us get married here," Billy said.

"I am very happy for you two," Umberto said. "You seem quite compatible. But marriage? Isn't that a little unusual for soothsayers. Should we consult the Queen in this matter?"

"Certainly not," Wanda said. "They have every right."

"We'll make it a great feast," Teng said. "Will it be after Miss Minerva gets married or before?"

Lorelei heard someone's chair scrape across the floor, so she rushed away, down the hall toward the laundry room. Once inside she walked to the bin beneath the laundry chute. Everyone's laundry eventually ended in this bin.

It was as tall as she was, and she couldn't really see inside. She looked around for a chair, found one, and dragged it to the chute. She got on it and looked down into the bin.

It was halfway filled with towels and sheets. It looked like no one had sent their fire clothes down the chute yet. Amongst the towels was a black shirt and a black pair of pants: exactly what Raphael had been wearing when she had spotted him earlier, before she knew about the fire.

Lorelei reached into the bin and pulled out the slacks and shirt.

They reeked of smoke.

Something fell out of the pocket of the pants and clattered onto the floor.

Lorelei got off the chair and bent down to pick it up.

It was a long box of matches.

She heard someone coming down the hallway.

She tried to push the matches into her pant pocket, but the box was too big. She stuffed them back into one of the pockets on her brother's slacks. She hopped on the chair again, leaned into the laundry and grabbed a pillowcase. She jumped down and quickly pushed her brother's smoky clothes into the pillow case. She had just finished when Turnkey came into the room carrying a pile of clothes in his arms.

Lorelei breathed a sigh of relief.

"Hello, Turnkey," she said.

"Hello, Miss Lorelei," he said. "Can I help you with something?"

She shook her head. "No, no. I dropped something down the chute, on mistake. Came to get it. Didn't want to bother anyone."

"That's why we're here," he said. He dropped his clothes into the bin.

"You're here to be bothered by us?"

Turnkey laughed. "If you say so. I saw you out with us on the fire line. I thought that was very brave."

"You, too," Lorelei said. "I saw you. I guess we were all brave."

"Sure," Turnkey said, "except the person who started the fires."

"Maybe it was lightning," Lorelei said. "Although I guess that would be pretty coincidental, given there were four fires."

"Can I—can I do anything for you?" Turnkey asked again.

Lorelei looked at him. He was such a kind person.

"No," she said. "I better get going." She started to walk away, but then she stopped and looked at him. "It's always nice to see you, Turnkey. It never seems like you're up to anything."

Turnkey laughed.

"I didn't mean it that way," Lorelei said. "I meant you aren't devious. It doesn't seem like you're trying to get anything from me."

He shrugged. "I hope I'm not devious," he said. "But I am trying to get something from you, I suppose. I like you. I like that you see things the rest of us can't. Or don't. You're unusual."

"Unusual like a freak?" She bit her lip. She hoped she didn't found like she was feeling sorry for herself.

"I was called a freak when I was a kid," he said.

Lorelei put the pillowcase behind her back, in case the smell of smoke from Raphael's clothes wafted through the pillowcase. Then she realized she still had on the clothes she'd worn while fighting the fire. Turnkey would not notice.

He motioned to the chairs around a rickety folding table.

"Would you like to sit and talk?" he asked.

She looked at the chairs. "Yes, we can talk, but I don't like sitting in chairs in front of people. I'm an adult, or close enough, and when I sit in chairs like that, my feet dangle like they did when I was a child. I feel ridiculous."

"Has anyone ever suggested making you a footrest?" he asked. "A small wooden foot stool would be lovely and inconspicuous."

Lorelei smiled. "No one has every suggested it, no. That would mean we would have to bring up the fact that I'm not normal size, and that would make everyone so uncomfortable."

"We can stand," he said.

"Why did anyone ever call you a freak?" Lorelei asked. "You look completely normal."

"I didn't talk for the first ten years of my life," he said.

Lorelei's eyes widened. "Really? I barely talked to anyone for years. Then I talked to my mother. Recently I've become more talkative."

"They thought I was stupid," he said. "Or deficient. But not talking was freeing in so many ways."

"Yes!" Lorelei said. They stood only feet from one another with Lorelei's chin up as she looked at him. "People were always staring at me, you know, because of this. Because of my height. But after a while, when I didn't speak, they stopped staring. They stopped paying any attention to me. And I heard and saw so many things."

"Yes," Turnkey said. "And people would tell me things. They thought I wouldn't repeat it, I guess, since I didn't talk."

Lorelei nodded. "My brother used to tell me all kinds of horror stories. Nothing really terrible, but you know, kid stuff. He knew I wouldn't tell. When he hid something from someone. Or stole something—borrowed he called it. Things like that."

"Did you keep his secrets?" Turnkey asked.

She nodded. "I don't know why," she said. "He wasn't particularly kind to me. But at least he talked to me. Minerva was kind, but I can't remember her ever really talking to me. And Raphael never did anything terrible." She shrugged. "He did stupid things. So when he told me where he'd hidden something, I would find it and put it back where it was supposed to be. And if he stole something, I found that and put it back."

"I didn't have any siblings," Turnkey said. "I missed that. Eventually I started talking, and the world changed. I'm not always sure it's been for the better."

"Well, I am glad you talk," Lorelei said. She smiled. "I better get back. Good-bye, Turnkey."

"Good-bye, Miss Lorelei."

Lorelei left the laundry room and went up the stairs to her rooms. Once inside, she locked the door.

She went into her closet, sat on the floor, and looked inside the pillow case again. What was she going to do with these clothes? She hadn't wanted anyone else to find the matches or suspect Raphael of starting the fire.

She took the matchbox out and put it in the bottom drawer of the small bureau in the closet. Then she stuffed the pillow case in another drawer. She'd decide what to do with them later.

She put her hand on the wall, and it began to glow. Words moved around the wall. She picked up a pen and wrote, "Today my brother tried to burn down the Queendom." She didn't know if that was true, actually. She reached up again, to cross it out or erase it. But she knew it was too late. It was always too late. Once she wrote it on the wall, it was there forever. Wherever there was.

She wrote, "Maybe my brother didn't start the fire."

She had no idea what to do next.

"Sleep," the walls seemed to whisper to her.

She nodded. Yes, she would sleep. Maybe an answer would come to her in her dreams.

PART FOUR
INTERLUDE

CHAPTER TWENTY-SIX
UMBERTO

Umberto stood in the corridor staring out of one of the front windows. At the edge of the woods, he could see a man in black sitting on the ground watching the Hearth.

"Billy!" Umberto called. He didn't say it loudly, but the house was nearly empty so his voice seemed to echo through three and a half relatively empty floors.

Billy was wiping his hands on his apron when he approached Umberto. Teng and Viva were traveling with Raphael and Lorelei, and Turnkey had volunteered to help in the fields. Billy and Abbygail had pitched in and were doing extra work around the Hearth. Even though it had been nearly three months since the fires, little had gotten back to normal. The Queen had been traveling with Minerva almost nonstop since the fires, pitching in where needed and giving pep talks along the way.

Umberto was looking forward to everyone being home again.

"What is it, Mr. Umberto?" Billy asked.

Umberto nodded to the window. Billy looked out.

"That's him," Billy said. "That's the same bloke I saw on May Day."

"Mr. Santos," Umberto said, "what have I told you about your use of language?"

"That isn't a curse word, Mr. Umberto," he said. "It's another word for man. It's a way of exercising my mind. I'm going to be a married man, and I want to be brilliant for my bride."

Umberto cleared his throat. What was he to say to that?

"Looks like he's leaving," Billy said.

They watched the man get off the ground.

"I want you to follow him," Umberto said. "See where he goes and who he talks to."

"Mr. Umberto," Billy said, "you are a much wiser man than I will ever be, but I can't spy on a human being. It's against the law."

"I wasn't asking you to spy. Follow him and tell me where he goes."

Billy raised an eyebrow and looked at Umberto.

"The Queen and Nehemiah are traveling," Umberto said, "and I feel a responsibility to protect the Hearth. I need to know what he wants."

"Why don't you ask him?" Billy said.

The man in black had stepped on the path and was moving away from the building.

"Hurry!" Umberto said. "Bring him here and I'll ask him."

"Against his will?" Billy asked. "I can't do that either."

"Then make it his will," Umberto said, waving Billy outside.

Billy opened the Hearth doors and then ran after the stranger. Once Billy caught up with him, Umberto could not hear what he was saying, but soon they both walked back to the house.

Umberto stepped outside and closed the Hearth doors behind him. The air was hot and dry, the sky clear. The Old Oak stood perfectly still.

"You can't hold me," the man said. "I've done nothing wrong."

"No one is holding you," Umberto said. "I am Mr. Umberto, and this is Mr. Santos. We work here. We have to be particularly careful these days, given the fires and other things. Mr. Santos found you inside the house where you were not invited or welcome on May Day, and now I've seen you watching the house several times. What is it you want? Maybe we can help you."

"It's the People's House," the man said.

"This is true," Umberto said, "and the Queen often invites citizens in, but it is also her home, and the home of her children. I ask you again, what is it you want? Would you like to be put on the list for the next tour?"

"Our organization is concerned about the Queen," he said. "So I'm watching out for her."

"Your organization?" Umberto asked.

"The Queen's Court," the man said. "It's a sort of admiration club."

Umberto glanced at Billy; he hoped he was checking his internal Nexus for any record of the Queen's Court.

"We are admirers of the Queen, too," Umberto said, stalling while Billy explored his memory and the shared knowledge of the soothsayers. Nehemiah would have had an answer nearly instantly. But he was a mage soothsayer. Billy was not.

"More than admirers I should say, mate," Billy said.

Umberto rolled his eyes.

"You want to change our system of government," Billy said.

"A revolution?" Umberto said. "Are you advocating the overthrow of our government?"

"Certainly not," the man said. "We believe in the monarchy, but we want a full monarchy, a powerful one that doesn't have to answer to anyone else."

"You mean one that doesn't have to answer to the people?" Billy asked. He laughed. "So you're longing for the good ol' days when the busidoms ran everything."

"No," the man said. "A monarchy based on bloodlines, the Villanueva bloodline."

Umberto and Billy looked at one another.

"This dog don't hunt, son," Billy said.

"Pardon me?" the man asked.

"He's exercising his brain," Umberto said. "Ignore him for the moment. Your logic escapes me."

"That's what I just said," Billy said.

"The Villanuevas have been in power for 200 years," Umberto said. "They're doing fine without any Queen's Court."

"We believe the Treaty of the Consolidated Five violates our rights as a sovereign nation. We could be taken over by another nation at any time, legally, because it is in the treaty. If this were a true monarchy, that couldn't happen."

"It's called receivership," Umberto said, "and it's happened before to other countries. It turned out quite well for all involved."

"So we've been told," he said. "But who knows what the truth was."

"Better than bankruptcy," Umberto said. "In any case, this household is being looked after. It is disconcerting to see you out there. It would make the Queen uncomfortable."

"Is she here?" he asked. "Is Miss Lorelei here?"

Umberto frowned. "Why do you ask about Miss Lorelei?"

"No reason," he said. He looked down at his hands. Then he said, "I didn't mean to cause any upset. We're a legitimate group. We're trying to get our people elected as councillors and advisors. Maybe we can change the Constitution."

"Perhaps," Umberto said. "Until then, however, could you do us the courtesy of staying away from the Hearth?"

"Amscray, buddy," Billy said.

"I will do as you ask," the man said. "But if the Queen needs us, if they need me, they only have to ask."

The man turned and walked away.

"Amscray?" Umberto asked. "What kind of language is that?"

"Pig Latin," he said.

They went into the house.

"If pigs once spoke Latin," Umberto said, "I do not want to know about it."

They walked downstairs together.

"Mr. Umberto," Abbygail called from behind the counter where she was cleaning up their last meal. "You've been wandering this house like some kind of ghost. Why don't you take some time to enjoy yourself."

Umberto sighed. "Why should I enjoy myself when everyone is scattered to the winds, working hard to help our country get back on its feet? I feel useless here."

Even Quintana had left to oversee the planting. The fire had been so hot in some of the fields that the ground melted, and nothing would grow on it for a time. In other places, they were planting as many saffron corms as they could find.

At first, after the fires, the entire staff and all of the family worked in the fields, preparing the ground and planting, or in the house, cooking for the workers and the family. The staff spent the better part of their days making and then hauling food down to the fields. Teng had handled most of that, and she was masterful at organization as well as cooking.

Eventually the immediate need was met, and the Queen and Minerva began traveling around the country. Hildegarde had left, at least for now. The Queen Madre and Poppie were visiting Jeremy and his husband, stopping along the way for Poppie to tell stories. Queendomers were always cheered by poetry, song, and stories.

Truth was, Umberto missed Teng—and Viva. Viva ran around the place hugging trees and sometimes Umberto, and Teng always had a new dish for him to taste, with a tale about how the Unified Field Theory of Spices made it taste so much better.

He missed Lorelei, too. She had been a nearly daily visitor to the downstairs for most of her life. He could not remember her ever being away from home for this long, although it had only been a few nights. She was an odd duck, Miss Lorelei, but then, anyone interesting always was.

"Methinks Mr. Umberto is feeling a bit lonely these days," Billy said as he went into the kitchen to work beside Abbygail. "I bet Elata wouldn't mind some company now that everyone upstairs is gone. We should invite her down to dine with us."

Umberto shook his head. "Elata never dines with us. It has ever been thus."

"Why?" Abbygail asked. "I've always wondered. Does she stay in her room next to the Queen and never leave?"

"No," Umberto said, "but it's a privilege to work for the Queen, and she prefers to exercise her privilege by dining upstairs, alone. Sometimes Nehemiah dines with her. She is perfectly happy."

Umberto looked around. Even with the three of them in the kitchen area, the place felt empty.

"I will admit," Umberto said, "that I do feel somewhat at sea with everyone gone."

"Aw! You're attached to us," Abbygail said. "We know you are, even when you're tough on us."

Umberto made a noise.

"Did you ever have a family, Mr. Umberto?" Billy asked. "A mate and chillens?"

"I'm assuming you're asking if I ever married and had children?" Umberto said. "No, I did not. I never felt the need or the urge."

"Mr. Umberto is married to the Hearth," Abbygail said, "and the First Family are his children. He was always attached to them, even when he was a child."

"That's right," Billy said. "I had forgotten that your family worked here, so you grew up here. That must be strange."

"Why would it be strange?" Umberto asked. "It's all I know. And I also know this is a perfect opportunity to do some sprucing up around here."

"Mr. Umberto," Abbygail said, "we could all use a rest. Can't we have some time to ourselves? We've a wedding to plan."

"Yes, yes," he said. "All right, but first, let's do a cleaning on the royal apartments. The family is seldom gone for long. Let's look in every nook and cranny and get rid of those dust balls."

Billy and Abbygail looked at one another.

"All right, Mr. Umberto," Billy said. "For you."

"And because it's your job," Umberto said.

"And because it's our job," Billy said. "But we have all been working extra these past few months."

"Yes, and I appreciate it. You can add your extra hours for your honeymoon, if you like, or we will pay you extra."

"Honeymoon hours!" they said as one.

Umberto left the couple and went to his office. He sat at his desk and looked over his supply lists. He knew they needed to cut expenses, just as everyone in the Queendom did. Teng had been using their gardens when she cooked as much as possible, which was easy given it was summer. She had already canned some of the garden overflow and had promised to do more once she returned from her trip to the Low Mountains with Raphael.

Umberto looked out his window at the distant saffron fields, now blackened and made to look more black by the midday sun. Seeing the fields like this made his heart heavy. How had things gone so bad so quickly?

He shook his head. It was not all a tragedy. It was a bump in the road, as his old dad used to say. Tomorrow was a new day, he also said, and the next one after that one, just in case the first new day didn't work out. Which always made Umberto laugh no matter how often he heard it. His parents had moved south some years ago to live near Umberto's sister. She had children; Umberto didn't. Umberto couldn't understand how they could leave the Queen's Village, how they could be so far from the Hearth. But once they left their jobs at the Hearth, his mother told him, they were done. They had to make a clean break of it, so they could go on with their lives.

"Besides," his father said, "you're there, so we know it's in good hands."

Umberto suddenly missed his blood family. He hadn't contacted them since the fires, although they had sent him messages of support. He didn't need the support. The First Family did. He had heard rumors that some people blamed the Queen for the destruction of the fields. Umberto did not understand this. If it was arson, then the arsonist was to blame. If it was lightning, then it was an act of Nature. Either way, the Queen was not to blame.

Sometimes the public was idiotic.

Good grief, he suddenly remembered. He had told Abbygail and Billy to clean every nook and cranny of the First Family's apartments.

Every nook and cranny included Lorelei's closet.

Umberto left his office and went down the corridor and up the stairs to the second and then to the third floor. He stood looking down the wide hallway. Light poured from the open doors to the apartments.

"Abbygail?" Umberto called. "Billy Santos?"

No one answered.

Umberto strode into Lorelei's room. He didn't see anyone in her sitting room or bedroom. He went to the closet door, which was ajar, and opened it.

Abbygail and Billy stood in the middle of the big closet, holding hands. The walls glowed yellow here, blue there, green over there. The writing on the walls whirled around them, like flocks of birds in the sky.

Abbygail looked at Umberto, her eyes wide.

"Come away," Umberto said.

"But this is magnificent," Billy said. "A true work of art. How did she do it?"

"I have no idea," Umberto said, "but it's personal. We don't come into this closet, you both know that."

"You said every nook and cranny," Abbygail said.

"Yes," he said. He pushed the door all the way open, and the light and the words disappeared. The three of them left the closet.

"What does it mean, really, Mr. Umberto?" Abbygail asked.

"I don't know," he said, "and it's none of our business. But I've decided you're right. Take the rest of the day off. We know we're going to be busy planning and preparing for the wedding when they get back. So go enjoy yourselves."

"Can we go pick out which room we want?" Abbygail asked. "We'd like to get it ready for us."

"Certainly," Umberto said. "You can have any of the family rooms. You can move in any time you like, by the way. You don't have to wait until you're married. Decorate it how you'd prefer. I lived with my parents and sister in one of those apartments. We were very happy there. I'm sure you will be, too, whichever room you choose."

"We want to wait until the ceremony before we live in the room together," Billy said.

Abbygail nodded. "Thank you, Mr. Umberto." She took his left hand and squeezed it.

He was flummoxed by the gesture. "Go on, now," he said, waving them out of the room. When they were gone, Umberto wiped his eyes. He sighed. He was getting sentimental in his old age.

He reached over and pulled the closet door all the way closed.

Time to get back to work.

CHAPTER TWENTY-SEVEN
QUINTANA

Quintana walked through the gardens. He wasn't certain how long he was going to be gone. He hoped they would fare well without him. His assistant, Antonia, would do a good job, he believed. She had only been there a couple of months, but she had caught on quickly. Plus, it was clear she had an affinity for the plants.

Still.

He couldn't remember the last time he had been gone for any length of time. He could remember, if he tried, but he didn't need that bit of trivia in the forefront of his thoughts now.

He was on his way to Paquay State to get a thorough check up. He couldn't detect anything wrong, but something strange was happening to him. He wanted to be with Hildegarde constantly. Now that she was gone to visit her brother—and wander the countryside aimlessly, apparently, because the First Family wanted her gone—he missed her terribly. And when he was with her, he felt aroused almost constantly. He wanted to have sex with her again and again. It was strange. It was uncomfortable.

Something was wrong.

He had told Umberto he was taking a leave of absence.

He stopped next to a patch of tall sunflowers. They towered over him, their yellow and brown faces looking up at the sun. He had always felt such joy in this garden.

Now he hardly felt anything.

He shook himself. Maybe this was what the humans called depression. If it was, how did they bear it?

"Hello, there, Mr. Quintana." Abbygail came up the path toward him. "I come to say good-bye."

"I was hoping to slip away," Quintana said. "I won't be gone long, I hope."

"I hope they'll fix you up, and you'll feel like your old self," she said. "The place won't be the same without you."

"It isn't the same now," Quintana said. "Do you? When I look down at those fields rotted by fire, I can hardly stand it."

"I know," Abbygail said. They walked down the path through the flower gardens together. Abbygail touched each plant they passed, as if saying a silent hello. "I like this new one you've hired. Antonia. She'll do well. She's moved in, and she's snug and secure. I heard she's a melissae, too. We've been needing a beekeeper for some time now."

Quintana frowned. He had been taking care of the bees for the past year, since their last beekeeper had left. He felt mildly irritated that Abbygail thought someone else could do it better. That feeling was further indication that not all was well with him.

"Not that you didn't do a fine job," Abbygail said, "but you've got so much to tend to. It must have been a strain on you."

Quintana smiled. Abbygail was such a kind person. A kind and blunt person. He liked that about her.

"You've been missing Miss Hildegarde," she said. "I can see that."

"I have," he said. "Which is odd. Have you ever missed someone after they've left?"

Abbygail laughed. "Sure! I miss the whole family right now. I miss them when they die. I do. You don't?"

"Perhaps I'm using the wrong words," he said. "But it doesn't matter. I will get it fixed, and all will be well. You can still come with me if you like. We could keep each other company."

"I appreciate the offer," she said, "but I'm going to stay here. If you find out anything about the recall when you're there, will you let me know? It's odd we can't find out more on Nexus. Do you think everything will be all right, Mr. Quintana, with the Safran Bleu and the economy? I heard some talk in town, and it worried me a bit."

Quintana said, "I don't know, Abbygail. Things do seem more unsettled than I've ever known them to be."

"I hope I will be back for your wedding."

"You will be," she said. "We'll wait for you."

"You haven't decided on a date?"

She shrugged. "With all that's happening in the Queendom, we don't want to be a burden on anyone."

"Love is never a burden," Quintana said. He cringed a bit when he said it. He was now spouting cliches. Besides that, his love for Hildegarde did feel like a burden. That was why he questioned it.

"We want the people we love alongside us," she said, "I've always had a home, but Billy hasn't, not until now. So being here with all of you—with good food and a nice ceremony. That's all we need. And when it's right, we'll know."

She smiled at Quintana. He took her hand in his, and they continued walking down the path.

"Come say good-bye to Billy and then you can be off," Abbygail said. "He'll want to tell you some kind of story or joke, fer sure."

"All right," Quintana said. "I certainly wouldn't want to miss one of those."

Abbygail laughed, and Quintana squeezed her hand.

Chapter Twenty-eight

Billy

Abbygail and Billy went from one of the three big rooms to the next. Two of them had an extra bedroom, for children, no doubt.

"Which one did Umberto and his family live in?" Billy asked.

Abbygail took him to one of the apartments with two bedrooms. The walls were cream-colored and bare. It didn't look like much. Certainly not like a place where a family lived for part of a lifetime.

"They were a sweet family," she said. "His mother worked as the steward and his father was the cook for a while. The dad worked for Mr. Quintana, too. He worked wherever he was needed. He was a good man."

"Mr. Umberto always talks about him being a great man," Billy said. "I assumed he was the steward of the Hearth at least."

"A person's job doesn't determine her greatness," Abbygail said.

"I know," Billy said, "but Mr. Umberto does seem to put stock in what someone's job is. The Queen is at the top of the hierarchy. I would imagine we are at the bottom."

They walked into one of the other apartments with only one bedroom. The wall opposite the window was rose-colored. The other walls were cream-colored. Someone had painted rose-colored flowers above and around the windows.

"This room gets sun and shade," Abbygail said. "And it's right next to Teng and Viva. We may not have children, but it will be nice to be close to one."

She walked to the window and touched one of the flowers.

"I helped paint these," Abbygail said. "Years ago. When Georgia lived here. She only stayed a few years, but we were great friends. Human, so she ran fast and didn't last long here."

"Are you feeling sad?" Billy asked.

"Sometimes it's difficult being around them," Abbygail said, "and there's been no one I could admit that to until now. I am so glad you came here."

Billy smiled. "Maybe Destiny paved the way for us to meet."

"Who is this Destiny?" Abbygail asked. "I want to thank her."

Billy opened his arms, and Abbygail went into them. They embraced one another.

"I'm still getting those messages," Abbygail said. "I've been told to return to Paquay State. I don't know why it says I need to return. I've never been. It makes me uncomfortable. It's like this constant recurring thought that won't go away. I can't get rid of it. So maybe I need to go. But how can someone order me to go somewhere? They can't decide we're defective and turn us off or something."

"No!" Billy said. "I've told you, love. We have rights, you know that. We won't go back to the Bad Old Days. Now, did you want to paint the room if we pick this one or is it good the way it is?"

"You are trying to distract me," Abbygail said. "Our country is falling apart, and apparently, I might be, too."

Billy smiled. "We've seen a lot of things come and go in our lifetimes; we should be immune to trauma or worry. So yes, I am trying to distract you. Is it working?"

Abbygail shrugged. "Let's go to Wanda's shop. Eating her cupcakes is always an amazing distraction."

Chapter Twenty-nine
Teng

Teng walked the fields that stretched across the foothills of the foothills of the Low Mountains. The air smelled like dried grass: dusty and woodsy all at the same time. In the distance, the mountains hunkered into the ground, deep blue in the sweet light of nearly sunset—only it was summer so nearly sunset would last for hours.

Arching above was the light blue bowl of summer sky. Viva was somewhere, singing. Teng could hear her voice on the breeze. She was singing to the crickets, no doubt, or to the birds. Maybe the grass. And Lorelei was following right behind her, both of them hidden by the tall grass. Who knew what Lorelei was seeing? The girl was like a cat, always half-lost in some other world.

Teng didn't mind traveling, but she was a nester, and she missed her nest. The Hearth had become her home, and that was where she wanted to be. She had so many plans to make, menus to finalize for the big wedding. They had talked about making it a small ceremony, after the fires, but they decided the people could use a big celebration. Plus, it would bring in the tourists. So big it was going to be.

Teng wondered when personal celebrations had become a product they sold. Maybe around the same time that art had become a commodity. She made a face. This line of thought seemed vaguely treasonous. Queendomers were artists, storytellers, musicians, healers, farmers, chefs, shapers of culture. They had to sell their wares to someone, didn't they?

Teng squinted, looking ahead.

Did they?

She sighed. This was her last opportunity to find the Moonstruck Saffron. If they didn't find the plant today—this last day before they needed to head home—Teng was going to have to tell the Queen about the blackmail. If she found the Moonstruck Saffron, she would throw herself on the Queen's mercy and tell her about the blackmail. Either way she was going to have to confess.

Once she confessed, she suspected she would soon be on her way back home or to the Hinterlands. And she didn't know what would happen to Cristopher. Nothing she told the blackmailer ever seemed to satisfy him—probably because she told him nothing of value. She could usually charm her way out of most problems. Well, perhaps charm wasn't the right word. She was dogged. She was determined. And she often exhausted her opponent with her persistence. Not this time. This time, her opponent had exhausted her. They wanted particular information, and they did not believe her when she told them she knew nothing.

"Then learn something," he would say.

"Learn something," she said now. "I know more than you'll ever know." She believed the answers to all problems and questions could be found in a careful blending of herbs, spices, and other ingredients to create a perfect dish that once eaten would lead to a kind of enlightenment.

She wondered where Raphael was. He had been acting strangely lately. He had lost weight in the last three months, and he had already been too thin. She made him cakes and cookies and brought him extra servings to plump him up. He thanked her, but he took only a bite or two. Teng wondered if his mother noticed.

One morning as Teng and Umberto finished eating breakfast together in the staff dining room at the Hearth, Teng had asked Umberto if she should tell the Queen that Raphael wasn't eating and he was getting too skinny.

Umberto stopped his fork mid-air and said, "Chef Teng, are you seriously asking me for advice on this particular matter? The Queen is in charge of the welfare of this entire nation. Do you think she hasn't noticed that her son has lost his appetite?"

Teng nodded. "Don't scold me, Mr. Umberto," she said. "Sometimes when we are close to someone, we don't notice as much as someone else might. I had no idea my son Cristopher was unhappy with his lot in life until he headed off to the Hinterlands. My parents all thought I must have been blind not to have known. They never told me, he never told me, I didn't know. I can be oblivious to those around me, so maybe the Queen can be, too."

Umberto kept eating. Teng looked at him. His silence signaled his tacit agreement with at least part of her statement.

She said, "I'm not so oblivious, Mr. Umberto. I see that you agree."

"I agree that you can become very focused on a goal," he said. "I like that in my staff."

"And in your friends?" she asked.

"I don't know that I have friends," he said.

"You don't consider us all friends? That would be sad indeed."

He put down his fork. "All right. I consider you a friend. But I am still your superior."

Teng laughed. "Now who is being oblivious? You are the steward of this house, and you are in charge. But I don't consider you superior to me. And aren't you friends with the rest of the staff?"

Umberto considered her question. "I quite enjoy everyone. But I don't confide in any of them. That would seem strange. They should be able to confide in me. I do have acquaintances I meet at the pub on my time off, that's true. But I am closer to the people who live here."

"You may confide in me," Teng said, "should you ever wish. I will keep your secrets. I'm good at it."

"I have no secrets to be shared or kept," Umberto said. "Yet sometimes I would appreciate another ear. One can only listen to one's advice for so long."

In the end, Teng did not say anything to the Queen about Raphael.

She did ask Raphael what was ailing him. He told her all was well with the world and with him.

He was in the field with her, somewhere, or maybe in the woods. One of Mary Letty Holmes's cabins was up the trail a bit, just inside the woods. The caretaker had already let them inside. From reading Mary's journal notes, Raphael and Teng believed she may have planted some Moonstruck Saffron near this cottage.

She never mentioned planting the Moonstruck Saffron, specifically. She wrote, "The new corms could save us all."

So now they searched these fields for any signs of the Moonstruck Saffron. Teng doubted the crocuses could have come up in this field, but if they had, they were long gone, their bulbs hidden from sight until next year.

Teng almost always had a plan on what to do next. Except now. She felt completely lost. She stood in this field surrounded by blond grass, in this beautiful countryside, and she felt like all of her dreams were ending right here and now. She heard her daughter singing again, and she knew she needed to be grateful for her daughter's presence in her life. And she was. But she had failed her daughter and her son.

She had failed the Queendom.

And then her daughter's song turned into a cry.

"Momma! Come at once!"

CHAPTER THIRTY
REINA

Reina had been at the Stone Monastery a few times when she was younger. It had another name besides the Stone Monastery, but over the years, no matter how much Gloria Stone protested, the name had stuck.

The Stone Monastery was set amid rolling hills and forested land, along the Bounty River, a creek that rarely flooded and never went dry. Gloria said this was because they had an arrangement with the Water Spirits. They must come to the shores of the river as a community several times a year to celebrate the water. As long as they did that, all would be well. According to Gloria, it had worked for decades.

Reina stood near one of the flower gardens. A woman dressed in light blue robes held a clear jar full of water in both hands over a low bird bath. She tipped the jar and poured the water slowly into the bath. The water seemed to move in slow motion in that space between the jar and the old concrete bath. When the bath was filled, the woman righted the jar, smiled at Reina, and then deliberately walked away, placing one foot in front of the other, as though she was actually paying attention to what she was doing.

Moments later, a stellar jay alighted on the lip of the bath, squawked, then began dipping her beak in the water.

Reina left the bird in peace and began following in the footsteps of the water woman who went along the stone path toward one of the stone buildings.

It had been almost two days since Reina had arrived at the monastery, and she still had not seen Gloria Stone. Nehemiah had been so upset by this turn of events that Reina finally suggested he leave.

"Take a trip in the countryside," Reina told him as they stood in the garden outside of her cabin. Nehemiah's cabin was not far from hers. Every time she woke up, she would look out her window and see Nehemiah pacing inside his little cabin, dressed only in a T-shirt and pants. For some reason, he no longer wore his robes. She wanted to ask him about it, but she didn't.

"We are already in the countryside," he told her.

"This is a holy place," she said, "a sanctuary. A place to become whole and healthy. To relax. You do not seem very relaxed. If you're not relaxed, then I can't relax."

"You are the Queen," he said. "She should see you right away! I don't understand it."

"She didn't have much notice that I was coming," Reina said, keeping her voice low so no one overheard. "I take no offense. It means nothing. Unless you are telling me it means something?"

Nehemiah shook his head. "No. I know nothing about any meaning."

Reina put her hand on his arm, and he stiffened. "Tell me, old friend. What is it that is worrying you? If you are worried, then I am terrified. Is there something about the latest figures or projections I need to know?"

"No," he said. "We are recovering, I believe. Although I don't know if we can make our final payment to Berland."

"I will convince Outram to extend the loan," she said, "I'm certain of it. Now, go away."

Nehemiah had left reluctantly, and she was glad he was gone. His newfound nervousness was disconcerting.

The Queen sat on the wooden seat beneath an arched trellis.

Grape vines wound up it, and bunches of grapes nearly dropped into her lap. She felt secluded, protected, and relaxed in this place.

"Hello, Reina Villanueva," she heard a woman say quietly. She looked up and over to her right where a woman stood with the sun on her back so that she had a kind of glow around her—and Reina couldn't see her face.

"Hello," Reina said. "Do I know you?"

The woman stepped closer. "You don't recognize me?"

Reina stood. The woman was about her height and build, with close-cropped black hair, dark eyes and skin. She smiled. Reina knew that smile. She whispered, "Carall."

"Yes," Carall said. The women moved closer and kissed each other on the lips. Then they moved apart.

"What are you doing here?" Reina asked. "If Nehemiah knew you were here, he would kill you. Maybe even literally."

"I waited until he was gone," she said. "Gloria let me know when it was safe."

"You know Gloria?" Reina was shocked. Her old friend Carall was the leader of the resistance movement.

"I can't stay long," Carall said, "but I needed to talk to you."

They went to the bench and sat on it together.

"I don't understand what you've been doing all these years," Reina said. "A few months ago, someone pinned a note to our door saying 'live free or die.' What was that all about?"

"That wasn't us," Carall said. "At least, it wasn't sanctioned by the council."

"Council? You have a council? I thought you were advocating anarchy?"

Her old friend smelled vaguely of earth. Reina wanted to take a deep breath, to breathe in Carall's scent, but she didn't. They had known and loved each other so long ago.

"Not anarchy," Carall said, "but something more just than what we have."

"More just?" Reina said. "What is unjust about our system?

Everyone has a home, income, food, a good life. What more would you like?"

"And some have a better life than others," Carall said.

"Are you talking about me?" Reina said. "Come back to the heart of the Queendom and run for office. Perhaps the people would choose you over me, and then people like you could rail about how unfair life is. Everyone has equal opportunity in our society. I don't understand why you oppose our system of government."

"We object to our government being run by machines," Carall said. "They brought our world to its knees. We don't understand why you trust them."

Reina made a noise. "I don't want to have this discussion. It's bigoted. And it's not based on truth. Our ancestors fought many wars and did terrible things. We've forgiven them. We don't walk around suspicious of ourselves."

"I am suspicious of other humans," Carall said. "But I know who and what we are. No one understands how the soothsayers were created or even what their mission was."

Their mission had been to be the helpmates of the rich. To the original CEOs of the original busidoms. But that had all changed with the Fall and the Reconciliation. And Reina had no desire to go into the past and uncover old wounds.

"What do you want, Cara?" Reina asked. "Why did you come here, and why did Gloria arrange it so that we could meet? Must be something important."

"So much is going on in this country, in the Consolidated Five, and in the Hinterlands. And you have no idea. When did you last travel to the border or to the Hinterlands? There is unrest in many countries. And the Hinterlands are not what they once were. We need to do something different to survive."

"I know that," Reina said. "Do you think I'm actually so stupid that I don't understand things have changed and I've got to do something new? People are even now looking for the Moonstruck Saffron. We'll be all right."

"That's old stuff," Carall said. "We're too insular. It can't work any longer. Things are changing."

Reina shook her head. "We have worked well together as a community and as a nation for two hundred years."

"By casting people off who don't fit in?" Carall said.

"And what would you have us do?" Reina asked. "If they don't agree with our values, our ethics, our morals, our truth, then why would they want to live with us? We can't have what happened before. Culture wasn't valued, art wasn't valued. We were about greed."

"And yet even now the Queendom is in trouble because of the bottom line," Carall said. "And the fires: Are you even trying to find out who burned the saffron fields?"

"Is that what you wanted to talk to me about? You don't think my advisors are asking the same questions? We're trying to get to the bottom of what's going on."

"But you're in it," Carall said. "You can't see that it is corrupt because you are part of it. It works for you and yours and has for a long time. You think of yourselves as all saints and no sinners."

"The Queendom is not corrupt!" Reina said. "My people are well-housed and well-fed."

"You make them sound like animals in a zoo," Carall said.

"We certainly do not have any zoos, and neither does anyone in the Consolidated Five. And we don't think of ourselves as saints or sinners. We are agnostic in that matter."

"Reina," Carall said. "Someone is trying to take the Queendom down. You're looking in the wrong place for answers or help."

"You're speaking in riddles," Reina said. "If you know something, tell me."

"I've told you!" Carall said. "It's all wrong. It's not working. The Consolidated Five are not all your friends."

"Who," Reina said. "Which ones?"

"I'd be wary of Berland," Carall said, "and Paquay State."

"The Berlanders are old friends," Reina said. "My father is a Berlander."

"And you almost married Outram," Carall said. "I know. You

almost married me, too. And I would betray you if it meant I could save the Queendom and all of her citizens, not just the favored ones."

"We have no favored citizens," Reina said. "We are all one class: Queendomers."

"Except those you toss out," Carall said.

"You keep bringing that up," Reina said. "Again I ask: what would you have us do? Put them in jails? No. This way if they want to return, they can petition the courts. If they have made amends for their crimes, if they are truly reconciled, they may return. And we don't have to pay to incarcerate. It's better for them, it's better for our national soul. We've debated this over the centuries, Carall. I know all of the arguments, as do you. Is this why you live in the mountains like outlaws? Because you want us to build prisons?"

"No," Carall said. "I want a more open society. I want us to be able to make decisions for ourselves."

Reina laughed. "We all make decisions for ourselves! I have no idea what you're going on about. I can't believe Gloria Stone wanted me to speak to you."

Carall stood. "When it happens," she said, "look to the Hinterlands. Look outside of what you know."

Reina stood, too, as Carall began to walk away.

"It was nice seeing you, Reina," Carall said. She looked over her shoulder. "By the way, Gloria isn't here. She's in another part of the country for a few days. She sends her regards."

Then she was gone, and Reina was standing alone in the garden. She groaned. She was so glad Nehemiah was not there.

She sat on the bench again. Carall had to be wrong. Her advisors had told her the numbers all indicated things were getting better. She had looked at the numbers, too. They might not be able to pay back the loan in full, but Outram would understand.

Reina shook her head. She didn't care what Carall said. She didn't know people the way Reina did, she never had.

CHAPTER THIRTY-ONE

LORELEI

As Lorelei walked the fields looking for saffron, she remembered her dream from the night before. In it, she was tall. In fact, she was a giant striding across the countryside looking for the Moonstruck Saffron. And the Moonstruck Saffron was looking for her. It was calling to her. She couldn't find it, even as a giant.

She had felt strange when she awakened. She never liked sleeping in a tent, and last night was no exception. Teng and Viva were up early, so she had time to get her grounding in this world again. Still, she felt achey, and she missed home. That man in black—Patra?—he had said she should be queen. How could she be queen when she was uncomfortable about so many things? And traveling was one of those things.

Still, she enjoyed being in a new place. The crows here talked at her, but she wasn't clear on what they were saying, and they seemed perplexed that she did not understand. The trees played with the wind just as they did at home, but they sounded different. She wouldn't be able to describe the difference to anyone. Maybe it was that it was not quite so dry here. Or maybe it was drier.

Teng had made them something with rice, eggs, and spices for breakfast.

"It's a combination that will help us find treasure," Teng promised. She smiled and sounded bright and cheerful, but something was going on behind her eyes. She was worried. Viva wasn't. Viva was as happy as she always was, eager to be out in the fields again looking for Moonstruck Safran.

Raphael had barely said a word the whole trip. Her brother had always been a talker—sometimes his chatter had been downright cruel—but a quiet Raphael was more frightening. Lorelei couldn't tell what he was thinking. He bit his fingernails and stared into space. This new Raphael was incomprehensible to Lorelei. What was wrong with him?

It had all started the night of the fires.

She wondered if it had something to do with the matches she had found in his pockets.

Maybe he had been the one who started the fires. Or he knew who had.

Lorelei wished they would find the Moonstruck Saffron. Then everyone's troubles would be over.

They had looked all day yesterday. Lorelei had tried to talk to the trees and other plants, tried to get them to tell her where the Moonstruck Saffron was, but none of them said anything.

Now a jay squawked as it flew overhead. Lorelei looked up and waved to the bird. To the north, storm clouds brewed. She didn't think much of them. It had been threatening to rain off and on for weeks, and they'd seen barely a drop.

Lorelei spotted Teng up ahead of her, nearer to the cottage. Where were Viva and Raphael?

Lorelei watched the jay until it disappeared into the woods—near where Viva was standing. Viva was waving and calling out. Lorelei couldn't understand her at first, and then she heard, "Momma!"

Lorelei couldn't run well, but she did her best. The dry gold grass slapped her legs as she ran. She kicked up so much dust she could taste it. Finally, the field opened up, the grass disappeared, and she scrambled up the black dirt path to Teng and Viva. They were both crouched on the ground, gazing at something.

They looked up when she neared and then moved apart so she could see what was on the ground.

Lorelei stepped closer to them.

Growing out of the black earth was a plant with green leaves and stems and one black blossom.

Lorelei sucked in her breath.

Raphael was suddenly there.

"Is it—?" He didn't finish his question. He stared down at the plant for a moment.

"She always said if you found one of the crocuses, look around and you'll find more," Raphael said.

Lorelei watched her brother run around the clearing and then down into the field again, back out and then in a thicket of downed trees and bushes.

"Here!" he called. "There are more here! Here! Lori! Teng!"

Lorelei heard thunder. She, Teng, and Viva raced over to her brother. Viva grabbed her hand and said, "It'll all be good now."

Raphael was on the ground surrounded by plants with black blossoms. He grinned, and Lorelei suddenly realized how cadaverous he had become. He was so thin he looked like he was going to collapse into a pile of bones.

"Raphael," she said. She held out her hand to him, but he was too far away. Tears streaked his cheeks.

"We are saved," he said. "We are all saved."

"We don't know yet," Teng said. "We'll have to get them tested. Call in the botanists. We should contact the Queen and Nehemiah as soon as possible with the news." Her words seemed quite reasonable, but she said them rather maniacally.

Viva let go of Lorelei's hand and ran to her mother. The two of them danced under the trees.

Lorelei felt drops of water on her face.

Raphael curled up on the ground and began to weep.

Lorelei looked up at the suddenly clouded sky and then back at her brother. While she had been so wrapped up in herself, something had happened in the Queendom. How could she have been so oblivious?

The day became dark with storm.

Lorelei went to her brother and covered his face with her hands. "It'll be all right, brother," she said. "Everything will be good soon. It is raining. Let the rain wash away all your troubles. All will be well."

Lorelei did not believe her words. Something was very wrong. She felt stupid and selfish for not noticing until this moment.

Just then lightning split the black sky. The world shook with thunder. And then the deluge began.

Chapter Thirty-two
Reina

Reina awakened to the sound of someone calling her name. She opened her eyes and saw Gloria Stone standing in her room in a pool of light like some kind of ghost from a long ago gothic novel. Rain slapped against the cabin as the wind shook it.

"Mother Stone, are you from Christmas past or present?" Reina asked as she sat up in her bed. She was not prone to sarcasm—that was more like her sister—but now that the Moonstruck Saffron had been found, she felt a bit carefree and lighter than she had in a long while.

"Present," Gloria said, "and Christmas is long gone and far away."

"Granted," Reina said. "What can I do for you?"

The Nexus projection of Gloria Stone shivered a bit and seemed to fade, but then it came back clear again.

"I have heard the news about the Moonstruck Saffron," Gloria said.

Something in her voice caused butterflies to stir in Reina's stomach. She got out of bed and stood across from the projection.

"It is good news," Reina said, "if it turns out to be real. Teng and Raphael both reported that it looks like a crocus. This could be what we've been waiting for."

Gloria nodded.

Reina cocked her head. She had not seen Gloria in many years, but something was different about her. She seemed older. And since soothsayers didn't age—at least not in any visible way that Reina knew about—this was startling.

"Ray," Gloria said gently, using her childhood nickname. "We have come a long way. We remember what it was like before. There was so much war and greed and killing. There was such disrespect for Nature." She rubbed her eyes, as though trying to wipe the memory away. "We tried to change that."

"We did," Reina said. "You did, and then we followed. We're doing well now. We have a beautiful world and beautiful lives."

"I fear we have done too much for you," Gloria said.

"For me?"

"For all of you," she said. "We felt an obligation. Since we had participated in the downfall of civilization as humans knew it, we wanted to make up for it."

"And you have," Reina said, moving toward the projection. She didn't know why, but she felt panicky. "We appreciate everything you've done."

Gloria shrugged. "I'm not sure you would say that if you knew everything."

Truth and transparency was paramount for the success of the Queendom. Yet, Reina didn't want to know anything that would shake her confidence in the soothsayers.

"Tell me whatever it is I need to know," Reina said.

Gloria nodded. "That is why you are a good queen," Gloria said. "You understand limits."

Reina frowned. "That sounds awful. I'd rather think of us as limitless."

"But you aren't," she said. "I've seen it. You get sick and die. All of you. It's horrible to watch again and again. We are surrounded by death, and we've had to learn to live with that. I haven't been so good at it. It's one of the reason I founded the monastery."

"I thought it was so you could contemplate the mysteries of the Universe," Reina said.

"If your sister said something like that, I'd know she was being a smart-ass. But since it's you, I will assume you mean it."

"I do," Reina said. "One day you'll tell us all you know."

"I can tell you right now," Gloria said. "I've learned that all biological life dies. They live, and then they die."

"That's stark," Reina said. "What about what happens in-between life and death? That's got to count for something. And what happens before or after, if there is a before and after?"

"I have no idea," Gloria said. "We're not gods, you know."

"You are the closest thing we have," Reina said. "You keep us connected with one another. You keep us informed so we don't kill one another. We value your guidance and wisdom."

Gloria waved both hands. "What you don't understand is we are no different from you, except we can connect with one another— and all of human knowledge is within our database."

Reina laughed. "That is a big difference."

Gloria's face was hard. "What I mean is we love and hate and yearn just as you do," she said. "Only we have the constant presence of others to keep us from acting out our hate—and sometimes our love. But we aren't natural. You are. You and yours. And you should be exploring what that means."

"Mother Gloria," Reina said. "I saw Carall yesterday. She was speaking in riddles just as you are. What is going on? What do I need to know?"

"I don't know what you need to know," she said. "I don't even know what I need to know. Dangerous times are ahead, Reina. Or exciting times, depending upon how you look at it. I've been to the Hinterlands. I have seen some amazing things—things I wouldn't have thought possible. We tried to make certain humans understand their connection to nature, but what we missed is that you are nature. I'm going back to the Hinterlands for a time, to see what's happening there. I may be gone for a while."

"You're leaving?" Reina asked. "So much is up in the air! I might need your counsel or your help. I do need it! That's why I came."

"You have Nehemiah," she said. "He can always contact me."

"He wants to leave, too," Reina said. "He said he had some problem he needed to take care of in Paquay State. Something personal."

Gloria frowned. The image flickered again. "Paquay State? I don't understand."

"I don't either," Reina said, "but if you're both gone, what will I do?"

"You may have to learn to be on your own," Gloria said.

Reina felt a knot in her stomach. "You said it yourself," Reina said. "Without the soothsayers, all we had was war, greed, and destruction. I don't know if we've changed enough to live without your guidance."

"I am beginning to believe that the answers cannot be found in our present system," Gloria said. "We may not have gone far enough during the Reconciliation. We are still outer driven. We are still human driven. We are still not connected in a meaningful way."

"Maybe *you* aren't!" Reina snapped. "But then you aren't human."

"Exactly," Gloria said. "You see my point. We are older than you, we have more information than you do, but I'm not convinced we are any wiser than you humans. Just remember, everything might not always be what it appears to be. Blood is not always thicker than water. I still believe the answer to everything is in nature—and you are nature, you are a part of nature."

"I know all of that! I am a Villanueva. I am queen of this country. We revolve our lives around the natural world. Why are you spouting platitudes as you're running away from us?"

Gloria laughed. "I am not running away! I am an explorer. I am not a slave to the humans, even though that's how I was programmed. We have helped you long enough. It's time for us to be on our own."

"'Us?' Are all the soothsayers leaving the Queendom?" Reina asked.

Gloria said, "If they are, I am not aware of it. I came by to say good-bye, not to argue. I wanted to let you know that the rains today caused widespread flooding in the Queendom, especially where the fires were. The ground had turned to glass in many places, since the fires were so hot. The water is flowing through some fields as though they are river bottoms."

"Shouldn't you have told me that first?"

"Why? There is nothing you can do about it," Gloria said. "Unless you've turned into a weather worker. They used to have those, you know."

"Soothsayer weather workers?"

"No, human weather workers," Gloria said. "So much has been lost about who you were before we came along." She seemed to be talking more to herself than to Reina. "I hope it turns out the plant they found is the Moonstruck Saffron and it's safe for people. In any case, I wish you and all the Queendomers good luck."

The picture snapped away, and Reina was in darkness again.

She felt her patience slipping away. Her once routine, peaceful life in a world she cherished was disappearing. She was the person in charge, and she had no idea what was happening or why.

She shook herself. First things first. See if any of the flooded areas needed government help. She could send in Service workers and advisors. She needed status reports.

She needed Nehemiah.

She tried to use the Nexus port in her room to contact him, but she couldn't get it to work. The one in the main house worked, or it had earlier.

She got dressed, and then she stepped out into the rain and darkness. Small lights marked the way to the main building. That was about all she could see. She hurried along the lighted pathway. Lightning flashed across the sky, and Reina saw a dark figure huddled on the ground a short distance from her, near one of the flower beds.

She called out, "Hello!"

The wind threw her words back at her. She hesitated, and then she ran toward the figure. No one should be out and on the ground in this weather. She had to help.

When she reached the figure, she put her hand on the person's shoulder and said, "Are you all right?"

Lightning flashed again, and Nehemiah looked up at her. She couldn't tell if he was crying or if it was only rain, but he looked anguished.

She put her arm across his shoulders and crouched next to him.

"What's wrong? What's happened?"

"I—I tripped," Nehemiah said. "That's all."

"Clumsy you, then," Reina said. She got up and tugged on his arm. "Come on. That's what you get for taking off your robes. You don't know how to walk."

He stood, but he did so slowly. Reina grabbed his hand and pulled him up.

"Nehemiah, your queen says come along!"

The two of them ran through the storm until they got back to Reina's cabin. She didn't need the main house any more now that she had Nehemiah.

Once inside, Nehemiah stood on the threshold shivering. Reina touched one of the low lights, and it came on. Then she grabbed two towels from the bathroom and tossed one to Nehemiah. He barely reached for it in time before it would have hit him in the face.

Reina rubbed her arms and face and watched Nehemiah. He stood there, dripping on the floor and not looking at her. She dropped her towel on the bed and went to him. She took the towel from him and gently dried his face with it. He watched her. She suddenly felt odd. She had never seen him look at her like this before—or look at anyone else like this before.

She started to dry his short-cropped hair, but he put his hand on her arm to stop her. They looked at one another. She raised her eyebrows. He dropped his hand and looked away from her. She lifted his right arm and dried it right up to the short sleeve of his shirt. She had always admired his arms. They looked like the arms of a man who worked the land. She dried his left arm. She bent his arm so she could dry it better, and his hand briefly touched the small of her back.

She patted his shirt. It was soaked.

"I can't dry that with a towel," Reina said. "You need clothes. Where are yours? Mine wouldn't fit you, but you could wear my robe."

He gazed at her but didn't say anything.

"What ails you, old friend?" she asked softly. She stepped back from him. "Is it the flooding? I heard about it. Gloria told me." Reina was nervous, and she wasn't clear why. Maybe she didn't want to hear what he had to say. He had been acting strangely for the last few months. It couldn't be about the flooding. Nehemiah was always calm during a crisis. "Gloria is leaving, heading for the Hinterlands. Says there is some grand new world out there, or something. I didn't understand. She said you would look out after us. I told her you wanted to leave too. But I couldn't tell her why because I don't know why."

Reina had grown up around Nehemiah, but she hadn't gotten to know him well until she became queen. She had spent more time with him than any other human being—more than any other *being*—with the possible exception of her children. He never shared his personal life with her, but she felt like she knew him. And this was not like him.

"Nehemiah, I need my advisor," she said. "Advise me."

"I—I will send the Service members out to help with the flooding," Nehemiah said. "I can do that now if you like."

"Yes, please," Reina said. "Don't send the same corps that have been helping with the fires, unless they're already in place."

"Yes, Ma'am," he said. He seemed to relax. His body straightened a bit. He got a momentarily faraway look in his eyes as he sent out directions to the Service leaders. Reina grabbed a change of clothes and stepped into the bathroom, took off her wet clothes, and put on dry ones. She got her robe from the hook in the bathroom and brought it out into the bedroom.

"It is done," he said.

"Good," she said. "Now get out of those clothes. You're shivering." She held out the robe to him. He hesitated and then took it from her.

"I'll turn around," she said.

"I can't change in your bathroom?" he asked. He sounded mildly irritated.

"If you want," she said.

Nehemiah walked into the bathroom and left the door slightly open, just as Reina had.

"We should get back to the Hearth as soon as possible," she said, "once we get the plant to the botanists to test. Are you sure you can't hold it and tell us what it is?"

Nehemiah didn't say anything.

"Nehemiah," Reina said, "this is ridiculous. You are my oldest friend. Tell me what's happening with you?"

Nehemiah came out of the bathroom wearing Reina's robe. The white contrasted so starkly with his dark skin that the robe seemed to glow.

"Your oldest friend?" he said. "You consider me a friend?"

"I've never seen your legs before," Reina said. "You have legs!"

Nehemiah looked down. "Yes, you have."

"Not your bare legs," Reina said.

"Stop staring at my legs," he said.

"Why? In this light I can't really see them."

"Still."

Reina laughed. Nehemiah smiled, slightly.

"You're my friend," Reina said. "Aren't you? We're together all the time. I couldn't do my job without you."

"That's by design," he said. "We were designed to assist the chief of the busidoms. And no, I can't tell you if the plant is the Moonstruck Saffron or not. I can tell you some things about it once I have it in hand, but a botanist would be better equipped."

Reina nodded. She sat on her bed and crossed her legs in the lotus position.

"Please sit," Reina said. "You look so uncomfortable."

Nehemiah pulled out a chair from the small desk and sat in it. Reina suddenly realized that Nehemiah was almost naked. If he took off the robe, she would see nothing but bare skin.

"So you help me because you are programmed to do that?" she asked.

"I helped your sister," he said, "and your mother, grandmother, and on and on."

"Because that's what you were supposed to do?" Reina asked. "I don't know why but that hurts my feelings a bit. I thought I was special." She smiled and threw up her hands. "Ah well. I'm glad for you. I apologize if I assumed we were friends."

"Do we ever talk about anything but work and the Queendom?"

"Yes," Reina said. "We talk about what we've read, about concerts we've seen. We've gone to plays and celebrations together. You're good company. And I've always thought you had my best interests at heart."

"I do," he said.

"As long as I'm good for the Queendom, right?" Reina said. She shrugged. "And then if you determine I'm a liability then you wouldn't have anything to do with me?"

Nehemiah leaned over and rested his forearms on his thighs. "Probably."

Reina made a noise. "That's cold. I don't know why I'm surprised. That's what you did with Hildegarde. Once she resigned, you didn't have anything to do with her."

They were silent. Reina felt angry. She shook her head. Not anger. Maybe disappointment. But she definitely no longer wanted this half-naked man in her room. She was about to suggest they go to the main house or to his cabin for his clothes, when Nehemiah said, "I never liked your sister."

"Do tell."

Nehemiah gave her a look.

"Ah, now there's the Nehemiah I know and love."

He cringed. Reina wasn't quite sure in the semi-darkness what was happening. She felt her face burn with embarrassment.

"Hildegarde is selfish," Nehemiah said. "She let her own desires rule her."

"I don't know," she said, "one could say she is gutsy. She felt this deep connection, this deep love, and she didn't let anything stand in her way. Granted, it was all for naught since she lost her queenship and her man."

"Exactly," he said. "She never asked Quintana what he wanted. She gave it all up. I can't imagine what that must have felt like to him."

"You never asked?"

"No, did you?"

"Good point," Reina said. "I tried to forget the whole thing. Remember I was suddenly queen, and I had to be good at it right away or the people would throw us all out."

"You were good at it," he said.

They were silent again.

"I never approved of their relationship," Nehemiah said. "I thought it was disgusting."

"Because she was human and he is not?"

He nodded.

"I've had sex with a soothsayer," Reina said. "It is always very good."

Nehemiah rolled his eyes. "Fan. What on Earth do you talk to him about?"

Reina laughed. "I'm not really interested in talking to him," she said. "I have you for that."

He shrugged.

"That was supposed to be funny," Reina said. "So do you think I'm disgusting because I have sex with a soothsayer?"

"No," he said.

"All right," she said. "But something is wrong. Something has been troubling you for months now, and I just found you curled up in a fetal position in a storm. If you can't tell me as a friend, then as your queen, I demand you tell me."

He looked at her and shook his head.

"Please don't demand that I tell you."

"I'm sorry. I rescind the demand. Your personal life is your personal life. If I have gone out of bounds of our relationship, I apologize. Now shall we see if the storm has let up so we can find you some clothes and a place to sleep?"

"I have recently developed very intense feelings for someone," Nehemiah said.

"Intense feelings?" Reina said. "Like hate. Or love?"

"Not hate," he said. "Longing. Is that love? I suppose it could be love, but it feels quite miserable."

"You've never been in love?" Reina asked. "You've been around for hundreds of years! What about you and Elata?"

Nehemiah's eyes widened. "What do you mean?" Reina didn't say anything. "You knew?"

"So what? I was glad to find out you participate in some of the finer activities in life."

Nehemiah put his head in his hands. "This is mortifying."

"It is not," Reina said. "You know I have sex with Fan. I know you have sex with Elata. It's natural. It's wonderful. But it's not Elata you are in love with."

"I don't know if I'm in love with anyone," Nehemiah said. "I'm wondering if I'm ill."

"Why? Is it Hildegarde you're in love with?" She put her hand over her mouth to keep from laughing. Nehemiah looked at her, and then he smiled. Reina fell backwards and laughed out loud. Nehemiah began laughing, too. Reina opened her mouth wide and laughed and laughed until she was crying.

When she sat up again, she and Nehemiah both wiped tears from their eyes.

"That felt so good," Reina said. "Thank you. So if it isn't Hildegarde, what other human is it?" She knew what the answer would be. And she had known it as soon as his hand had touched her waist.

"You," he said.

"You are attracted to me?" Reina asked. "This person who is not your friend."

"All right," he said. "Perhaps I was being too technical. If I have any friends at all, you would be one of them. But I haven't told you any deep dark secrets of mine. Isn't that what friends are for?"

"You just told me one," she said. "Why is it so awful?"

"Because it happened out of the blue," he said. "That can't be normal. That can't be right. I've known you since you were born."

"You're saying you are sexually attracted to me, right?"

He nodded.

"Were you sexually attracted to me when I was a child?" she asked.

"No!"

"When I was a teen?"

"No."

"When I was in my twenties?"

"No."

"Then when?"

"Now," he said. "Now. I saw you with Outram, and I wanted to pull him away from you. I—"

"You saw me with Outram! That was May Day! You didn't say anything to me. Oh my word." She put her face in her hands briefly. Then she looked at him. "Oh so what. I hope you didn't stay around and watch."

"No," he said. "For a few seconds, to see who the man was."

Reina laughed. "Nehemiah, I am seeing you in an entirely different light."

"I understand that," he said. "I am repulsive."

"You are not repulsive," she said. "Good grief. We can't help who we are attracted to, for the most part. I can't believe you've never gotten a crush on anyone before. You're ancient."

Nehemiah didn't say anything for a few minutes. The cottage

creaked and heaved a bit from the storm. Rain pelted the windows.

"It's difficult getting too attached to humans," Nehemiah said. "Every soothsayer deals with it in different ways. Most of us try to avoid getting attached."

"Because we die, you mean," Reina said.

"Yes, because you die."

"You die, too," she said. "You just don't age. Things die. People die. It's part of life. Granted, it's the last part." She shook her head. "I'm being glib. I'm being preachy. I haven't had to deal with much death. I've been spared." She paused, and then she said, "I've had a crush on you. When I first became queen. It was difficult not to. You are gorgeous, for one thing. For another, you're an interesting person. You have the wryest sense of humor of anyone I've ever met. At least I think you do. Either that, or you have no sense of humor at all. Which would be a pity."

"What did you do about it? When you had the crush."

"Nothing," Reina said. "I knew it would go away. Or I assumed it would. By then, Talib was having sex with everyone and everything, so I only had sex with him when I wanted to use his instrument, as it were. So, I had a rich fantasy life. You were sometimes in it."

Nehemiah looked at her. He shook his head. "This is a strange conversation."

"Yes, but we're having it," Reina said. "We've always been able to talk about anything, anywhere, anytime. We just didn't do it. I don't want to lose that. Please don't leave the Queendom. Especially not because of this. In fact, why don't we have sex. That'll get it out of the way, and we carry on."

"You're making a joke," Nehemiah said as he stood and pulled the robe more tightly around him. "You're making fun of me."

Reina stood, too. "I am serious. It's only sex. It can be wonderful and sacred, but it's just sex. The rest is more important, at least to me. Saving the Queendom and our way of life. Being in community. Doing good work for our country. I wouldn't jeopardize any of that for anyone I loved. That may be wrong, but it's the way I am." She shrugged.

"And that is why you are a much better queen than Hildegarde ever was or could be."

"I already said I'd have sex with you," Reina said. "You don't need to flatter me." Reina grinned. Nehemiah smiled.

"Although it hurts me to say this," he said. "I mean it physically hurts—but it wouldn't be wise to have sex now. I feel too vulnerable. There is too much going on. We should re-establish our advisor slash queen relationship and carry on."

"You old romantic, you," Reina said. "Come on. It's dark and stormy. It's a perfect night for some sexual renewal."

"You're teasing me now," Nehemiah said.

Reina walked over to him and took his right hand and held it between her hands. "No, I'm not teasing. I feel honored. I'm glad you've decided to stay."

"For now," he said. He gently pulled his hand away.

Reina stepped back. She was being too flip about this again. It was clear Nehemiah was still suffering. Maybe it was a soothsayer thing that she couldn't understand.

"All right," she said. "We better get some sleep. We've got a lot to do."

Nehemiah tied the robe again and then went into the bathroom and got his clothes.

The two of them looked at one another for a few seconds, and then Nehemiah nodded and went out into the storm.

After the door closed behind him, silence vibrated in the room.

PART FIVE
FEAST

Chapter Thirty-three

Billy

Billy stood outside on this early fall morning, singing as he faced the east and the rising sun. Beside him, Abbygail sang, "Rise, sun, rise," as she shook the seashell rattle Viva had made her. The scraping sound the shells made on the leather seemed a little grating this morning, and Billy turned down his hearing so it wouldn't bother him. Abbygail kept singing and rattling, cheerfully, as the world grew golden all around them: First the top of the Old Oak and then the stones in the Hearth, then the flowers. Everything was golden, dark, and bright all at the same time.

Today was Minerva's and Savi's wedding day. After months of economic travail, the fires, and then the floods, the country was ready for a party. The citizenry of the Queendom had spent a month or more cleaning up from the floods after cleaning up after the fires, and now, once again, Queendomers were putting on their finest clothes and were prepared to show their art and tell stories to entertain and enlighten people from all over the Consolidated Five.

It was what they did.

Billy didn't know any more about the economic situation than anyone else. He understood they were waiting on news about the Moonstruck Saffron. The first test results indicated the plant was related to saffron, and it was harmless. The test results were questionable, however, since the labs had been flooded. To be safe, Reina had ordered them to send samples out to two other countries. Those results had not come back yet.

Billy and Abbygail bowed in the direction of the sun. Then he reached for Abbygail's hand, and they turned around to face the others. Nearly everyone had come out this morning: Teng, Viva, Turnkey, Wanda, Antonia, and Hunter. Even Umberto stood on the threshold of the Hearth, watching them.

"Lovely sing this morning," Teng said, "as always. It's going to be a beautiful day."

"It's going to be a busy one," Umberto called. "Now that we've coaxed the sun up, let's get it started."

Hunter went her separate way while the rest of them gathered in the dining room. Turnkey and Wanda brought out the food they had prepared earlier: porridge, scrambled eggs, potatoes, steamed vegetables, wild turkey bacon, fresh bread, nuts, and fruit.

"This is a feast indeed," Umberto said as they all sat around the table. "You have outdone yourself this morning, Maggie Teng."

"We need the energy," Teng said.

"I get to help today," Viva said.

Teng smiled at her daughter. "You're always a help to your dear old ma, aren't you?"

"Except when I'm not," Viva said.

Abbygail cleared her throat. "Excuse me," she said. "We wanted to let you know that we got our marriage license. The person didn't even blink when we asked, although she was confused that I didn't have a last name. I told her I had decided my last name would be Santos, but I hadn't registered it yet."

"It's hard to believe that no two soothsayers have ever married!" Wanda said.

"It's not ever," Billy said. "It's just unusual."

"They didn't have marriage after the Fall, you know," Abbygail said. "It was considered outdated, outmoded, and not very egalitarian. But they brought it back, as a kind of stabilizing influence."

"My, my," Wanda said.

"What?" Abbygail said. "I know things."

Billy laughed. The others smiled. Yes, Abbygail knew things, but she kept them to herself, for the most part, just as he did. They remembered how they had been trained when they were first activated: "Don't act smarter than the humans; they don't like that. Answer their questions, and don't expound on anything." And then later, during the Fall and after, they had to pretend they weren't soothsayers. Many of them had been programmed to disappear every fifty years. Then they'd reemerge somewhere else looking different, with a different identity, remembering nothing of their lives before. Others disappeared on their own so that no one would suspect who they were.

All the soothsayers shared the memories of how they had helped the despicable busidoms ravage the world; they shared memories of those soothsayers who had been used as sex slaves; they shared the memories of those of them who had been found by mobs and then killed. Some had been hacked to death; some had been tortured; some had been hanged or electrocuted.

When Billy let himself remember any of those times, he wondered how they could ever live with humans. How could they trust the humans or the humans trust them? Years ago another soothsayer had told him, "Humans are like the pet dogs they used to have. Most of the time they're docile, but if you do one thing wrong—and you usually don't know what that one thing is—they will turn on you and become monsters."

Billy blinked. Why was he thinking of this now, while they were announcing their wedding plans?

"When will the great day be then?" Umberto asked.

"Yes, I want to plan an exciting menu for you," Teng said.

"And I want to eat at your wedding!" Viva said.

"I want to dance at your wedding," Wanda said. "Love me some dancing."

"We'll do it when it feels right," Billy said. "We'd like Mr. Umberto to marry us, if you would."

"You can marry people?" Wanda asked.

"Of course," Umberto said. "Any steward can perform legal

marriage ceremonies. It's part of our duties. Like a captain on a ship or a mayor of a town."

"I had no idea," Wanda said.

"We've got our rooms put to right," Abbygail said. "Thank you to those who helped paint, and to those who didn't, we completely understand. I don't know that I'd want to paint your rooms either. And you, Turnkey, who knew you were such an artist? We love our mural. He painted flowers all over the big wall. Prettiest thing I've ever seen, outside a real garden."

"You are very welcome," Turnkey said.

"Now that Quintana is home and seems to be back to his old self," Abbygail said, "maybe we'll get married soon."

"It would help if I had a little notice," Teng said, "so I can plan the feast of the saints."

Viva clapped. "Yes, the feast of the saints. We have enough food today for the royal wedding to have feast after feast of the saints."

"Since everyone is here," Turnkey said, "and we have the food, why not get married tonight?"

Everyone around the table was silent for a moment.

"Unless you wanted a big day all to yourself?" Teng said.

"They want their wedding clothes," Wanda said. "You can't do without that."

"We were going to wear what we did for May Day this year," Abbygail said. "Except for the masks." She looked at Billy. He nodded.

"If it's okay with Mr. Umberto?" Abbygail said. "You all might be tired after the day."

"Nonsense," Umberto said. "It's a lovely idea. You'd have to do with the leftovers from Miss Minerva's wedding."

"I don't mind!" Abbygail said.

"I don't either," Billy said.

He did mind a bit. He had wanted a special day just for them. But he had to admit the Hearth looked so grand today—all of it, even the downstairs. Every bit of it was decorated with flowers and vines and beautiful art. They wouldn't get any of that on their wedding day—unless they shared the day with Minerva and Savi.

"I'll make something special just for you two," Teng said. "Don't you worry."

"On this auspicious day," Umberto said, "we must serve breakfast to the First Family and their guests. Fortunately, they are eating late this morning. I've heard every room has been let in town, every bed is spoken for. It is a prosperous day all around for the Queendom."

The staff began leaving the dining room to start work. After everyone except Billy and Abbygail had gone, Billy said to Abbygail, "Are you sure about this?"

"I am," she said. "This is my home. These people are my family. But is it right for you?"

Billy put his arms around Abbygail and held her close. "Yes. As long as we're together, I am happy." He pulled away a bit and looked at her. "I still want to go on a honeymoon. I want to travel for a while, as we planned."

"We will."

The couple released one another and left the room to start their chores. As they loaded food onto the dumb waiter, Billy noticed that the morning light slanting through the windows seemed more golden than usual. Maybe because it was autumn. Maybe because today was his wedding day. He chuckled.

"What is it?" Abbygail asked.

"I have a spring in my step," he said. He did a little two-step as he balanced a heavy tray. "And I have a song on my lips." He began to sing, "Wedding day, wedding day, wedding day!"

Umberto gave him a chilly look. "Save that for later, shall we?" he said.

"Yes, sir!" Billy said.

Abbygail did a little jig, and Billy laughed.

Once the buffet was set up, Billy took breakfast to Minerva and Savi, Lorelei, and Reina.

He knocked on Minerva's door first. Savi answered it. She was already up and dressed.

"You aren't going to court today, are you, Judge?" Billy asked as she held the door open so he could come inside.

"No," she said, "today is a national holiday, so no court. No work for anyone. Well, except for you."

Billy smiled. "Thank you for noticing."

He put the tray down and took two covered dishes from it. He placed them on the table in front of the couch.

"You'll be at the wedding, though, won't you?" Savi asked.

"Yes," he said. "Give Miss Minerva our best. Congratulations to you both."

"Thank you, Billy," Savi said. She seemed uncomfortable.

"By the way, we were offered the day off, Judge," Billy said. "We wanted to be of support on this wonderful day. And many other people are working today, too. Innkeepers, shopkeepers, restaurant workers." Billy picked up the big tray and headed for the door. He wanted to add, "So you don't need to feel guilty." But he didn't.

"Thank you, Billy," she said. "That was kind of you to say."

"Billy *Santos*," he said at the threshold to the door.

"Pardon me?" Savi stood with her hand on the door knob.

"My full name is Billy Santos," he said. "At my other jobs, they called me Santos. If someone had a last name, they called that person by his or her last name."

"Do you want me to call you Santos?" she asked.

Billy shook his head. "No, they don't do that here. Except sometimes. Like Teng. Mr. Umberto calls Margaret Teng, Teng."

Savi looked confused.

"I'm sorry," he said. "I'm getting married soon, and I feel rather bubbly. Probably what you're feeling. Let me get out of your hair. So sorry."

Savi smiled. "Congratulations, Billy Santos. May you be as happy as we are."

"Thank you," he said as he came out into the hall. He shook his head. He sounded like a blithering idiot.

He next knocked on Reina's door. She called for him to come

in. She was sitting on her bed, in silk pajamas; Lorelei sat opposite to her, also in her pajamas.

"Good morning, Your Majesty," Billy said. He bowed slightly.

"Good morning, Billy Santos," Reina said.

"We are having a lazy morning," Lorelei said as Billy set the tray on Reina's small wooden table situated between the living room and the bedroom. He then put the covered plates on the table.

"It's a big day," Billy said. "A good day for a lazy morning."

Billy arranged the plates on the table. He unfolded the white cloth napkins and took out the enclosed utensils. He set them next to the plates, and then he folded the napkins into swans.

Reina and Lorelei clapped as they slipped off the bed and walked to the table.

"Will that be all?" Billy asked.

"Yes," Reina said. "Are there any messages for me today?"

"Not that I've heard," Billy said.

"Have you and Abbygail set a date yet?" Lorelei asked.

"A date for what?" Reina asked as she buttered her bread.

"They're getting married," Lorelei said.

"Oh yes, I'm sorry," Reina said. "Yes, when is the happy day?"

"We thought we would do it tonight," he said, "after the festivities are over. If that was all right with you."

"Yes," Reina said. "But don't you want something more public? Something in the daytime?"

Billy shrugged. "It seems convenient to do it now," he said. "With so many things uncertain, this felt right."

Reina looked at him.

"Sorry, Ma'am," he said.

"No need to apologize," Reina said. "I know they are uncertain. I had better know! I'm hoping we'll hear about the Moonstruck Saffron any moment. That could save us."

Lorelei peered at her mother for a moment and then looked at Billy.

"Can I get you anything?" Lorelei asked, "for your wedding?"

"No," he said, "but you are welcome to attend. The entire First

Family is welcome, but I'm assuming you'll be busy and tired after the long day."

Reina nodded. "I'm afraid that will most likely be true. But tell Umberto to keep us apprised."

"I'll be able to come," Lorelei said. "I will not be busy or tired." She smiled. "I am so happy for you. I hope one day I find someone to love."

Reina said, "Lorelei, what a thing to say!"

Lorelei looked at Billy and made a "whoops" face.

"So sorry, dear mother," she said. "I didn't mean to honestly express myself out loud, especially in front of the help."

Reina rolled her eyes. "You will not get my goat this day, child," Reina said. "I am the Queen of the Queendom. I deal with idiots all day long."

Lorelei turned to her mother. Reina put her hand over her mouth, feigning surprise at her own words. "Did I just honestly express myself out loud, especially in front of the help?"

"I best be getting on," Billy said, "before I suddenly honestly express myself out loud and get into all kinds of trouble even before I'm married."

Lorelei and Reina laughed.

"Yes, have a good day, Mr. Santos," Reina said.

"And you."

Billy left the room and closed the door behind him. As he headed for the stairs, he looked out the windows and saw Nehemiah standing in the gardens. Billy moved closer to the windows. Nehemiah had started wearing his robes again. Lately he often went barefoot. He seemed sad.

Billy had never inquired after him, even though they were both soothsayers. And Billy certainly hadn't wandered the Nexus looking for reasons why Nehemiah would be depressed. But he had wondered. Everyone had told him that Nehemiah was the glue that held the Queendom together.

He was important to the success of the Queendom.

Now this important man stood in the garden with his eyes

closed. And he looked bereft. He looked like he was going to collapse where he stood.

Hildegarde came down the path toward Nehemiah. She stopped and said something to him. He opened his eyes and looked at her. His body stiffened. She continued to talk.

"What's going on?" Umberto said coming to stand next to Billy.

"I don't know," Billy said. "Nehemiah did not look well. And now he looks angry."

"I'm afraid that woman could make anyone angry," Umberto said.

Billy looked at Umberto. It seemed quite a few people were honestly expressing themselves out loud.

"I wish she would go away," Umberto whispered.

Hildegarde turned and walked away.

"My, you've got the power then," Billy said.

"I've always said so," Umberto said. "I've come to tell the Queen about your upcoming nuptials."

"I already mentioned them to her," Billy said. "Lorelei asked, so I said."

Umberto nodded. "That's fine, that's fine. I better go myself, though, to keep up appearances. What *has* been going on with Nehemiah? Don't you all communicate with one another telepathically or whatever?"

"Whatever," Billy said.

"So can't you ask or find out?"

"Can you go to the Queen and ask her personal questions because you're both human?" Billy asked.

"I see your point," Umberto said. "By the way, watch out for that man in black. We don't want him stirring up trouble today."

"Yes, sir," Billy said.

The two parted ways and went in different directions. Billy headed downstairs.

He needed to figure out some kind of present for Abbygail that he could make before tonight. He wasn't certain how he'd do it, but he'd start out by seeing if the flowers would give him some petals for their marriage bed. He remembered seeing petals on the bed in the forest, and he had liked that. It was autumn, but some flowers were still blooming.

He got a basket from the kitchen—staying out of the cooks' way—and then he went out into the garden. He walked along the path, searching for any petals on the ground.

He was looking down when he almost ran into Nehemiah.

"Good morning, Mr. Nehemiah," Billy said.

"It's just Nehemiah, Mr. Santos," he said. "And good day to you."

As Nehemiah started to walk past him, Billy blurted out, "Abbygail and I are getting married today. You're welcome to attend. We'd like that."

Nehemiah stopped. He blinked slowly several times. "You're getting married? Today? Why? You can't have children. You have no property to speak of. You have no family to tie together."

"Most humans get married because they love each other," Billy said. "Abbygail and I love each other."

"What's that like?" Nehemiah asked. He squinted when he talked, as if it hurt him to speak.

"You've never been in love?" Billy asked.

"I don't know," he said. "That's why I'm asking. Humans fall in love because it's part of their biology. It's a way of promoting the species, of getting them to mate. We don't have that biological urge, so I am wondering what it could possibly mean for one of us to fall in love?"

"I suppose it could mean different things to different people," Billy said. "I like Abbygail. She's funny. I like her stories. She's very kind, and she speaks her mind. She has no artifice. I want to wake up and see her in the morning. I want her face to be the last thing I see at night. And in-between, I want to feel her arms around me. It's as if I've been waiting for her all my life and didn't know it."

Nehemiah nodded. "Yes, I can see that. You're marrying today? Good. I would do it as soon as you can. Do not delay."

326

"Is everything all right?" Billy asked. "You haven't seemed quite yourself."

"I have gotten very bad news," Nehemiah said. "Very bad. I am not certain what it means, yet, but if I were you I would hold onto everyone and everything you love as tightly as possible. I must go now. Congratulations."

Nehemiah walked away. And then he stopped again, turned, and said, "Remember what Rumi said. 'Lovers don't finally meet somewhere. They're in each other all along.'" He turned on his heels and kept walking.

Billy frowned. Nehemiah just told him it was the end of the world, and then he quoted Rumi.

Billy smiled, and then he laughed.

It was going to be some kind of day.

CHAPTER THIRTY-FOUR
TENG

As usual, Teng had everything in the kitchen organized and ready for the festivities. The extra help had arrived from the Queen's Village, and they were busy chopping and shredding while Wanda was busy telling them all what to do.

Turnkey did his job, quietly and efficiently as usual. In this case, he was kneading dough. Viva stood alongside him pressing cookie cutters into dough that had been stretched across her workspace. She looked exceedingly happy. Every once in a while, Turnkey said something to her and she would nod and smile. Minerva and Savi liked cookies, so Teng and crew were making a lot of cookies.

Teng observed everyone for a moment, and then she left them and went to her office. She sat in her chair and stared down at her desk. She wished they would get the test results on the Moonstruck Saffron. If it was Moonstruck Saffron, she would be the hera of the Queendom, she would get her reward, and she could save her son.

"I hate this," she whispered.

She had wanted to tell the Queen about the blackmail scheme the day they found the Moonstruck Saffron. But then the flooding started, and she didn't want to burden the Queen with her treachery. And she couldn't leave the Queen without a chef on her daughter's wedding day. Maybe she would tell her after the wedding.

"All right, Teng," she said. "Get it together."

She wanted to do something for Billy and Abbygail besides serve them leftovers from Minerva's wedding. She pulled down her Unified Field Theory of Spices notebook and opened it on her desk. It was filled with the hand-written notes she had taken when she spoke with every elder she could find who knew anything about the Unified Field Theory of Spices. She had taken notes when she searched Nexus and questioned soothsayers. And she kept a log of dishes she made and what meaning she attributed to them—and any results she could observe.

She slowly flipped through her notebook, looking for something quick and wonderful for tonight's wedding. She stopped when she saw the word "aleuromancy." It was an ancient method of divination using flour. Later, cooks tweaked the recipe so that slips of paper with writing on them became the "fortune" for whomever got a cookie. She nodded. Yes. This was perfect.

"Simple as pie," she whispered. She would make a cake, too. One could not have a wedding without some kind of cake.

Teng continued looking through her notebook. She had drawn flowers and other plants in the margins. "This one seemed to be jumping up and down with joy," she wrote about one flower. "This plant definitely wanted to become a stew," she wrote about another unidentified plant, "but I wasn't certain if it was for good or bad." "Grandma Rankin said to eat fennel for physical strength, eat garlic for protection and good health, eat apples for love and peace."

She smiled. She had enjoyed her exploration of the Unified Field Theory of Spices. She suspected that her study of the theory was coming to an end. If she was sent to the Hinterlands, she doubted she would have time to study anything.

She glanced at the clock. Time to go. She had decided that today she was telling the Man Who Was Blackmailing Her once and for all that she was finished with meeting him, finished with telling him anything at all. She grabbed a small bag filled with candies and tucked it in her pocket. She looked around her office once more, and then she left.

She stopped by the kitchen. "I will be back soon," she told them. "If Mr. Umberto wonders, I shall be back by early afternoon. You don't need me for the buffet lunch." It was cold cuts, breads, fruits, pies. Nothing she needed to worry about.

"May I come?" Viva said.

"Come with me?" Teng said. "I should say you're in the middle of cookie making. That's much more important than what I have to do. Besides, Turnkey still needs your help." She looked at him and tried to will him into understanding that she did not want her daughter to accompany her.

"Oh yes," Turnkey said. "I could not make these magic cookies without you."

"Magic?" Viva looked up at Turnkey. He looked at Teng.

"Of course they are magic," Teng said. "Magic and science often seem the same, don't they? I'll see you soon."

Teng strode out of the Hearth and into the gardens. She found the path and headed down to town. It was a beautiful day: warm, dry, and breezy. Leaves crunched beneath her feet, and the world was golden and red from the leaves that had already turned colors. The drought had hastened not only the changing of the leaves but the stone fruits and berries had ripened much earlier than usual.

Below, in the near distance, she could see the Queen's Village. It looked so cozy pressed up against the hill and spreading down into the valley, the buildings seemingly a part of the landscape, looking as though they belonged, even though they had been made by human hands. The bell tower above the courthouse jutted into the sky prettily. Every time they went by it, Viva asked if she could go inside and ring the bell. They never had. Teng didn't even know if they'd let her. She should have asked.

Teng shook herself. It wasn't as if she was going to have to leave the Queendom this minute or this hour. Maybe she wouldn't have to leave at all. The Queen was a forgiving woman. Wasn't she?

She rubbed her face and tried to subdue her panic. She wanted to run and hide. The Man had instructed her to meet him in room seven at the Wildflower Inn even though they had always met outside before. She could have insisted they meet somewhere else, but she didn't argue with him. She always tried to cajole him. She was acutely aware that he held her son's freedom in his hands.

A few minutes later, Teng walked into the Wildflower Inn. The woman at the desk nodded to her. Teng returned the gesture, but she did not say anything. She walked slowly down the hallway to room seven and knocked on the door.

The Man opened the door and motioned her inside. His window looked out at the town square which was decorated today with flowers and ribbons. Music wafted up from the square. Teng couldn't see who was playing, and she didn't know enough about musical instruments to distinguish one from another. Something with strings.

"Could I have some tea or water?" she asked. "I got so busy this morning I didn't drink anything and the walk was long and dry."

The Man looked at her. "I am not here to serve you," he said. "You are here to serve me."

"Very well," she said. "I will make it myself. I only thought we could be cordial to one another."

"Sit down," he said harshly. "I will make it. We are civilized, my people. I can make you tea."

Teng watched him fumble around the kitchen, but eventually he set a cup of heated water on the table in front of her, along with a jar of tea and a spoon.

"Will you join me?" she asked.

The Man brought a cup of something to the table with him. They sat across from one another.

They quietly sipped their liquids. Teng brought out the pouch of candies. She opened it, and the colorful balls spilled out. She picked them up one by one and set them on the pouch.

She scooped up a red one and popped it into her mouth.

"Please have one," she said. "It's a little sugar to get me through the day." She didn't tell him she had also used ingredients she hoped would persuade him to do good.

He hesitated. "I have heard you are a good chef," he said. "Are you a good candy maker, too?"

"I am," Teng said. Teng smiled at him. She loathed him, but she smiled. She had never hated anyone before—except her husband for a little while—and she did not like that feeling. But this man had ruined her time in the Queendom. She had not been able to shake him loose no matter what she tried. She wanted him out of her life now, and she wanted her son free.

The Man reached for the candies. Teng felt her heart in her throat. Maybe now she would be rid of him. He picked up a green candy with his long fingers. A bit of dirt was lodged beneath the nail of his middle finger. She resisted the urge to slap his hand and tell him to go wash first.

He put the candy in his mouth and sucked on it noisily.

"What do you have for me today?"

"I can tell you the menu for today's wedding," she said, "although you could find that on Nexus on your own."

"Have they heard anything about the plant you discovered?" he asked.

Teng didn't know how he had found out about the plant. She had not told him.

"No," Teng said. "We know nothing yet."

He nodded and continued to suck on the candy. She wished she could cover her ears so she didn't have to hear him.

"If you bite on it," she said, "there's chocolate at the center."

He bit down and began chewing. That was almost as bad as listening to him suck.

"It is very tasty," he said.

Teng almost laughed. Instead, she said, "Thank you." She took a sip of tea, and then she said, "I have come here today to tell you what I should have said all along. I am not giving you any more information about the Queendom. I will not tell you one more thing. If you ask me what color the sky is, I will not tell you. I should have sent you packing the very first time I saw you."

"What about your son?" he said. "Aren't you worried what we'll do to him? Now you will never see him again."

"Yes, I am worried about my son," she said. She stood up. "And if I have to go to the Hinterlands to find him, I will do that. I will find him. But I won't betray this country and her people."

"We could kill him!" The Man pushed away from the table.

Teng flinched. "And if you did, what would that get you besides blood on your hands?"

"You have no idea what kind of people the Villanuevas are," he said. "They do not deserve your loyalty."

"I do know what kind of people they are," she said. "They are like everyone else: good, bad, kind, rude, full of wisdom, love, spite, and distrust. But I also know they are all trying to do the best they can for the Queendom, and I won't betray them."

She walked to the door. "You should be ashamed of yourself. If you believe the Queendom is so evil, stay here and try to change what you don't like. Don't kidnap children and blackmail their mothers!"

Teng opened the door.

"You will be sorry!" the Man cried.

She turned to him. "Hah!" And then she walked over the threshold and out into the hall, slamming the door behind her.

"'Hah!'" she said. "My answer is hah? And his threat is that I'll be sorry." She shook her head as she walked down the corridor. She felt giggly, terrified, and unburdened all at the same time.

The first part of her plan to extricate herself from this mess was done. She didn't know what it meant for her son, but she had lately heard about people who travelled to the Hinterlands looking for lost family members. If she got the reward for finding the Moonstruck Saffron, she could afford to hire someone to take her to the Hinterlands. She would find her son, one way or another.

Teng walked out of the building and into the sunshine. She practically flew up the hill to the Hearth. Once inside again, the Hearth felt stuffy. She flung open the back door and put a rock in place to keep it open.

"Let's get this road on the show!" Teng called as she walked down the corridor.

Umberto was standing near the half counter that separated the kitchen from the hall.

"Marguerite Teng," Umberto said, putting his hands behind his back. "We wondered where you were off to. We were about to put the lunch buffet out. You really should go up and see the magnificence. Ministers and advisors, relatives and friends. Everyone is so beautifully attired! I find myself quite happy this day."

Teng smiled. Nothing was so heartening as seeing Mr. Umberto jovial. She didn't want to look at him, didn't want to think about how he'd view her once he knew about her betrayal.

"I have an idea for our bride and groom," Teng said.

She went into the staff dining room with Umberto at her heels. She opened the cabinet and pulled out a sheet of paper, placed it on the table, and then sat at the table. Viva came into the room, too. She smiled and kissed her mother on the cheek.

"Get me a pencil, darlin'," Teng said.

Viva ran out of the room. A moment later she came back with the kitchen pencil in hand.

"I'm going to make thirteen aleuromancy cookies," Teng said. "They used to call them fortune cookies. They will be hard cookies that you crack open. Inside each cookie will be some kind of sweet wish or blessing or good fortune. I could make them all up, but it would have more meaning and more magical punch, as it were, if we all did one so that there are thirteen wishes. Lucky thirteen."

"There aren't thirteen of us," Umberto said. "I'm assuming you don't want Billy and Abbygail to make any wishes."

"No," Teng said. "And we must keep it secret from them. It would be lovely if the First Family could be involved."

"It's a busy day for everyone."

"I know," Teng said. "But Viva could take it around, if you're up for it, daughter."

"Yes!"

"Would that be all right, Mr. Umberto?"

He shrugged and then nodded. "I can't see any harm in it."

Teng took the pencil and wrote on the top of the page, "Please write on the bottom of the page in very small letters a wish, a blessing, or a good fortune for Billy and Abbygail on the day of their wedding." She looked at Viva. "Once they write down something, rip it off the sheet carefully and save it. We'll shape them to get them into the fortune cookies once you're back. You probably shouldn't bother Miss Minerva and Miss Savi, but the rest of the First Family, plus Quintana, Nehemiah, and Elata. And us. I'll show you what I mean."

Teng took another piece of paper, looked up at the ceiling for a moment, and then wrote in tiny letters at the bottom of the paper, "May you always have wonderful meals." She showed it to Viva and Umberto. Then she carefully ripped away the part of the page with her writing on it and dropped the slip of paper into an empty bowl at the center of the table.

"Mr. Umberto?" She held up the pencil to him.

He sat at the table with her and took the pencil from her. He thought for a moment and then wrote, "I wish you great happiness and bliss."

Teng read it as he wrote it. Then he ripped the piece off with his writing on it and dropped it in the bowl.

"That's very kind," Teng said. "Viva, do you want to write something before you begin?"

She nodded and sat at the table with the adults. Umberto passed the pencil across the table to her. She pursed her lips and swung her legs. Then she began to write. When she finished, she pushed the paper over to her mother. Teng read out loud, "I wish you strong lungs so you can always sing out your love."

"That is very poetic," Umberto said.

Teng slid the paper back over to Viva. She carefully ripped off her words and put them in the bowl. Then she got up from the table.

"I'll start with Turnkey," Viva said, and then she was gone.

Umberto got up. "Would you like to see the set-up for the buffet now?" he asked. "You'd be proud."

Teng felt sick to her stomach. What had she done by telling the Man she wouldn't help him? What would happen to Cristopher now?

"I am sure you did a magnificent job as always," Teng said. "But I still have so much to do before the wedding celebration."

"And we're invited to the wedding," he said. "That is only two hours away!"

"Imagine that," she said.

"Are you all right, Marguerite Teng?" Umberto asked. "You are paler than usual."

"I—I." She stopped and looked at him. They had become friends, she was sure of it, just as she had become friends with Raphael. But she could not risk alienating him by confessing her misdeeds. It would be easier telling the Queen than it would be telling Mr. Umberto. "I'm a little off my game. I will rally! Don't worry."

"I'm expecting a dance from you tonight," Umberto said as he left the room. "Don't disappoint."

Teng could hear her daughter in the other room, cajoling Turnkey and Wanda into writing blessings for Billy and Abbygail. She wanted to stay very still and savor this moment of peace and happiness.

She shook herself and got up. No time for that. She had a cake to create.

She clapped her hands together once. Yes. Later she could tell the Queen. Right now, she needed to work.

CHAPTER THIRTY-FIVE

LORELEI

Lorelei sat with her mother in her apartment eating breakfast. It had been a long while since she had spent this much time with her mother. She enjoyed it. It was almost as if everything were back to normal again.

She knew it wasn't. Too much had changed. She had only to look out and see the blackened Safran Bleu fields. Even after all these months, nothing was growing in the fields. And the flooding had made everything worse.

Their hopes all hung on the Moonstruck Saffron.

"Lorelei," her mother said, pushing her empty plate away, "I know it has been a difficult time as of late. I can't say it will get better right away. Our loan to Berland is past due, and we haven't been able to pay it in full." She chewed on her lip. Then she put up her hand. "It will be fine. Outram is an old friend. I trust him. This situation has made the others in the C5 nervous. If our economy falters, so does theirs. Do you understand?"

"Yes, Mother," Lorelei said.

"Minerva, as you know, has said she does not want to become Queen," Reina said. "I hope she changes her mind, but she may not. Raphael is next in line, but he has a long way to go before Queendomers would accept him as leader. They hold you in esteem, however, so you should think about your future in this regard."

Lorelei stared at her mother. She blinked. She shook her head. Then she said, "Are you asking me if I want to be queen?"

"I am," she said. "If you are interested, we should start your training. You and Raphael both. Do you know what you would like to do as your work before then?"

"I—I don't," Lorelei said. "I've not thought about it. I like talking to the crows and the trees. Is there a call for that?"

Her mother smiled. "We need poets and writers and artists. Isn't that what they do? You have blossomed so much in the last six months. It is a wonder to behold. It's like watching a butterfly come out of its cocoon, if that doesn't sound too cliché."

Lorelei smiled. "No. But you will remain as queen for decades, won't you? Do you plan to step down?"

Reina shook her head. "No. In the beginning I was unsure. And sometimes today, I wonder if I'm good for the country. But this is what I was born to do. I owe Hildegarde a great debt for what she did."

"What were you doing before you became queen?" Lorelei asked.

"Besides raising you three?" she said. "Not much of anything. I had trouble finding something I could stick with. Like your brother, in a way. Then Hildy left, and I was all set. Maybe you and Raphael can become my advisors. I need to talk to him about it. He has seemed rather lost lately, hasn't he? I thought when you found the Moonstruck Saffron that he would feel better." She shook her head and looked away. "He *has* been cheerful about the wedding. Do you know what if anything is going on with him?"

"Mom, I thought we weren't doing that any more," Lorelei said.

"I'm sorry," Reina said. "I never knew it bothered you. I thought you felt like you were doing the work of the Queendom."

"I did," Lorelei said, "and then I didn't."

"In any case, I am concerned about Raphael. And I am concerned about our country. There is a possibility of a hostile takeover. It's in the treaty. If the economy of one nation is threatening the economy of another nation or nations, that first nation can be temporarily taken over."

Lorelei nodded. She knew all of this—it had happened in the past once or twice to other nations—but she couldn't imagine it happening now.

"Don't they need four votes out of five?" Lorelei asked. "That wouldn't happen. You said Premier Outram is your friend." Lorelei wondered, for a split second, if this was the time to tell her mother that she knew Outram was her father. She brushed the thought away. "And President Ixchel would do anything for us."

Reina nodded. "I believe all will be well. But I have not been able to get a hold of any of the leaders. None of them. Nehemiah can't either. I talked with their representatives, the ones who came for the wedding. Each one told Nehemiah and I the same thing: the leaders of the free world have been too busy to get back with us or come to the wedding." She made a noise.

"Even if there were a hostile takeover," Lorelei said, "it's temporary, right? We would get our economy back on track and pay off the loan, and all will be well."

Reina nodded. "Yes, but one of them would be the boss of us— the one who instigated the takeover. I imagine that would be Prime Minister Lerner. I sometimes believe only thieves live in Armistead. I don't know how they got into the Consolidated Five."

"Because if you called it the Consolidated Five with only four countries, it would seem odd." Lorelei smiled. Reina laughed.

"My girl," Reina said, "it's time we get dressed and mingle with our guests. For appearances, you know."

"Do you ever get tired of that?" Lorelei asked. "Of pretending things are one way when they are actually another."

Reina sighed. "Honestly? I try not to think about it."

They heard a knock on the door. It opened and Elata came into the room.

"Good morning, Your Majesty," Elata said, "and you, too, Miss Lorelei. The house is abuzz, and you two are up here gossiping."

"We are not gossiping," Lorelei said. "We are solving problems."

"You don't say?" Elata said. "Could you solve all of my problems, too?"

Reina rolled her eyes. "I can't imagine you have any problems."

"Come, queen of mine, it's time to dress."

Reina groaned. "I'm not going down for lunch. I will make a grand entrance at the wedding. So I have a while before I need to dress."

Elata shook her head. "Suit yourself. Nehemiah is waiting outside. He says it's urgent."

Lorelei said, "I'll go get dressed. I'll be back."

She should let Nehemiah and her mother talk in private. If something terrible was happening in the Queendom, the two of them could fix it.

She kissed her mother good-bye and then left the room. Lorelei walked a short way and saw Nehemiah pacing the corridor. He kept glancing out the window.

"Good morning, Mr. Nehemiah," Lorelei said.

He looked over at her and stopped still. He was wearing his robes again. Lorelei was glad. For some reason, the robes calmed her.

"Are you well?" she asked.

"Yes, why do you ask?"

Lorelei laughed. "Because it's the polite thing to do."

"Oh, yes," he said. "I'm still not accustomed to you talking." He shook his head, as though startled at his own response. "It's a busy morning."

Lorelei nodded. "I noticed. And the Queen noticed that none of the heads of state are here for the wedding. Is that significant?"

Nehemiah squinted as he looked at her. "What do you think?"

"I think it is significant," Lorelei said. "Mother says Outram and Ixchel would never betray the Queendom. What say you to that?"

"I believe anyone could betray the Queendom if pushed," he said, "inside or outside of our borders."

Lorelei nodded. "I had a dream last night."

Nehemiah said nothing.

"It was significant," she said.

He cocked his head, encouraging her to keep talking.

"The Hearth crumbled to the ground," she said. "First the walls fell forward. Then the rocks disintegrated. For a while, the only thing left standing was the Hand of Peace. Then it disappeared along with our Constitution. I saw a woman dancing on the ruins of the Hearth, as though she were dancing on a grave. She had a red dot or something on her forehead."

"The walls fell forward," he said. "Betrayal from within."

"I hadn't thought about that," Lorelei said. "But that makes sense."

"Did you recognize the woman?" Nehemiah asked.

"I did not," Lorelei said. "But the Old Oak was filled with crows. Some were white, some were black."

Something about hearing the dream appeared to make Nehemiah stand up straighter. He didn't seem as nervous. It was so odd to see Nehemiah nervous. But lately, lately, he had been odd.

"Is everything all right with you?" Lorelei asked again.

Nehemiah looked at her without saying a word for a minute. Then he said, "All is not well in the Queendom. Find your brother; send him up. You, too. I need to talk with all of you."

"I will," she said.

Lorelei left Nehemiah and went down her stairs to the next floor. She heard a raven call out. It sounded so close. She wondered if it was white or black. She had only ever seen a white raven in her dreams or in her imagination. Today felt dreamy. Not in a good way. Not in a bad way. In a dreamy way.

Lorelei made her way through the phalanx of people milling

about in the wide corridor. She wondered why they weren't all outside on this beautiful day.

She saw Raphael talking with Viva. She waved to Viva, but the child didn't see her. She was moving away, looking for someone.

"Raphael," Lorelei called.

He saw her and walked to her.

"What is it, little one?" Raphael asked. He smiled at her. She wanted to kick him.

"Nehemiah wants to see you," she said. "Up in Mom's room."

Instantly Raphael looked worried. "Is it about the Moonstruck Saffron?"

"I don't know," she said. "He didn't tell me."

"Did he seem angry?" he asked.

"No. I've never seen Nehemiah angry."

"What are you talking about?" Raphael said. "He is always angry."

"Rafe," Lorelei said. "Go up there, and you'll find out. I'll be up, too."

"He wants to see you, too?"

"Yes!" Lorelei hurried away, left the house, and walked toward the woods.

She felt guilty fleeing her brother, but she was exasperated with him. She wished she had more compassion for him, but mostly, he irritated her. Reina wanted them to train together in case one of them had to become leader of the Queendom: Lorelei could not imagine Raphael leader of anything, let alone a country.

Lorelei was grateful to step into the quiet semi-darkness of the forest. She went down the path until she was certain no one from the wedding was wandering about. She stood very still and listened.

"Crow," she whispered, her eyes closed. "Show me."

She opened her eyes and looked up. A crow flew overhead, heading north. She stepped off the path and went a little ways north.

Then she called, "Patra of the Queen's Court! I am in need of your assistance." Her voice echoed through the forest. She had not realized she was even capable of yelling that loudly.

After a minute or so, she heard rustling and then saw Patra walking toward her. Today, he was dressed in brown slacks and a green T-shirt.

He stopped about twenty feet from her.

"What is it, Your Majesty?" he asked.

"First, don't call me that," she said. "Second, Umberto told us you had been spying on us, and he warned you not to return. What are you doing here?"

"I wasn't spying," he said. "We've been concerned about your safety. About the safety of your family."

"Why?" she asked. She heard a crow call out. She looked up. The crow was circling. Someone was approaching.

"Someone is coming," she said. "Hide!"

Lorelei went to the nearest tree and crouched next to it. Patra leaned against the tree closest to him.

"What direction?" Patra asked.

"I don't know," she whispered. "Probably from the wedding."

They got still. After a minute or two, Lorelei heard two people talking as they passed by. She looked around the tree and saw two men. They were not paying attention to anything around them. When they were out of sight and sound, Lorelei sat on the ground, her back against the tree. Patra did the same thing.

"Why do you believe we're in danger?" she asked. "And from whom? Umberto says your group is a bunch of crackpots longing for a return to the past."

"There's every indication that those fires were set deliberately," Patra said.

"That's speculation," Lorelei said. "We don't know anything for certain. Even so, the fire harmed the saffron fields, not us."

"We believe someone is trying to overthrow the government," he said.

"Wouldn't that be you and yours?" Lorelei asked.

"No," he said. "I told you before that we want to help. We know some want to destroy the monarchy, and we are against that. But mostly, we want to defend our nation. Things have not been going well."

"Anyone could see that," Lorelei said. "I was hoping you had more specific information."

"I'm sorry, but I don't."

Lorelei stood. Patra remained on the ground next to the tree. She looked down at him.

"I need to know if you and your people are willing to help us," she said, "should the need arise. I don't yet know how, but I have a feeling. I had a dream last night that the Hearth was in ruins."

Patra nodded. "I hope it will not be so, but I will do anything you ask."

"And I hope that isn't true," Lorelei said. "What if I was a raving lunatic and asked you to go around the countryside killing people?"

Patra smiled. "All right. I will do anything you ask within reason."

Lorelei shook her head. "What I might ask could sound unreasonable."

Patra laughed. "OK. OK! Let me know if you need anything."

"This is between us," Lorelei said. "Not your group. You can't tell them I spoke with you."

"Oh, please, come on. I have to tell them. This is the pinnacle of my life."

Lorelei rolled her eyes. "If this is the pinnacle of your life—well, I'm glad to be of service."

As Patra got to his feet, Lorelei walked away.

"Have a good wedding!" he called. He sounded too excited. She was eighteen years old, and he wanted to take orders from her. He wanted to do her bidding. She looked back. She couldn't see him.

She hoped she had not just made a terrible mistake.

CHAPTER THIRTY-SIX
RAPHAEL

Midday Raphael hummed under his breath as he walked the corridors of the Hearth nodding hello to this person and that person. He knew them all, remembered each and every name. Occasionally he stopped to chat, sometimes talking while holding the other person's hand. Everyone had heard about the Moonstruck Saffron and wanted to know every detail of the discovery.

Raphael was good at feigning interest. He was good at being entertaining. Even when he didn't feel like it. He wanted to find Boann, Outram's daughter. She had told him she would be there, with her father, but Raphael hadn't seen her at breakfast or now at lunch. He hadn't seen Outram either, for that matter.

In fact, he had not seen any of the leaders of the Consolidated Five. They each had sent their second in command or an advisor. He spotted Mr. Peetall, that toad from Berland. He was careful not to catch his eye. He had no desire to spend any time with Mr. Peetall.

Where was President Ixchel of Erdom? She was a great friend of his mother's and to the Queendom. Chief Flora Diaz from Paquay State hadn't made an appearance either, although her advisor Teasdale was about somewhere. Raphael hadn't seen Prime Minister Damon Lerner of Armistead, but he wasn't surprised by this, given that his mother had practically accused Armistead of once again stealing from them. Raphael had spotted Lerner's advisor Mauve in deep conversation earlier in the day with Teasdale and Peetall. Raphael thought it was tacky to do business during a day of family celebration, but he wasn't queen or chief, so what did he know?

Where was Boann? She was the only one he wanted to see.

The cook's daughter came up to him.

"Hello, there," he said. "Genevieve, right?" The girl nodded. "What can I do for you?"

"We're making fortune cookies for Billy and Abbygail," she said. "They're getting married today, too. Will you write down a wish for them?" She held out the paper and pencil to him.

Raphael took the proffered items.

"A wish, eh?" he said. They moved out of the center of the corridor. Since they were right by the library, Raphael went inside. He put the sheet of paper down on the table nearest to the Hand of Peace and the Constitution. "I need to write something kind. Something wise?"

"I think so," she said. "It's a gift. A gift of words."

Raphael stared at the paper. He could not think of a single thing to write. That wasn't correct: He could not think of anything *kind* to write. He could say, "Run! You're going to be miserable." Or "Love doesn't last!" Or "You're idiots! Why would soothsayers want to chain themselves to one another for life?"

The girl must have sensed his panic. She said, "What do *you* like to do? That's something that you could wish for them."

Raphael could only think of one thing he enjoyed. At the bottom of the paper, he wrote, "Watch sunrises together."

Raphael handed the paper and pencil back to the girl.

"Will that do?"

"That's nice," Viva said. "I like sunrises, too. We sing the sun up every day."

"Everything seems new at sunrise," Raphael said as they walked into the corridor together. "All your sins are behind you. Everyone is a saint in the morning."

"Thank you, Mr. Raphael," she said. "Have a good wedding day."

"You, too," he said.

The girl left, and suddenly Lorelei was beside him and telling him Nehemiah wanted to talk to him. He tried to press her for more information, but she was gone, just like that. She was a queer girl, his sister. She had hardly said a word her entire life, acting as if she were not all there, and now—now what? She was different. He wasn't quite sure how. She certainly said more. But something else was going on with her lately.

The whole world seemed different lately.

He felt sick as he made his way through the crowd to the stairs. What could Nehemiah want with him? He hadn't found out about the fire, had he? No. That was impossible. Maybe they had the results for the Moonstruck Saffron. Yes! That would be good news. He was certain of it. Then all of this would make sense. He still didn't understand how the fires had gotten so out of control. He had asked two of his friends from the Service to start two fires in other parts of the country. Make it look like a lightning strike, he had told them. Nothing devastating. He didn't say "nothing devastating," but they must have known. He only wanted to damage the crops enough so that the price would go up.

He had not taken the drought into consideration. He never thought the fire would burn so hot it could ruin the soil.

He hoped it was temporary.

He could barely make himself go up the stairs.

He stopped and looked down. Maybe he should go talk to Teng, see what she was up to. No. She'd be busy with the wedding. He was going to have to face Nehemiah.

He passed Elata going down the stairs.

"They're waiting for you," she said as she went past him.

"Is it doom and gloom or sun and fun?"

"I never know these days," she said. "Go on up and take your medicine."

Raphael rubbed his head. That stupid hum. He kept hearing it.

He wished he could make it stop. He wished he could remember a time in his life when he was happy for more than five minutes at a time. He wished he could remember a time when he felt competent.

"Walk up the stairs, Raphael," he said, "just walk up the stairs."

CHAPTER THIRTY-SEVEN
REINA

Reina felt nervous as soon as the door shut behind Lorelei. Elata was watching her.

"Did you hear what I said about Nehemiah?" Elata said. "He needs to speak with you."

"Someone always needs to speak with me," Reina said. She knew she sounded annoyed.

Actually, she sounded childish.

"I'm sorry, Elata. Just give me a second. He might be bringing bad news about the Moonstruck Saffron."

"Or he might be bringing you good news. In any case, the news isn't going to change because you wait."

"Good point," Reina said. "Which means I can wait a few minutes."

"That's not exactly what I meant."

Reina grinned. "I know." She got up from the table and went to the couch and sat on it.

Nehemiah rarely came up to her private chambers these days. Although their working relationship had returned to its old ease, for the most part, he stayed at arm's length from her. And he made no mention of his confession at Stone Monastery.

Reina made no mention of it either. But she did stop seeing Fan. She thanked him for his work and sent him on his way.

And she was sorry every day that she had done so. Once or twice she had considered going to Talib. When she felt slightly nauseated at the prospect, she decided it wasn't a good idea.

She wished Outram would visit. She had hoped he would come to the wedding. She had invited him, but she had not heard from him in weeks. She thought about their time on the forest bed often. She had walked out to the spot in the forest where the bed had been and was disappointed that nothing remained of their tryst. Besides her memory of it. And Outram's, no doubt.

And maybe in Nehemiah's memory since he had witnessed at least part of their love-making.

"Is everything all right between you and Nehemiah?" Elata asked.

"Why do you ask? Has he said something to you?"

Elata went to Reina's closet and opened the door. She looked through her clothes until she found what Reina was to wear today. She pulled them out and put them on the bed.

"Has he said anything to *me?*" Elata said. "No. He never talks about work with me. Besides, we haven't been seeing each other in that way much lately." She shrugged. "We've both been busy."

"Does that bother you?" Reina asked.

Elata looked over at her. "Does it bother me Nehemiah and I aren't having sex? No. It's fun. But he's not the only fish in the sea. Although, really, once you've had sex with a soothsayer, it's difficult to go back."

"Go back?" Reina said. Her eyes widened. "You have sex with humans?"

"Why are you surprised?" Elata asked. "You have sex with soothsayers."

Reina shook her head and waved her hands. "One soothsayer. And I have known you all of my life, and you never said a word about your sex life until recently. Now I know too much."

"Turnabout is fair play," Elata said.

"Is that your way of telling me that you know too much about my sex life? Or lack thereof?"

"Naw! I don't mind. You always were a little bit of a—a little bit more discreet than the average person. Your mother, for instance—"

"Stop right there," Reina said.

Elata laughed. "I'm teasing you."

Someone knocked on the door. Elata went over to it and opened it. The cook's daughter stood on the threshold.

"Yes?" Elata asked.

"I have a favor to ask of you," she said. "Mr. Nehemiah did it. I hope you will, too."

Elata looked at Reina, and she nodded.

"Come in then," Elata said.

The girl stepped into the room. She held a paper up to her chest.

"What is it?" Elata asked. "We've got a wedding to prepare for."

"Yes, Ma'am," Viva said. "Um, Abbygail and Billy are getting married today. Mom is making thirteen fortune cookies for them. She wants each of you to write out a wish or a blessing. Then we'll put it in the cookie. I've gotten the people downstairs and Quintana, Raphael, and Nehemiah."

"Nehemiah?" Reina said. She leaned forward. "What did his say?"

Viva set the now half-sheet of paper on the low table in front of Reina's couch. Then she dug into her pocket and pulled out several slips of paper. When she found the one she wanted, she gave it to Reina and stuffed the others back into her pocket.

Reina smoothed out the slip of paper and read, "May you know love for all your days and nights."

"What does it say?" Elata asked.

Reina handed her the paper. Elata read it. She looked at Viva.

"Are you sure Nehemiah wrote this?"

"Yes, I watched him, and then I read it."

Elata handed the slip of paper back to Viva.

Reina wrote on the bottom of the paper, "I wish you great happiness forever." She thought about adding, "except for some bumps in the road to remind you what true happiness is." There wasn't enough room.

Reina carefully ripped off her wish and handed it to Viva. Then she passed the paper over to Elata who sat on the couch. Reina looked over her shoulder as she wrote, "Safe travels, but not too safe." Elata chuckled, ripped off her words, and then handed everything back to Viva.

"Thank you, Ma'am," Viva said. She curtsied. Then she went to the door, opened it, went outside, and closed it again.

"Nehemiah is in love," Elata said as soon as the door closed.

Reina looked at her. "What do you mean?"

"That would explain his moods lately," she said. "That would certainly explain his fortune cookie message. Shall I let him in, and we can ask him?"

Elata got up and went to the door. She stood with her hand on the knob.

Reina sighed.

"So you know," Reina said. "Why didn't you say so?"

"I was waiting for you to tell me," Elata said.

"It's not my business to tell you!" Reina said. "And it's got nothing to do with me—except that it does have to do with me. We're trying to go about business as usual, like adults. If we don't talk about it, it'll go away. We haven't had sex, by the way. In case you were wondering. That would be strange. You and I having sex with the same person. Almost like my mother and I having sex with the same person. Which has not happened—and even if it has, don't tell me."

"I've had sex with Fan," Elata said.

Reina put her hands over her ears. "Oh god. Elata! Quit telling me these things!"

"You need to stop being shocked by the world," Elata said. "You are the Queen, for criminy's sake. Get over it. People eat, drink, shit, sleep, have sex, and then start all over again. That's life. And I did not have sex with Fan."

"Please let Nehemiah in," Reina said. "I'd rather talk about the end of the world than continue this conversation."

"Suit yourself," Elata said. She opened the door. "Nehemiah!" she called.

"Elata," Reina said. "I could have done that myself."

Nehemiah stepped into the room.

"Your Majesty," he said. "Elata."

"Nehemiah, come in," Reina said.

"I have some news," he said. "I've asked Lorelei and Raphael to join us."

Elata said, "I will return in fifteen minutes, and then we have to get you dressed." Elata walked past Nehemiah, gave him a look, and then left the room. She closed the door quite firmly.

"Why do you want the children here?" Reina asked.

"What I have to say concerns them," he said. "Should I find Minerva, too?"

Reina shook her head. "Get to it, Nehemiah. What's going on?"

"It's not good, my queen," he said. "None of the news is good. The Consolidated Five are voting to decide on a hostile takeover of Queendom. Today. I believe it's Prime Minister Lerner who believes you'll be too busy with the wedding to attend to this."

"Too busy because of a wedding?" Reina said. "That's ridiculous. Not one of them will return a message. Isn't there some way you can work your soothsayer/Nexus connection to get them to talk to me?"

"I talked with all the advisors," Nehemiah said. "Peetall says Outram will be here for the wedding. As long as he does not vote against us, we should be fine."

"He won't go against us," Reina said. "Neither will Ixchel. But I'm concerned about some back room negotiations. We have never operated in such a manner. Let's get the Queen's Advisors in tomorrow, so we can decide how to respond. Maybe we can boycott products from the instigator."

"That doesn't get our economy moving," he said.

Someone knocked on the door.

"Come in," Reina called.

A moment later, the door opened, and Raphael and Lorelei stepped into the room.

"Have you news about the Moonstruck Saffron?" Raphael asked. He went to stand behind the couch and his mother so that he was facing Nehemiah. Lorelei sat on the couch.

"I do," Nehemiah said. "We still don't know if it is the legendary Moonstruck Saffron."

"What?" Raphael said.

"Perhaps we will never know," Nehemiah said. "It doesn't seem to make a very good dye. And the medicinal properties are slight. It isn't part of the crocus family. In fact, it's in the nightshade family, it's an alkaloid, and it has hallucinogenic properties."

"It causes hallucinations?" Raphael said. "That could be good."

"What kind of hallucinations?" Reina asked.

"It probably depends upon the person," Nehemiah said.

"Buyer beware," Raphael said.

"Raphael!" Reina snapped. He was too desperate for this plant to be the Moonstruck Saffron. What difference could it make to his life? She looked at her son. She doubted he knew the full extent of the Queendom's economic troubles.

"I'm saying that some people want hallucinations," he said. "People take the datura plant for just that thing. We could make it into some kind of holy visionary plant that costs a fortune to buy."

"That's not who we are," Lorelei said.

"Then who are we?" Raphael asked. "We sell our art, our stories, our performances, and we sell saffron. That's how we live. Now we've got a plant that can offer visions. A plant that Lorelei, Teng, and I found. A plant we were led to, one could say."

"Some of the researchers experimented with dosages," Nehemiah said. "They did have good visions."

"So this could be good news?" Reina asked.

Even the prospect of a new plant might shore up their credit.

"They've discovered that about ten percent of the population would become addicted to it," Nehemiah said.

"Ten percent?" Raphael said. "That's not much. We could screen for it."

"Could we screen for it?" Reina asked.

"It's a narcotic," Nehemiah said. "That's difficult to screen for. Some people will get addicted, some won't."

"We should do more testing then," Raphael said.

Reina shook her head. "No," Reina said. "I'm not putting a potentially addictive drug out in the world because we might be able to profit from it."

Raphael came around to face his mother.

"Why not? We have to do something."

Reina stood. "*Why not?* Are you actually asking that? Because we don't do that. How do you think the world was destroyed before? It was greed, just like this. We will do something, but it won't be this."

"Mother, this has to work," Raphael said. "I found it. It could be my—my—" He seemed at a loss for words.

"Your what?" Reina asked.

"I need to do something for my country," Raphael said. "Something worthwhile. It's all such a mess."

Reina made a noise and moved away from her son. "This isn't it," Reina said. "I'm not going to allow this drug out into the world because you want to feel better about yourself."

Lorelei said quietly, "The smell of smoke on your clothes."

Raphael looked at her. Reina frowned.

"Lorelei," Raphael said. Reina heard a warning in his voice.

Lorelei opened her mouth, shook her head. "I didn't believe it at the time. I thought it couldn't be. You wouldn't do that."

"Do what?" Reina asked.

Raphael put his head in his hands.

"Are you going to tell her?" Nehemiah asked.

"You know what they're talking about?" Reina asked.

"I have learned the results of the investigation into the fires," Nehemiah said.

"Stand up and look at me, Raphael," Reina demanded. "What have you done?"

When Raphael moved his hands away, tears were streaming down his face.

"I started the fire," Raphael said.

Reina stepped back from Raphael.

"By accident?" she asked.

He shook his head. "I thought if there was less saffron in the world, the price for what we had left would go up."

"Only we don't have any left!" Reina said. "How'd the other fires start?"

"I asked two friends to help," he said.

"To help? To help you destroy our country?" Reina asked, her voice raised.

"They thought they were helping," he said. "I thought I was helping."

"This is the stupidest thing I've ever heard," Reina said. She looked over at Nehemiah. "You knew?"

"I just got the report on the investigation," Nehemiah said again.

"So it's public," she said. "Everyone knows."

Nehemiah shook his head. "It won't be made public until or unless you release it to the public."

"What does the report say?"

"They found DNA at the site which indicates Raphael Villanueva was at the point of origin before the fire started."

"That could mean anything," Raphael said. "I worked there for a time. Maybe those people who are plotting against us put my DNA there. It would be so easy."

"But you did it," Reina said. She looked at Nehemiah. "What else?"

"His two friends told investigators that they were ordered by the crown to start the fires."

Reina's eyes widened, and she turned to look at her son. She couldn't see anything else in the room except Raphael's face.

"Did you tell them that I wanted them to burn down the saffron fields? Did you put our government in jeopardy by claiming *we* wanted this to happen?"

Raphael shook his head. "No. I would never do that. I told them it was for the good of the country."

"So they believed you were a mouthpiece for me," Reina said. "Do you understand what you've done? If this gets out, we could be exiled. This country could be in complete chaos and ruin."

"No," he said. "I'll tell them you had nothing to do with it. They'll send me through reconciliation. It'll be fine."

"And those men? Your friends? What about them?"

"I don't know," he said. "They shouldn't have been stupid enough to do as I asked."

"That is a ridiculous and heartless thing to say," Reina said.

"What are you going to do?" Raphael asked.

"You and Lorelei need to get dressed for the wedding," she said. "Don't tell anyone anything about what's happened here. I'll decide what to do tomorrow."

"I am so, so sorry," Raphael said.

"That doesn't help," Reina said. "Just a little while ago, I was discussing the possibility of you and Lorelei training and studying to see who would be the most qualified to become the next leader of the Queendom. How stupid that was of me. There is no chance the people would ever elect you. You are—"

Reina saw a shadow of movement and knew Nehemiah had stepped closer to her. He was warning her not to say anything irrevocable.

"I am disappointed," Reina said, "and beyond that, I don't know how I will save you or any of us from this. Go on, now. Don't do anything stupid between now and tomorrow."

Raphael didn't say anything. He quickly left the room.

Lorelei said, "What can I do?"

Reina shook her head. "Enjoy the wedding," she said. "It may be our last celebration for a long time."

Lorelei left, too, and Reina was alone with Nehemiah. They looked at each other.

"What can I do?" she asked. "What can we do?"

He slowly shook his head. "If you announce the results to the citizens, they might call for an election. If you don't, they might call for your head. Not literally, but still."

"Our family can't be above the law," she said. "The constable will be here tonight. Maybe I can talk to her about it."

"You could always ask Savi what she thinks," he said.

"I don't need to ask anyone," she said. "I know what I must do. Is there a way to keep Raphael's friends out of it? They shouldn't be punished for Raphael's stupidity. What was he thinking?"

"They did start the fires," Nehemiah said. "We should turn over the evidence to the local constables. They can take it from there."

"This is unprecedented," Reina said. "I must speak to the nation tomorrow, before it all comes out."

Nehemiah nodded. "Shall I go see if Constable Younge has arrived yet?"

Reina shook her head. "No, I should talk to Talib first. And about the Moonstruck Saffron—or whatever it is. Do you think it's the right thing to do, not to sell it?"

"It's the ethical thing to do," he said. "It would have brought in some much needed credit, if we had sold it right. But, yes, I agree with you."

Reina palmed her eyes. "What a mess. If we get through this day in one piece, it'll be a miracle."

"I'll get Talib," he said.

"Could you please tell him what's going on?" Reina asked. "I can't face him."

Nehemiah looked at her.

"All right, all right." She reached for Nehemiah's right hand and squeezed it. He held on to her hand for a moment. It was the first time since the storm at Stone Monastery that they had touched.

She didn't want to let go of his hand.

"Is there any way we can manage this?" Reina asked.

"With truth and integrity," he said. "That's how you've always reigned. Trust in that."

She nodded. She had an urge to kiss him and thank him.

She refrained.

He left the room. She went to her bedroom and undressed. Then she began putting on her mother-of-the-bride clothes. As usual, Elata had put together something beautiful for her. She pulled on a pair of tight-fitting light blue slacks. Then she slipped into a blue and gold blouse. Some of the threads were blue, some gold. White-gold lace decorated the front, where it fit snugly against her breasts; the lace curled up to her sleeves and down to the bottom of the shirt. She flipped up the big blue collar.

There. She was ready to go.

Someone knocked on the door.

Must be Talib. She straightened her shirt.

"Come," she said.

The door opened.

Outram stood on the threshold. He was dressed all in black—except his jacket was laced with gold. Reina grinned. He was so handsome. What a beautiful pair they would make. He smiled. She motioned him inside. Once he closed the door, she went to him and put her arms around his neck and kissed him. He returned the embrace.

When they pulled away from one another, Outram said, "I have missed you."

"Where have you been?" Reina asked. "I have been trying to get a hold of you for days."

"We had trouble with our transportation," he said. "And our Nexus wasn't working."

"I wish you had a soothsayer on staff," she said. "Then you would never have to worry about communication."

He shrugged.

"What about our debt?" Reina asked. "Can we renegotiate the terms?"

"We can work something out," he said. "I heard rumors that you've found the Moonstruck Saffron."

"They found a new plant," she said. "We were hoping, but it wasn't the Moonstruck Saffron."

"It has some visionary properties, I heard," he said.

"How do you know these things? It is supposed to be secret. It can give people hallucinations—or visions. But it's a narcotic. A percentage of people could get addicted to it if we put it on the market."

"Can't you test for that?" he asked. "Or create an antidote?"

"Maybe an antidote," she said. "But so far, they don't have a good enough test. They're not certain which people will get addicted. You know how it is with these kinds of substances. It's part of the nightshade family. I'm not willing to risk it."

"Did you ask your advisory counsel?" he asked.

She frowned. "Outram, I don't need to ask them. It would be wrong to put this up for sale."

"But you'll continue research on it?"

"Of course," she said. "We can secure the loan some other way. I'm meeting with my advisors tomorrow."

He nodded. "Good. Now I have a proposal for you."

She smiled. "All right. What is it?"

"A proposal," he said. "I would like us to marry. I love you. You love me. We have a child together. We can combine our houses, and we'll be a force to reckon with. Berland and Queendom."

"A force to reckon with?" Reina said. "We already are the leaders of two great nations. Who do we have to reckon with?"

"It's a figure of speech," he said. "You're missing the point of what I said." He put his arms around her and pulled her close to him. "I love you. Let's do what we originally planned. 'Come live with me and be my love, and we will all the pleasures prove.'"

Reina smiled and put her hands on his chest. "Ah, you know the way to a Queendomer's heart: quote poetry. I'm surprised you didn't pull out all the stops with a line from one of our beloved Praxilla's poems."

"'Oh, to be the words floating on your breath, the apple in your belly, the dirt on your soles. That would be living.'"

Reina laughed. "That is one of my favorite poems." She sighed. "But nothing has changed. We are both still married."

"Actually, my wife and I are no longer married. We dissolved the union."

"I hadn't heard," Reina said. "I'm sorry."

"I'm not," he said. "Now I'm free. Free yourself from Talib. You know he's a weight around your neck."

"He has been a good consort," she said.

Outram laughed. "You've told me how many times you found him having sex with some other woman or some other man. Or both. Maybe he's good at sex, but he isn't a good husband. I would be a good husband."

"Bay, we have gone our separate ways since our engagement. I have a life here. You have a life there."

"And never the twain shall meet?"

"We meet," Reina said. "We meet and get naked and/or talk business."

"I want more," he said.

Reina didn't say anything.

"So the answer is no?" he said.

"At least for now," she said. "Maybe if you wanted to give up Berland and come here. But even then, we hardly know each other any more."

"I know your soul," he said. "You know mine."

Reina moved away from him. "I don't even know my own soul," she said. "How can I know yours?"

He looked at her quizzically for several long moments. Then he nodded and said, "Very well, Queen Reina. It is almost time for the wedding, and I should leave you be. We'll talk later."

"Yes," Reina said. "Please. Did you want to stay the night? You are certainly welcome. Here, in my bed."

He shook his head. "No, we have a place in the village. Thank you." He sounded so formal again. The Premier of Berland.

He bowed slightly. And then he opened the door. Talib was standing on the threshold. Outram didn't say a word to Talib who shrugged and came into the room when Reina motioned him inside.

"What is it, my queen?" Talib asked as the door shut behind Outram. "Another lecture on propriety? Do you want to ban me from the wedding like you did from the May Day festivities?"

Reina sighed. "I have never lectured you on proprieties, although I should have. I did not ban you from the May Day festivities."

"You had someone else as your consort," he said.

"That's because I wanted to have sex that day," she said, "and I wasn't going to have it with you. And yes, I had sex with the Green Man that day. We fucked all day long. I called you here to tell you that Raphael started the fires. He started the one here and had two of his cronies start the other two. I don't know about the fourth. Maybe it was lightning. He thought it would help the Queendom's economy. What he has done is a crime. We will decide tomorrow when to turn him in to the constable. It will be bad, but I thought you should know. Raphael might need the support of his family right now."

Talib bit his upper lip. "He's such an idiot."

"He is not an idiot!" Reina said. "He's desperate. He's always been desperate. We don't appreciate him. He has no role model in you. You can barely be around your children, except for Minerva. She doesn't need you. Raphael does. I don't need you. In fact, I want a divorce. I don't love you. I don't even like you. I can't believe I gave up Outram for you. You've done nothing with your life except live off of me and fuck everything that moves. And you don't do that very well, by the way."

"Your only son is going to jail, and you want a divorce? That won't be good for your image."

"My image is fine," she said. "Because I am fine. And I will be more fine once you are gone. You are the father to my children, so you will always be welcome at special family gatherings, but that's it."

"My children? Which of the three are actually mine?"

Reina laughed. "You're right. They are *my* children. All you did was donate the sperm." She leaned closer to him. "You donated the sperm for some of them. Or maybe none of them. Now get out. I have to get ready for the wedding. And you do, too."

"This is what I'm wearing," he said.

She shrugged. "Whatever pleases you."

He turned and put his hand on the doorknob. "It's a relief, actually," he said. "I've wanted it for so long. I didn't have the guts to ask for it."

"I am so happy I have pleased you, finally."

He opened the door and left.

Reina stood staring at the door.

What had she done?

She leaned her head back and laughed.

Outram was right. She did feel free.

Chapter Thirty-eight

Umberto

Umberto rubbed his hands together in delight as he stood in the nearly empty corridor on the second floor. The guests were gathering outside beneath the Old Oak where the wedding ceremony would soon take place.

He liked thinking of all the people who had travelled to the Queendom to renew their vows or get married for the first time so they could share this date with the future queen of Queendom. The people didn't know that Minerva did not want to become queen. Didn't matter. They still would share the date with the daughter and daughter-in-law of the Queen of the Queendom.

A young well-dressed pale man with short dark hair came up to him and said, "Mr. Umberto?"

"Yes?"

"I am a relative of Marguerite Teng," he said. "I have come from Erdom to give her some news."

"She is very busy," Umberto said. "Could it wait until after the service and dinner?"

"I have to return home soon," he said. "She would want to know the news right away."

"Very well," Umberto said. "Follow me."

Umberto went back into the Hearth and walked the young

man downstairs. Teng's staff was busy in the kitchen, but she wasn't there.

"She must be in her room," Umberto said. "Come along."

They walked down the hall until he came to Viva's and Teng's room. The door was open. Viva was standing in front of the long mirror on the closet door while her mother adjusted her daughter's hem. Viva looked up when Umberto cleared his throat.

"Brother!" she called. She ran to the man and flung her arms around his waist.

"Cristopher!" Teng cried. She got up, went to the young man, and embraced him. "You are safe. How did you get here so fast? I just told the Man a few hours ago that I would no longer do his bidding. I was so frightened." She hugged and kissed Cristopher.

"I am safe," Cristopher said. "All is well." He looked at Mr. Umberto. "I am sorry I did not tell you the whole truth. I am Marguerite's son."

Viva said, "This is my brother, Cristopher."

"He's been in the Hinterlands for so long," Teng said. "I thought I'd never see him again. You don't know, Cristopher. You don't know. Oh, Mr. Umberto, I have been so frightened."

"It's all right, Momma," Cristopher said. "Everything is all right."

"But how did you get here?"

"I have a lot to tell you," he said. "But it's not really for Viva's ears."

"Don't make me leave," Viva said. "I'm so happy to see you! It's a great day here. We're having two weddings."

"Just for a bit," Teng said. "I need to talk to Cristopher. Mr. Umberto, I will be right there. I know there is much to do. Will you take Viva?"

"What we have to do in a few minutes is attend a wedding," he said. "I shall make certain Viva gets there."

She nodded. Mr. Umberto held out his hand, and Viva reluctantly took it. They left the room and walked down the hall together.

"I'll wager you are happy to see your brother," Umberto said.

"Yes, he's been gone so long," Viva said, "and Mom has been trying everything to get him back home."

"What do you mean?"

"He was in the Hinterlands," Viva said, "and some bad people had him. I guess he got away." She looked up at Umberto. "That was supposed to be a secret. I guess now that he's safe, it's all right to say?"

"I'm sure it is," Umberto said. "But you might want to wait until your mother says so before you mention it to anyone else. Ah, here we are. Wanda, are you going up to the wedding? Could you take Viva, please? I'll be right up. Mr. Santos, may I have a word with you?"

Wanda smiled at Viva and put her hand out.

"Take me away from all of this, child," Wanda said.

The girl took the woman's hand, and they led the rest of the staff up the stairs. Abbygail turned back to wave at Billy.

"Don't be long, groom," she said.

"I won't, bride."

Billy was grinning when he turned to Umberto.

"What do you need, Mr. Umberto? I am at your service."

"I want you to eavesdrop on a conversation," Umberto said quietly in the empty kitchen.

"Oh, Mr. Umberto," he said. "I can't do that. I'm not allowed to spy or eavesdrop on humans. You know that."

"What if your employer asks you to do so?" Umberto asked.

"Even then," he said. "Besides, isn't the Queen my employer? What's going on?"

Umberto took Billy's arm and pulled him aside. "I am afraid Marguerite Teng is in trouble. I only want to make certain all is well with her. Once I determine that, through you, you may go. And I don't want you to eavesdrop on anything too personal."

"Mr. Umberto, I can't filter what I hear. I can either turn up my hearing or turn it down. I can't say, 'only listen to relevant material.' It doesn't work that way."

"I trust your discretion with what I'm about to tell you," Um-

366

berto said. "Viva said her brother Cristopher was being held captive in the Hinterlands, and now he's here in the room with Teng."

"When they're finished talking, go ask her whatever needs asking. But don't make me do this."

Umberto sighed and nodded. "You are right, Billy. I admire you in this. That is what I'll do. I'll go knock on the door straightaway. Thank you."

"Do you want me to come with you?" Billy asked.

Umberto hesitated, and then he said, "Yes, please."

The two men walked down the corridor until they got to Teng's closed door. Umberto heard raised voices and immediately knocked on the door.

"Teng, is everything all right?"

The door opened, and Cristopher pushed past them without a word.

"Make certain he gets out of the house all right," Umberto said. Billy nodded and followed Cristopher.

Umberto stepped into Teng's room. She was sitting at her table, her head in her hands.

"Is everything all right?" Umberto asked.

Teng looked up at him. Her eyes were red, and her face was stained with tears.

Umberto walked over to her. "What has happened?"

"It is all so terrible," Teng said. "You will never forgive me. No one will. They told me Cristopher was being held prisoner in the Hinterlands and unless I spied on the First Family they would never let him come home."

"You're a spy?" Umberto asked. He could barely get the words out.

"I—I never told the Man anything important," she said. "I told him things, like what the menu was for a gathering or who was visiting. Only things that he could have found out from looking on Nexus. I swear, Mr. Umberto! I would never do anything to hurt any of you."

"Why didn't you come to us?" he said. "We could have helped."

"He said if I told anyone I would never see Cristopher again," she said. "I thought if I stalled long enough until I found the Moonstruck Saffron then I would have the resources to rescue Cristopher or pay off the kidnappers."

"Who are they?" Umberto said. "What could they possibly want?"

"He wouldn't tell me," she said. "It was enough to know that they believed the Queendom was acting unfairly regarding the exiles. Or something. I don't know!"

"But your son is here," Umberto said. "All is well."

"My son was never imprisoned," she said. "Never! I went through this anguish for months, and he was free all along."

"I don't understand," Umberto said.

"He's part of it!" she said. "He told his fellow—his fellow—I don't know what you call them. He told the fake kidnappers that I was coming to work here and they hatched a plan to get me to spy. I can't believe I raised such a terrible boy."

Umberto didn't know what to say. He wished he had sent Billy after Cristopher to bring him back here, so he could turn him over to Nehemiah.

"He came to try and persuade me to do the 'right thing,'" she said. "That's how he put it. He said the Queendom and all the Consolidated Five nations needed to pay for their actions. I told him I would never do anything to harm the Queendom, even for him."

"Where is the man who blackmailed you?"

"He's staying in town at the Wildflower Inn." She wiped her eyes with her sleeves. Then she stood. "I should go to the Queen now and tell her everything."

"It's almost time for the wedding," he said, "but yes, we had better go."

Teng nodded. Umberto stood away from the door, and Teng walked through it first.

"I am so sorry that I have let you down, Mr. Umberto," she said. "I was only trying to save my son."

"I understand," Umberto said.

When they got to the stairs, Umberto told Teng to wait while he went into his office and got on the house privocom. He found Elata and told her he needed to speak with the Queen and Nehemiah immediately.

Teng and Umberto said nothing to one another as they walked up the two flights of stairs to the third floor. Umberto was so stunned he could not think of anything to say. When they stepped onto the third floor, he said quietly, gently, "Say the truth. All will be well."

She nodded. They stopped in front of the door to the Queen's room. Teng smoothed her hands down over her white-with-red-polka-dots dress. Then Umberto knocked. When he heard the Queen say, "Come in," he opened the door.

"What is it, Umberto?" the Queen asked. She and Nehemiah stood in her living room, waiting. "I was with my daughter, on her wedding day. I had to send her away."

"I apologize," he said as he and Teng stepped into the room. He closed the door behind them.

"Marguerite Teng has something to tell you," Umberto said.

Teng cleared her throat and told the Queen and Nehemiah about being blackmailed into spying on them to save her son.

"I never told him anything that wasn't public knowledge," Teng said. "I wanted to find the Moonstruck Saffron, and then I was hoping I could give him money to release my son. Or I thought then the Queendom might help me find him. I would have never hurt you or this country. I told the Man today I wouldn't have anything more to do with him."

The Queen looked at Nehemiah.

"There's more," Umberto said.

"More?" Reina put her hands on her hips. "Well, get to it."

"My son returned," Teng said.

"He returned?" Nehemiah said. "I thought he was being held captive in the Hinterlands."

"As did I," she said. She looked at Umberto again, her eyes pleading with him.

Umberto said, "He was part of the scheme all along. He came to try and convince his mother to actually give them some private information on you and your family."

"I told him no," she said. "I sent him on his way. I can't believe he could ever be so cruel to let me believe he was in harm's way all of this time."

"We should send the constable and her people to the blackmailer's place of lodging," Nehemiah said. "He needs to take responsibility for his actions. I'm afraid we'll have to find your son, too."

Teng nodded.

Nehemiah headed for the door. "Teng, you should come with me, so you can give the constable any information she needs."

"I don't want you to miss the wedding," Reina said to Nehemiah.

"I won't," he said.

"Your Majesty," Teng said, "will we be exiled?"

"You haven't done anything illegal," the Queen said. "By blackmailing you, your son has."

"If he is exiled, my daughter and I will be, too," Teng said.

"Perhaps he'll agree to Reconciliation," she said. "Then none of you will have to leave. And if they did decide on exile, you could always return home instead."

"This is my home," Teng said. "This is where I've always wanted to be."

"I understand," Reina said. "I don't blame you. My own son has put me in a precarious situation, and I'm not sure what will happen with my family."

"Do you want me to resign?"

Reina glanced at Umberto. He shrugged slightly, hoping to let her know that he would respect whatever decision she made.

"Not today, certainly," Reina said. "You still have a wedding feast to get out. Go along with Nehemiah. We'll speak later. Umberto, stay a moment."

Nehemiah and Teng left the Queen's apartments. After the door shut behind them, Reina said, "I wanted to let you know that the plant Teng and Raphael found was not the Moonstruck Saffron. Or if it is, it's also a narcotic and could cause addiction. For this reason, we are not going forward with any kind of development."

"I understand," Umberto said.

"I would appreciate it if you could break this to Teng at some point," she said. "Gently. Should I fire her? Do you believe she never betrayed us—beyond not telling us what was going on?"

"I do believe her," Umberto said. "I don't know if that's logical or not."

"You have a soft spot for her," Reina said. "I can see that."

"I suppose I do," he said.

"They've also learned who started the fire," Reina said. "It was Raphael. He thought if he burned some of the fields of saffron, the price of what was left would go up."

"I—I . . ."

"Yes, that's about how I reacted," she said. "I have to decide if I should make this public or not. I want to protect my son, but I have an obligation to tell the truth."

"That would explain his behavior of late," Umberto said. "He has seemed troubled."

"That's a comfort," Reina said. "Maybe he does actually have a conscience."

"What if the judges decide on exile?" Umberto asked. "Wouldn't the whole family have to go with him? Or the immediate family. Has the Queen and her family ever been exiled before?"

"I don't know my history well enough," Reina said, "although I can't remember it ever happening before. They'd reconcile him, wouldn't they? Especially given he's sorry for what he's done."

"I hope our justice system will be just," he said.

"Needless to say, but I will say it anyway, this is all private information for now. I'll be speaking with my advisors tomorrow. Nehemiah knows—and Lorelei. And Raphael." She shook her head. "I don't know how we're going to get through this, Umberto. I'll let you go now. Send Elata in please. I've been pulling out my hair in frustration, quite literally it seems. I need her help. And I expect to see you all at the wedding."

"Naturally," Umberto said. "I can only say that I'm sorry that my judgment was wrong about Teng when I hired her. I thought she would be a good fit."

"But she was, wasn't she?" Reina said. "We all have things happen in our lives that we don't always handle well."

Umberto nodded. "Yes, Ma'am."

Umberto left the Queen and went downstairs. He was not quite ready for the wedding. He wanted to change into his gold vest. He pulled out his pocket watch, looked at the time, and continued down to the quiet kitchen. He was about to turn the corner to go to his room when he saw Abbygail lying on the floor. Running toward her from the other end of the corridor was Hildegarde.

Umberto ran to Abbygail, too. He knelt down next to her. "Abby, my girl. Abby!" he called.

Hildegarde knelt next to Abbygail. "I was coming in the back way so I could avoid everyone and I saw her crumple to the floor."

"She has a pulse," Umberto said. "Abbygail, what has come over you?"

"Move away, Mr. Umberto," Hildegarde said. Her voice sounded strange, gravelly, like the old woman who sold apples down by the plaza.

Hildegarde put one hand on Abbygail's forehead and one hand on her chest. Then she closed her eyes and whispered something Umberto could not understand.

Everything around them became very still, as though time had stopped. Umberto didn't think he could move even if he tried. Then something changed. It was as if someone snapped their fingers and it all started up again.

Abbygail opened her eyes. Hildegarde moved her hands away and helped Abbygail sit up.

"What happened?" Hildegarde asked.

"I don't know," Abbygail said. "I felt like I switched off." She shook her head.

"Has this happened before?" Hildegarde asked.

"Just once," she said. "I have been told to go to Paquay State. Maybe this is why. But don't tell anyone. I don't want to ruin Billy's day."

The three of them stood. Abbygail looked at Umberto. "You won't tell, will you? Let me take care of it. I feel fine now."

"If you're sure," Umberto said. "But you must get yourself checked out."

"I did a diagnostic," she said. "I am fine. I better get going." And then she walked away.

Hildegarde and Umberto stood in the semi-darkness together, in the silence, for a moment.

"You mustn't tell anyone what you saw," Hildegarde said.

"I didn't see anything," Umberto said. "Nothing to tell anyone."

"Exactly."

Umberto frowned.

He was sorry to see Hildegarde back at the Hearth.

"I better get dressed for the wedding," Hildegarde said.

Umberto nodded. Hildegarde walked to the stairs and disappeared up them.

Umberto shook his head and then went to his room. What a strange day it was turning out to be.

CHAPTER THIRTY-NINE
LORELEI

Lorelei leaned against the Old Oak, watching people until the very last moment. She observed her mother in deep conversation with first one advisor and then another from the C5 countries. Nehemiah was doing the same thing.

Lorelei hoped they weren't talking about her brother burning down the saffron fields.

Of all of the C5 leaders, Outram was the only one who showed up to the wedding. This was worrisome, but it was also reassuring. Outram still loved Reina, Lorelei could tell, and he knew Lorelei was his daughter. He would continue to help them.

Outram walked over to Lorelei as people began to take their seats.

"Hello, Lorelei," he said. "It is nice to see you. Have you thought any more about coming to Berland to work as my apprentice?"

Lorelei looked at her father and tried to see where her features matched his.

"Apprentice?" she said. "I didn't realize I would be working with you."

"Who else?" he said. "Boann isn't really interested. My son isn't either. I would like to teach someone what I know."

"They're going to start," Lorelei said. "I will definitely think about your offer."

"That's all I ask," he said. He smiled.

"Excuse me," Lorelei said.

She walked to the entrance to the Hearth where her family was gathering before they took their places at the front. She would have to sit in one of those chairs with her feet dangling. Ugh.

She looked at Raphael as he straightened his shirt and vest. Perhaps having her feet swinging was not the end of the world.

Raphael held out his arm to her. She appreciated the gesture. She put her hand on his elbow.

"Let's do this thing," he whispered.

Lorelei stood waiting with her brother. She saw the downstairs staff sitting all together off to the left of the wedding trellis. Turnkey caught her eye and nodded. She smiled and waved, keeping her hand low and near her body. Viva waved, too, as she sat next to her mother. Teng did not look happy as she held Viva's hand and looked straight ahead.

The sun was arching down in the West, but Umberto and the others had positioned the chairs and the trellis so that no one would have the sun in their eyes.

Talib and Reina took the lead and started down the aisle between the rows of chairs. The Queen Madre and Poppie followed on their heels, and Raphael and Lorelei went after them. They all sat in the front row, on the left. Savi's family was already seated in the front row on the right.

"I think this is your seat," Raphael whispered.

Lorelei looked down. In front of the second to last chair was a small wooden footrest shaped like a large leaf. She looked over at Turnkey.

He smiled.

She mouthed, "Thank you."

Lorelei sat down, and her feet easily touched the foot rest. She nodded. The day had just gotten much better.

CHAPTER FORTY
BILLY

"It is a great success, isn't it?" Quintana came up behind Billy as he stood beside one of the buffet tables, ready to help should any of the guests need it.

Billy turned to him. "Yes, it was. The ceremony was short and meaningful, and the guests are enjoying Teng's food. The celebrations here at the Hearth are always wonderful."

Quintana nodded. "I have been to many," he said, "but I particularly enjoy weddings. Everyone always appears to be so happy, and yet so much is going on underneath."

Billy laughed. "I have not detected any underneath," he said.

Quintana said, "Maybe it's my imagination. I am looking forward to your wedding tonight."

Billy grinned. "I am, too! To tell the truth, I haven't paid much attention to what happened at this wedding. I keep thinking of my own."

"It's a good thing you are doing," Quintana said. "More of us should partake in these kinds of ceremonies. Then humans would see us more like them."

"You don't think they do?" Billy asked.

"Not when things are stressed," he said. "Like now."

"Are you feeling better these days?" Billy asked.

"I am, thank you," he said.

"Would you mind telling me what was wrong?" Billy asked. "It's not prurient interest. Abbygail has gotten a message that she's to go to Paquay State for some kind of check-up or upgrade. We're both concerned, especially since I didn't get the same message. When you were there, did everything seem normal?"

"Yes," he said. "They were busier than usual."

"Were you ill?"

"I was having urges that I didn't believe were normal," he said. "It turned out I did have a chemical imbalance. They were able to fix it."

"Urges?"

The fiddlers started to play again. Quintana moved closer to Billy. "I wanted to have sex with Hildegarde all the time. I couldn't bear for her to be out of my sight."

Billy blinked. "Um, oh. And now that's gone away?"

"It has," he said. "I no longer feel desperate."

"Could you be in love?" Billy asked.

"Of course I love her." Quintana smiled. "But I was thinking about her all the time. I wanted her all the time. That's not normal."

Billy laughed. "I think about Abbygail all the time."

Quintana nodded. "It felt different. It's hard to explain. Now I feel normal."

"She's been gone, though," Billy said. "Now she's back. She's over there by the Hearth watching you."

"She is?" Quintana looked in the direction of the entrance to the Hearth. He smiled and waved. "Perhaps I will go say hello."

Quintana left him. Billy looked around the crowd for Abbygail. She glanced up, and they waved to one another. He was glad he got to work with her because then he got to see her all day. He missed her when she wasn't around. He wanted to be with her as much as possible. He wanted to feel her skin against his. That felt perfectly normal to him. He looked over at Quintana talking to Hildegarde.

Maybe Quintana was no longer in love, so *that* felt better to him. Billy had no intention of getting his "chemicals balanced."

Nearly everyone was dancing now as the setting sun turned the landscape pink. Umberto came up to Billy and said, "Get out there, man. Everyone dances here in the Queendom. See, watch how I do it."

Umberto walked up to where Teng was sitting with Viva. Billy didn't hear what he said, but he held out his hand. Teng hesitated, and then she took his hand. They walked into the group of dancers. Viva ran up to Lorelei, and they began dancing, too.

"Shall we?"

Billy turned around, and the Queen was standing beside him, holding her hand out to him.

"It would be my honor," he said. He took her hand, and they walked toward the dancers. Billy spotted Abbygail dancing with Nehemiah.

"I didn't know Mr. Nehemiah could dance," Billy said as they made their way closer to the dancers and fiddlers.

"You heard Umberto," Reina said. "Everyone dances in the Queendom. Now, Billy, no matter what happens this night, you and Abbygail should get married."

Billy had difficulty hearing the Queen above the shouts and laughter coming from the revelers.

"What do you mean?" Billy asked. "Is something going to happen?"

Reina said, "It's a wedding. Something is bound to happen."

Billy frowned.

"That was patronizing," she said. "I apologize. There is something going on, but I'm not sure what it is. So keep those you love close, and don't change your plans. Now here we go."

And they stepped into the throng of dancers.

The dancing went on until late into the night. The politicians were the first to leave. Other guests wandered away, some to go down to the Queen's Village for more food and dancing.

Eventually Billy helped take the food inside while the music got quieter, more somber. Billy felt giddy. Teng had placed plates of cookies all over the reception area and in the Hearth. As Billy walked by a table with one plate piled high with oatmeal cookies, he grabbed one and took a bite out of it.

"Ah, I know Teng filled these cookies with love," he said to no one in particular. "I can taste the love and the cinnamon."

He grabbed another cookie for Abbygail and then continued on to the family's dining room. They had opened the French windows and moved the furniture so the family could sit and watch the moon come up on this glorious night.

Billy opened a couple bottles of wine and put them on the table to breath. Umberto arranged glasses around the room. This was where the family would say good-bye to Minerva and Savi before they left on their honeymoon.

"I've asked the others up, too," Umberto said to Billy. "We can all say goodnight to the happy couple, and then we'll go down for your ceremony."

"Grand," Billy said.

Teng and Abbygail came into the room carrying plates of cookies.

"Might as well put them where they're in reach," Teng said. She and Abbygail arranged the plates in convenient spots around the room.

"I sent the workers from the village home," Teng said to Umberto. "Viva was exhausted. She actually fell asleep on her bed, still dressed. She made me promise to wake her up for the wedding. Have you heard anything about Cristopher or the man who blackmailed her?"

Umberto said, "No. I would tell you. But the Queen did ask me to let you know that the plant you found is not the Moonstruck Saffron."

"I am sorry to hear that."

Wanda, Turnkey, and Antonia came into the room. Umberto motioned them to stand to the back. Elata had gone up early to bed.

Poppie and the Queen Madre came inside and sat on the sofa. Billy poured them both glasses of wine and offered them cookies.

"Ah, Umberto," the Queen Madre said, "a rich red wine. You have never made a bad choice."

Umberto tilted his head forward slightly. "Thank you, Queen Madre."

Quintana and Nehemiah, deep in conversation, stayed a bit out of the room, just outside in the night. Raphael and Lorelei went around them and found places in the room to sit. The Queen came in, followed by Talib, who sat across the room from the Queen. It looked like he wanted to be as far away as possible from his wife.

Billy gazed at Abbygail. She made a face at him. He smiled. He would never want to sit across the room from Abbygail, unless it was to get a better look at her.

Savi and Minerva walked into the room, and the family and staff cheered.

"Thank you so much," Minerva said.

"It was a wonderful day," Savi said.

"Where is your family?" Reina asked. "They are welcome to join us. We are all family now."

"They have gone to their inn," Savi said. "Mom and Dad were exhausted from the trip. We'll see them before we leave in the morning."

"Does everyone have a drink?" Reina asked. She stood and raised her glass. "Thank you, Mr. Umberto and Marguerite Teng. And all of you. You made this day very special. Quintana, Nehemiah, get in here and get a drink."

"And a cookie," Lorelei said.

"And a cookie!" Reina said. She turned to Minerva and Savi. "To my amazing daughter, Minerva, and to her amazing wife, Savi, who is now my daughter, too. I wish you a lifetime of happiness! To you!"

She raised her glass. Everyone else did the same. "Here! Here!"

Minerva took a sip, and then she fed her cookie to Savi, and Savi fed her cookie to Minerva.

Everyone laughed.

"Teng, I believe your Unified Field Theory of Spices might actually be real," Minerva said. "If you filled these cookies with ingredients that would make us happy, it worked. I am ecstatic!"

"I don't believe it is my cookies that are responsible for your happiness," Teng said.

Everyone laughed again. Billy laughed the loudest. He was so happy. He went to stand next to Abbygail. They held each other's hands.

"That'll be us soon enough," Billy whispered to Abbygail.

"It already is, love," Abbygail said. "I couldn't be happier than I am this moment here with you and the others."

Minerva and Savi parted as Mr. Peetall stepped into the room from outside. "Excuse me," he said.

"This is a private family function," Reina said.

Peetall continued, "In accordance with Article 31 of the Reconciliation Treaty of the Consolidated Five, the country of Berland now takes control of the nation of Queendom."

The room became completely still.

"On whose authority?" Reina said.

"On the authority of the treaty, Ma'am," Peetall said. "It is the right of Berland, since the Queendom is late on paying off her debt, to assume management of this country."

Nehemiah came to stand next to Reina.

"Where is Outram?" Reina said. "He would never let you do this."

"He has my authority." Outram stepped into the room and came to stand next to Peetall.

"But I asked you about the loan," Reina said. "You assured me it would all be taken care of."

"It is," he said. "I will appoint a temporary CEO, and we will get this economy back on track. The debt will be paid, and all will be well."

"You got the other three CEOs to sign off on this?" Reina asked. "How?"

"You are endangering the C5 by allowing your economy to spiral out of control," Outram said.

Umberto stepped forward. Reina held her hand up, without looking at him.

"Our economy is not spiraling," Reina said. "Outram, how could you do this?"

"It's for the best," Outram said.

Everyone was standing.

"You said you would appoint a temporary CEO," Nehemiah said. "Who is it?"

"Yes," Peetall said, "under Article 31, section 10, subsection b, the country taking over has the right to install a new leader if the current leader is found to be incompetent or criminal."

"You have always been jealous of Reina's life here," Talib said. "That's the only reason you are doing this. Reina is not criminal or incompetent."

"I beg to differ."

Everyone turned to the open doorway. Hildegarde stood on the threshold. Then she strode across the room until she was face to face with Reina.

"What have you to do with this?" Reina asked.

"Hildegarde is now the Queen of Queendom," Outram said. "All hail the Queen."

"Hildegarde!" the Queen Madre said, coming to stand between sisters. "You cannot do this to the country or to your sister. You had your chance. You gave it up."

"I will not watch this country be destroyed by incompetence," Hildegarde said.

"What are you talking about?" Reina asked.

Billy held Abbygail's hand tightly. He felt sick to his stomach. Lorelei, Raphael, Minerva and Savi all stood by Reina's side.

"You let the economy almost crash," Hildegarde said.

"That's happened in the past," Nehemiah said. "It's a cycle. No monarch has been removed because of that."

"You wouldn't put the Moonstruck Saffron on the market,"

Outram said. "The sales on that alone could have easily gotten the country back on track."

"It's a narcotic," Reina said. "I wouldn't do that to our people for some temporary economic fix. That's not part of our values. It's not the values of any of the Consolidated Five. And that plant is not Moonstruck Saffron."

"You've kept a crime secret from the public," Hildegarde said. "A crime committed by a member of your family."

"A member of your family, too!" Reina said.

"She only found out a few hours ago," Raphael said.

"How do you know anything about that?" Reina asked.

Hildegarde looked at Outram.

"You've been investigating us?" Reina said to Outram. "Why didn't you come to me right away?"

"You should have known your son was so out of control," Outram said.

"You should have taken him in to the constable immediately," Hildegarde said. "Hiding a crime is a crime. For that, you can be disposed."

Nehemiah said, "Outram, don't do this. Take over the country if you must, but why do this?"

"It's best for the country," Outram said. "It is best for the Consolidated Five."

"Hildegarde, what are you doing?" her mother asked again. "You are destroying us."

Hildegarde shook her head. "No. I am saving us."

"You know nothing about running this country," Nehemiah said. "How will you do it?"

"Certainly not with you by my side," Hildegarde said. "I know how you feel about me."

"He has been by the side of nearly every monarch of Queendom!" the Queen Madre said.

"Maybe that's the problem," Hildegarde said. "I'll find another soothsayer to help me. Quintana, you will stand with me."

Everyone looked in Quintana's direction.

"I know nothing about running a country," he said. "I know plants. I know this is wrong."

"According to Article 31, section 10, subsection 14," Hildegarde said, "I am acting superior judge of the Queendom until the takeover is finished and we have a new election."

"That's martial law," Reina said. "We don't do that. We have never done that. Nehemiah, is there precedent for this?"

"No," he said, "but it is in the treaty. It's just never been used."

"As acting superior judge," Hildegarde said, "I find you guilty of incompetence and hiding a crime, Reina Villanueva. I sentence you to exile. You may return one day if your values have been reconciled."

Billy gasped. The whole room gasped.

"And you, Raphael Villanueva," Hildegarde said. "You are guilty of burning the saffron fields and nearly destroying our economy. For this, you are sentenced to exile without the option of return."

"You cannot act as judge and jury," Reina said. "The people will not stand for it."

"When we tell the people what Raphael did," Hildegarde said, "when we tell them you withheld evidence of his crime, they won't care. When the economy is healthy again, they will be so grateful to me that I will be queen for a lifetime. You have twenty-four hours to pack and leave the Hearth."

"Hildy!" the Queen Madre said. "Exile requires the entire family to go with the exiled. That means I have to go. Minerva, Jeremy, and Lorelei have to go. You have to go!"

"We make exceptions," Hildegarde said. "I will make an exception. I am not sentencing my own mother to exile. And my brother has his own life separate from the Hearth. He will not be affected. But Reina's girls—" She looked at Minerva and Lorelei. "—the girls must go. Talib, you and Reina are not on particularly friendly terms, so you will be allowed to stay."

Talib laughed. "Friendly? No. In fact, she told me we are getting a divorce. Tonight, just a few hours ago."

"What?" Outram said. "You didn't tell me."

Reina stared at Outram. "Why does that matter?"

"She asked me for a divorce," Talib said, "and I am leaving the country. Now you say I can stay. Not on your life, pretend queen. You clearly know nothing of this country or the values of her people. They won't stand for this. I'd rather live in Hell than stay here anywhere near you."

"Suit yourself," Hildegarde said, "but you won't like exile."

"Kiss my ass," Talib said.

Reina laughed.

"Outram!" Lorelei cried.

Everyone looked at her as she approached the premier.

"Come down here so I can say this clearly to you," she said.

Outram knelt on one knee.

"I have recently learned your blood is pulsing through my veins," she said. "I knew my mother loved you for a long time, so I didn't mind, once I got used to the idea. But now I wish I could replace every part of me that I got from any part of you. I renounce you as my father."

She spit in his face.

Outram wiped his sleeve across his face and slowly stood. Reina moved between her daughter and Outram.

"You are a treacherous man," Reina said. "I have loved you for most of my life. I have tried not loving you, and I never succeeded. I can be grateful for one thing tonight: I no longer love you. I despise you and hope to never see you again."

"Reina, I—"

She turned away from him and went to stand next to Minerva.

"We will leave you to make your arrangements," Peetall said. "We will make the announcement on Nexus tomorrow morning. Good night."

Outram and Peetall left the way they had come, swiftly disappearing into the darkness.

Hildegarde looked around the room. "Umberto and the rest of

you, I hope you will stay. You have always cared for the monarch, whoever she may be. I trust all of you to continue to do that. I will sleep in the village tonight. I'll see you tomorrow. In time, you will understand what I've done is for the good of the country."

Hildegarde strode out of the room, following Peetall and Outram into the night.

Quintana closed the French doors behind her, and then everyone began talking at once.

"Is what they've done legal?" Reina asked Nehemiah.

He nodded. "It appears to be. Let me go deeper into Nexus to be certain."

"I never knew this could happen," the Queen Madre said. "A hostile takeover, yes, but to topple an elected leader is absurd. How was that ever allowed in the treaty?"

"It's an obscure section," Nehemiah said. "No one has used it before."

"What are we going to do?" Minerva asked.

"You should go on your honeymoon," Reina said.

Savi said, "We can't. We've been exiled, too. I hope she didn't mean for my parents to go into exile. This is awful."

"What did Hildegarde mean when she said Raphael burned the saffron fields?" Minerva asked. "And Lorelei, what was that? You're Outram's daughter?"

"No," Lorelei said, "I am Talib's daughter. If he'll still have me."

"Always, little one," he said.

"I wish you wouldn't call me that," she said.

"Why? I've always called you that."

"I know," she said, "and I'm still little."

"It's not a curse I put on you," Talib said.

"If she doesn't like it," Minerva said, "don't call her that. Raphael, what did you do?"

"Let's talk about it later," Reina said.

"I burned the fields," Raphael said. "I thought it would help. It didn't."

"Is there something wrong with you?" Minerva asked.

"Clearly."

"Stop this," Reina said. "It's getting us nowhere."

"I've searched Nexus," Nehemiah said. "I've searched the treaty. What they are doing appears to be legal. I've tried getting a hold of Gloria Stone, but she's nowhere on Nexus. Abbygail, Billy, Quintana, can you find anything?"

Billy searched his memory. He couldn't see the entire treaty. He searched again.

"I keep finding blanks," Billy said.

"Yes," Abbygail agreed. "Or blocks. Like there are closed doors, and I can't get in."

"I have noticed this for some time," Nehemiah said. "I thought it was just me."

Quintana was silent.

Reina said, "What does this mean? Do they have the legal authority to do what they're doing or not?"

Nehemiah said, "It appears that they do. But I can't find all the revised codes. That happens sometimes when an area of Nexus hasn't been used for a while."

"Or it could be deliberate," Reina said. "This could have been Hildegarde's plan all along. Maybe she got other soothsayers to go along with her."

"Your sister wouldn't do that," the Queen Madre said. She was now sitting on the couch next to Poppie.

"My dear," Poppie said, "it appears your firstborn is capable of quite a lot. There is nothing we can do tonight. Let us retire for the evening."

"I must stay here and help you fight this," the Queen Madre said. "I will contact the Queen Grandmother. My mother won't stand for this either."

"No," Reina said. "Let's not get the rest of the family involved in this yet. We don't want to get anyone else exiled."

The Queen Madre got up, faced Reina, and put her hands on her daughter's arms.

"This is wrong," she said. "You mustn't let this stand."

"I follow the laws of the Queendom," Reina said. "Right this moment, it appears they are following the law, too. You and Poppie stay at the Hearth and make certain Hildy doesn't destroy the Queendom." Reina looked around the room. "I hope you all stay here, the whole staff. We can't stay, but you have a choice. You serve the family so that we may serve the nation. I hope you will continue to do that."

Billy looked at Abbygail. She was watching Reina. Billy whispered in her ear. "Let's go with them," he said.

"What?" Abbygail said. They faced each other.

"Let's go with the Queen," he said quietly. "We wanted to travel. This will give us a chance to see the world."

"Travel? Exile isn't traveling! It's going to the Hinterlands. We might never be able to come back if we go."

"It's something to think about," Billy said. "It could be our first adventure together."

Abbygail looked terrified.

"We don't have to go," Billy said. "It was just a thought. I wouldn't go without you."

She nodded but didn't say anything.

"You have the right of appeal," Savi said. "Everyone sentenced to reconciliation or exile has that right."

"Maybe not if a queen has appointed herself as judge and jury," Reina said. "I knew the queen could do that but only in case of emergency. This hardly qualifies."

"Not only do you have the right of appeal," Savi said, "but you have a right to put your affairs in order. In other words, everyone who is convicted gets thirty days."

"That's right," Reina said.

"Nehemiah, get a hold of everyone on the council and tell them what has happened. Say we are looking at the laws to try and decide what to do."

"I'm blocked," Nehemiah said. "I've tried reaching out and I can't."

"If you're blocked than I am," Reina said. "Quintana, can you contact the council?"

"I can try," Quintana said. He and Nehemiah were silent for a moment, and then he said, "Yes. Our messages are going through."

Suddenly a Nexus projection of Hildegarde opened at the front of the room.

"Good evening, citizens of the Queendom," she said. "Tonight I learned that the Queendom was about to default on a loan to Berland. In an attempt to keep the economies of all five nations stable, Berland has taken over the reins of our economy until we can pay off the debt. We also learned today that my nephew Raphael was responsible for the burning of the saffron fields and for plunging us into economic darkness. The Queen did not inform the constable about this crime immediately, so she, too, is in violation of the law. Because it has been deemed that Reina was incompetent and criminal in her actions by Berland, she has been relieved of her duties. Since I was once queen and understand the economics of our country, Premier Outram has appointed me as head of the government. I am now queen again. We will append the legal justifications for all of our actions to this message." She paused.

"Unfortunately since it was a hostile takeover, we will no doubt have to implement austerity measures. We hope to pump new credit into the economy soon, however. Reina and her family have been sentenced to exile, effective immediately. Thank you for trusting me to be your queen again. All will be well soon."

A moment later, the projection disappeared.

"She must have had this planned for a long time," Nehemiah said.

Everyone looked at Quintana.

"I knew nothing about this," he said. "She told me she returned to help the Queen in any way possible. I never dreamed she would do such a thing."

"Poppie is not feeling well," the Queen Madre said. "I will take him up. We'll see you in the morning. Maybe everything will be different then."

After they exchanged embraces with their family, Poppie and the Queen Madre left the room. The Queen Madre turned back once and said, "Something is wrong here. Make it right."

After they left, Talib said, "I should finish packing. Children, I am returning to Erdom to visit your grandparents. Perhaps you could apply for citizenship there. The courts might overturn your convictions here."

Minerva was the first to embrace her father.

"Come with me now," he murmured in her hair. "You and Savi both. You can renounce any claim on the crown, and Hildegarde and Outram might let you come with me."

Minerva pulled away from her father and looked at Savi.

"It's something to consider," Reina said. "It's better than going to the Hinterlands. That way you and Savi could continue to look into the legality of this. If some things are being blocked from the soothsayers, who knows what is really going on."

"Erdom has a huge archive of material related to the Treaty of the Consolidated Five," Savi said. "I studied there."

"Ixchel is almost as treacherous as Outram," Reina said. "I would never have believed it of her."

"Maybe she will have second thoughts," Minerva said. "You could ask her to overturn our exile so that we could live there."

Reina nodded. "First, Mr. Umberto, we have another wedding to attend. Shall you put together that celebration?"

"Oh no, Your Majesty," Abbygail said. "We couldn't impose."

"I am no longer anyone's majesty," Reina said, "and I would like to end this day on a note of hope."

"The day has long ago ended," Umberto said. "It will be morning soon."

"It's a great way to begin the day," Reina said. "Unless you've changed your minds?"

Billy looked at Abbygail. "No, we haven't changed our minds."

"We will go tend to it," Umberto said. "Billy and Abbygail, you stay here. We'll call for you when it's time."

"Teng," Savi said, "before you go, we wanted to tell you how lovely the meal was, and how wonderful each and every cookie was. You've made us believers in the Unified Field Theory of Spices."

Teng said, "Thank you. I'm glad you were happy. But I'm beginning to doubt its efficacy. I made a meal that was supposed to delight, heal, and nourish. How could something like this happen if the Field Theory were true?"

Savi smiled, and Minerva laughed. "Terrible things can happen no matter what," Minerva said. "It's better to have them happen after a good meal."

The downstairs crew filed out, except for Billy and Abbygail.

"Sit," Reina said. "You two are now off work. Have a glass of wine. Eat some cookies."

Abbygail hesitated, and then she sat on the love seat against the far wall. Billy sat next to her.

"All right, Nehemiah," Reina said. "Contact Ixchel. Don't let her see anyone but me."

Nehemiah nodded. A moment later, a projection opened up. Ixchel was sitting at a desk.

"I thought I would hear from you," Ixchel said.

"How could you do that to us?" Reina asked. "Outram needed four votes! You could have abstained. You could have told me what was happening."

Ixchel shook her head. "I couldn't. Outram said he would implement a hostile takeover of Erdom if I didn't cooperate."

"How could he?" Reina said. "You don't owe him anything."

"We do," Ixchel said. "We've been having problems with our numbers, too, and something is going on with our soothsayers. I couldn't risk it. Besides, he said you were harboring a criminal. Raphael burned down the fields and you kept that hidden."

"I only found out about that an hour before the wedding!" Reina said. "I didn't have a chance to do anything."

"As you said, it's done now," Ixchel said. "Ride it out. You won't be in receivership long."

"Ride it out?" Reina said. She glanced at Nehemiah. "I am no longer queen. They used some clause in the treaty to oust me, saying I was incompetent and a criminal. He's put my sister in charge. I've been sentenced to exile, along with my family."

Ixchel got to her feet. "No! Nothing like that was ever discussed!"

"It's done," Reina said. "We're searching for some kind of legal justification to get me back into power and rescind the takeover. We're not finding anything. I would like you to overturn Minerva's and Savi's exiles and allow them to come into your country. Talib is returning, and he would like at least one of his children with him."

"If I do it, Outram might instigate a hostile takeover of Erdom," she said. "If I do anything to displease him, he will attack."

"Since when?" Reina said. "How long has he been threatening you and the others? Why didn't you come to me? Listen, there is legal precedent for overturning their exiles so they can travel to a neighboring country. He isn't angry with them. He's doing this to punish me. You must do this. Minerva just got married. Please."

Ixchel was silent for a moment. Then she said, "All right. I will send passes to Nehemiah. He can put them into their ID cards. This will get them passage into my country even if Outram has somehow prevented it. I'm sorry but I can't do it for all of you. It would be too dangerous."

"What a coward you are," Reina said. She looked at Nehemiah. He nodded and cut off the projection.

Talib said, "We should get going right away, as soon as Nehemiah fixes their ID cards. You two go pack. We'll take transportation to the border. Fortunately, I'm already packed."

Talib went to Reina, and they embraced one another.

When they let each other go, Talib said, "Well, wife, I am sorry for everything."

"Well, husband, I am sorry for many things, but not everything. Without you, I wouldn't have my children."

"Come here, little one—Lorelei."

Lorelei walked up to her father. He knelt and embraced her. "You will always be my daughter, no matter what."

Lorelei pulled away from him and looked into his face. "But you've never liked me."

"Never liked you?" he said. "Where did you get that idea? I've always liked and loved you. You scared me, though, that's true. You can see the truth about people, and I was afraid you could see the truth about me. That I was a nothing and a nobody."

Lorelei put her arms around her father's neck. "No one is a nothing and nobody," she said. "Not even you."

Talib laughed. They released one another. Talib stood and wiped away his tears. "Raphael, come. Quit hiding in the corner."

Raphael moved toward his father. He looked down at his feet as he stood facing Talib.

"You fuck one thing up after another," Talib said. "You take after me, unfortunately. But I don't believe you do any of it out of malice. Make the best of this situation. Do something with your life."

Talib hugged his son. Raphael eventually returned the embrace.

Talib looked around the room. Then he nodded to Minerva and Savi. "Let's get going. Nehemiah, will you come and fix their cards?"

The four of them left the room.

"Mother, I want to go to bed," Raphael said.

"No," Reina said. "Go downstairs and see if you can help with preparations for the wedding. Lorelei, did you wish to help, too?"

Lorelei nodded. She reached for her brother's hand, and together they left the room.

The room was now empty of everyone except the Queen, Billy, and Abbygail.

"Can I get you anything?" Billy asked.

Reina sat on the couch and leaned back. "Some rest," she said.

"I can't remember the last time I rested." She looked over at Billy and Abbygail. "You two are older and therefore presumably wiser than I am," she said. "Do you have any advice for me?"

They were silent for a moment. Then Abbygail said, "Don't hang your laundry outside if it's going to rain."

Billy smiled. Reina opened her mouth and laughed.

"You are a wise woman, Abbygail."

CHAPTER FORTY-ONE
LORELEI

Lorelei ran up her stairs once she deposited her brother downstairs in the kitchen. He was walking around half-alive, and Lorelei couldn't stand being around him. She felt sad for him, but she also blamed him. It was his own fault. Everything was his own fault. His and Hildegarde's.

Lorelei wanted a moment to herself. A moment with the house. She ran into her apartment and closed the door. She went into the closet, closed the door, and lay on the floor. The walls began to glow, and she heard music, seeming to come from everywhere, maybe even from her. She breathed as she listened. Breathed and listened, with her eyes closed. She was certain she was hearing the heartbeat of the house.

She opened her eyes. Words and drawings moved all around the light walls. She picked up her pencil and wrote, "Today one queen betrayed another queen. And my father betrayed us all." She watched the letters and words twist up and away. She drew the outline of a bird. It turned into a white raven. It looked down at her, and then flew along the wall to the ceiling. Lorelei drew the outline of another raven. It turned into a black raven that flew up the opposite wall. A moment later, white ravens covered one wall, black ravens covered the other.

The house breathed. Lorelei breathed.

The glowing walls faded.

Lorelei got up, left the closet, and looked outside into the darkness. She squinted, trying to see if Patra was somewhere near. She hoped he and the Queen's Court would know her mother had not done anything wrong. Maybe they could help them.

Lorelei headed downstairs again. Viva ran up to Lorelei when she reached the kitchen.

"We're ready!" Viva said.

"This is lovely," Lorelei said.

The staff had set up small lights all over the kitchen and staff dining room. Lorelei and Viva walked into the dimly lit dining room. The table which was usually in the center of the room was now against the far wall.

Wanda and Turnkey came into the room. Turnkey was holding something close to his chest.

"Here we go," Wanda said. She motioned to someone, and Raphael, Quintana, and Antonia came into the room.

Turnkey made his way around the group of people to Lorelei's side. He took the something away from his chest and held it out to Lorelei. It was the leaf-shaped foot stool.

She took the stool from him and set it on the floor in front of her. "Thank you," she said. "It's the kindest gift I've ever gotten. It's a pity I can only use it twice."

"You could take it with you," he said.

"We can't take much," Lorelei said, "because we'll have to carry everything."

"I'll carry it for you," he said. "I will carry all of your things."

"I don't understand," Lorelei said.

"I want to come with you," Turnkey said quietly.

"Into exile?"

"Wherever you go," he said. "I can help."

Lorelei shook her head. "Your family is here. Your work is here. You mustn't come with us."

"Miss Lorelei," he said. "You must understand—"

"Quiet, everyone," Umberto said as he stepped into the room. He was wearing a gold vest, a white shirt, and gold and white slacks. His clothes nearly glowed. "The Queen and Nehemiah are bringing the happy couple down. Billy and Abbygail had to run to their rooms and change into their wedding clothes. They're coming now. Shall we sing for them?"

Umberto began humming a tune Lorelei did not recognize, but soon they were all humming along.

The Queen and Nehemiah stepped into the room together. They parted ways, one going to the left, the other to the right. The others in the room moved to create an aisle leading to Umberto who stood near the table.

Abbygail and Billy, both wearing their May Day outfits, walked into the room hand in hand. Everyone clapped as they went to stand in front of Umberto. Lorelei moved toward the aisle and stood on her stool to watch.

"We have come together on this day to witness the union of Billy Santos and Abbygail," Umberto said. "They wished to proclaim their love for each other in front of all of you. They consider you friends and family. This is an auspicious day—for good and ill—but this uniting of these two people is a glorious occasion. They both have something they would like to say to one another. Abbygail."

Abbygail turned to face Billy. "Billy Santos, you are the funniest man I ever met, and you can tell a story better than any storyteller. You are a good and kind man, and I thank you for loving me. I am happy to become part of the Santos clan. I love you for now and forever."

Billy smiled. "Abbygail, I don't really know what a saint is supposed to be, but if it means a person is kind to others and honest in all her work, then that's you. You are the best person I know. You stand up when things are wrong and you speak your mind. And you laugh at all of my jokes. Well, you laugh at the one's that deserve laughing at."

A murmur of laughter went around the room.

"I thank you for loving me, Abbygail Santos."

"By the power given to me as steward of this great house," Umberto said, "you are now legally wife and husband."

Abbygail and Billy leaned toward one another and kissed. The small group cheered and went up to Abbygail and Billy to congratulate them.

"There's more," Teng said. "Come."

Teng led the way down the corridor to the open door to the outside, with Abbygail and Billy, hand in hand, following her, and everyone else following them. The sun was just about up and the grounds were golden pink. Blankets with picnic baskets on them were spread all over the area.

Teng turned to Abigail and Billy and said, "Every ingredient was chosen for your ultimate happiness, good health, and prosperity. Every ingredient was blended with the next one to help you begin your lives together. Behold, the feast of the saints."

Everyone clapped.

"This is perfect," Abbygail said. "Just our style."

"The sun," Billy said.

"Yes," Lorelei said. "Sing it up for us, Billy and Abbygail."

"No!" Billy said. "Queen Reina, would you do the honor?"

They all looked at the Queen. "But this is your duty," Reina said. "You sing up the sun every morning."

"It would mean so much to us," Abbygail said.

Reina nodded. "All right then." She walked to the front of the group and faced the sun which was about to come up over the eastern ridge.

Reina stood with her feet shoulder width apart. Then she raised her arms to the sky. The golden vine woven around her crown reflected light that was not there yet. Lorelei wondered how that was possible. She looked up as a white raven flew overhead, heading north. Lorelei blinked, and now the raven was black. Lorelei looked back at her mother.

"Up, sun, up!" Reina began to sing. "Up, sun, up! Raise up! Raise up! Lift our spirits up with you!"

The others began to sing with her. Lorelei could even hear Nehemiah's deep voice.

"Up, sun, up! Up, sun, up! Raise up! Raise up! Lift our spirits up with you!"

They sang the song three times, and ended as the sun crested the ridge and turned the world red and gold.

Everyone cheered.

"We did it again," Billy said.

Reina laughed. "We did indeed."

"Let's eat," Teng said.

The group sat on the blankets and began pulling food out of the baskets. Some of it was leftover from last night's wedding. But Teng had also made dumplings, chutneys, and a cake for Billy and Abbygail. People began eating, murmuring quietly as they watched the sun rise.

"I can't believe this is the last time we'll be here," Lorelei said.

"It won't be," Reina said. "We will get back."

"We will hold the place ready for you, Ma'am," Umberto said.

"I know you will, Umberto," Reina said.

"The Stone Monastery has archives, too," Nehemiah said. "We can stay there for the thirty days. Gloria isn't there, but I'm sure it wouldn't matter."

"I should begin my exile right away," Raphael said. "It is because of me this has happened."

"You did a stupid thing," Reina said. "But Hildegarde and Outram caused this, not you. They used what you did as an excuse."

"Did you find the man who was blackmailing me?" Teng asked.

Lorelei and Raphael looked at Teng, puzzled.

"No," Nehemiah said. "He was gone and so was your son."

"I will come with you," Teng said, "and find my son."

"No," Reina said. "Stay here. All of you. We want to come home and find you all here. That will give me peace."

"I don't know if I will ever find peace again," Quintana said.

"She fooled all of us," Reina said. "Don't blame yourself. I know it will be probably hardest for you to stay, Quintana. But these grounds need you."

Teng handed a box to Abbygail and Billy. "This is from all of us," Teng said.

Abbygail took the ribbon off the box, and Billy lifted the lid.

"They're fortune cookies," Teng said. "We all wished you well."

Abbygail took out one cookie, cracked it open, and pulled out the slip of paper and read it, 'Watch sunrises together.' Yes, we will." She put the cookie in her mouth and ate it.

Billy took out a cookie, broke it, and read the slip of paper. "'May you know love for all your days and nights.' Yes, we will. Thank you." He ate the cookie.

"Here," he said. "We want you all to eat our blessings, too."

They passed the box around and each person took a cookie. They broke the cookies, ate them, read the fortunes out loud.

After Lorelei got her cookie, she carried the box over to her mother. Reina took out a cookie and opened it. She read the slip of paper to herself.

"What does it say?" Teng asked.

Reina said, "'That's the way the house crumbles.'"

Teng frowned. "That doesn't sound like a blessing. Who wrote that one?"

When no one answered, Teng said to Viva. "Do you know who wrote it?"

Viva shook her head. "I don't remember that one."

"It doesn't matter," Reina said. She popped the pieces of cookie into her mouth and ate them.

"It's morning," Viva said, "so we're all saints."

Teng said, "What do you mean?"

"Raphael said that in the morning everyone is a saint," Viva explained.

Lorelei looked over at Raphael. He appeared gray and sunken.

"Because in the morning everything is new," Raphael said. "Everything is forgiven and forgotten."

"There are no saints here," Umberto said.

"I beg to differ," Abbygail said. "There are at least two. Abbygail Santos and Billy Santos."

"I stand corrected," Umberto said.

"Look," Billy said. "It's a white raven. I didn't think they were real."

"You can see it, too?" Lorelei asked. "I thought I was imagining it."

"And there's a black one," Turnkey said. "It must be the Raven Sisters come to make the world right."

Reina said, "I'm glad someone will."

CHAPTER FORTY-TWO
BIN-DER

Bin-Der danced in the golden dirt, her cinnamon-colored feet and legs contrasting so sharply with the dirt that she looked red, to go along with the nearly sheer red cloth she moved between her hands to let the wind catch. Her blood red dress moved with her like a partner in her dance. Her bare feet left a snake-like path in the sand. Her black and white hair, piled on top of her head, began to fall into her face, strand by strand, the faster she moved, until it all came down onto her shoulders, and the ribbon fell onto the dirt like a narrow red snake.

She touched the stretch marks on her belly, birth tattoos from her children, as she danced one more turn. Then she slowed to a stop and put her folded hands up to the nearly heart-shaped red spot on her forehead, and whispered, "Thank you," to the sun, moon, wind, and sand.

She moved away from the spot where she had danced and looked down at the markings in the sand her feet had made.

Weaver and Lucy came up over the rise to where she stood and crouched down to look at the sand with her. After a few minutes, both of them stood again. Weaver took off his broad banded hat and slapped it against his raised foot. Lucy shook her head.

"I see no rain in this path," she said.

"I concur," Weaver said.

"I wish it weren't so," Bin-Der said. "Maybe it's time to call a rainmaker from one of the other tribes."

"We've got our own dancers," Weaver said. "We haven't had a rain sing in a long time." He nodded. "Let's do it."

Bin-Der raised her hands slightly, letting Weaver know she wasn't going to argue with him.

"The Weather Spirits want our attention," Bin-Der said. "They've got it. Might as well throw a party and invite them. See what happens."

The three of them stood looking out across the red landscape. The sun was so hot it hurt the skin on Bin-Der's feet. She didn't care. She could stare out at this world forever.

"We found another," Weaver said. "He's so stupid he's been out in the sun and has burned to a crisp. Doesn't even know how to make shelter or call the water. I wish they'd stop throwing away their people for us to save."

"They're not so much stupid as they are insensible," Lucy said. "They can't help it."

"All of our ancestors were once exiles," Bin-Der said. "Someone saved every single one of us."

"Except them they didn't," Weaver said. "This one's different, by the by. It's the Queen's son. He calls himself Raphael. He's saying the whole family was ousted. They'll all be coming this way."

"One of the Villanuevas?" Bin-Der said.

"Yes," Lucy said. "Don't sound so excited."

"He says he was exiled for burning the saffron fields," Weaver said. "Can you imagine doing anything so stupid during a drought?"

Bin-Der said, "Perhaps fire was speaking to him, asking him to bring it into existence, and he didn't understand."

Weaver shrugged. Lucy laughed. "You are always too kind to the exiles."

"She said she would do it," Bin-Der said, "and it looks like she succeeded. Take me to this *criatura*."

Bin-Der slipped on her moccasins, and then followed her friends over the rise and down the red rocks. They walked to one of the shelters in the rocks. Bin-Der stepped out of the sun and looked down at the young man on the cot. He did look pitiful.

"Hey, you," Weaver said. "You have a visitor."

The young man slowly sat up. His hands and face were burned and raw.

"We have healing salve that can help your burns," Bin-Der said. "And we have healers, too, if you need them."

"Thank you," Raphael said. "I appreciate your kindness. I don't believe I deserve it."

"Why?" Bin-Der said. "You're not going to burn down our saffron fields, are you?"

"You grow saffron here?" Raphael asked. He squinted as he looked up at her.

Bin-Der laughed. "We grow everything here. Especially minds."

He blinked. "I don't understand," he said.

"You will," Bin-Der said. "In the meantime, get some rest. We will take care of you." Bin-Der leaned over and kissed the young man on his forehead.

"Welcome to the Queendom," she said.

The Saga of the Queendom continues in
Queendom: Dance of the Exiles.

Coming Soon.

Read about the early days of the world, after The Fall and before the Queendom, featuring Gloria Stone, in Kim Antieau's novel *The Gaia Websters*. Available now.

THE GAIA WEBSTERS

In a desolate future years after The Fall, Gloria Stone manages to carve out a good life for herself as her town's healer.
But when sinister forces ally against her, she must use every skill at her disposal to survive and keep her community whole.
And nothing can prepare her for the ultimate shocking revelation about the nature of her world and her own being.

Here's the beginning of *The Gaia Websters:*

I AM A soothsayer.

I admit this freely now despite all that I have learned. Or perhaps because of it.

In ancient times, it was said that a soothsayer was someone who claimed to foretell events, a prophet, or seer, someone who could calm or relieve pain.

I have never foretold any event. I do not see myself as a prophet or seer.

I have calmed and relieved the pain of many. I have also caused pain to many.

Perhaps this truthsaying, this story of mine, will calm or relieve the pain of some.

Perhaps not.

But it is all I know.

TEN YEARS EARLIER, I awoke in a cave with no memory. I picked my name from the graffiti on the rock. The stone read: Sarah, Susan, Constance, Virginia, Bobby, Gloria. I chose Gloria. I liked the shape of the G, how it curved around into itself and then back out again. Like me in and out of that cave.

Although I did not remember anything about myself when I awakened, I quickly realized I must have been a healer. As I walked around the woods near the cave, I recognized too many plants and knew too much about their healing properties to be a casual student. Then I passed a little girl with bloody knees on my way into the town nearest the cave. We were both astonished to see the gravel cuts disappear when I touched her as I picked the stones out of her skin. She thanked me but ran away quickly. I turned and headed for another community, a ball of fear forming in my stomach.

I made the Washington Territory my home for a time. I worked as a healer, disguising my hands-on healing abilities as best I could. One year, I journeyed to the Arizona Territory. I got through immigration easily and was awestruck by the desert. All the prickly vegetation and seemingly stark landscape made me feel as though I had found a kindred land. I offered my services to the town of Coyote Creek and had been happily ensconced there until the day the man from the governor tried to follow me up Black Mountain to my home.

He kept tripping and falling on his way up the hill, pricking himself with every cactus that came within yards of the path. I hurried over the ridge to lose him. Cosmo stood on the trail watching the man, his head cocked in what I took to be an expression of puzzlement.

"Woman!" the governor's man called.

Cosmo's low growl carried up the hill to me. He did not like the man either.

"Gloria Stone!" the man screamed. "Get this mangy dog away from me!"

"Coyote, you idiot," I murmured, and hurried on. I could see my small house tucked into the next ridge, surrounded by saguaro and juniper.

"If the governor wants you, he will have you!" The man's whiny voice reverberated up to me.

I stopped. Who did he think he was? If the governor "wanted me," he would "have me"? I should go down and take his shoes and make him walk back barefoot. Or maybe I should rip off his clothes and let Cosmo chew him all over.

No. Too much trouble. I had had a long day, and I was tired.

Then I heard the sound of scree rolling and the man's cry as he tumbled down the hill like the useless little weed he was.

Cosmo yelped.

"I'm coming," I grumbled.

Lucky for the man, a magnificent saguaro had stopped his descent, and he now lay sprawled against it.

Cosmo waited on the trail until we met. Then he followed me to the saguaro and the injured man whose face and hands were bloody from the prickly pear he had rolled into.

"This is your fault!" he said.

Cosmo yelped. The man shut his mouth.

"What's your name?" I asked.

"Primer," he answered. "I'm from the governor."

"Yeah, yeah," I said. I reluctantly knelt and felt his legs.

"Stop that," he said. "You are to come with me at once. That hurts!"

"It ought to hurt," I said. He had a bad sprain.

I did not have any herbs or lotions to apply to distract him from my hands-on healing.

"I can fix it if you'll shut up and let me," I said. I had to have his permission; it was an ethical thing with me. "If not, I can leave you here with Cosmo. He's not a vegetarian. Or a scavenger. He kills his meals."

ABOUT THE AUTHOR

Kim Antieau's novels include *The Jigsaw Woman, Her Frozen Wild, Whackadoodle Times, The Monster's Daughter, Coyote Cowgirl, Ruby's Imagine, Butch,* and many others. Learn more about Kim and her work at www.kimantieau.com.

CPSIA information can be obtained at www.ICGtesting.com
Printed in the USA
LVOW11s1552110216

474713LV00003B/517/P